MATCHLOCK
AND THE
EMBASSY
A THIRTY YEARS' WAR STORY

1

Matchlock and the Embassy
A Thirty Years' War Story – Book One.

When Diplomacy Fails Publishing

For requests and business inquiries, contact the author
matchlock@wdfpodcast.com

For Anna.
History Friend for life.

Before we begin…

If you enjoy this book , please consider giving it an honest review wherever you get your books from. If you enjoy this book , please consider giving it an honest review wherever you get your books from.

Reviews are the ___lifeblood___ of books like these, and really do make the difference between people ignoring this book, or reading it and enjoying it (hopefully) just like you!

If you wish to keep up to date with all things Matchlock, including behind the scenes details, fascinating facts about the Thirty Years' War, and special offers, make sure you become a Matchlock Messenger by clicking here:

https://www.subscribepage.com/matchlockmessengers

For everything else Matchlock related, see our website

www.matchlockbooks.com

- CONTENTS -

- ACKNOWLEDGMENTS -

First and foremost, I must thank the reader for reading.

Thank you for taking a chance on the first work of fiction from this author. I hope you enjoy the time you spend in this world, and that you'll come back for more!

Next, I have to thank my history friends.

Matchlock would never have come to life if not for the phenomenal support provided by listeners of my history podcast *When Diplomacy Fails*. It was in that medium, and on that platform, that I first gained confidence in my abilities, and started to think beyond the box I had always put myself in. A community of history enthusiasts, some even nerdier than myself, now surround everything I do. I can't ask for a greater blessing than that.

Of course, behind every creator is a long-suffering other half. I must therefore thank my wife, the hardest working and most caring nurse I know. Anna was the first person to lay her eyes on the string of words that eventually made this book. For that, she is owed an apology. For believing in this story, for encouraging me to tell it, and for getting occasionally more excited than me, I cannot thank her enough. We finally did it, love. Now let's watch *Matchlock* conquer the world!

And then there's the family. There's my dad, John, who (along with Anna) served as a free editor and proof-reader, for this novel. He offered no end of brilliant advice and attention to detail, as I knew he would. I would pay him if he let me. My mum, Angela, contributed tons of moral support, and always believed I was in control of things, even when I wasn't one hundred percent sure myself. Their love helped nourish this author along, even when he *really* wasn't feeling it.

And then there's the more obvious person to thank – my literary inspiration. I was twelve years old when I first read a book by Bernard Cornwell. Even though I had no idea what was happening, I was so captivated by his exploration of history, that the genre always stuck with me.

Without Cornwell, there would be no Twamley. His back catalogue is the blueprint for my career. My ultimate goal, if I could be so bold, is to do for the Thirty Years' War with *Matchlock* what Cornwell did for the Napoleonic Wars with *Sharpe*. If I can bring legions of new readers and enthusiasts into this underappreciated era in history, then I will consider my mission accomplished.

It probably goes without saying that producing a work of fiction, let alone historical fiction, is something I have always wanted to do. I have *always* loved to write stories. I was the guy in class who asked for more paper during the English exam (yes, really). I've been writing since I was young, but those tales were never finished. I would write feverishly for several days, only to give up, and move onto something new and shiny.

In 2012, I started my history podcast *When Diplomacy Fails*, which provided twenty-year-old Zack with a brand-new platform for writing stories, and letting his creative juices flow. This time, the stories were true, and were communicated, like a radio program, in audio format, to anyone who was interested. As it turned out, quite a lot of people were!

After close to a decade, two degrees and a nearly finished PhD later, my love of history and storytelling has only grown. Now, I make a living by exploring history, wrapping my head around it, and making it accessible to people, so that they can enjoy it as much as I do. It has been a privilege, an adventure, and a pleasure.

Matchlock, you might say, is a natural evolution of this profession, and I can't wait to see where his journey takes me. I hope you'll join me for the ride.

Zachary Twamley
August 2021
County Wicklow,
Ireland

.

THERE IS NOTHING IN LIFE THAT A MAN
SHOULD MORE DESIRE, OR THAT BRINGS HIM
GREATER GLORY, THAN TO SEE HIS ENEMY
PROSTRATE IN THE DUST AND AT HIS MERCY.

BUT THIS GLORY IS DOUBLED BY HIM WHO USES
THE OCCASION WELL, THAT IS TO SAY, WHO
SHOWS MERCY AND IS CONTENT WITH HAVING
HAD THE VICTORY.

- FRANCESCO GUICCIARDINI (1483-1540) -

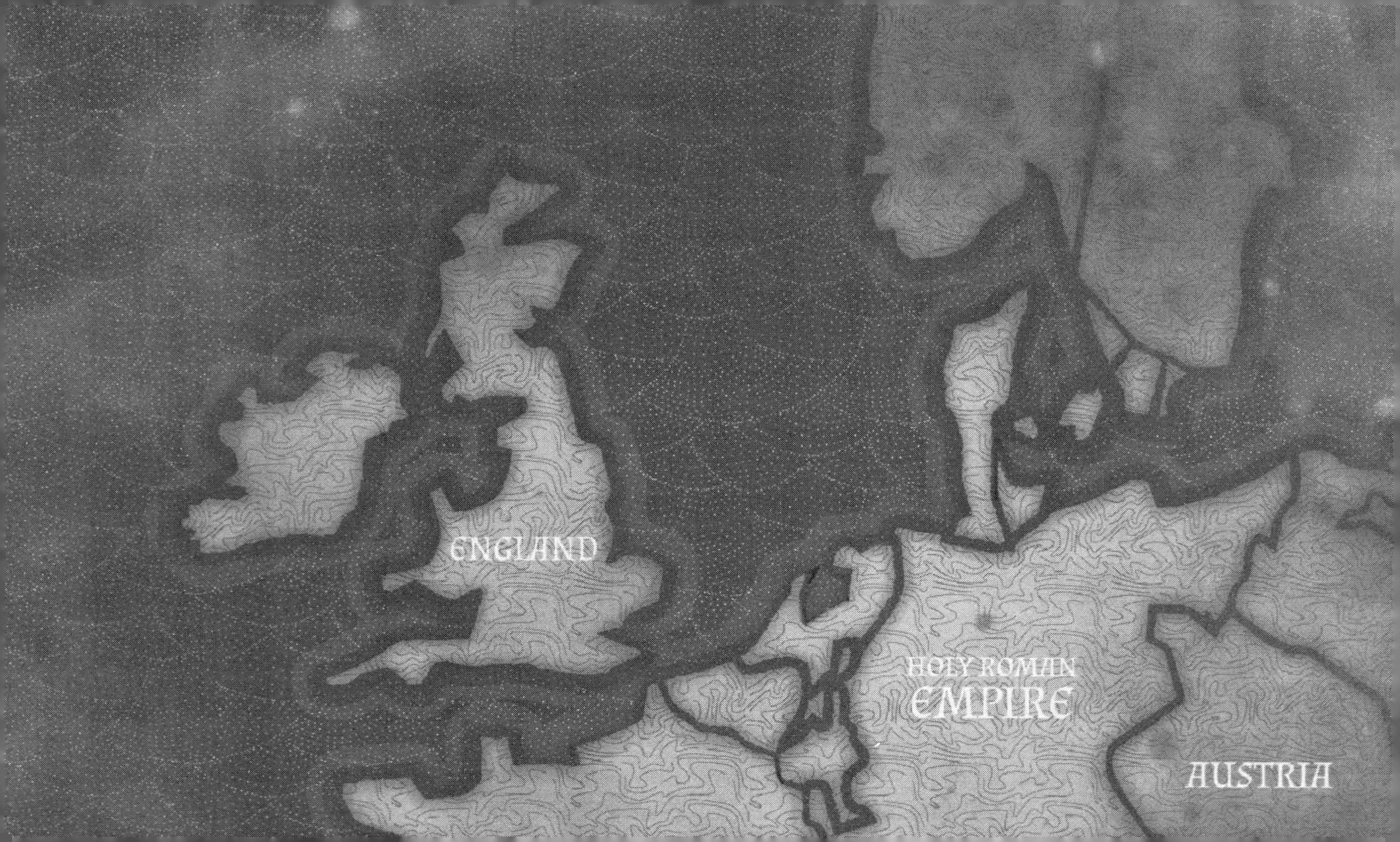
ENGLAND
HOLY ROMAN
EMPIRE
AUSTRIA

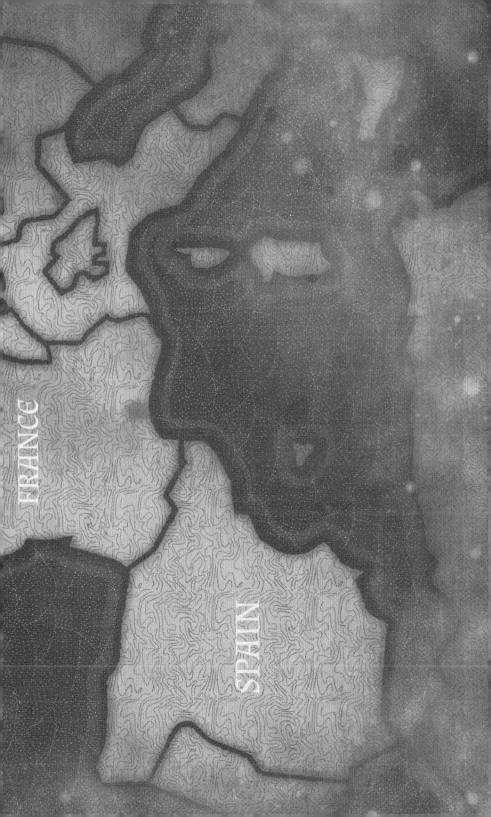

FRANCE

SPAIN

- PROLOGUE -

11 March, 1613.

10KM SOUTH OF LEEUWARDEN,

FRISIA, UNITED PROVINCES.

The musket was ready to fire, but the boy could not pull the trigger. Even worse, his enemy knew it. They saw him flinching, hesitating. They sensed his weakness. They saw his soft frame. His flushed face. Perhaps they also saw his trembling arms. They could not know the war underway in the pit of his stomach, but there was more than enough evidence to suggest that they were not in any danger.

But the boy was in danger, that much was plain.

He had heard the commotion when the party of men had broken into his home. He had crept gingerly down the creaky stairs. He had grabbed Father's musket. He had stood in the doorway, and attempted to plan his rescue.

Then he had been spotted, and ordered into the dining room.

Judging by their attire, from their black clothes to the fearsome black masks, these men had seen and endured many sights worse than that of a boy clinging to a loaded musket.

The boy remembered Father's safety measures. He remembered that the musket had been preloaded and preprepared in case of an emergency.

The circumstances certainly qualified as an emergency. Father had never permitted the boy to fire a musket, but the boy had seen one fired.

The trigger merely needed to be pulled.

How hard could it be?

Yet the boy could not pull the trigger. Not even the urgent glances from Mother, or his brothers, could egg him on. He could not pull it, and his bluff would only be tolerated for so long.

His hand was frozen. His whole body was ice. He was fixated on the masked men who had entered his home. All six men were now focused on him. They had hesitated at first. After all, he was only a boy, armed with a volatile weapon.

But that hesitation had passed.

Now they were creeping gradually towards him.

Time was running out.

One masked man stood by his brother, James. Such a stellar young man. Mother's favourite, without a doubt. But now, James was a hostage. His face, normally full of colour, was drained and sweating.

There was no explanation.

No reasons given for shattering the joy of this family holiday. Instead, there were just six masked men.

The standoff was interrupted with a stark raising of the stakes. The masked man next to James unsheathed his sword with a swift, shimmering movement. Although the darkness of the evening had arrived, the light from the room's spluttering candles caused the blade to glisten.

The steel was then pointed at James' throat.

'Put it down boy,' the masked man hissed. 'Put it down or I open his neck.'

But he couldn't. The boy couldn't move. He was stuck fast. His arms ached from the weight of the firearm. His legs ached from tensing in one place. His breathing came in fits. Sweat ran down his neck.

A thin whisp of smoke rose above the lit piece of match cord, which confirmed that the musket was as ready as it would ever be. But the confirmation was irrelevant. The act of firing the weapon was impossible. And where to retreat? It was safer to stand still, or to close his eyes, and pretend it was all a horrendous nightmare.

'Look at me *boy*,' the man barked. 'Put it down. I won't ask you again.'

The boy stared at him. The black mask covered his whole face, leaving only the whites of his eyes and the curve of his mouth actually visible. That was enough to paint a vivid picture. A picture of evil.

The boy tried to speak. There was no air in his throat.

Then there were two hands on him. One on his right shoulder, the other on his firearm.

It was another masked man.

This one was gentler. Still a villain by virtue of his actions, but somehow less fierce and less malicious. Like he was simply doing a job.

The musket was lowered slowly into the masked man's hands, and the cord was extinguished. The boy heaved a sigh of relief. His hands were empty. He was defenceless.

He had done as the masked man had demanded.

But the sword was not lowered.

Instead, the masked man let out a sickening chuckle, and with a flick of his wrist, arched the blade upwards through James' throat.

In the time it took the boy to gasp, blood was flicked from his brother's throat and onto the carpet. A horrific gurgling sound escaped from James' throat, and the murderer pushed his victim roughly to the floor.

Mother screamed, and broke free of the two men holding her and her youngest son. She ran to James' side, sobbing, wailing. She cradled his head.

The boy had only seen death once before, when grandmother had died in her bed. James' eyes now looked the same as hers once did. Glassy. Vacant. Empty.

The masked men seemed conflicted. The one who had taken the boy's musket shouted at the other who had taken James' life. One looked out the window. Other masked men stood on the edges of their feet, unsure how to react.

And then, the killer locked eyes with the boy.

For whatever reason, the boy held his gaze. Did the killer see this as a challenge? The boy felt no anger. He had not even cried out at the atrocity. He was numb.

The killer made for the boy with frightening speed. He pushed past the objections of his masked peers. With a final step, he struck the boy with the middle of his right fist.

The world seemed to stop.

The boy's vision blurred, but he knew he was on the ground. The carpet cushioned most of his fall, but the back of his head cracked against a stone tile.

Was his nose broken? His eyes watered.

But it was not over. The mask was on top of him.

Bearing down on him.

Striking him.

Again. And again.

What could be done? Nothing. There was no pain. Perhaps James had felt no pain either.

The boy gasped.

The limp hands he held up were swatted away. Resisting was useless. The killer hissed and spat at him as he struck. Over and over again.

And then the assault ended.

Was it all over? Was he to join with James, and grandmother?

He tasted blood. Was there blood in Heaven?

No. He was still here.

Curses bounced off the walls and into the boy's ears.

The boy could hardly move his body, but he could move his head. He angled it towards the commotion. The masks were arguing among themselves.

But why?

Had they not wanted James to die?

But James *was* dead.

Mother still cradled her favourite son's head. She begged him to get up. She cursed the man responsible, but did not look up from his victim. James' open throat had spilled his entire life onto his chest. It had once been a full life, but now James' face was ashen, and drained of everything.

The youngest son stood to the side, shivering. He had soiled himself.

Candles flickered, as men rushed around the room to interrupt a standoff. They traipsed mud all over the carpet.

Mother would normally have dragged such offenders out by their ears. She would have forced them to scrub the carpet clean. The three sons had already been reminded several times that this house did not belong to them, and was only on loan. But now she just sobbed quietly into James' chest.

A creeping darkness stalked the room, as several flames were extinguished.

The youngest son whimpered, and called out in vain to his distraught mother.

The boy watched the nightmare unfold, silent and still.

There were shouts in the distance.

And then the masked men began to run.

The one who had handled the boy's musket paused for a brief moment. His head seem to dance between the different sights. It locked onto James, and then back to the boy.

The boy squinted at him, and momentarily held his gaze. The boy wanted to call out to this gentler masked man.

He had so many questions. Too many.

It was overwhelming for a mere boy.

The boy's neck gave out. He rested his head on the hard tile.

A familiar voice loomed into his ears.

Father.

Father had come back. He had gone for a walk. He and Mother had been fighting again.

The boy had not been meant to hear it, but he had.

A door was forced open.

Father demanded to see the masked men, but they had all gone.

The boy did not see Father until he was over his face. Father's rough hands were placed gently on the boy's face.

Words were poured onto him.

First concerned.

Then angry.

Like mumbled blurs of words. The boy could not respond.

Just like he could not fire the musket.

The boy's eyelids fluttered.

Perhaps when he woke, everything would be better. Perhaps he would dream of a better time. Of a time without men in black masks, or of a time when he had been able to pull the trigger.

A haunting wail filled his ears.

Mother's despair had been unleashed for the whole province of Frisia to hear.

The only escape from the nightmare was sleep.

Merciful sleep.

And then there was darkness.

The flickering candles were gone. All was silent.

But Matthew Lock knew that he had failed.

- CHAPTER ONE -

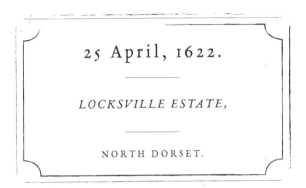

25 April, 1622.

LOCKSVILLE ESTATE,

NORTH DORSET.

'Ooh. Hard luck Matt. Sixty-eight seconds.'

Matthew Lock winced. Looking up from his weapon, he rubbed his hands on the edge of his buff coat and shook his head. Everything was black with powder stains.

'I was better yesterday. You saw me make it in under a minute.'

'I saw you make it in *sixty-three seconds*,' Arthur corrected. He focused on the target his brother had just punctured with multiple holes.

'We'll agree to disagree then.'

'Hold there, I'll check the target,' Arthur said, as he walked fifty yards to the bale of straw.

Lock sighed. If he was to make Father proud, sixty-eight seconds simply would not do. Most soldiers would be delighted with three shots in that time period. Most soldiers would be delighted to fire a single shot in a minute. But Matthew Lock wasn't like most soldiers. He wasn't even truly a soldier.

'You missed twice,' Arthur called back. 'But two misses in thirty shots is a good record.'

Arthur traced his finger around the edge of the square target, mumbling to himself.

Lock called back to him. 'Alright. That's enough lead expended for one day. Let's head home. I'll have time to practice tomorrow.'

'When are they due back?' Arthur asked, as he sauntered to his brother.

'I'll have to check with Gus. I think he said before noon. I'll be up early.'

'Father will scarcely have time to pack before heading off again with you,' Arthur said, a hint of jealously palpable in his tone.

'Father said the embassy would supply food, so we need only bring our clothes. Mine are packed already. I am sure Gus has taken care of it.'

Arthur whistled as he ran his hand along the musket Lock had brought as a spare. 'Wouldn't mind a trip to Europe myself someday. Sounds like a great adventure.'

Lock scoffed. In truth, he was fearful that Father would decide to bring Arthur along. 'You'll have your chance brother. This way, I can let you know what it's like. I can warn you of its dangers, and recommend only the worthiest of sights.'

Arthur grabbed a spare bandolier near Lock's feet, and appeared to weigh it in his hand. The twelve powder charges, known as the twelve apostles, were still intact. 'I had half a mind to practice myself today.'

Lock rolled his eyes, and gestured towards a gathering mass of grey cloud in the distance. 'If it rains and we wreck the powder again, Father will keep these under lock and key.'

Arthur smirked at him. He clicked, and his horse turned its head lazily towards him. 'Come, Ferdinand. Race you back to the stables, Matt?'

Lock grimaced. He knew what Arthur was up to. His brother was like lightening atop his beast. Ever since Father had brokered an arrangement to purchase Ferdinand and Isabella, two powerful Frisian mounts, Arthur had made it his mission to establish his horse as the quickest. It consumed him like the musket drill consumed Lock.

'Stay clear of the woods this time, will you?'

'Don't you be changing the rules now,' Arthur grinned, as he threw himself onto his mount. He was graceful and strong, but still young. Lock watched him, a picture of confidence, as he turned Ferdinand around, in the direction of home.

Lock whistled, and cursed lightly when he saw that Isabella was several yards in the distance. 'Come on you silly girl,' Lock moaned. Isabella could not have been less interested in Arthur's challenge. She trotted absent-mindedly to the stream that flowed gently through a clump of trees.

Arthur laughed. 'She's just trying to give you some exercise. Perhaps she wishes to run this race without you?'

Lock waved his arms in vain at Isabella. She pretended not to see him, and snorted at him as he approached. 'Why do you have to embarrass me like this, girl?' Lock asked, as he placed his foot gently in the stirrup, and prepared to clamber onto her saddle.

'We're still waiting over here brother,' Arthur teased.

Lock gritted his teeth and persuaded the beast to turn. Father had been so excited to purchase two foals from the same mother, he had not paused to consider whether two stallions would have been better than this mare. Isabella was somewhat smaller than the stallion, though the horse breeder has assured Father that each horse came with its own unique strengths. Lock had yet to locate Isabella's.

'*Come on* girl,' he urged. Balancing his firearm on his knees was far from easy, but Father had insisted that the act would improve his coordination, and make him more comfortable with riding.

'We are *waiting*, Matt,' Arthur tutted. 'You'll make me miss my supper.'

'Perhaps it would be good for you,' Lock scoffed. In truth it was he who had overindulged over Christmas, and Arthur's silence suggested that his brother knew it too. Isabella had finally stopped her protesting, and she shuffled casually to Arthur's side.

'Smell that?' Arthur asked.

Lock inhaled deeply. 'Beef, is it?'

Arthur laughed. 'Not *food* you glutton, it's the smell of your defeat.'

'You're welcome to swap mounts, if a challenge is what you're after.'

'Matt if I wanted a challenge, I would have requested a contest in the drill. I've had enough of you showing me up for one day.'

Lock smiled. Though his brother rarely offered a complement, he always seemed to pick the right moment. The sun was suddenly eclipsed by a grim collection of cloud. Lock glanced to the sky just as Arthur began to countdown from three. His brother was nearly standing in his stirrups, his back arched, his arms tensed. He grinned at Lock.

'*Go!*' Arthur shot ahead like a ball from a cannon. Clods of earth were kicked up behind him, as Ferdinand rejoiced in his task.

Isabella was in no hurry, in spite of Lock's best efforts.

'You could at least pretend to care.' She turned her head back to him and blinked. 'That's right, I'm talking to you. Don't you want to catch your brother? I bet he badmouths you to his friends too.' Lock sighed, and pressed his spurs as gently as he could into Isabella's sides.

The beast's whole body flinched, but it did the trick. She picked up speed, and wind rushed through Lock's overgrown hair. He brushed it from his eyes, the same group of brown curls that Mother always complained of. Rounding a bend, and over a bridge, he spotted Arthur's mount in the distance.

There was no hope of catching them, and his brother knew it. He had slowed Ferdinand to make the turn comfortably. It was the same turn where, over a decade before, Lock had fallen to disaster, and been laid up in bed for a fortnight. Arthur always insisted on riding past it.

'You'll never overcome your fear of the danger until you face it so often that it ceases to move you,' Father had insisted.

As far as Lock knew, Father had never been thrown from his mount into a shallow, stony stream ten feet below. But he was at least partially correct. Lock's heart was no longer in his throat as he approached the site. He said a quick prayer as he passed it, on instinct at this stage. Down the valley and into the distance, a trail of smoke emerged from a large, brown brick structure.

Locksville. Home was in sight.

Isabella seemed to recognise it too. The excitement began to rise through her, and Lock couldn't help but become swept up in the task. He pushed her to move quicker, to at least retain Arthur in his sight. Lock returned his eyes in front just in time.

He gasped, as a wayward duck waddled from the lake directly in front of Isabella's thundering hooves. She skirted slightly to avoid it, but the bloody bird didn't get the message. It flapped and stumbled into Isabella's path, who had no choice but to halt entirely. Lock surged forward, grasping Isabella's neck roughly, and just managed to stay upright. Isabella snorted at the startled bird, and Lock shook his head as it waddled back to where it had come from.

'You're alright girl,' he soothed, patting her neck and calming her sufficiently to resume their trot. Lock allowed himself to calm down.

'Alright girl, just get us home.' The race was over, and Lock could already hear Arthur's witty retort when he learned that a duck had been the source of his brother's delay.

The stables loomed into view, and rain drops pattered onto the back of Lock's neck. Isabella began to speed up slightly. Her hooves grasped the cobbled road, and the rich clopping sound reached Lock's ears. It was a familiar sound. A favourite sound. It meant home was near.

Lock saw the stable boy, busy at work outside the paddock, shovel in hand. Arthur and Ferdinand were nowhere to be seen.

Lock pulled on the reins to slow Isabella down. He halted a few feet from the stable boy, who nodded at Lock with a smile. 'Terry, have you seen Arthur come through here?'

Terry shook his head lightly. 'Not so far Master Lock. Did you beat him this time?'

Lock turned his mount 180 degrees on the cobbles. 'It would appear so...' Something was off. Arthur would normally have his mount delivered by now, and would be waiting, arms folded, on the outside of the stable, to bask in his triumph. 'I'll go look for him.'

'Tread carefully Master Matthew. Weather is due to worsen I reckon.'

Lock turned without answering. Could Arthur be in trouble? Arthur was the best rider he knew. Lock called for him as he rode back the way he'd come. When he came to a fork in the road, he paused. He patted Isabella's neck. 'Where have our brothers gone, girl?'

Clumps of trees on his right and left swayed nonchalantly in with the light gusts. Raindrops pattered onto their outstretched leaves. The smell of the rain travelled on the breeze.

Lock called again. Still nothing. Perhaps Arthur had taken a shortcut, to further enhance his victory? Would he be so foolish? The edge of the estate's grounds could be dangerous. Father had warned them of poachers and the like, who could occasionally be desperate enough to turn to violence.

Lock's stomach growled. He was starving. His hips strained from the saddle. He called again, moving Isabella on the road which led out of the estate. If one continued due south, they would reach Sherbourne, and after a full day's hard riding, Dorchester. And if one went *that* far, it was only an hour's ride further south to Weymouth, where the refreshing sea air could be taken in.

Mother had always insisted that Dorset was England's greatest county. It was one of the few things Mother and son agreed on, though Father could always be counted on to declare his undying love for Scotland's rugged highlands.

Lock had only embarked on the gruelling ride to the seaside town a handful of times. He generally preferred to take the family's carriage. The journey took almost twice as long, but it at least gave him time to read. On those rare occasions when he did push his mount so far south, he was never alone in the journey. It was a three-man trip, concocted by Father, who tended to mix business with the pleasure of his sons' company when he could.

After a near ten-hour ride through the countryside, they would reach their destination. He and Arthur dismounted, stinking and thirsty, and Father purchased a round of bitters. Lock missed the smell of the sea. He could still taste the bitter ale. Perhaps he would request some with dinner, if Gus allowed it on a Sunday.

Lock called again, forcing Isabella into a gallop. Perhaps she could sense her brother was in danger? She did not protest as Lock drove his spurs in. Rounding a corner, calling Arthur's name, Lock spotted something a few yards ahead. It was the bandolier Arthur had reached for back at the musket practice. It had been tossed, or left behind. Father despised wasted powder. Arthur would not have left this here voluntarily. Lock's breathing accelerated.

The rain had begun to intensify. Still, Isabella did not protest. Lock couldn't persuade her to stop if he'd wanted to. Then, rounding another corner, where a low stone wall met with woodland, and demarked the boundary of the Locksville estate, Lock saw him. Ferdinand, unsecured, and grazing leisurely just off the road. Arthur was not with him. Lock called for him again.

He realised he was praying, though in truth, it was hypocritical. The two had skipped the morning service. Arthur had insisted that if he'd been forced to hear Cain and Abel's story one more time, he would convert to Rome. He had been sure to say it out of Gus' earshot, of course.

Lock moved Isabella closer to her abandoned brother. He dismounted. He lacked a sword, or any means to defend himself save his musket. The driving rain would make any firearm useless, but it would suffice as a club.

Lock struggled to imagine himself actually resorting to such means. He called again, wobbling slightly on his tensed legs as he led her from the road.

He made a loop from Isabella's reins, and tied them to a pillar which jutted up from the low stone wall. '*Stay*, girl,' Lock whispered. She was somewhat sheltered here, next to her brother. Rainwater dripped down his back, and Lock shivered. He walked briskly to Ferdinand's saddle, but there were no clues he could see. No spurs had been caught in the stirrups. It would seem his brother had dismounted in good order, but why?

Lock pulled his dolman close. The large, dark, knee-length coat was not waterproof, but it provided an extra barrier against chilly wind. Its thick back and torso lining was reminiscent of a gambeson, which also protected the wearer in a fight, Father had insisted with a wink.

Was Lock wandering towards a fight now? Perhaps shouting Arthur's name was bad strategy in that case. As he vaulted over the stone wall, he spotted it, one of Arthur's boots. It seemed to suggest that his brother had clambered over the wall, and wandered into the dense forest.

The wood provided a picturesque buffer between Father's land and that of his neighbour. They frequently went on hunting expeditions together, but Lock hadn't seen Lord Crawly since the previous winter. He normally stayed in London during the spring and summer, a decision which Father could never understand.

Lock resisted the urge to call out again. He scanned the horizon rapidly, and his eyes scanned past tree trunks dead and living. Birds sang joyfully, unaware of the crisis below them. Rain dripped through the canopy. A twig snapped. Rustling behind him. Lock spun around and gasped as a red squirrel sped innocently up a dead piece of bark, and into a small hole high above.

Lock pushed forward, until his ears fixed onto a strange pattering sound. The rain had intensified. Or, perhaps, it was not the rain. It was voices. Lock moved gingerly in their direction. He noticed marks in the forest floor. The leaf litter had been disturbed. Had someone been dragged through here?

A collection of thick trunks lay ahead of him, and as he moved around them, he saw it. A low structure made entirely of wood. The old shack, which he and Arthur had once built with Father. They had made it shortly after James' death. The plan had been to keep it their secret, and to escape there together. Just the three of them. But then Arthur had been unable to keep his mouth shut. Mother had made such a fuss about its dangers. It had since stood derelict.

A slight clearing opened before him, with the shack in its centre. The voices had become louder. They were clearly within the shack. The voices were slightly strained, but Lock could hear no sense of panic. The door, that wretched door which he had spent a full day constructing, rested lazily on a single hinge. The combination of wind and rain caused it to creak intermittently. Lock could barely hear himself think with the rising roar of the rain. He was relatively protected here. Once he emerged from the trees, Lock would be easily seen.

He listened carefully. Three voices, two low and one slightly higher, and then Arthur's tone. Arthur shouted something unidentifiable, and Lock surged forward involuntarily. He emerged from the safety of the trees, and closed in on the shack. Five steps. Four steps. Three steps. Two.

Lock exhaled. He stepped to the shack, and tried not to overthink his next move, as he pulled the creaking door back on its hinge.

- CHAPTER TWO -

'You've a good voice for begging bacon,' Captain Augustus Frank had said, when he had been shown the shack for the first time. Father did not argue with his friend. Creating the wooden cabin had been a labour of love, by three people who had no idea what they were doing. It had been too unstable, too draughty, even to spend a single night in it.

He and Arthur had been incredibly disappointed, but Captain Frank swore that he would help Father repair it, and bring it up to a liveable standard. He never had found the time.

And then, Lock had been busy himself. Once he commenced his musket training in earnest, and once Father permitted him to hold a true firearm, and not merely practice with a broom, Lock found that he was hooked. Lock fired the matchlock by himself on the evening of his sixteenth birthday. That, Lock decided, was a better present than spending a night in a draughty shack.

As a child, the wooden cabin had seemed so large within. Had they slept prone on its decaying floor, one would have tripped over themselves on the way to the door in the middle of the night, in the event nature called. A different form of nature called Lock back to the shack now.

The call to defend one's own blood.

Three men were standing with their backs to him, one was kneeling. The rain pattered so loudly on the shack's weathered roof, and the draught blew so freely through the structure, that his opening of the door did not even register with the men. Grass grew in its corners, and rain leaked in several places.

With their backs blocking the view, Lock could not see what the men were so focused on, but he had a suspicion. As he stepped lightly towards the middle of the room, gaps between the men revealed a pitiful sight. Someone was tied to a chair, the single piece of furniture remaining in the entire shack. Lock resisted a gasp, as the victim's wide-eyed expression came into view.

It was Arthur. His brother did not see him, transfixed as he was on his tormenters, but he presented quite a sight. His confidence from barely an hour before had vanished. It was replaced by a look of desperate terror. Blood streamed from his mouth, and cuts were present on his left cheek. He wore only one boot, and the sock had been removed from his foot. This foot was held by the man in the centre, as the other two watched the scene with arms folded. Still, somehow, nobody had noticed him.

'Six shillings, Arty boy,' the kneeling man said. 'Six bloody shillings. Did you think your rich papa would stop us looking for you?'

'I'll get the money,' Arthur hissed. 'You know my Father will pay.'

'We don't want your *Father* to pay, Arty, we want *you* to pay. You lost the game. You pay. That's the rule.'

'What's the bloody difference?' Arthur challenged, half gasping, as the man's grip on his foot tightened.

Lock was frozen solid.

In the corner of the shack, there was a lantern, perhaps brought by one of the men. It rested a near his feet, and was still lit.

'The difference, Arty, is that your Father's foot isn't in my mitt right now. The difference is I won't take papa's toes, but I will take yours.'

'You're insane, all three of you. Call yourselves gentlemen? Release me, and you'll have your bloody money.'

Lock kept his eye on his brother, while he stooped to the lantern, and opened it carefully. Its rusty metallic door creaked, but the sound was lost amidst the hammering crescendo of rain.

The man holding his foot laughed, and his lackeys parroted the sound. 'Who said we was gentlemen, Arty? You should have thought better than moseying up to Scarlet as you did, shaking your money and fluttering your pretty eyelashes at her.'

Lock knew his musket's powder was damp, but the match cord, fortunately, had remained dry in its dedicated pouch. He touched the cord to the lantern candle. It ignited. Slim whisps of transparent smoke wafted towards the roof, and were seized by the elements.

Arthur struggled in his restraints. 'I did not know Scarlet was your woman.'

'All the women in Sherborne are my women, ya sleazy lout. Don't you know who I am?'

'You're the knave that wants to take my toes,' Arthur said, and Lock managed to catch a glimpse of a smirk on his ashen face.

The man laughed. 'I admit Arty, you were a good lad to play cards with, and you're a good lad to jaw with, but I am bad man to owe money to. I will ask you one more time, and then we take your little baby one. I'd like to see you swagger around with a limp, so I would Arty.'

'I told you, I have the money. It's in a safe place on the estate. I would be more than happy...' Arthur gasped as the point of the man's knife was pressed into the underside of his baby toe. 'I would... I say, I would, be more than happy to bring you there.'

The man with the knife grunted, and one of his lackeys seemed to hesitate. He stammered slightly as he spoke. Lock recognised him instantly as the elder brother of Terry, their stable boy. That explained how Arthur had been ambushed and why he had willingly dismounted.

'Maybe we should leave it Billy. He could tell his Father...'

The man called Billy turned to his lackey with a glare. 'I'm not afraid of Charles Lock, do you hear me? The man's been coasting on his reputation for too long I say. His soft son the same. Group of blow ins, the whole lot of them. Lord Crawly never should have sold his land. Though I wouldn't mind giving ol' Catherine a turn.'

The hair rose on the back of Lock's neck, but he focused on his lit cord. He blew it gently, the sound barely audible even to him.

Arthur struggled in Billy's grip, 'Release me you bastard, you know I'd clobber you in a fair fight.'

Billy laughed in a rough cackle. 'Silly Arty. I ain't no gentleman. I don't fight fair like you. I take what I want, when I want it.' He then offered the tip of his chin for Arthur to strike, safe in the knowledge that he was bound to the chair.

Lock's heart raced in protest. He could stay silent no longer. The cord still smouldered, the smoke snaking to the ceiling, as it was sucked through its patchwork of holes. Carefully, he slid open the pan where the powder lay. All that was needed now was to pull up the trigger, and the cord would dip into the pan, setting off the weapon. He was as ready as he'd ever be. He exhaled quietly, and prepared to shout as loud as he could above the sound of hammering rain.

'I'll take whatever you've got Arty,' Billy jeered.

'Perhaps you'd be willing to take some advice.'

The three men paused and then turned, each face telling a different story. Panic, curiosity, confusion. The lackeys were dumbfounded by the sight. Only Billy seemed truly invested in his mission. Lock also noted, to his relief, that he recognised his second lackey as another son of a local farm hand.

Their eyes rested on Lock, and the firearm grasped in his two hands. They saw the lit piece of cord. A flash of recognition momentarily crossed their faces. They knew Lock's reputation with the musket. Everyone within a day's ride of Locksville did. All Lock could think of was how damp his powder was. Perhaps they would be too startled to think the same.

Billy stood upright, and Lock avoided the temptation of checking on his brother. He had to focus on the man in the centre of this conflict. He was taller than Billy, and thicker as well. But Billy knew how to fight. He knew how to fight far better than he knew how to play cards.

'And just what the bloody hell do you want, Matty boy?'

Lock steadied himself, planting his feet firmly on the ground. He looked at the three men down the limited sights of his musket. There was no time to blow on the match cord. He would only have a minute, at most, to maintain his threat. 'As I said, I am here to offer advice. Back off, now, before you hurt yourself and your... accomplices.'

Billy smiled, and arched his back. Tilting his head, he looked down his nose at Lock and his weapon. Lock maintained eye contact.

'You ain't got the guts, coward,' Billy barked.

Lock knew he was right. Even with dry powder, firing a musket in this enclosed space could blow the eardrums of everyone present. But Billy's accomplices didn't have to know that. They were the easy targets. With some work, three against two could become four against one.

'I spoke to Terry, earlier,' Lock said, his eyes still focused on Billy. Terry's brother winced visibly. 'He's looking for you. Says you've been associating yourself with...' Lock considered his next words. '...unsavoury folks.'

'No, no I told Terry not to tell Ma, he swore he wouldn't tell a soul.'

'*A soul*?' Lock faked a chuckle. 'He told me, Captain Frank, and everyone in Locksville what his brother has done. Such a shame, he said. He used to look up to his brother. Now he's become a knave.'

Terry's brother barely held it together. His current role was out of character. Perhaps he had been desperate. He threw his hands to his face to cover his shame. '*I'm ruined*, I'll never work here again!'

Billy rolled his eyes, but he didn't attempt to calm him down. Perhaps he knew the cause to be lost, yet he still stood his ground.

The cord still trailed smoke.

'And what about you, Edward?' Lock tutted.

'*Me*?' the other lackey panicked. He hadn't counted on Lock's memory for faces.

'Yes, you. You served us well. Father always spoke well of you. Is this how you repay loyalty? Are you truly behaving as a Christian should?'

Billy put up his hands. 'Alright enough Matty boy, I see what you're doing. What you don't realise is that these boys are my friends. I paid them well, and they're sick of taking the scraps from your table.'

'You can't be much of a friend if they require payment to be around you,' Lock said. Somehow, his voice remained calm. His knuckles turned white as he strengthened his grip on the musket.

Still the smoke trailed lazily into the ceiling.

The two lackeys were unsteady now. One scratched his filthy scalp, the other glanced anxiously at Arthur, and then back to Lock. Edward broke first.

'We didn't mean it Master Lock, it was all Billy's scheme, I swear! You must not tell papa.'

'*Get out*,' Lock said quietly, as he flicked the musket in the farm hand's direction. Edward rushed past Lock and burst through the door. After a few moments' hesitation, Terry's brother followed him, bringing a sudden burst of draught into the shack as they left. Their footsteps padded through the wet undergrowth, before dying away.

'You conniving little lout,' Billy hissed. 'Shouldn't have surrounded myself with such weak men.'

'Shouldn't have captured my brother, Billy. Shouldn't have messed with my family.'

Lock had to pretend not to notice that the smoke had ceased rising from the cord.

He would no longer be able to fire his weapon.

'Oh no, Matty boy? See, I ain't afraid of your kind. You give yourselves airs and graces. Your Father buys a big house, but I don't need a big house. I've got my respect. You ever been to Sherbourne, Matty? They don't respect you there.'

'I don't need the respect of Sherbourne's residents.' Lock said flatly. His limbs ached from holding his tense pose, but Billy still seemed unaware that he could do him no harm, so Lock maintained it.

'They mock you, boy. They call you a coward.'

'Don't listen to him Matt,' Arthur called. Lock's eyes moved momentarily to his brother, who looked in a bad way. A large gash on his right shoulder, which Lock had missed before, leaked blood into his white shirt.

'And you are a coward, aren't you boy?'

'I'm not a coward. You're a swine.'

'Oh aye, Matty, I'm a swine as sure as the sun is bright, and the rain is wet. But I don't hide who I am.'

'Perhaps you should.'

'I know all about your brother, Matty. I know you killed him.'

'The heck you say?' Lock's knees quaked slightly.

Billy grinned widely. 'You didn't pull the trigger, did you Matty? You had the chance to kill the bugger that had a sword to James' throat, but you didn't do it. Why not, Matty? Eh?'

Lock stayed silent. He stared emptily down the barrel into Billy's glistening eyes.

'If a bastard had a sword to my brother's throat, I would have helped him finish the job. Awful bastard he was. But your James was different, I hear. He was a good man, even Sherbourners say so.'

Lock could find no words. No wit. No sarcasm. No cutting comeback. Just tightening hands.

'They all wonder why you didn't save your brother when you had the chance. They curse you for being weak. They curse you for being a coward. But mostly, Matty, they curse for not pulling the trigger.'

Lock arms shook with the effort. His muscles were failing him.

'You couldn't pull the trigger, could you Matty? You couldn't pull it then, and you can't pull it now.'

As he uttered the last word, a sick smile spread across Billy's face. It seemed to feed off Lock's despair, growing bigger and bigger as he watched it. Lock stared at Billy's beady eyes. His cheeks flushed from years of drinking. A nose burnt from hours spent in the sun.

'Billy, get out ya bastard,' Arthur hissed. Billy turned to Arthur and gave a mocking bow.

'*Lord Spineless*, that's what they call you Matty. Lord Spineless of –'

The shack erupted with noise.

Lock wasn't sure why he pulled the trigger. The powder was surely soaked, and the match cord had gone out, yet he still pulled his fingers up. The act moved the piece of cord, held by the serpentine, towards him. He always thought serpentine an odd name, but as Father had explained, serpents could spit venom. Dragons, of course, could spit fire, and muskets were among the most fearsome firebreathers of all.

Having not expected the weapon to fire, Lock hadn't braced himself properly, and the weapon had pushed him off balance against the shack's flimsy wall. But he was in far better shape than Billy. He struggled on his haunches, holding his hands to his ears and crying out. Blood leaked out of them and onto his tattered grey coat. A large hole had been burned into his clothes, and the skin underneath was scorched red.

Somehow, in all his activity, Lock had neglected to insert a musket ball. But the weapon's discharge still inflicted nasty burns, as Billy was learning. The right side of his face was badly singed, and his eardrums were certainly burst. In his agony, he shouted furiously at Lock, who heard nothing but ringing. Lock recalled the questions he had once posed to Father. They were now much more relevant.

'*What happens if the enemy closes on you and you've expended your shot?*' a young Matthew had asked.

'*Then, Matthew, be ready to improvise. You grasp the barrel with both hands, and prepare to club his skull with the stock.*'

This seemed like the moment when such improvisation would be necessary. Billy was wounded and dazed. He rose to his feet, took his hands from his ears, and shouted to overcome his newfound deafness.

'You... you mad bastard. You just made the worst mistake of your life...'

Could he bludgeon this man, who he barely knew? Lock considered that he could, if he had to. But he preferred to fight with words.

'Get out Billy. Go home to Sherbourne and tell your knavish friends that the Lock family won't stand for these insults.'

Billy grimaced, and carefully felt for burns. His countenance softened. He knew he was vulnerable. He knew Lock had the advantage.

'You will pay for this Lock. I swear it on my Mother's grave, you will pay for this.'

Billy half stumbled past Lock, making for the door. Steadying himself by its frame, he glanced back at Arthur. Lock met his eyes, the musket still brandished like a club, adrenaline surging through him.

'Touch my brother again, Billy, and next time I won't leave a mere burn, I'll rip a hole in your chest.'

Billy seemed dubious, but the pain was persuasive. 'Your brother... owes me money,' he hissed, as he stood at the doorway.

Lock reached into a pouch in his back pocket. 'Here,' he thrust a collection of coins at him. 'Now be gone!'

Billy looked at the pennies that clinked and spun on the wooden floor, before turning his gaze back to Lock. 'No, *your* money won't do. The debt has increased. It must be paid.' As he said the last few words, he turned and pushed through the door. It closed behind him.

Lock gasped, dropped the musket, and now came to terms with the ringing in his own ears. His head was throbbing from the entire interaction, and his muscles ached. Then he moved on Arthur, who had gone quiet. He knelt behind his brother in the chair, and began pulling through the knots that had been tied behind him.

The rope was thick and sinewy, and it took several minutes before he made any progress. Arthur groaned as the process continued. The rope cut into his shoulders, and blood continued to seep from several cuts, but the wound on his right shoulder was the most problematic.

Finally, the ropes were undone, and Arthur could be moved from his chair. Lock lifted him carefully, with his body under his brother's left side. Arthur's legs seemed good for nothing, at least not yet. As Lock walked him to the door, Arthur muttered an apology, his eyes fixed to the ground.

'I'm sorry... Matt...' Arthur whispered.

'It's alright Arthur.'

But it was not alright. Was Arthur dying? Would he need a physician? Did he really owe a man like Billy so much money? *Six shillings*? That was enough to purchase a new horse. How had Arthur come by so much money, and why had he deigned to waste it on cards?

He would grill him when he returned home, but he was more worried about what Gus would say tonight, and what Mother and Father would say when they returned tomorrow. Mother, of course, would rush to her perfect boy's side, and somehow blame the elder brother for what had happened. Father would wait in the wings before assigning blame, but he would only ever commend him when out of Mother's sight.

Lock grumbled to himself as they emerged from the shack, and made for where he hoped their mounts would still reside. If Billy truly was so desperate, perhaps he would steal them? Then again, a man with a face full of pain tended to retreat, not raise the stakes. Billy was a problem for another day.

Arthur began to stir. 'My shoulder,' he moaned. 'I think it may be broken.'

'It's not broken Arthur, it's merely a flesh wound.' Though he had no idea. He didn't even have the full story of how his brother had ended up here. Certainly, the two lackeys would be made to pay, but Terry didn't have to pay for his brother's sins. He had always been a good lad.

Arthur coughed a few times, and turned his face up to the rain. Lock welcomed the continuing downpour. It had soaked him through. Torrents of water flowed from his hair all the way down his back, but it seemed to mollify the pain.

It could not wash away the painful memory of what had just occurred. Did all of Sherbourne know of 1613? Truly? Lock forced himself to believe that Billy had been lying, but the act was in vain. There was no escape from his shame. He was doomed to have his failings follow him wherever he went.

- CHAPTER THREE -

Lock had known Captain Augustus Frank his whole life. There was scarcely a memory he possessed that Gus was absent from. He had been father's brother in arms, until, tiring of war, father had asked Gus to join him on his estate. The offer was one of companionship, as much as employment, for Captain Frank was an accomplished physician.

He had been there for Lock's own birth, and had helped deliver Arthur as well. Whenever Gus was absent, bad things tended to happen, like on that night in 1613, when the Lock family had holidayed in Frisia without him.

Perhaps he was like an uncle, or perhaps he was more like a friend, Lock was never quite sure. Sometimes Captain Frank could be possessed by a righteous anger. His jowls would quiver, and his whiskers would twitch with emotion. On other occasions, he was a picture of restraint, upheld by a steely nerve that overcame even the most dangerous of situations. Perhaps, he had once been reckless, and had since learned his lesson.

When he drank with Father, Lock would overhear their tales from time to time. Gus always seemed to be in place to save Father's skin, and just at the right moment. He was perhaps a decade older than Father, and certainly wiser. Father was a doer; Gus was a thinker. That was what Mother said. As a result, they had argued often.

Father complained when people would gossip about him. Gus would reply that people were too nosy for their own good. There was something unspoken that haunted many of their disputes, this was Lock's impression. But the two men had always stuck together. Father knew deep down that he needed Gus around. His sons needed someone to take care of them when he travelled abroad. More than once, Gus had proven his worth.

He had given one vagrant a good hiding when they'd attempted to steal

Father's prized Frisian stallions. On another occasion, he stood alone, like a brick wall against a storm, when a group of knaves had broken into Locksville late at night. Armed with only a lantern, he had scared the villains away. Gus joked forever after that their real reason for running was that he had neglected to button up his nightrobe as he swung the lantern at them.

Captain Frank had been part of the family for all of Lock's twenty-two years, and in all of those years, Lock had never seen the man cry.

Until today.

The day when Lock returned with Arthur on the front of Ferdinand's saddle, with Isabella trailing obediently behind. The horses clopped their way into the courtyard, and Gus had been there to meet them, hat in hand.

Then he had seen the state of the two brothers, and he had fixed that problem first. The trauma had overcome Arthur, and he drifted into a wistful sleep after Gus had carried him upstairs to bed and tended to his wounds. But when he returned to the hall, fulfilled some small talk, and seated himself next to Lock, the huge bear of a man broke down.

Lock nearly dropped his book in shock. Tears erupted from him, and Lock hardly knew what to do. Gus leaned forward in his plush burgundy chair, his grey locks tied back from his face, exposing his tired, wrinkled eyes. Those eyes ran like streams, as he shook his head in apparent disbelief. After choking on the sight, Lock practically leapt out of his chair and crouched beside him, his knees pressing into the soft rug where his young feet had once trodden.

'Captain Frank?' Lock said, gripping the man's arm. 'You need not worry about Arthur, he'll recover. I will make sure he pays Billy the six shillings, and then some.'

Captain Frank just shook his head and stared at the ceiling. He moved his ham hands to his face, and wiped away tears in vain.

'I tried... I tried...' Captain Frank managed to say, before exhaling steadily, and swallowing a new wave of sorrow. 'I tried to keep it together, for Arthur's sake. He's been through enough today.'

Lock leaned back from Gus' chair. 'What do you mean? Whatever is the matter?'

He looked at Lock's earnest face and shook his head. 'Oh Matthew, it is so terrible.'

Lock rose to his feet and straightened his back. 'Whatever the matter is,

I'm sure we can work it out.'

Captain Frank shook his head again. 'I fear you will hate me if I deliver this news.'

'I could never hate you Gus, not after everything you've done for our family, and for me.'

He had not intended to call him Gus, but the statement was true. He loved the man like a second Father. Perhaps, more than his Father.

'It's your parents, Matthew...' Gus began. He shook his head again. 'They...'

'What? Are they delayed? If I have to miss the embassy with Father I do not mind.'

'Oh Matthew you poor boy, you have your whole life ahead of you.' Gus put his head in his hands, and appeared to psyche himself up for his task. He blinked at Lock several times, before beckoning him to come closer. With both of his hands, he seized on Lock's right hand. His hands had never been in Lock's before. Lock was taken aback by the act, but Gus' expression moved him to remain. Gus took one great heaving breath, before uttering the news that would change Lock's life forever.

'Matthew, it's your parents. I learned this morning that both were found murdered. In The Hague.'

Lock's ears latched onto distant birdsong, and the faint sound of the last drips of rain. His mouth fell open. He blinked at Gus. It was too much to comprehend. There were too many questions to be asked. Lock took a few dazed steps backwards.

Captain Frank stood up from the armchair, seized Lock's shoulders with his hands, and shook him slightly.

'Say something lad, say something,'

Lock could not speak. He could not think. He could barely breathe. His knees shook. His eyes fixed on the portrait from 1612, just behind Gus' head. Mother had always hated it, but it was Father's favourite, so it had stayed.

A family of five, a perfect family of five, with a loving couple and their three sons and their two boisterous wolfhounds. Lock used to look at the work and mourn for his elder brother, and then for the dogs.

It hit him, like a swift thrust in his gut, that he would now have to mourn for his parents as well. He collapsed into Gus' awaiting frame.

He sobbed. They were gone. Both of them. And he'd never had the chance to make up for what he'd done. He'd never had the chance to make them proud.

Time seemed to stand still as he rested in Captain Frank's arms. Eventually, he was gently set down into a chair. Captain Frank ran through various details that went in one ear and out the other. Talk of inheritance. Of how to tell Arthur. Of the ongoing investigation into his parents' demise.

'How?' Lock had managed to say, as he pulled his knees up to his chest to warm his heart.

'They're... not sure yet,' Captain Frank had said, as he placed a blanket over the shivering man.

'Who would do such a thing? Who could do it? Why? *Why*?!' Lock had shouted the last word, consumed by a sense of injustice. Gus had done his best to comfort him, but Lock burst forth from the chair, nearly tangling his legs in the blanket. He ran out of the hall, down the corridor with its gaudy mahogany panelling and marble pillars, before bursting through the front door.

He ignored Captain Frank's shouts and pleas to stop. Matthew Lock ran. He ran as fast as his legs could possibly move him. He ran to escape from Locksville. He ran to escape his past. He ran to escape his shame. Yet he could not run quickly enough. There was only one solution. There was only one way to fix what he had broken nine years before. He would go on the Embassy alone. He would go to The Hague, and he would find out for himself what had happened to Charles and Catherine Lock.

- CHAPTER FOUR -

Lock sat at the end of Arthur's bed. The sun's rays pressed forcibly into his bedroom, and Lock had pulled the curtains aside, so that his brother would feel the warmth of the sun on his skin, before he received the coldest news imaginable.

Lock had insisted on delivering it, though Captain Frank had offered. As his brother stirred, and looked up at him with dark eyes that sparkled with kindness and care, Lock found that words failed him once again.

He delivered the gutting news through bitter, angry tears, and he watched as his brother crumbled into pieces. He now understood Captain Frank's agony. Giving such news was akin to attacking a loved one with a deadly weapon, an unavoidable assault, which filled the stomach with bile. Arthur had demanded answers immediately, and Lock regurgitated the same information that Gus had passed to him. As before, it was not sufficient.

'Why are the bloody Dutch taking so long to figure it out?' Arthur demanded. '*Who killed them?*'

'I don't know, Arthur, I wish I did.'

'I swear, I'll get the bastards who did this.' Arthur's body quivered with a potent mix of fury and grief. Lock recognised the combination. It still surged through him.

He decided to wait for the worst of Arthur's rage to pass. There was nothing he could do for the moment. Lock had promised to return to his room after a while. He left Arthur prone and, on his side, still sobbing quietly in bed.

Lock stared out the window and shook his head, as the sun rose on the hardest day of his life.

It had already been the worst night of his life. But once Captain Frank caught up with him, shivering and sobbing in that run down shack where he had retrieved Arthur from, Matthew Lock had sworn an oath. He swore to find out the truth, and get justice for his parents. He could honour them in death, even if he could not honour them in life.

He had returned with Captain Frank, and after he had been plied with considerable shorts of whiskey, and no shortage of food, he found that the pain had lessened, and the practical sphere of his mind began to whir into life.

Captain Frank had not objected to Lock's insistence that he make the trip on the Embassy alone. It was, Captain Frank said, a fitting way to honour his Father's memory, and the journey was something Father had deeply wanted for his son.

The last four years of an Oxford education would be for naught if Matthew Lock never ventured into the wider world, and put this training to the test. There was also the matter of his skills with the musket and sword, skills which had been honed furiously after many years of relentless practice.

There was also a personal motive. The Embassy's destination was Frankfurt, but made landfall in The Hague. This granted Lock a unique opportunity to conduct an investigation of his own.

'I would come with you lad, but I want to be here for Arthur.'

Lock found that he had acquired a new sense of anxiety over his brother's wellbeing. He was riven by further sobs when it dawned that his brother was the last member of his family left. He was all he had in the world. The only one to also hold the Lock name. But certainly not the only one to suffer from his parents' loss. Lock had never seen Captain Frank's frame absorb so much alcohol.

The funeral, Captain Frank explained, could not be completed until the bodies had been returned, but repatriation was a difficult matter, particularly when crossing over the Channel. Lock could leave Bristol with the Embassy, visit The Hague, and then guarantee the swift return of his parents' remains.

Captain Frank's eyes then glistened, and he mentioned a name Lock had not heard in some time.

'Sir Horace Vere, Matthew, that's the man you need to see.' Frank had said the words while staring into a small glass, as he swirled the liquid around it.

'*Vere*?'

'Your godfather, Matthew. He'll be able to tell you more about your Father's life. He may even be able to shed some light on who was responsible for... you know.'

'Do you think?'

'It is difficult to say Matthew, but I know your Father intended to visit Vere when he was there recently.'

'Where is this Vere character staying? Somewhere in The Hague?'

Captain Frank shook his large head. 'No, lad. Vere is a soldier of the highest order. He commands the English garrison at Frankenthal.'

Lock had never heard of the place, and Captain Frank knew it.

'It is, shall we say, a good distance south of The Hague. Follow the Rhine, it's on the left bank, near Mannheim.'

'How on earth do I get there?'

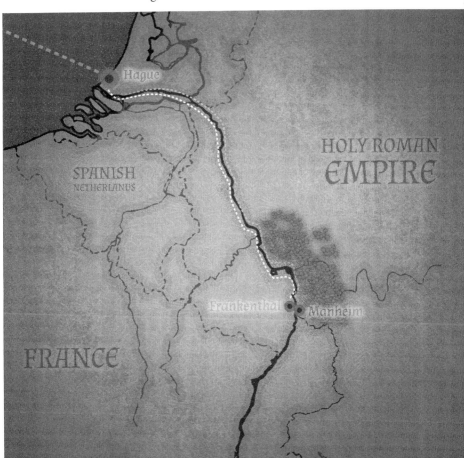

'The Embassy will go as far as Frankfurt, lad. Not sure how quick they'll travel, but that'd be a good way to start. From Frankfurt, you can head due south. Another's day's ride south-west, perhaps two. You'll have to arrange safe transport with the Spanish, but that shouldn't be too great an issue.'

Lock nodded. Grief and rage numbed him to any logistical problems. Perhaps, he was simply going through the motions, and the penny would drop once he left Locksville.

The task was clearly great, but his nationality did offer him a certain degree of protection. The King of Spain's daughter was on the verge of being pledged to the Prince of Wales, and neither Britain, nor Spain, would wish to jeopardise this arrangement with a scandal involving a travelling Englishman.

'Perhaps you'll even run into our Baron John in your travels,' Captain Frank said with a weak smile.

Baron John Digby of Sherbourne was England's ambassador to Spain, and had been knighted for his service to the King. His estate was just a short ride to the south, centred on Sherbourne castle, and it dwarfed that of Locksville. Father had always marvelled that Digby had been rewarded for the same reasons as himself – exemplary service in the field of diplomacy.

'I should be so lucky, but I doubt I'll see Madrid.'

'Baron Digby has been quiet over the last year, so your Father said, but yes, Matthew, it is probably best to stick to the plan.'

'I will stop in The Hague, and then onto Frankfurt, and then to Frankenthal?'

Captain Frank grunted in affirmation, and gazed at the bottom of his empty glass.

'Do you know what I might find?'

Captain Frank rose from his chair, and walked to within inches of the ground floor window. He gazed at a sprawl of green forested land. The sun's rays made him wince as they shimmered into his eyes. His bushy eyebrows were drawn, but when he turned to Lock, he maintained his composure.

'You should know, Matthew, that there is a war going on. You will have to tread carefully, and ensure you do not involve yourself in it. You are a neutral observer. On a... fact-finding mission, that is all.'

Lock nodded. Past conversations with Father ensured the situation in Europe was at least vaguely known.

The continent had become a hotbed for conflict in recent years. First, there had been the Bohemian revolt, which had been exacerbated by the decision of a Rhineland prince to seize the Bohemian Crown. The forces of the Holy Roman Emperor had defeated his armies, but this rebel, Frederick, the Elector Palatine, had retreated to The Hague to continue his rebellion. Lock's journey would take him through the heart of Frederick's lands, but this wasn't the only conflict to consider.

In April 1621, a truce between the Spanish and Dutch that had lasted a dozen years, expired. War raged in the Netherlands and in Germany, and it seemed certain that the Habsburg dynasty, which fought in both contests, would pool its resources and soldiers together, so that all the conflicts would be transformed into one.

This, at least, had been Father's theory.

'You should find the Spanish commander near Mannheim, lad. He'll be able to authorise your travel across the Rhine to Frankenthal, so that you're not pestered by Spanish soldiers.'

Lock moved to Captain Frank's side. 'I will, Gus.'

'When will you leave?' the captain maintained his stare into Locksville's distant reaches, perhaps unable to return his gaze to his surrogate son.

'The Embassy departs from Bristol on Friday, so I have a few days, but I will not delay. I intend to leave today. I am already packed.'

'And, how do you feel?'

'I feel... I feel like I don't know if I can do this.' The confession evoked shame, but it was cathartic to admit it.

Captain Frank nodded and smiled weakly out the window. He cleared his throat. 'Did I ever tell you the story of how Matthew Lock became the most accomplished musketeer in all of England?'

'Oh, come now Gus.'

'I believe it was not less than two weeks after James' murder. You were face to face with the musket again. Naturally, its inner workings were as mysterious to you as an unknown language. The five-foot-long piece probably felt large and unwieldy in your young, fleshy hands.'

'It did,' Lock said quietly.

'And you *hated* the weapon, didn't you? You hated it like you'd never hated anything else.'

Lock just nodded, and sniffed lightly.

'Your anger may have been justified. After all, had the secrets of the musket been easier to decipher, had the mechanism been more accessible to a complete novice, James might still be alive.'

'Gus I'm not really sure –'

'But this grudge against the matchlock musket was pointless. It was a source of power, to be harnessed, to be directed against one's enemies. It simply required training, like any other language.'

'A *lot* of training.'

Captain Frank stepped toward the window and opened it, permitting a light breeze into the room. He leaned on the low sill with his elbows, and breathed the air greedily. 'Indeed, Matthew, a soldier could train for years in the drill, and they would never achieve fluency in the language of the musket. But they could at least come close. For a non-soldier, the dreary drill manual by Jacob de Gheyn was the only possible route to proficiency.'

'And for the twelve-year-old boy?'

Captain Frank turned his head to smile at Lock. 'For the boy with protective parents, who denied their son a musket, a broom would have to suffice.'

Lock winced. 'I try to erase the broom period from my memory.'

But Captain Frank evidently had not. 'For nigh on a year, you went to the corner of the Locksville estate, dark wood broom in hand, Jacob de Gheyn's manual propped open with a stone. Each of the forty-three steps were rehearsed, one by one. A piece of string doubled as a match cord, and imagination did the rest. Your Father's powder was securely locked away, so there could be no practice with the real thing.'

The initial protests had since vanished. It was comforting to dwell on anything other than the current state of grief. Lock's teenage years seemed a blur of drilling and powder. Was this how the mind coped with trauma?

Captain Frank took the hint, clearing his throat, and embellishing for effect.

'Matthew Lock's mission was simple. To learn the drill inside out. To equip himself with the necessary knowledge, so that if the masked men ever returned, he would know how to expel them. The masked men did not return, except for when Lock closed his eyes, and they invaded the sanctity of his dreams. When he slept, the hesitation, the helplessness, the failure, all haunted him like so many relentless ghosts.'

Lock stared at Captain Frank's front-facing frame.

How did Gus know so much about his internal struggle?

'My physician's notes recorded the symptoms. Matthew Lock, victim of trauma, prone to bouts of night terrors, recommend plenty of fresh air, and... the occasional dash of port.'

Lock sighed. 'Never did see that port.'

'That's because my recommendations could do no good, not truly. No, if Matthew Lock wished to banish the terrors, he would have to master the new techniques. Then, surely, the haunting would end.'

'I couldn't tell anyone about it. Not the practicing, and certainly not the nightmares.'

Captain Frank shook his large head. 'Naturally, you kept your new obsession secret, not that your parents showed much interest anyway.'

'True,' Lock said quietly.

'But... a certain... Captain Frank noticed something. At first, he suspected crime.'

'*Crime?*'

'Indeed. A teenager acting out in anger against his parents, or against the world. One morning, I followed you to your favoured destination at the edge of the estate, just where the stream runs at its shallowest.'

'You did?'

'I watched you in... fascination. You stood for hours, repeatedly, obsessively, furiously, rehearing the movements.'

'Gracious, did you have no other duties?'

'This was more important. I watched you for perhaps a month, and then two, unsure of precisely how to approach the subject either with you or your parents.'

'You watched me for all that time?'

Captain Frank swallowed hard. 'I also watched you get better. I watched the satisfaction and confidence grow on your face as the techniques became more natural. I watched you switch between the different steps with increasing smoothness and speed.'

'You never said anything, during that whole time?'

'The secret observations had become... precious to me.'

'*Precious?*'

Captain Frank sighed and dabbed the corners of his eyes with a handkerchief. 'Those mornings… were the only point of the day when a smile could be seen on your face.'

'It was… a difficult time.'

Captain Frank cleared his throat, determined to maintain his narrative tone. 'Yessir, otherwise, Matthew Lock was a picture of misery. An outsider in his own home. Blamed unfairly, but understandably, by parents crippled and hounded by grief.'

'I beg your pardon?'

Captain Frank raised his index finger with intent. 'But, I was stuck in a crisis. If I shared the secret with Charles Lock, your Father would surely intervene. He would be guaranteed to act. To force you to cease with these fruitless exercises.'

'He would?'

'Charles Lock could be… cruel like that. He could also be blind to crises happening under his nose.'

'Such as?' The story was verging on impertinence.

'It was not the second son, but the youngest son, that was the true black sheep. Discipline was difficult for a Father who was too gutted even to speak to his remaining sons, so Arthur roamed uncontrolled.'

'He was a brat, that much is true.'

'And then, the day arrived. The day when Arthur's mischief caught up to him. Arthur had returned, basket of brambly apples under his arm, from an orchard far from the estate's grounds.'

'*Apples*?'

Captain Frank nodded. 'The fruit was easily recognised. They belonged to a poor family of little means. A family that depended upon the income from these apples to get them past winter. Then a pig could be purchased. Then the family would not starve.'

'I see.'

'But Arthur had seized their apples.'

'*No.*'

'Indeed, Matthew, Arthur had stolen them without a care for the family's well-being, or the consequences it would bring. I was steps away from reprimanding the boy, an awkward mission, considering his position in the family.'

'You shouldn't have hesitated, you should have –'

'There was no need for me to act. You, Matthew, acted in my stead, and in your Father's.'

'Are you sure?'

'You ripped the basket of apples from Arthur's arms. Carefully, though, ensuring not to drop any. You condemned your brother for his selfishness. And when Arthur had protested, you explained the bigger picture.'

'And Arthur learned his lesson?'

A smirk grew in the corner of Captain Frank's mouth. 'The younger brother knew he had erred. But in his shame, he also felt anger. In this anger, he sought to get even by using the only weapon he had against his brother.'

'My rehearsals,' Lock whispered. Vague whisps of the confrontation floated through his memory, few of them tangible.

Captain Frank nodded. 'Your daily rehearsals by the stream were no secret to Arthur. Who could imagine the punishment which would follow, when the Father would arrive to chide the son, and take away the one thing which seemed to bring him joy?'

'Arthur did that... to me?'

'The secret was shared shortly after, and the following morning, the Father acted.'

'God sakes, why are you telling me this now? You mean to turn me against my brother when I need him most?'

Captain Frank sighed heavily through his blocked nose, before continuing. 'You had been allowed to go to the stream, as normal, armed with your broom, the piece of string, and Jacob de Gheyn's increasingly tattered drill manual. You made it perhaps... halfway through his routine, when clattering hooves sounded in the distance.'

'Did I run?'

'No. You were frightened, though. You knew your Father never came this far from the home. He had hardly seen this portion of his estate since it had been purchased. Charles was accompanied by Arthur, and... myself alongside him.'

'You were all there? Truly, I do not remember.'

'I watched, as your Father dismounted, and marched towards you.'

'At times, he terrified me.'

'Charles could be a terrifying man, and you always bowed to him. But not today. Perhaps it was bravery that dissuaded you from frantically hiding the evidence, as he may have expected. Perhaps it was anger. Perhaps it was a determination to hold onto the one thing that brought you meaning and joy. Whatever it was, you stood your ground.'

'He reprimanded me?'

'Your defiance seemed to have been the wrong decision. Your Father seized the broom from your hands. There was no protest from the boy, only muted despair. I... shielded my eyes.'

'He struck me?'

'No, Matthew. Your Father had not come to reprimand. He had come to reward. I remember him now, reaching to his back. He produced the five-foot-long musket which you had not dared to use. He placed it in your hands.'

Lock gasped, failing to block another wave of grief.

Captain Frank turned to face Lock, his eyes bloodshot and moist. 'For a precious, fleeting movement, your Father embraced you, and held you tight. You hesitated, before holding your Father's waist. Though your tattling brother had not realised it, Arthur had jolted your Father back into... well, Fatherhood.'

'I... I don't know –'

Captain Frank seized Lock's shoulder with his right hand. 'The very notion that his second son could engage with a routine for nearly a year without his knowledge left your Father deeply affected. He worried you were drifting away from him. He feared he might lose you... like he lost James.'

'He could never,' Lock managed, just as his voice broke.

'*If the boy wishes to drill*, your Father said, *if he wishes to practice until his fingers become calloused and his arms ache, then let him practice with a real musket*. And if you wished to take these rehearsals to their logical conclusion, and become the best bloody musketeer in all of England, then *that* was an outcome your Father wished to help you achieve.'

'I made it this far, thanks to him, and thanks to you.'

'Indeed you did. Within three years, you fired your first shot, filthy from powder, but swollen with pride. By now, your passion had become an open secret. Much of the estate had come out to watch you shoot.'

'They had?'

'Among those that had clapped feverishly when the musket cracked, and the musket ball surged from Matthew's musket into the nearby stream, was... was me. As proud of you as I've ever been, and as I am now.'

The strain had become intolerable. Lock collapsed into Captain Frank's frame for the second time. He sobbed into his shoulder, holding nothing back. 'I couldn't save James, and now that they're gone, I feel like I... like I killed him all over again.'

'Don't you dare, Matthew. I don't care what those bastards say, because I know you, and I knew your Father, and I know what he would say.'

'*What?*' The desperate tone was palpable, though the question was muffled by Captain Frank's dolman.

'That you were a *child*, not a soldier, and that it was the duty of the parents, not the *child*, to protect the family from harm.'

'It doesn't matter what age I was, Gus, I failed them. And I never got a chance to make up for it, or make them proud.'

Captain Frank forced Lock's frame away from his. He held Lock firmly by both shoulders, and shook his head. '*Proud?* Your Father scarcely shut up about you.'

'I don't believe you.'

'The career your Father chose... I believe it hardened him. But if you think he wasn't proud, then you did not see the change in him when he returned home.'

'The change?'

'He used to count down the days when he'd be able to return home to his family. And once you took up the musket, God, I'd not seen him so excited since he met your Mother.'

'I thought he spilled his drink on Mother the first time they met?'

Captain Frank hesitated. 'That... that was a natural reaction to her beauty, and her charm.'

'How can I do this without him? I don't know how to be a soldier-statesman. I'm a fraud.'

'You are Matthew Charles Lock. You are your Father's son. You are an Oxford graduate. You are a bloody good shot, a good man, and a valued friend.'

'Don't forget mediocre horseman.'

Captain Frank raised an index finger. 'But even in that, you persevered. When that beast threw you off, and you fell so far, you got back up, and you did what you had to.'

'Things were easier then, James was alive.'

'That miserable physician, from Sherbourne, do you remember him?'

Lock nodded.

'He recommended I take your left arm, and remove it, since it was so badly mangled from the fall. But I knew you were made of stronger stuff. *Matthew Lock is a fighter*, I said. And I sat with you, for those first few shaky weeks, as your small body was racked by fever. Through it all, Matthew, I knew you could pull through.'

Lock instinctively flexed the fingers in his left hand, and Captain Frank nodded at the act.

'Seems I was right to believe in you. Tell me, Lock, how many people need to believe in you, before you believe them?'

Lock had no answer.

'The world doesn't know what Matthew Lock is capable of, but I do.'

'Do you now?'

'You will do great things, Matthew. It is a grave crime that they won't be here to see it, but they are watching.'

Lock nodded slowly, and contributed a weak smile.

Captain Frank sniffed gently. 'You know, your Father wished it to be a surprise, but I was meant to come with you, on the Embassy.'

'*Why?*'

'He... he had his reasons, lad. It's not important now. I don't wish for you to go. In truth, I wish to keep you here forever, where you will be safe. But I also know you're the only one who can get justice. I am far too old to pursue it in a continent riven by war.'

Lock nodded gently. Both men watched a heron in the distance. The prehistoric bird tip-toed gingerly around the edge of the lake, before sourcing his meal, and making a dramatic exit.

Lough Lock, the lake was called. The name had been chosen by James, and it had made Father laugh and long for the Scottish Highlands at the same time.

The calming body of water had been a constant reminder of James' absence. But now they were all gone, the people who were supposed to lead the Lock family forward.

Captain Frank sighed in the silence. 'I'm also far too cranky to put up with the politics that comes with repatriation. But Vere will help you. Go to Frankenthal and speak with him, lad, and he'll sort this business out.'

Lock indicated that he would. 'I would speak to Arthur before I leave. He should know why I am going, even if he will surely beg to join me.'

'He will know he cannot join you, particularly with his wound, but you may tell him that he has the rest of his life to leave the nest.' Captain Frank said the words breathlessly, as though he dreaded the moment when his adoptive family no longer needed him. He cleared his throat. 'Go on lad, get your business together. Let's not keep each other with our grief.'

Lock nodded, and made for Arthur's bedroom.

- CHAPTER FIVE -

A fitful night of sleep had done little to soothe Arthur's condition. "I'm coming with you,' he had insisted, when Lock had revealed his intentions.

'Don't be ridiculous brother, you can hardly use your right arm.'

'It's fine. Gus says it isn't broken, just a deep wound. I won't have to be bled. He merely recommends bedrest.'

'Exactly,' Lock soothed. *'Bedrest.* You must listen to the doctor.'

Arthur winced as he sat upright in bed. His right arm hung by his side. Lock sat on the bed beside him. It was like the reverse of what had happened when they were young. Mother would abide no fearful sons, and in the event of a thunderstorm Arthur would creep bashfully into Lock's bed. They'd barely say a word to each other, nor would it be mentioned the next day, but by the sound of his brother's peaceful sleep, it did the trick.

'Gus just wants to hold me here, to stop me from leaving.'

'In fact he does not. He said you could leave next year, when you're ready to depart from your studies.'

'My studies,' Arthur rolled his eyes. 'I have no need for studies, Lock. I wish to become a soldier of fortune.'

Father's war stories had inspired both his boys, but Arthur had been captured far more than his elder brother by the appeal of the lifestyle. Father had always seemed dubious about it. He seemed to believe that Matthew was suited for the life of a soldier-statesman, whereas Arthur was not. Father even made his eldest son promise to persuade Arthur away from this life when the time came. Saving Mother's favourite was no minor task. Lock understood that this responsibility would now also fall entirely upon him.

'It is not what Mother wanted for you,' Lock said, his voice close to cracking.

'God, Matty, what are we going to do without them?'

Lock moved his hand to Arthur's uninjured shoulder. 'The same thing we've always done Arthur. We will make it through together. We'll make the Lock name as fearsome as it was when Father was arranging peace and war between the great powers of Europe.'

Arthur smiled at the suggestion. The straight cut under his right eye had begun to scab.

'That could scar, brother.' Lock said.

'Let's hope so. If you get to be the tall brother, I should at least get to be the scarred one. *Arty One-Eye*, they could call me.'

'You have both your eyes still.'

'For now. Billy could return to finish the job.'

'He won't, Arthur. I told him in no uncertain terms to steer clear of our family.'

'And he agreed?'

Lock realised that Arthur had been delirious during much of the showdown. 'He did. But if he returns, Gus is here. He could rip Billy apart with his bare hands.'

'I'm sorry, you know. About all of it.'

Lock shook his head. 'It's alright. Billy is a nasty piece of work. A manipulator and a schemer if there ever was one.'

'I did it for you, you know,' Arthur said quietly.

'What do you mean?'

'I was in the King's Arms in Sherbourne, having just ridden Ferdinand rather harder than usual. I was parched beyond belief, and to slake my thirst, I requested some bitters.'

'Not simple water?' Lock smirked.

'I felt I'd earned the bitters. Save the water for the horses, didn't Father used to say?' Arthur's smile broke as his eyes moistened. He coughed the sorrow from his throat. 'I was enjoying my drink, when Billy caught sight of me. I knew he wanted my money. Man is always without coin of his own.'

'Why did you not just walk away.'

'He insulted my honour.'

Lock sighed. 'Arthur, he cannot insult your honour. He is below your station. Well below it. Only men of our rank can make a mark on your name.'

'It wasn't my name he lambasted; it was yours.' Arthur stared at the rosewood vanity in the corner of the room.

'*Mine*?'

'I was a fool for letting him trap me. Perhaps it was the bitters, but I could not stand to hear your good name defaced by such a common tramp.'

'What did he say about me?' Lock wasn't sure why he wanted to know. He also suspected he knew what ammunition Billy would have used.

'It's not important now Matt.'

'It is to me.'

Arthur sighed. 'It was about 1613, of course. The rat bastard has no clue of what he speaks, but he said it with such venom that the whole tavern seemed to pause.'

'He called me a coward?'

'At first. I could handle such lies. But when he saw the taunt failing, he worked himself into a more ridiculous frenzy.'

'Saying what, exactly?'

Arthur paused for a few seconds, before closing his eyes and uttering the filthy collection of words. 'He... he claimed that you had not saved James because you wanted him to die, since then you would be the heir, and Locksville would be yours.'

The anger returned to Lock like a flood. His body shook on the bed. 'What utter bollocks that man spews. I regret now that my musket contained no proper ball.'

'It is untrue, no words exist to describe the audacity of the lie. We both adored James, everyone did. But when I saw the tavern pause with horror, I couldn't help myself.'

'I wish I'd been there, I would have brought him outside.'

'Duelling is illegal, Matt, you know that.'

'Who says we'd be duelling? I wouldn't give him a chance to draw a weapon of any kind. I would crush him like a beetle.'

Arthur shook his head and sighed. 'He would never have said such things if you'd been there. All ruffians like him are the same. All words, and no action.'

There was a brief silence. Lock tried to swallow his rage. Arthur failed to swallow a yawn. Lock then yawned in turn, and Arthur chuckled. As boys, one of their more favoured activities was to try to elicit a yawn from Captain Frank.

The task was all the more entertaining when the captain was engaged in serious business, and was made to appear bored by the involuntary act. One particularly successful game of yawns saw the entire dinner table, servants included, captured by the uncontrolled urge to join in.

'I just... I can't believe they're gone,' Arthur whispered. 'Not just ma and pa, but James as well.'

'I think we should remove that portrait,' Lock said sadly.

Arthur turned towards Lock on his rear. 'Absolutely not, it was Father's favourite.'

'It is... painful to look upon it now brother. We could keep it stored for a while, and take it out later.'

Arthur nodded slowly. 'We should acquire more wolfhounds. If Father's contact is still on location in Ireland, we should write to him and request more pups. Those hounds were incredible fun. I wouldn't mind a lick of fun right now.'

Lock returned to the scenes of whooping joy which had greeted his Father when he brought two Irish wolfhound pups back with him from the Pale. The pups had grown exponentially, and rivalled some of the horses in size. The gentle giants required considerable care and attention, but were as loyal as foresworn knights on a medieval crusade. Both brothers adored them, so much so that the dogs had been featured on the official family portrait, on their insistence.

Persuading the beasts to sit still as the painter did his work had been a mammoth task, but it had been a magical day. The dogs had filled a hole when James had died. It was as if they had sensed something had changed in Locksville. They had only passed recently, and had been themselves mourned like family members.

Lock basked in the fond memories, and was almost crushed when he was forced to return to reality.

'It's not your fault. You do know that, don't you?' Arthur said quietly. 'Those masked men, whoever they were, *they* were the true villains, not you.'

'I couldn't save him,' Lock said.

'You were a *child*, Matty. You had barely seen Father fire his musket before, how were you to know how the bloody thing worked?'

'If those villains crossed my path now...'

'If you saw those masked men again brother, I have no doubt you would fire upon each before any have a chance to recite their prayers.'

'Yes.'

Arthur cupped his left hand on Lock's right shoulder. 'You must let it go, brother. Focus on our parents. Focus on getting justice for them.'

'And what of getting justice for *James*?' Lock said, perhaps to himself. The quest had once animated the two brothers, but it had been abandoned by the family long ago. Nine years was a long time. It had been too painful even for Mother and Father to speak of the firstborn son any longer.

Arthur withdrew his hand. 'Justice... does not always follow evil deeds. What is it Reverend Burrell says? That some things are not resolved this side of heaven?'

Lock nodded at the expression. It had always brought him comfort, though he had simultaneously questioned why God did not work to punish evil, particularly where it was so manifest.

'I will miss you, brother.' Lock said, his voice cracking slightly. He looked to see Arthur's face already streaming tears.

'It shames me to cry, but I've scarcely been able to do much else in the last while. You must go. You must go the continent. Find this Vere character, and find justice for ma and pa. If you can, retrieve for me a souvenir.'

Lock smiled wearily. He was reminded of his lack of sleep by another round of involuntary yawns.

'You should fetch Father's clothes. They are yours now, after all,' Arthur suggested.

The words caused Lock's stomach to flutter. 'I suppose.'

'You can represent the Lock name while in Europe, and you should do so while in his finery.' Arthur then smiled. 'They should fit, just about.'

'Perhaps an expedition free from cakes will do my physique the world of good,' Lock grinned. 'I should surely visit the barbers as well. I'd imagine there are few shaggy looking envoys around.'

'Be safe, brother. And remember, as long as I breathe, you are not alone in this world.' Arthur turned to Lock with difficulty, clutching his right arm as he did so. 'We will make them proud.'

'We will,' Lock said, as he slid his body off the bed. 'I swear it.'

- CHAPTER SIX -

B ristol had been father's favoured point of departure for his varied continental adventures. London took far too long to reach, whereas Bristol was a single day's ride from Locksville if one pushed their beast hard enough. This time, the journey had taken Lock two days, and was broken by an overnight stay in Frome, a town of perhaps three thousand souls.

The stop was not truly necessary, but Frome had been Father's traditional 'midway' point when on the way to Bristol. The argument for pausing and resting, and of course eating, had never seemed particularly logical to Lock, but Father had insisted. He made sure to avail of the town's superior wool and clothing producers, and always returned with something of value for Mother.

But Lock had not perused Frome's wares, he had instead shut himself into his room, and contemplated his mission. It was a somewhat miserable exercise.

Billy's words still rang in his ears. The contemptible lie – that he had deliberately allowed James to suffer murder at the hands of the masked men – haunted him. He drank too heavily, toasting the memory of his parents in his solitude, and he suffered for it the next morning.

Upon leaving Frome for Bristol, Lock had requested that the carriage driver move at a gentle pace. There was, after all, no rush, and his stomach was tender. By the time Bristol had loomed into view in the early afternoon, the worst of the hangover had washed over him, but Lock was starving. The kind of bottomless pit hunger that demands a substantial feed.

His hunger had been cured with a heavy meal at an inn perched conveniently on the quayside. While there, seated at a simple wooden table in the open air, Lock had the ideal opportunity to watch Bristol in action. The city buzzed with activity, and thanks to his Father's instructions, Lock knew why.

Situated in a strategically optimal location, and blessed by geography, as much as the industry of its citizens, Bristol had become a metropolis of unrivalled importance. With the River Avon to its south, and the River Severn emptying itself in an enormous mouth to the north, Bristol was the epicentre of trade and commerce in south-west England. Availing of the manufacturing capabilities of Frome, in addition to the less savoury trade in slaves, the city had ballooned in size. Lock swore it had grown since he had last been here, perhaps five years before.

This was a city prideful of its accomplishments. Great pioneers like John Cabot, the first European to land in North America, departed from here. That was more than a century ago. The abundance of vessels cruising in and out of the port was a stark testament to the fact that the citizens of Bristol were now well used to such travels.

Lock eyed up several cargos as they arrived. The smells were what always drew him to the docks. It was, after all, where he would wave Father goodbye. Father would try to redirect his son's attention from the human cargo that arrived. Now, with no parent to forcibly avert his eyes, Lock stared in fascination at the abundance of black slaves, weighed down by chains, and staring vacantly into the distance.

One particular scene, perhaps fifty yards away, then drew his eye. Something stirred within him, as a rotund, sweating man with puffy red cheeks and a long whip began to attack the backs of his property. Lock winced, and silently cursed the man's cruelty, but knew from what Father had told him that he could do nothing.

Once they wore the chains, Father said, these were not human beings anymore. They had no more rights than would a vase, or bushel of corn. Some claimed they even lacked souls, and that the hard, back breaking work they were bound for on distant plantations would help nurture such a soul.

Lock scarcely believed that, and he glared fruitlessly at the distant rotund figure as he waddled maliciously after his bony charges. Father had been wrong. Slavery was not the natural order of things. He couldn't help but wonder what Jesus would have said to the rotund man, who would likely huff and puff his way into a Sunday service each week.

So fixated was he on the suffering that Lock did not see a portly, well-dressed man enter his field of vision, and wave warmly at him. Lock eventually came to, and rose from his table to shake his hand.

'Sir Henry Vane, your servant Sir! Thank you so much for meeting with me.' Lock said.

Sir Henry Vane was an MP and a rising star in Britain's political establishment. He had made the journey from Bristol to The Hague several times, most recently the previous summer, which was why Captain Frank had arranged for him to meet Lock just before he departed. He was also, crucially, one of Father's friends.

Lock had only ever seen him at a distance. Then he had been in the prime of his youth, a lawyer and intimate of the king, and only in his twenties. But the last decade had worn on him. He had a paunch, double-chin, and his moustache had begun to grey. Lock wondered how age could change a man so drastically. He also feared how the diplomatic life would transform him when he reached his mid-thirties.

'Matthew Lock, a pleasure. May I please offer my condolences for the loss of your parents. They were exemplary people, and did this nation a fine service.' Vane gestured for Lock to sit down, and he pulled out the chair opposite Lock.

'Thank you, Sir Vane,'

'Henry, please, call me Henry.'

'Henry it is!'

'I am sorry we could not arrange this meeting in happier circumstances. I believe your Father, God rest him, wished for you to hear from someone other than himself what the journey would be like.'

Lock nodded. That had indeed been Father's intention. Generous though he was with his advice, often when it was not even requested, Father had insisted that Lock receive perspectives of the world from as many minds as possible. Minds which were, of course, screened by him beforehand.

'Your Embassy is the same arrangement which departs annually. The war has slowed down the functions of most businesses that work across the Channel, but I think you'll find we English are masters at improvising when the money is right.'

Vane leaned back in his chair, and began smoking a tobacco pipe, an act Lock had not expected. Mother had always frowned upon the habit. Father had always despised the smell. Vane's sharp eyes seemed to sparkle even through the transparent puffs of smoke. He held the pipe as though it had been attached to him from birth.

'How many men tend to travel with the embassy, Henry?' Lock was careful at all times to maintain eye contact. This, Father had told him, was the best way to ensure you always received an answer. Whether that answer was honest or not was another matter.

'Oh, a good few, I dare say. Perhaps two hundred or more.'

'*Two hundred*? And these are all ambassadors or envoys of some sort or another?'

Vane chuckled and waved his hand through a lingering cloud of smoke. 'No, no Lock. Embassy is surely a... traditional affectation, rather than an accurate description of its intent. Truly, it is mostly merchants, travellers and adventurers now. Not much diplomacy to be had so long as His Majesty wishes to tie this nation to Spain.'

Some believed that the marriage of the Prince of Wales to a Spanish Princess could end the war between the Holy Roman Emperor and the Elector Palatine. King James had, after all, arranged the marriage of that Elector to his daughter, the Princess Elizabeth. That union gathered the pillars of Protestant Europe together, and was seen as a great coup.

But the effort to create the equivalent Spanish, Catholic union had been less successful. Critics could also argue that there was no guarantee the King of Spain would be able to persuade his cousin, the Emperor, to reinstate the Elector Palatine in his lands.

Indeed, some whispered that an Anglo-Spanish marriage would only serve to restrict and shame England, particularly if the Prince of Wales was compelled to convert to Rome.

'You do not commend the policy?'

'I do not, Lock, I do not. I know your Father felt quite dubious about it.'

'He detested it,' Lock said, shaking his head. A seagull landed a foot from him, eying up his leftovers. Vane shooed it away with some effort. 'He was also disappointed that the Twelve Years Truce did not last.'

Vane held up his hands. 'Ah, of course, *the Truce*. Your Father's greatest achievement. Shame it did not stand the test of time.'

'I think it lasted long enough Henry. Father used to say that the Dutch and Spanish were bound to make war again in the future. I think he just believed that the King of Spain would not resume the war so soon.'

Vane rubbed his chin for a few moments, before nodding. 'I fear he has resumed the war to capitalise on his expanded powers.'

'What do you mean?'

Vane smirked, before producing a rudimentary map which he lay on the table. 'This is a map of the Rhine. You will find an abundance of forces loyal to the King of Spain are now garrisoned there.'

Lock looked at the yellow piece of parchment. It was really just a drawing of Western Europe, with rough borders for France, the Dutch Republic and the Spanish Netherlands detailed. The Holy Roman Empire, that conglomeration of polities with no equal in the world for its byzantine complexity, clearly confounded even this cartographer. The label *German lands* were simply indicated on land across the Rhine, and the map's detail stopped before it reached the Empire's centre.

'*Here*, Lock,' Vane pointed at the Rhine River, which snaked its way from the Swiss mountains, all the way to the Dutch lands, where it emptied into the North Sea via three smaller tributaries.

Upon these watery barriers, the Dutch had based their main defences. Uniquely for this map, portions of the Rhine were highlighted. Vane placed his finger upon them.

'The Spanish are concentrated in *this* area, just below the Dutch. I would hazard a guess that Spain's generals are poised to attack the Dutch from the south with a major campaign later in the year.'

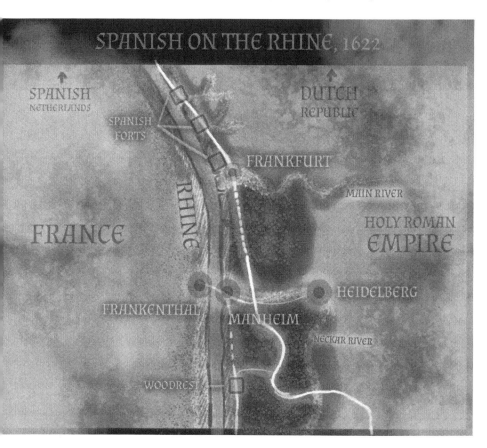

'Is it safe, to travel through the Republic, I mean?'

Vane nodded. 'For an Englishman of noble birth, yes. But be sure to keep your papers on hand. You have your accreditation?'

Lock nodded.

Reaching into his bag, he retrieved one of his most prized possessions. On the surface, it was a simple piece of parchment like any other. But a closer look revealed that the individual was authorised to travel in the company of the Embassy as far as Frankfurt. This made official the individual's claim to protection, and this claim to safety was the greatest defence Lock had against impatient Spaniards. At the bottom of the parchment, the seal of His Majesty himself was found. The document had been delivered late the previous year.

'Who should I show this to?' Lock asked, holding the parchment in front of Vane's eyes. Vane skimmed over the document and smiled knowingly.

'What are the odds, Lock, that you will find yourself outside of Frankfurt?'

Lock hesitated. If Frankenthal was to be reached, and if Vere was to be plied for information, venturing outside of the parameters of his instructions would be essential. 'It is... possible.'

Vane's smile became a grin. 'In that case, Lock, I would recommend checking in with the Spanish commander just below the city of Mannheim.'

'Mannheim?' the city sounded familiar, but not familiar enough for Lock to find it himself. The memory of Captain Frank's pep talk had largely vanished. The so-called map contained no information about the placement of cities, only the supposed placement of soldiers.

Vane made a gesture towards the map to acknowledge its worthlessness. 'I told them this would be a problem. I want a map, I said, not a bloody sketch. Mannheim is easy to find Lock. It sits at the confluence of the Rhine and Neckar Rivers, and you'll be able to reach it by following the course of the Main, another tributary, directly south from Frankfurt. But first... Lock, are you paying attention?'

Lock nodded, but in truth, the geography lesson seemed to wash over him. How had he gotten this far without a proper map? It would be wise to secure one upon landing in The Hague. Failing that, befriending a knowledgeable travelling companion would suffice.

'Charles Lock was a master of these river systems. He knew them as well as the inner workings of a man's heart.'

'Yes, Henry, he did try to teach me.'

Lock searched his brain for Father's lessons on German geography, and the complex system of tributaries that fed into and flowed from the Rhine. It was a wet maze, Father had said, but once you knew your way, you could glide along its courses, and make for any destination. Lock wished to play it safe.

'How long will it take, by carriage, to reach Frankfurt from The Hague?'

Vane chuckled. 'A week, if you're lucky, and if your driver is generous. It can feel like a year if your company is wretched, though. Be wary of the company of merchants. Their talk of coin will bore you to tears, I'm sure.'

'Very well, and from Frankfurt, how long is the journey to Mannheim?'

'Riding solo would be quickest.' Vane gathered his chin in his right hand. A fold of skin on his neck, the by-product of an easy lifestyle, squeezed itself over his unnecessarily tight collar. 'I would hazard a guess that you could make it in two days of hard riding. Then, you must cross the Neckar upstream from Mannheim, if you wish to avoid too much attention.'

Lock must have grimaced at the news, because Vane held up a hand to appease him.

'Not to worry lad, the journey is easy enough. Just tell any Spanish you meet that you're English, on business for the King.'

'And if they check my instructions, and see that I'm only authorised as far as Frankfurt?'

Vane smiled. 'You do as all good envoys do. *You act.* Feign confusion at first, and then disgust, and then anger at the suggestion that you would attempt to steer the King of Spain wrong.' He appeared finished with his pipe, and the conversation as well. He stood up suddenly, the wooden chair grating on the cobbled ground.

'Am I officially an envoy now?'

Vane allowed a chuckle. 'You are an envoy if you say you are, Lock. Who else would dare say different with His Majesty's seal in your possession?' He then slapped his thigh in apparent excitement. 'Oh, Lock. This will be a fantastic experience for you. I only wish your Father could see it.'

Lock's face fell. 'As do I, Henry, as do I.'

Vane sought to change the subject. '*Officer* Lock, that's what you can go by.'

'*Officer Lock*?' Lock blinked at his newfound title. 'Is that not somewhat... vague?'

'That's precisely the point lad. It is vague enough to sound important, and to fit into the known professions. Are you an Officer of an ambassadorial mission? An Officer in the King's army? An Officer in the East India Company? Who can know but you! You must sell your act, Lock. Nobody else will be able to do it as well as you can.'

Lock turned the title over in his head. 'Officer Lock,' he said out loud.

Vane pointed at Lock's chest with an excited grin. 'Now you've got it! *God*, I remember my first embassy like it were yesterday. We went from London of course, but these Bristol adventures are capital fun. That was to Heidelberg, to mark the marriage of the Elector Palatine to King James' daughter, the Princess Elizabeth. Who would have thought then that the Elector would become the Winter King, and the scourge of the Emperor?'

Lock wasn't sure if the question was rhetorical, so he offered a polite shrug. 'Perhaps if I run into him, I will ask.'

Vane made a mocking bow. 'You can greet him as His Highness, the King for Winter, the Lord of let downs, the Master of nothing and the Elector of a few towns, held only by the good graces of the English volunteers.'

'That's quite a mouthful.' Lock then paused. 'Will I find many Englishmen in my travels, Henry?'

Vane, originally intending to leave the conversation, now found he was enjoying himself again. He retrieved his pipe, and began inserting some new tobacco. He beckoned for Lock to walk with him. 'You will find Englishmen and English soldiers, Lock. His Majesty is not at war with the Habsburgs, nor does he intend to be. But, this has not stopped many volunteers travelling with His Majesty's reluctant blessing, to defend fortresses and towns loyal to the Winter King, who is, after all, his son in law.'

'Do these towns still fly an English flag?' The idea made Lock's heart swell with pride, to see the banner of St George fly over the Rhine, but Vane's reaction blunted his enthusiasm.

'Unfortunately, yes. Those poor sods have no chance of relief. They're simply counting down the clock.' Vane then paused, to gaze at a shipment of cloth being lifted from a barge on his left that had likely originated upriver. 'I simply *must* have new linens.'

He turned to Lock, and gestured to a large wooden vessel with its sails folded tightly against the rigging. 'That's your ticket to Europe, Lock. I wish you the greatest fortune. Be sure to track me down when you return. I would love to share more stories with you. Love to Arthur, of course.'

Lock nodded in thanks. He didn't have the heart to tell Vane that his vessel didn't depart for another three days. A tiredness welled up within him, and Lock recalled how poor his sleep had been the night before. The Quayside Inn was far from upmarket, but it was likely better than the kind of board he could expect while travelling war-torn roads. The pull of bitters was in the air. He intended to make the next three days count.

- CHAPTER SEVEN -

The sea was perfectly calm as their vessel departed from Bristol's docks, so much so that Lock had watched the city slowly vanish into the distance. A light breeze ruffled his newly tended hair, but it helped to soothe his nerves. The sun was high and intense, and Lock did his best to relax, to make the most of the adventure. He had mingled with some of the moderately well-dressed figures, merchants mostly, who talked of great hauls of pepper, and the booming trade in tulip bulbs.

After a few hours though, rough conditions had forced Lock below decks. Once there, the distinctions of class and status were never more clearly spelled out. His own compartment was small, but perfectly adequate. Two simple cots, which his heels hung over the edge of, a single bedside table between them, and a distressed desk and chair constituted his furniture.

But the more sumptuous suites boasted twice the space, and he could hear loud, cheerful chatting, as well as the clinking of glasses, through his thin walls. These were made men. The kind who splashed out on needless luxuries simply because they could. Lock didn't envy their wealth, but he envied their easy lives. He wondered whether these men had ever had to struggle for their living, as Father had done, or if they'd been born into wealth, and their parents before them.

Lock clung to his credentials. He had travelled sparsely, but his musket, his short sword and two changes of clothes still weighed more than enough. Some gave him curious looks, and likely wanted to know what a tall young man, dressed and equipped like a soldier, but not actually a soldier, was doing in their midst.

The conditions became rougher still on the third day, when all sense of social order was thrown overboard, along with the contents of many travellers' stomachs. Lock had never been one for seasickness, but the lower decks reeked so intensely of vomit that he was forced to retreat above for air. The power of the sea had terrified him even from a young age, but from Father's insistence, he at least knew how to swim.

Father's favourite lesson to support this demand came from the sad fate of his maternal uncle, who had the whole world ahead of him. A picture was painted of a well-liked, honourable fellow of good means, and of great intellect, who drowned when his vessel sank on the way to the continent. He was twenty-two.

The similarities made Lock sweat. He said repeated prayers, and watched the unseasonably aggressive waves, as big as houses, churn back and forth into the distance. A moment of calm followed, and it seemed safe to brave going below decks again.

Lock returned to his compartment, and froze once he saw the bed. Someone had been in here, unauthorised. His bed was perfectly made up, but that wasn't the issue. It was what now lay on this bed that froze him to the spot.

It was a mask, a black velvet mask.

The same mask that he had first seen nine years ago, on the night James Lock was killed.

The room was empty now. Whoever had been here, and delivered this message, was now gone. But they were still on the boat. Somewhere, on this vessel, was someone who might know something about what had happened in 1613.

1613.

He had been so consumed with his parents' fate, that the fate of his brother had been pushed to the back of his mind. Here now was a stark reminder. It pulled him right back to that night in Frisia, on 11 March. His least favourite day of the year, when Mother was decked out in mourning clothes, and Lock had to hear how her favourite son was stolen from her.

Now he was locked in his compartment with this memento of his failure. But there was something else. Beside the mask, there was a small note.

Lock half stumbled to his bed, as the vessel veered on a wave, before coming to a rest. There could be no mistaking it. This was a note. And it was addressed to him.

Lock picked the thick piece of card up from the bed. A black wax seal had to be cut through, which was done with a small knife on his bedside table. The note contained only a paragraph. Lock slumped onto the bed as he read it.

Matthew Lock,

It has come to the attention of the Black Prince that you have left England, and intend to make for the continent. Depart from this course immediately, and return to your home. If you fail to heed this instruction, another message will be sent to you in person.

The Black Prince.

Lock stared at the simple paragraph. He read it twice, three times, many times more.

The Black Prince.

Lock had never heard of the man, if indeed he was a man. And what business was it of his where he went? The men in black masks, were they his agents?

Had the Black Prince killed James?

Did he wish to kill Lock now?

Perhaps he had also killed his parents?

But it didn't make sense. If indeed the Black Prince was responsible for these murders, why would he warn Lock away from the continent? Would he not prefer to lure Lock deeper into his web?

Lock read the paragraph again. Cold ice ran down his spine. He shivered, though his compartment was stuffy.

How had his personal mission come to the Black Prince's attention? Why did the Black Prince wish him to remain in England? What kind of message would be sent if he indeed failed to listen now?

For the briefest moment, it seemed ideal. The perfect reason to absolve himself of the mission before him, which grew more dangerous by the day. He could show Arthur the note, and his brother would be awed that a figure as mysterious as the Black Prince deigned to speak with him, and to warn him from his mission.

But this would be a lie. Arthur would scratch his head and wonder how a myth could have dissuaded his brother from seeking justice.

He would think less of him.

Arthur would take on the mission himself. He would not be deterred by such threats.

No. Lock had to continue onwards, to The Hague, to Frankfurt and then to Frankenthal, where Vere awaited him. This was the only possible course. Perhaps, as he travelled, he could pick the brains of his companions, and learn more of this Black Prince.

The mystery enthralled him, as did the possibility that it was all a bluff.

What entity could possibly wield the power to send a second instruction, this time in person? Could Vere know?

There was a knock on his door, and Lock jumped off his bed to his feet. The note was scrunched and shoved in his pocket.

'Yes?' Lock called.

'Pardon me Sir, just wished to inquire if you received it?'

Lock's stomach lurched. 'If I... *received* it?'

'Yes, Sir, your meal Sir, it was delivered an hour ago, but you did not sign for it.'

Lock exhaled a stone of breath and glanced around his room.

Sure enough, a plate of now cold food rested on his bedside locker. Lock had taken the knife from the plate to open the note, but had not even noticed the food.

He never failed to notice food.

The Black Prince, whoever he was, had made himself at home in his mind.

'Yes, thank you, I will sign for it shortly,' Lock called. A grunt was delivered in reply, and footsteps receded from his door.

Lock dropped back onto his cot. He looked at the black mask on his bed. He picked it up and held it close.

It was a vizard, a fantastical garment which adorned the faces of well-to-do ladies as they travelled. Father had once scoffed at a group of them, down by the docks in Bristol many years before.

The utility of the vizard, Father said, was to guarantee against any impression of the sun on the lady's precious face. The small slit in place of the mouth also ensured that the lady could not speak. To further guarantee this purpose, the lady held the mask in place by biting down on a bead. This would add to the lady's mystery, though it was hardly functional in social situations.

After 1613, Lock noted that Father did not scoff at the vizard any longer. Instead, he actively moved his family from the company of those that wore it.

Charles Lock seemed to make it his mission to ensure that Mother, particularly, never saw the wretched things again. The tactic had worked. This was the first vizard Lock had seen since 1613, not counting the visions of the mask that haunted his sleep.

This vizard was somewhat different in style. The mouth slit was larger, so that the wearer could speak. It was also wider and longer, so that it could fit on the face of a man. A piece of fabric at the back of the mask ensured that it would stay fastened to the face at all times.

Lock shook his head as he examined it. The obscene garment of the fabulously privileged had been transformed into the sinister mark of the villain. And all, it seemed, on the orders of the Black Prince. It was now a symbol of fear. Without the man behind the mask though, the garment lost some of its impact.

Without really thinking, Lock held the mask to his face. Then, with a flick of his index finger, he secured it there. Seeing the world through the mask was unsettling. Lock removed it abruptly after a few moments. He pulled open a drawer of his bedside locker and flung the mask within.

He eyed up his food, but could not bring himself to touch either the potatoes, the slice of lamb, or the turnip. Father had paid a high premium for a private cabin with meals inclusive, but it did not seem to matter now.

Lock still recalled the excitement in Father's eyes when he had explained the Bristol Embassy. '*The perfect opportunity to dip your toe in the soldier-statesman experience,*' he had said.

Lock had been sold from the first syllable. A holiday alone with Father, where even more knowledge could be mined from him.

What on God's earth could be better?

Lock looked over at the bed which Charles Lock would have slept on, had he been with him. It was still perfectly made up, just as it had been when he'd first opened the door. Lock sighed and stood up. He would sign for this blasted dinner, and then he would turn in for the night.

Mercifully, by the fourth day, the continent was in sight. Excited calls from the upper deck had moved Lock to join the party of travellers that waited impatiently for their journey to end.

This was a coast transformed by man's industry, and his relationship to the sea. Passengers pointed with excitement to Ostend, a port now in Spanish hands, which had been wrestled from the Dutch after a brutal three-year siege, two decades before.

Then, the Dutch coast loomed into view. A smattering of farmland continued far into the distance, surrounded by countless towns and villages. But the coast was where the Dutch had made their homes, and their fortunes.

Lock scanned his memory for Father's geography lessons. The province of Zeeland, the Republic's second largest, was spotted first. Then, following the coast, the province of Holland.

Lock smiled as he recalled how Mother had always referred to the Republic simply as *Holland*, and how Father had diplomatically reminded her of her error. '*Try telling a Zeelander that they hail from Holland, love, and see what they say.*' Lock could recall Mother's scrunched up face, her playful punch of Father's arm, and how the two had walked hand in hand to their Dutch residence.

Through the morning mist, the Dutch Republic's capital loomed into view. It was a built-up metropolis founded in wartime. '*Den Haag*,' Lock whispered to himself.

Father's insistence on Dutch lessons had always struck him as odd, particularly when Arthur had been forced only into German and French lessons. Father had claimed Lock would thank him one day, when the Dutch usurped the Spanish, and overcame England's paltry settlements in the New World. He was certainly thankful for the lessons now.

'Land, at long last, eh Officer Lock?' A red-haired man appeared on his right, his arms resting on the wooden railings which had saved Lock on many occasions already.

Lock smiled at the man he had met on the first day of the journey. He was one of the merchants. Patrick Murphy, a zealously proud Irishman, who had made his fortune in the pepper trade, and had travelled more miles by sea than Lock had managed to blink. He was short, middle-aged, and with a notable paunch, but fiercely talkative and almost unrealistically friendly. Lock took to him instantly, but soon realised that silence was not the Irishman's strength.

'Can you see the political district?' Lock asked. That was where the diplomatic personnel would congregate once the vessel docked. It was where he would be most likely to find a good carriage to share, and the good company to go with it.

Murphy pointed vaguely to the right, to a point beyond the docks. 'You'll want to head past the fisheries, to the right of the merchant's quarter. If you can smell turmeric, you've gone too far into the rich man's land.'

Lock didn't know what turmeric smelled like, or even what it was, but he'd already learned to smile and nod when unsure. The act, just like Sir Henry Vane had assured him, was the most important weapon in his arsenal.

As of yet, nobody had questioned his title of *Officer* Lock. As far as Murphy, and anyone else knew, Lock was on his way to Frankfurt, to serve as His Majesty's junior representative to the German Diet.

The vessel approached the docks, and activity could be seen and heard in greater detail the closer they came. Merchants loudly selling their wares, fishermen carrying loads of fish, a smattering of slaves gathering for auction.

'Well, Officer Lock, it has been a supreme pleasure to meet you. Should you find yourself as far afield as New Netherland, do look me up. I'm sure we'll have cause to meet again.' The Irishman winked at Lock, before going below deck.

Lock scarcely imagined he'd ever see him again, but he had been grateful for the company.

Murphy's vivid descriptions of his own family had brought Lock close to tears, but it had also persuaded him of a new mission, one which Captain Frank had not authorised. It was important that he bring himself to the political quarter, and prepare for his journey to Frankfurt, but it was also true that his parents Dutch home was in that same political quarter. What better way to better understand their fate, than to visit the place where they had been murdered?

Lock had initially bristled at the idea. His stomach performed somersaults merely from contemplating it. Dutch officials had insisted that they would get to the bottom of the mystery, Captain Frank said, and it was important to respect their authority. But it was also important to acquire justice. It was also important to uphold the Lock family name. A failed investigation would be ruinous.

Lock found that he had come to terms with the idea surprisingly quickly. He had bargained with himself. He had decided it was unlikely he would find anything, but that it might give him the opportunity to speak with the Dutch officials on the ground. It would also help speed the process along, if the Dutch knew that the son of the murdered couple was in the vicinity. For the sake of Dutch honour, they would have to find a speedy resolution to the issue.

The vessel jerked as it was pulled into the docks. Large, burly men with balding heads and beer bellies heaved on thick ropes, and the vessel was secured after a few minutes of effort. The sun shone with few clouds to shield it, and the sea glittered in the early afternoon. The waves lapped gently against the vessel. This was the North Sea, Murphy had said. It was the more relaxed cousin of that unruly knave, the English Channel.

Lock could barely contain the urge to set his feet on the dark wooden docks, nor was he alone. He ensured he was front and centre, as the bridge was extended and fastened. Perhaps four or five people were in front of him. Although it was known that the Republic was at war with Spain, the war seemed far away from here. Because of course, it was. Spanish armies were many miles to the south, and the best jewels that the Dutch possessed were protected by defences in depth, concentrated on the many strands of the River Rhine.

The Dutch navy had been as industrious in trade as defence, and the military blockade which protected incoming vessels had been cleared with some deft signalling by the captain. The flag of St George was an invaluable symbol in these difficult times. Its claim to neutrality, to commerce, and to potential gain for all sides, meant that English ships fared well as they approached the coast. This appeared true whether The Hague was their destination, or Antwerp, Spain's premier port in the Netherlands.

Lock stepped off the bridge and onto the docks, adjusting the sling of his musket as he did so. The weapon was not primed, and the match cord was somewhere in the depths of his bag, but it was good to have a weapon near at hand. Lock had put his sword away. It clinked off the contents of his bag. It had been just the right size for such a journey as this. A war sword would hardly be needed as he walked The Hague's calm streets.

In the business of not drawing attention to himself, Captain Frank had warned him of the mania for duelling which had emerged in the last few decades. Captain Frank recounted tales of roaming drunkards on the streets of Paris, The Hague, Vienna and elsewhere, spoiling for a fight. They would judge your prowess and rank based on your sword, and then deliver some wanton insult. If you failed to meet their challenge, they would proclaim your cowardice to the world. The last thing Lock wanted was another excuse for his honour to be impugned. Let his sword be hidden away. He didn't expect to need it now.

Lock availed of the service provided by the Bristol Embassy, which arranged for the bags of the travellers to be carried to the English Embassy building. This way, it was explained, travellers could take in the sights of The Hague without being weighed down by their luggage. Other travellers, with far greater baggage than Lock, were only too eager to hand over their weighty cases and bags. The wagon was packed high, and two mules trotted optimistically forward once it was filled.

The first mission was to escape the pong of fish. After a quick request for instructions, from a fisherman who seemed startled by his question, Lock was directed towards the political quarter. As Murphy had said, it was to the right of where the merchants had their homes, and where their warehouses stood. The more important the embassy, the more sumptuous the building was likely to be. His parents' house was a short walk from the embassy itself.

Lock scanned his brain for childhood memories of his many Dutch holidays. Gradually, the cobbled stone streets and distinctive paint became familiar. There it was, the English embassy. It was a large, ostentatious structure, cream with faint streaks of light orange and grey, battered by the elements, but with innumerable windows and multiple stories. He was getting close.

The area seemed so calm, a picture of culture and civilisation, that it was difficult to imagine murder happening here. For a brief, cruel moment, his mind tried to fool him. Perhaps there was a terrible mistake, and his parents were still alive. He forced the cruel hope away. It would do him no good to live in fantasy.

Some figures gave him curious looks. Lock noted that he was considerably taller than most individuals he encountered, which probably explained the fisherman's startled reaction. Some were drawn to eye up his musket, but looked away when they noted that it was not primed.

Some soldiers passed him by, officers among them, and Lock marvelled at their iron breastplates, faded white buff coats, and wide navy trousers. Veterans, surely, of Maurice of Nassau's armies. They marched in step and in groups of six, their feet clapping off the stones in a satisfying rhythm. Turning a corner, past a stall selling oysters, Lock saw it.

His parents' Dutch home.

His knees quaked slightly, but Lock forced himself onward.

He had spent many months here, before the family returned to Locksville permanently in the summer of 1613. After James' murder, the Netherlands seemed to lose much of its appeal. Mother declared her undying hatred of the country, but Father's responsibilities and rank still drew him here on occasion. Their recent trip had been the first time she had returned to the Dutch capital in nine years. That was how long it had taken to forgive the Dutch, to forgive God, to forgive herself.

That forgiveness had killed her.

Lock approached the door. It did seem curious that no officials were posted outside, to warn citizens of an ongoing investigation. If the Dutch truly were serious about dispensing justice, shouldn't that have been essential? As he reached closer to the door's dark red wood, his stomach lurched.

The door was not locked. It was not even closed. It was slightly open, perhaps by a few inches. Lock stared at the door, and his hand hovered in front of it.

Something was wrong.

Which careless investigator had left his home in such a perilous state? What of the danger posed by looters, or opportunistic burglars? Did no one care for his parents' honour?

Lock exhaled. He checked his back pocket. The spare key to the Dutch residence that he had swiped from his parents' room was still there. If he met any challengers, he had the perfect alibi.

He could do this.

He must do this.

Nobody else *would* do this.

Another exhalation.

Go into the damned house, he heard Arthur say.

Lock obeyed. It was time to make them proud.

- CHAPTER EIGHT -

Mother had protested when she had learned that the Lock family's Hague residence would consist merely of a two-storey dwelling. She called it an apartment. Father insisted on calling it a house. It had seemed so large when Lock had been young. He remembered running up and down the hallways that seemed to wind on for miles, chasing after Arthur, being chased by James.

Now, it was though Mother whispered *I told you so*.

It was much smaller than he remembered, there was no denying it. It was also darker, and surprisingly messy. Furniture was moved into strange places, and papers were strewn on the floor. It had been nine years since Lock had set foot here. He stood a few steps inside the front door, bombarded by nostalgia. The family had retreated here after James' death, before limping home on the earliest vessel that would take them.

How had Father put up with such mess, when he had always hounded his sons for untidiness at home? Lock found himself scoffing at Charles Lock's hypocrisy, when a thought loomed in front of him. It was a sinister thought, but the more his eyes scanned the halls, the more convinced he was of his theory.

Father had not been messy. Someone else had left this mess. The same person responsible for his death? Lock walked a few paces to the bottom of the stairs. He could walk up the soft carpeted steps to the floor where his bedroom had once been, or he could walk to the left, and continue down the hall towards the reception and dining rooms.

Lock did neither. He found himself frozen by the family portrait which he had not seen in nearly a decade. It was older than the one in Locksville. Here, he was cast as a child, barely finished crawling. Arthur was held by

Mother, his lower half wrapped in baby's linen. James stood, as a proud boy of six or seven. Even now, Lock could see his smile through the artist's impression. Lock reached out a few inches to touch the frame. It was slightly crooked.

He then flinched so heavily he nearly toppled backwards. *His parents.* They had been featured in the portrait.

But their faces. Look at their faces.

Lock's breathing accelerated.

Their faces within the portrait had been scratched at with such venom that holes had been cut where their heads had been. Lock gazed at the vandalised portrait with a mixture of horror and fascination.

Who would do such a thing?

Lock pulled himself away from the alluring familial memories. He snapped back to the present. The mess he had barely registered. The lingering sense of threat. The dread that gurgled in his stomach. He glanced past the stairs, down the polished wood which graced the halls. Mother had wanted marble flooring, but Father had scoffed at the excessive expense. Papers seemed to fill the floor.

Lock turned his gaze to the top of the stairs. Something drew him forward, to place a right foot on the bottom step to get a better view. He could see the landing. Shards of broken vase beckoned him to investigate. And there was something else. Clothing. Distinctive silk patterns torn and thrown carelessly around. He was on the fifth step now, and with every step, came more destruction.

Three quarters of the way up the stairs, Lock saw it.

Blood. There could be no mistaking it.

Accelerating now, he reached the top of the stairs, and the cream carpeted landing where his young feet had once trodden. The destruction was even worse up here. Paintings had been torn from the walls. Slashes had been inflicted on the plaster behind them. Pieces of carpet had even been ripped up.

And there was blood, more blood. At first it seemed random, but then Lock noted patterns. The blood rested in spurts, and in streaks. It seemed to lead to the end of the hallway, where his parents' bedroom had been.

Lock continued forward, his heart in his throat. The first doorway on the right. Arthur's bedroom. Lock looked into its interior. Arthur had been given the smallest room. He was, after all, the smallest child. Lock had never seen so much destruction squeezed into such a small space.

An unrestrained gasp fell from him. Arthur's cot had been upturned, and wooden splinters revealed it had been dashed to pieces. Holes in the wall suggested it had been battered to bits against the wall itself. The door balanced on a single hinge.

Lock moved on. His own bedroom, next door on the right. It was a similar picture of devastation. Here there were even holes in the roof, made by the legs of a stool, Lock supposed. A Dutch language bible was upturned in the centre of the floor. Lock nearly moved to fix it, to retrieve this relic from his childhood. But something moved him forwards.

Past James' room now, the room where he had longed to be as a child. James' room had always seemed the most inviting, the most interesting. On occasion, James had allowed him in. There was the dark wood floor his brother's room had boasted.

Joyful visions returned to him. The sound of tapping his toy soldiers' feet on that same floor, as James painted vivid pictures of these soldiers and their mission. Together, the two brothers authorised a battle plan, and the toy soldiers marched diligently forward to accomplish it.

The floor creaked below him. Lock had stepped onto a bare portion of wood, where the carpet had been ripped up. Still he moved forward. His eyes fixed on the streaks of blood that led to his parents' bedroom. This had been the holy grail of his childhood, and was the largest room in the house.

He neared the doorway. The grey wood door was slightly ajar, and Lock pushed it open. The familiar creak from a decade before rushed back to him. If they heard that creak in the middle of the night, the boys knew the jig was up, and they were in trouble. Father had always intended to get the creak fixed, so he said. It had been their early warning system.

But Lock had no warning for what came next.

The door opened into a gruesome scene. This was it. This was where Charles and Catherine Lock had spent their final moments. This was where they had been killed. Lock was certain. The bodies had been removed, but the evidence had not. Lock had never seen so much dried blood in one place.

Mother's prized rugs, sourced from the Orient, now served as sponges for his parents' life force. They appeared soaked, as though in need of a good wringing out. The right corner of the room, where the three boys had played while Mother and Father had watched lazily from their bed, was now a haunting shade of crimson.

Two large stains could mean only one thing.

Tears pricked Lock's eyes.

A portrait had been cast to the floor. Its characters stared emptily at the ceiling. This was the earliest portrait of his parents, from 1596. It depicted Catherine and Charles, both sumptuously dressed, and had been arranged for their first-year wedding anniversary. Two young adults, in the prime of their lives, stared out at Lock. Mother clung earnestly to Father's right arm. Father's moustache looked solid and mature in the artist's ink.

Lock walked to it, and his right foot crunched on glass. He paused and bent over. A distinctive smell filled his nostrils. Wine. The smell was clear to him even now. They had been interrupted and murdered as they relaxed in their bedroom with a drink. It was a fate too horrible to imagine. But why? Why had someone broken into their home, killed them in their leisure, and then proceeded to destroy the house? The sheer hatred required to power such behaviour made Lock shiver.

His eyes drifted to the left corner of the room, where the wardrobes stood, once full of garments, now strewn across the room. Lock smelled something else. Something barbaric. Urine. The smell became more concentrated the closer he got to Mother's undergarments. Lock's breathing ran away from him. His fingernails dug into his palms as his fists tightened.

How dare he. How dare he do this to them.

It had to be a man. No woman would commit such an atrocity. Or could it be a group of men? The brutish behaviour which had already been evidenced hinted that Mother had been the victim of the gravest dishonour. Had Father been killed first? Or had he been forced to watch? The scenario had been described by Arthur, when explaining the Rape of the Sabine Women, a more unsavoury tale in Ancient Rome's otherwise glittering past.

Lock was nauseous. He reached for the bedpost to steady himself. He had to remove himself from this room, from this house. He began to walk, and then, like a stabbing pain deep in his gut, his ears picked up a crash from downstairs, followed by a laugh.

They were still here. The bastards were still here.

Lock moved from the room, back to the landing. His heart thundered in his ears. He struggled for breath, for some sense of composure. *What would he do*? He had his musket. But what use was that? Could he prime it in time? Could he access the powder? What if they came upstairs once again?

Lock found himself moving quicker. His childhood memory returned to him, of how to move across the landing without making a sound. This had made eavesdropping immensely convenient. He had listened in on a wide range of conversations as a young child, when his parents were surely convinced that he was tucked up in bed. He could have scarcely imagined that skill would be needed for such a time as this.

The chattering intensified. Another laugh. Two men, perhaps three. They were below him. That was certain. But where? In the kitchens? In the reception room? He heard glass shatter. His mind painted a picture of the downstairs layout. Glass could only be in such abundance in the dining room, where large glass cabinets contained the delft and silverware that the servants would retrieve at mealtimes. He heard the clinking of metal.

They were stealing the silverware. The family silverware.

Were they looters? The wretched authorities had welcomed them with their carelessness. It was a calming thought to imagine that they were mere looters, and not the murderers, having returned to finish off the family's heir. Or, perhaps, the murderers had never left. Perhaps they had baited him to come here. Perhaps they had waited for him to walk right into their trap.

His legs pushed him to the edge of the landing. He had had reached the top of the stairs. The voices grew closer. Lock slowly retrieved his musket from his left shoulder. If nothing else, he could use it as a club. The voices were below him. Perhaps a few feet away. But what language was that? It was not Dutch.

What now? Would he rush down the stairs and demand an answer? Would he bluff them as he had bluffed Billy?

Lock froze. He saw the top of a head, and the back of another head. They walked with their backs to him towards the front door, where he had been standing mere minutes before.

Lock's back arched as he watched his enemy saunter through his home. *How dare they.* His fingers tightened on the musket's barrel. Two men. And then, another voice called behind them, a third voice.

The two men turned around, and Lock prepared to catch a glimpse of their faces.

His whole body froze in place.

No. Not them. *Anything but them.*

Black masks.

The same black mask that had been left in his cabin.

The same black masks that haunted his dreams.

The same black masks that had stolen James from him.

These black masks were here. They were back. They were in his home.

He had convinced himself that he had overcome this fear, when the mask had appeared in his cabin, and he had examined it up close. But it was an altogether different story when attached to the face of a malignant individual.

Lock moved his hand to his mouth to suppress a whimper.

All the fear, all the paralysing fear that had crippled him nine years ago. All of it was back. He was a boy of twelve, utterly helpless. Immobile before them. He could do nothing. He was a lamb before wolves. He was a coward.

Billy was right.

Tears pricking Lock's eyes.

Perhaps he should offer himself. He deserved to die for the crime of such wanton shame.

But Lock didn't want to die. He wanted to run.

He wanted to run from this house, from The Hague, from his Father's mission, and all the way home, until he could embed himself into his room, lock the door, and throw away the key. He squeezed his eyes shut.

The men in their masks continued their discussion, as they walked obliviously towards the back of the house. He heard them head for the kitchens. Minutes passed, or were they seconds? Was it safe to leave? Could he even move? Could he leave this place behind? Could he leave these bastards here, free to roam and trample on his family's honour?

He could.

He had to.

He could do nothing else.

He talked himself up to it, the mere act of walking down the stairs. His stairs. The stairs that were now his by right. His property. His home.

But Lock didn't want it.

He didn't want anything they had touched.

Lock stumbled down the last three stairs, twisting his ankle and whimpering once again.

He wrenched the door open. Sunlight struck his eyes. Tears trickled weakly from them. And he ran. He ran from the house. He ran from the embassy. He ran for minutes, perhaps half an hour. But he ran to nowhere.

He ended up in a dead end. Hopelessly lost. And then he crumpled. His back scraping itself off the rough wall of an unknown building.

His frame shuddered to the filthy ground, and Lock wept. He wept from fear. He wept from shame. He wept with empty-handed rage. He wept like he hadn't wept since James' death. He wept until his eyes dried out.

He was not cut out for this. He was not qualified to make Father proud. He was a knave. The lowest of the low. The boy who ran. The boy who failed his family for a second time.

- CHAPTER NINE -

A rthur. That was the only thing that moved him forward. Not the sense of personal shame or failure, or the burning desire to redeem himself. It was Arthur. Arthur's face when Lock returned home and told him what he had found. That was a face, that was a conversation, which would be worse than death itself.

And so he walked. He walked back to the political district. He walked slowly. Nobody noticed him. Nobody sensed this insignificant failure in their midst. Anonymity was his sole relief. To be recognised in this state of shame would be social death. And then, familiar landmarks returned. Before long, he was near the embassy once again.

He stood opposite it, gazing at the building.

Already, some individuals milled around its exterior, and Dutch officials prepared carriages, attaching them to impatient horses. Dust swirled off the cobbled stones, and people shielded their eyes from the sun with pamphlets they had purchased from the nearby vendor.

With his musket slung over his shoulder, Lock forced himself forward, unsure of what awaited him. Certainly, it was better than wallowing in his failure, or returning to the scene of the crime. Distant voices called names in English. He watched groups of well-dressed men and women pile into carriages with a laugh.

A horse clopped behind him and then passed him out, making for the embassy. Suitcases were piled high in the carriage's rear.

A rush of sickness was supressed when Lock recalled that all passengers had their contents transported to the embassy in advance. He would have to retrieve his belongings before leaving.

He walked forward, closing in on the ruckus outside. There was a definite queue, not particularly long. Names were called, and individuals in finery walked from the line to their awaiting carriage. Not for the first time, Lock was thankful of Father's thorough preparations. The ticket price had included a carriage ride from The Hague, all the way to Frankfurt.

Lock's eyes fixed on a bored man in a drab navy uniform, who stood guard over a wagon of bags and satchels. Lock scanned the collection for his own, as the figure eyed him with suspicion. A sword by his side, and several colleagues nearby him, suggested that security was taken very seriously. Lock spotted his own bag with a wave of relief. He made for the figure on guard.

'Name?' the man asked Lock in English.

'Matthew Lock, going to Frankfurt via the Bristol Embassy.'

The guard nodded, and turned to the wagon, as his colleagues maintained their steely gaze. After a few moments, he turned around, his hand full of Lock's tired looking pack.

'Thank you,' Lock sighed.

The man nodded, and waved Lock away. Lock scoffed at the man's briskness before returning to the queue. It had shrunk since he'd last seen it, but there were plenty of carriages remaining. Horse dung had begun to pile up near one of them, and after an aggressive wave, a young boy rushed from the side, and brushed the offending contents onto a tray, before making a quick exit.

This was a tightly run ship.

The order of precedence clearly dictated who was entitled to pile into a carriage first. Plenty of Lords and Earls were called, and many more individuals seemed content to commandeer their own carriages, or to purchase one outright. The fancier, softer models guaranteed the rider a comfortable journey. Harder benches meant harder times. Lock heard his name, and he snapped forward, as several eyes burrowed into him.

After a brief glance at his ticket, the caller gestured for Lock to join a shared carriage, which had one space remaining. Lock did not hesitate. He found that an inner sense of urgency to leave this city now possessed him. Nor was he the only one. To the front of his carriage, four horses pawed at the ground. Lock shuffled forward a few paces, before clambering onto the carriage, and pulling himself inside.

There was enough room for two people to sit side by side, with another couple opposite, but that was the extent of the space. Perhaps a few inches separated Lock's knees from the person opposite.

He had received the worst seat.

A backwards ride, next to a rotund, sweating man who argued incessantly with his partner opposite him about the finer points of tulip cultivation.

Lock folded his arms and leaned into the hard wooden bench. An elderly woman smiled weakly back at him, perhaps aware that he had received the short straw. But at least he would not be walking to Frankfurt, or riding alone. There was safety in numbers for the civilian during wartime.

How long had Vane claimed the journey would take?

A week? Trapped with *these* people?

A week to dwell on his thoughts.

On his failings?

The elderly woman clutched her bag, and retrieved a book from its interior. Lock stared at its cover, unable to hide his astonishment. The tattered book was a relic. It was Jacob de Gheyn's 1607 manual, *The Exercise of Armes for Calivres, Muskettes, and Pikes*. It was well-read, judging by its condition.

Lock then restrained himself when he noted the lady's eyes smiling back at him.

'Forgive me, madam,' Lock said.

'That is alright... Mister Lock, is it not?'

'Matthew, my friends call me Matthew.'

The lady nodded. 'Ah yes, such a lovely name. The caller was quite loud, which I suppose is his job. It is a pleasure to have a member of such a distinguished family for these travels.'

Lock's curiosity turned to mild panic. 'Forgive me madam, how do you know my family?'

The lady smiled and shook her head. 'Oh, forgive *me*, Matthew. I thought you might recognise me, but I suppose you were very young when we last met. Madame Jane Digby, from Sherbourne? I am travelling to Spain to visit my son, Sir John. He is quite accomplished you see, in his role as England's ambassador to King Philip IV.'

Her eyes twinkled even in the dimness of the carriage. There was a depth of warmth and sincerity to her, but there was also excitement.

'I have not seen my son for nigh on a decade, Matthew, can you fathom it? I know he is greatly tiring of life in Spain, so I thought a visit from family would be to his benefit.'

'You travel alone, Madame? Would your son not send a deputation to collect you, perhaps by sea?'

Madame Digby waved her right hand at the suggestion. 'I cannot abide sea travel, Matthew. The great swells unsettle my stomach, and cause... unsightly results.'

'A private carriage then, or one which would avoid the rank and file of this city?'

'Oh, I do not mind travelling among others. The journey is long, and company makes the duration more bearable. I see you travel alone as well. Are you going to Frankfurt? Without Arthur?'

Lock had to swallow his sense of discomfort at how much this lady knew. It was perfectly normal, after all, that the matriarch of the Digby family would be so well informed. Father used to complain that his own Mother was an expert in the accumulation of gossip.

'I'm afraid Arthur is indisposed. A... hunting accident has laid him up in bed, though he intends to join me next year, I am sure.'

Madame Digby tutted, before smiling warmly. 'Of course, Matthew. Perhaps it would be wise to prepare the way for him yourself. You head the Lock family now, after all.'

It was not new information, but it was still hard to hear. Captain Frank had insisted that talk of inheritance could resume once his parents' bodies were repatriated. The prospect of negotiating with Dutch authorities moved him to shudder, especially after their shoddy treatment of the crime scene.

It was almost easier to dwell on that challenge, rather than the one which would surely define him for the rest of his life. There was still much Lock did not know about the head of the family. How, for example, did one *lead* the family? Should he marry? Who could arrange the match?

Lock tried to change the subject, he gestured to her curious choice of reading material. Madame Digby smiled and opened the book before her. Even from this angle, Lock could see the illustrations of the different figures, spelling out the forty-three steps of the musket drill. If he closed his eyes, he could picture each one of them in vivid detail.

He no longer needed Jacob de Gheyn's book.

Since 1613, Lock had memorised each illustration, and each of the forty-three steps. With the help of Captain Frank and Father, these forty-three steps had been abbreviated to thirteen. Without trying, his mind began reciting each one internally.

Madame Digby laughed quietly to herself. 'Yes, it is an odd sight, is it not? In truth, I wished to see for myself what you men must learn. I have read so many books, Matthew, but I have never read this. Sir John has so many copies of this book, but this was his first. It... it brings me comfort to carry it with me, and flick through its pages. Look.'

Madame Digby turned the pages towards him, and Lock could see that Sir John, like any practicing soldier, had made extensive notes beside each illustration.

'He was quite a shot you know. Practiced even when other activities would surely have stood him in better stead. But I suppose, he proved me wrong in the end, did he not?'

Lock nodded respectfully. 'Sir John is well respected throughout Dorset. His estate is beautiful to walk through.'

She seemed delighted with the response. Then she paused. 'You are most generous, Matthew. I do hope he and your Father were able to make peace... before the end.'

Lock nodded briskly, and forced a smile. 'I believe that they were.'

In truth, he had no idea what she referred to. Father had scarcely mentioned Sir John Digby, save for when he complained that his estates were either too ostentatious for their own good, or were too overgrown and in need of maintenance. Then again, this did sound like the comments of a man who had fallen out with his neighbour. But something still did not add up. Lock risked a guess at Madame Digby's business.

'Forgive me, Madame. Does Sir John know you are coming? I can't imagine such a distinguished ambassador would permit you to travel in anything other than absolute luxury.'

Madame Digby's face fell, and she shook her head. By her crow's feet, wrinkled cheeks and weathered forehead, Lock guessed she was perhaps in her late sixties. Her grey hair retained a refined sense of dignity. The kind of dignity Mother forever sought to replicate. The confidence and grace which came from a lifetime of good breeding and privilege.

'Indeed, Matthew. Sir John has been quite aloof for the last few years. He has written only to update his family on the most mundane of matters, and to demonstrate that he still lives.' She smiled at the remark, but it was clearly a source of pain that her son had been emotionally absent. 'I fear that my days... may be numbered, Matthew. I wish to see my son, if I can, before I have occasion to meet my saviour. If he cannot find the time to see me, then I will endeavour to see him.'

Lock nodded politely at the response, and regretted his curiosity.

'And what of you, Matthew? Is this your Father's vaunted Bristol Embassy?' The smirk which accompanied the question moved Lock's expression to change, and Madame Digby chuckled. 'Oh my boy, it was hardly a secret how excited he was to take you. He was only recently explaining the itinerary to my butler. Could barely keep his mouth closed.'

'*He was?*'

She nodded. 'It broke our hearts when James was taken. I'm sure I don't have to tell you, how rare good a man he was.'

'You don't,' Lock said, less polite than he'd expected. 'I only mean...'

She put up a calming hand. 'There is no greater pain than to lose a child, Matthew, but to lose a sibling cuts just as deeply.'

'Yes,' Lock didn't know what else to say. No matter where he went, he couldn't avoid the reminder that he was all alone, and that the people who would lead the way were now gone.

Madame Digby gazed out of the window. 'What do you think of this city, Matthew? Impressive, for a Republic, is it not?'

Lock was weary of the conversation, and of speaking, but he didn't wish to offend. 'Impressive, although The Hague delivers quite an... assault on the senses.'

Madame Digby laughed, and then gestured to the couple, still arguing over their wares. Their conversation had now turned to salt. 'At least it gives men plenty to talk about.'

The carriage struck a rut in the road, and the interior wobbled slightly. Lock leant on his knuckles to relieve the pressure on his rear. Madame Digby sighed at his discomfort.

'Oh, Matthew, is this your first carriage ride? Did you forget your pillow?' She gestured to the soft cushion which she had wedged under her extensive plume of pale blue skirts. Before Lock could answer, she turned to her bag, and retrieved a smaller cushion.

'Here, Matthew. Take it. Consider it a gift from one distinguished Dorset family to another.'

Lock desperately wanted the cushion. It would solve all his problems. But such a gift, from a House above his own in status, would not come cheap. Surely, Madame Digby would leverage this favour in the future. She hadn't gotten this far merely by being kind. She was clever, too, particularly when it came to her friends.

'Thank you, Madame.' It was surely best to acknowledge the favour. 'And please, if you feel it necessary, do not hesitate to call on me in the future. I would be happy to help Sir John if I can.'

Madame Digby smiled knowingly. 'Well met, Matthew. We must look after one another, must we not? We are all that separates the Crown from the rabble, after all.'

Lock nodded awkwardly. 'I'm afraid I will have to beg your forgiveness one more time, Madame. The events of the last few days have me quite exhausted. I intend to catch as much sleep in the next week as possible.'

Madame Digby reused her calming hand, as though the request was barely necessary. 'Indeed, Matthew, indeed. Please, relax your head. Always had trouble sleeping, myself. I will be sure to wake you when we reach our first rest stop.'

Lock smiled. This partnership just might get him through the numbing journey. He glanced out of the carriage door. They were still in The Hague's outskirts. The trotting horses ensured that the carriage moved only gradually, along streets choked with other carriages. Soon they would be into the Dutch countryside, and then the carriage would hug the Rhine.

Placing the cushion under his rear, Lock sighed in relief. He caught Madame Digby smile at his reaction, and nod at him to rest. He did not have to be told twice. His only fear was what awaited him when he shut his eyes.

Visions of black masks, of grave personal failings, and of the Black Prince beating a path to his door.

- CHAPTER TEN -

Father had always complained of the perils of travel. There were bandits, thieves, the occasional lone vagrant. There was the threat of starvation. Of missed carriages. Of ill horses. But boredom, father said, that was the thing he truly loathed. His was a mind which needed stimulation.

He could barely sit still, even at dinner time. He would engage in feverish conversation, filling his belly with food and feeding his mind with theories, ideas and debates. He encouraged his sons to do the same. A talkative man, Father said, is eminently more amenable than a silent one. Mother offered that a silent man was better than one who talked when he had nothing to say.

Father's boredom from his travels had moved him to create a volume of wisdom and wit for his sons to draw from. It was based on the musings and reflections of Francesco Guicciardini, a distinguished Florentine citizen from the early sixteenth century, and Father's role model. This, Father claimed after a few too many glasses, was his true bible.

Lock had left the volume next to his nightstand, back in Locksville. Like everything else precious to him, though, he had memorised some of its more useful passages. It was these passages that Lock ran through, as he worked to pass the time and ease the numbing boredom.

The boredom had become particularly acute when his other companions had left. Not all, it seemed, were bound for the city of Frankfurt. The merchants had hopped off by the end of the first day, to follow up on an impossible breakthrough in the tulip trade, so they said.

Madame Digby had lasted slightly longer, journeying overnight, before transferring to a second carriage, which would take her overland to the Pyrenees, and then into Spain.

She had waved frantically to Lock as she departed, and never ceased urging him to get in touch with her beloved son. Lock lied that he would do his best. Hers was a journey of at least a month, and Lock did not envy her. But he did miss her.

For four full days since he had been alone. He had had plenty of time to curse Vane's vague instructions, and to curse himself for failing to locate a map.

The Rhine, it transpired, was riven by right bank tributaries, each one spanned by a bridge more unstable than the last. There was the Lippe, then the Ruhr, then the Sieg, and an exhausting sequence of streams in between. The arrival of each made Lock believe that, mercifully, the journey might soon be over, only to be disappointed.

Finally, that morning, the carriage had crossed the Main. It would next be necessary to follow its course, to the gates of Frankfurt. The driver had barked down to him that they should reach their destination by nightfall.

That he was headed in the right direction was certainly reassuring, but the silence bore down on him. The roads lost their distinguishing features, and blurred from one to the next. Lock spread out his body on the otherwise empty bench. The once cramped compartment was now his own. It was early in the afternoon, but as to where he was, he did not know.

The carriage jolted suddenly to a stop.

Lock shifted his stiff body on the bench. Had he fallen asleep? Could it be? Could the journey finally be at an end? He was about to remove himself from the carriage and ask the driver that very question, when the door opened, and three men clambered aboard. Lock's heart jumped to his throat as he saw them.

Each man was clad in a black velvet mask.

One sat beside him, and two sat opposite.

The men were effectively featureless. Moderate height and weight, clad in black, with black boots and a black mask. Each was equipped with a sword. The one directly opposite him had a small dagger in addition to the longer blade. No one spoke.

The man beside Lock handed him a note, and a small paper knife. Black wax sealed the note once again. Evidently, they found their charge so unthreatening that they were willing to hand him a weapon, however small. Lock's musket and his belongings lay on the middle of the carriage's floor.

There was no question of touching them, or of fighting back. He would be overpowered immediately.

Lock held the note in his hands, and fought to stop them from shaking. He cut through the wax. The small note was unfolded. A single paragraph met his eyes.

Matthew Lock

It has been nearly a week since the last message was delivered to you. You have failed to heed its instructions. This is disappointing. You will now be forced to comply. You will be returned to The Hague where you will be watched, until you are seen to return to England. Please do not resist. This will only make the job of my masks that much more difficult, and I will not be able to guarantee your safety.

The Black Prince.

Lock's eyes fanned over the note several times, his mouth agape.

Who the devil was this man?

Who did he think he was, ordering him around?

Now seemed like a good time to find out.

'*You*,' Lock turned to the man beside him, the note still in his hands. 'You killed my parents, and my brother.'

But there was no reaction. The man was like black stone. Lock virtually shouted at the side of his face.

'Do you hear me, you foul bastards? What makes you think I'd go anywhere with you?'

The masked man sat perfectly still, facing forward, his hands by his side.

'Are you deaf, man? Who is your master, *what does he want with me?*'

He had tried, probably unsuccessfully, to hide the desperation in his voice. He was now more angry than fearful. The Black Prince's message had not been a bluff, not when it was placed on his cabin bed, nor at this moment. The carriage turned, and had begun moving again in the other direction.

The prospect of the return journey, after suffering days of numbing travel, was more daunting than failure itself. He could not go back. They could not make him. But how had this happened? How had he been found?

The man directly opposite Lock, with the dagger, spoke in German. 'I do not know your parents, Matthew Lock. Nor do I know your brother. I am sorry for your losses.'

Lock squinted at the man in front of him. Was he the leader of this group?

'*Sorry*? I don't want your sorry, I want justice.'

'It is not my mission to get you justice.'

'Then get out. *Get the hell out of my carriage.*'

The masked man shook his head. 'Mister Lock, my men and I have been nothing but polite and restrained. But you must understand our orders. We will return you to The Hague. We will ensure you return to England. We will not fail the Black Prince.'

Lock maintained his stare of the leader opposite him. The masked man to his right shifted on the hard bench. So they were human after all. But they wouldn't be persuaded. Short of some miracle, they wouldn't be overpowered either. So how? How to overcome such odds?

The carriage offered no prospects for escape. But the journey was still young. He had a whole week to prepare himself, to look for an opening. And if he had to, he would go obediently to The Hague, and lose them in the city's streets.

'You won't succeed in your mission,' Lock whispered, half to himself. 'I don't know how, but I will disappoint your bastard master one way or another. He doesn't know who he's dealing with.'

The masked leader cleared his throat. 'You are Matthew Charles Lock, from Locksville Estate in North Dorset. You are the second son of the late Charles and Catherine Lock. You are the elder brother of Arthur Lock. Is that the truth?'

'Partially,' Lock did his best to appear unimpressed. 'It is also true that masked men killed my older brother. It is also true that I found masked men in my home, where my parents were murdered.'

'I do not know about that.'

'Well, you should. Does the Black Prince know about it? What kind of operation is he running? Are you happy to serve a master that butchers families?'

The masked leader was silent.

'Ask him, next time you see him. Ask him if all this is worth it. Ask him if it's worthwhile making an enemy of the Lock family.'

Still, the masked leader did not say a word.

'Perhaps my Father learned something about the Black Prince. Something he wanted to keep a secret?'

Lock searched in vain for a reaction, however slight. The masked leader was aggressively self-contained.

'What about you? What if your Father, or your brother, or your son, fell afoul of your precious Black Prince? Would you still follow his orders then? Or does your honour mean nothing to you?'

Lock couldn't help but be impressed. Though, it was highly likely that his subordinates would not be as equally disciplined. Lock turned to his right.

'And you? Would you follow this leader of yours, if he ordered an attack on your family? That's what he did to my family, you know. What if he ordered you to defend someone that defiled your Mother, or your sister? How far does your blind loyalty go?'

The man's fists clenched and unclenched slightly. Lock continued in the most condescending tone of German he could manage.

'Perhaps you would go along with it anyway. Perhaps your sister deserved it. Perhaps your Mother had a reputation, and she deserved it too. Perhaps you would encourage the Black Prince to have his way with her –'

The man shot out of his chair and struck Lock hard across the face. Lock was knocked from the bench with the attack, but it had been worth it. The attacker's leader reprimanded him harshly.

'Sit with the driver,' the leader barked. 'I will *not* tolerate anyone that loses their composure.'

Sure enough, the man left the carriage interior. He was replaced by the other figure seated by the leader. Lock was still surrounded, but now it was two on one. Much more manageable odds.

'I know you are an intelligent man, Matthew Lock. Otherwise, you would not have come this far. But you must behave. I will not warn you so gently again.'

Lock rubbed the side of his face. 'You know why I'm here. You know why I'm going to Mannheim and then to Frankenthal.'

'You have told me.'

'Yes, but were you in my position, would you give up without a struggle, and allow yourself to be pulled from your quest?'

The leader did not answer the question. To do so would have exposed his internal conflict, and thus his weakness. The leader nodded at his subordinate beside Lock. With a single, gradual movement, he withdrew his sword, and placed it flat on his right knee. This would serve to remind Lock that they were armed. Lock smiled at the act. Now, they were taking their charge more seriously.

After a few minutes of heavy silence, the interior became darker. Lock spied plentiful trees outside. The carriage wheel struck a rut, and bounced slightly on the impact. The man beside Lock cursed quietly, and the leader glared at him.

'Seems to me like a thankless occupation.'

His two guards said nothing. The man beside him tightened his grip on the sword hilt.

'You escort brats like me around for a living. Didn't you want to do more with your lives? Didn't you think you'd amount to more than as a slave to a master you've never met? How do you even know he's real?'

The man beside him was clearly itching to respond. Lock tried pushing the most obvious buttons first.

'Take this man, here. You must be, what, in your mid-twenties? You probably thought you'd have more excitement and meaning in your life, than rubbing your sword in a dim carriage for a week.'

He stayed silent, but relaxed his grip slightly on his sword.

'Does the Black Prince teach you how to use it, or just how to rub it?'

His right hand tightened on it again.

'I bet you the four shillings I was going to pay that treacherous driver that you can't even swing the thing.'

The man beside him exhaled, and turned his head to gaze out the window. The trees had become increasingly concentrated. They must be moving through a forest. The carriage had slowed down to compensate for the poor road. Lock raised the stakes.

'I bet you those four shillings that that prick in your hand is as useless as the one between your legs.'

The man beside him stood up and raised his hand, just as his leader let out a loud shout. Lock recoiled in expectation, but there was no strike. There was instead another sound.

Muskets.

Lock opened his eyes to see the man swaying while clutching at his throat. A musket ball had ripped through the nape of his neck. It had come from behind them.

'Get *down*,' the leader hissed.

Lock threw himself down onto the bench, lying as flat as he could. It took a moment before he realised that the leader was on top of him, shielding him with his body, or at least trying to.

What an earth was happening?

The unfortunate masked man with a hole in his neck choked and bled out helplessly on the carriage floor. The leader cursed. The carriage had sped up slightly, but to its detriment. A wheel struck an errant stone far too hard, and a loud crack rang through the interior. It was now stuck fast, like a perfect target. Another crack was sounded. And another. More musket shots. Wood splintered inside.

'Keep your bloody head down, Lock!' the leader shouted, looking frantically around.

'Who is shooting at us?'

'Germans, German rebels. They must have recognised us.'

'I think the black masks are a bit of a giveaway.'

The leader glared at Lock, and reached for his bag on the floor. 'We may have to run for it.'

'*Run for it*? Run to The Hague? You'll never make it.'

'Not me, Lock, *you*!' the leader kicked at the door on the carriage's left side, and it swung open, barely still on its hinge. A musket ball ripped through it just at that moment. The leader flinched and cursed.

'Go, now, while they're reloading!'

'I don't understand, I thought the Black Prince wanted me off the continent?' the protest was an odd one, but Lock was too confused to act. Something wasn't right.

'Other orders take precedence over those instructions Lock, now move!'

'What *other orders*?'

A musket ball splintered through the roof of the carriage, and the driver let out a loud yelp. His body thudded to the ground.

'Lock, *go now*,' the leader rolled sideways, so that Lock's body was pulled onto the carriage floor. He landed in a pool of the other man's blood.

'Don't look at him Lock, just get out, *go*! Run to the south, follow the Rhine. Tell them you're English. The Germans won't hurt you.'

The instructions caused Lock to crawl through the grisly scene. He moved to the edge of the carriage, where the door had been kicked open. He threw his bag out. Lock turned to look one more time at the masked leader, who had laid his sword by his side, and was pouring powder into his musket. He saw something in the masked leader's eyes which had been absent until now. Fear.

Lock exhaled, and scrambled to his haunches. Using his legs, he propelled his body out of the carriage, and into the mystery that awaited outside. He pushed aside branches and ran into the darkness of the forest.

His legs protested at the sudden activity, following a week of sitting. His bag clattered into his back. His ankles cried out, but Lock kept going. As far as he knew, his life depended on it. He ran to the south. Musket fire boomed through the forest, accompanied by shouts and protests. As he panted his way through the undergrowth, as quickly and carefully as he could, Lock heard a man scream.

Had the leader just been killed?

There was no time to dwell on it, he had to move.

The Rhine rushed loudly on his right. It was his sole point of reference. A cobweb was pulled onto his face, and Lock cursed as he picked its strands away. Finally, the sounds of musketry either ceased, or became too far to hear. Lock spotted a tree stump, with three red mushrooms protruding from it. The foliage was so dense he could barely walk, and certainly not in a straight line.

His heart hammered in his chest. Running had never been his forte. Lock practically collapsed to his rear on the stump. He glanced back to the scene he had escaped from. Had the German rebels just saved his life? Had the masked leader sacrificed himself to save his charge? It was easier to decide that the former had happened, but there was no way to be sure.

Lock spotted smoke rising in the south. He was without a horse, and certainly without a carriage, but he was free.

Free to go south to Mannheim.

Free to speak with Vere in Frankenthal.

Free to find out what on earth was happening.

- CHAPTER ELEVEN -

A German-speaking Englishman, on a mission for the King of the British Isles?

The innkeeper's mouth had fallen open, and he had profusely apologised for the behaviour of his countrymen back in the forest. The further north one goes, he said, the madder the German became. Lock ran out of ways to thank the innkeeper for his generosity, as he was showered with excessive hospitality from the moment he arrived.

To help Lock understand what had just happened, the innkeeper sat with him as his new guest stuffed his face, and gave a personal account of life on the Rhine since the war had begun. It was grim story, and Lock only absorbed half of it, but what he did learn was of immense value.

The Spanish had arrived in the summer of 1620. Thanks to the departure of Frederick, the Elector Palatine, and his quest for the Bohemian Crown in the east, Spanish armies had swept up the Rhine almost completely unopposed. They had occupied key strategic towns and crossings south of the Dutch border, just in time for their war with the Dutch to resume.

The information poured from the excited innkeeper, who showered Lock with attention, and even shared a mug of bitters with him. Lock was his first customer in a fortnight, a fact which the innkeeper did not let slide.

'The Spanish have scared travellers away, Officer Lock. We used to get adventurers from all over the continent. They would walk the length of the Rhine at their leisure, stopping at inns like mine along the way. But no more.'

Lock didn't challenge the innkeeper's claims. He could have noted that aspiring customers were unlikely to be impressed by the peeling paint, the draughty interior, or the chewy meat. But that would have been rude.

Courtesy and kindness, Father said, were two formidable weapons in an envoy's arsenal. And they were free. Their deployment could mean the difference between life and death. Or, in Lock's case, between a full belly and growling hunger.

The innkeeper had been an invaluable mine of information. Diego de la Barca was the name of the commander, and his army was based in the village of Woodrest, a short ride south of Mannheim.

De la Barca had been based there for over a year, and he had made space for his army by effectively tearing the village down. His men were often split between garrison duty, in the nearby Mannheim, and patrol duty, around the countryside.

Their arrival and subsequent behaviour had not endeared them to the locals, many of whom had taken to the forest rather than submit to the King of Spain's authority. It was because of this defiance that de la Barca's men had acted so harshly in the first place, but this was really just an excuse.

Some vile men had enlisted in de la Barca's service, and they had no reservations about behaving reprehensibly, no matter the victims. De la Barca, it was said, did nothing to discipline his soldiers, and his superiors were becoming restless with his slow progress. Although the Spanish controlled the region, the fortress of Frankenthal, with its English garrison, still held out.

The innkeeper's son had followed the Elector Palatine in his quest to Bohemia, and had since vanished. Lock promised to keep an eye out for him, but he forgot his name almost immediately. His mind was elsewhere.

It was deep in the Black Prince's organisation.

It was in his Hague residence.

It was back in 1613.

'How long is the journey to de la Barca's camp, at Woodrest?'

The innkeeper took a long swig from his tankard, wiped the foam from his lips, and tilted his head to the right. His scraggly beard moved with his chin, as though frozen to his face.

'By foot, Officer Lock? Two days, perhaps three, depending on how fast your feet move.'

'Do you have a horse I can buy?'

The innkeeper shook his head. 'I've had to sell them, to keep the inn alive, and to keep food on my family's table. To my shame, I sold them to the

Spanish.'

'You had little choice,' Lock reassured him. 'A mount is of no use when your family is starving.'

The innkeeper grunted in appreciation. 'I can offer you some bread for the journey, and you're welcome to stay here, for as long as you wish, of course.'

'You are very kind. I will depart in the morning, Herr...'

'Kleppe, Pieter Kleppe. Please, call me Pieter.'

'Call me Matthew,' Lock smiled.

'You travel without a weapon, Matthew?' The concern on Kleppe's face was etched deep into his wrinkled brow.

'I have a sword, but I'm afraid I had to leave without my musket. There was no time to retrieve it during the ambush.'

Kleppe clicked his sausage fingers and rose from his chair

'Stay here, I've got something that might take its place.' The innkeeper headed for the waist-high wooden table that passed for a bar. Lock assessed Kleppe's setup. He did not feel particularly confident about the firearm which Kleppe would produce, if his inn was anything to go by, but Lock was immediately made to eat his words.

'This was my son's second musket,' Kleppe said, rubbing the dark wood along the barrel. 'You should take it with you, and when you return it, bring me more customers.'

Lock began to protest, but Kleppe would not have it.

'I haven't had a conversation with anyone but my dog for the last ten days, Matthew, and that was with a group of rude Spaniards. I want you to have it, please.'

The donation of the musket suggested that Kleppe knew his son wouldn't miss it. It suggested, more poignantly, that he knew his son was lost. Perhaps vaporised by cannon during the battle of White Mountain, the day that the Elector Palatine lost the Bohemian Crown. Or, maybe he had been shot to pieces by Count Tilly's professional Catholic League army.

Or, then again, the younger Kleppe could have decided to leave his Father behind in his rundown inn on the dark side of the Rhine. It brought Herr Kleppe more comfort to imagine that the latter possibility had not occurred. Dying in battle for a worthy cause, after all, was much easier to stomach.

Kleppe lowered the musket onto the table, and Lock's hands rested on it. 'Thank you, Herr Kleppe. I will take good care of it. I will think of your son when I have cause to use it.'

Pieter Kleppe nodded, and indicated his intention to prepare Lock's room. Lock turned his attention to the musket. It had seen better days, but with a clean and check, perhaps a few rounds fired, it would be ready for service.

It was roughly five feet long. The firing mechanism was that of a matchlock, identical in function to every musket Lock had seen. The weapon was slightly heavier than the one he had left behind, but the calibre of musket ball would not have to be changed, so long as he was careful. Lock ran his index finger along the cold steel barrel atop the weapon. A slight whiff of powder evoked a host of memories.

As he aged, the training muskets became heavier, and Lock became stronger. Once the forty-three steps had been learned, they could be sped up and adapted. They were eventually divided into thirteen steps.

Lock imagined Captain Frank call out each step in his gruff, hearty voice, as he aimed at the rustic wall and his fingers pulled up the levered trigger.

This weapon had a past. Was it as weighted a past as his own? A deliberate pattering of steps suggested that the innkeeper had returned to Lock's presence.

'I didn't ask you to *marry* the weapon, Officer Lock,' Herr Kleppe joked, though it was plain that the innkeeper was pleased to see his guest treat the heirloom with such respect.

'Your son was very fortunate to have such a firearm,' Lock said, his eyes now fixed on the inscription which was etched into the lock plate.

'You seem to know your way around it. Did your Father teach you?'

Lock simply nodded. The answer would be too complex to explain. Lock could fire off two shots in under a minute, the quickest fire rate in Dorset, and, Father loudly proclaimed, the British Isles as well.

Lock had never been sure of that, and per Mother's objections, he was never entered into any shooting competitions. The heir to the estate, she insisted, should be tasked instead with learning how to be a landowner, and not wasting his time with frivolous games. But word had escaped the Locksville estate nonetheless.

'Shame you couldn't see the weapon he took with him. A wheellock. Are you familiar with it?'

Lock nodded, though he had never seen one up close.

'Fearsome firearm that. Expensive though, mind you, and hard to maintain. My boy won it in a shooting competition, if you can believe it. The wheellock does pack a punch, and doesn't require that blasted lit match to follow you around everywhere.'

'My Father used to say that the lit match kept warfare civilised. It prevented ambushes, and made men honourable.'

The innkeeper snorted at the view. 'If he thought it kept men honourable, then I fear he hasn't seen enough of the world.'

Lock nodded politely.

Herr Kleppe had a point. However much of the world Charles Lock had seen, his own demise was anything but honourable, and was surely delivered by thoroughly knavish men.

'I have your room ready, Officer Lock. You look like you could sleep for a week. Carriage travel leaves much to be desired, I'm sure you'd agree.'

'I do, Pieter, I do. If not for a kind lady's donation of a seat cushion, I fear I'd have limped through your door.'

'Ah, Officer Lock, these things will be learned with time. Come.' Kleppe gestured to the stairs which led to the inn's upper level. Lock obliged. His eyes were heavy, and his legs were like lead. Kleppe patted him on the back as he made it to the landing.

'It is a humble room, but you can have it for as long as you need it.'

Lock could already tell that his heels would hang over the edge of the bed, but he didn't care. The sight of linen bedsheets, rather than straw, was enough to draw him into the admittedly humble room. It was a touch larger than his cabin on board the vessel, but it was the bed that mattered.

'Shall I wake you in the morning, for a breakfast of bread and sausage?'

'Herr Kleppe, if I don't get out of bed for bread and sausage, you'll know I've been replaced by a Spanish spy.'

A deep belly laugh erupted from the innkeeper, as he closed over the door. Lock was already on the bed before it had fully closed. There was much to think about, but his mind had other ideas. It had begun to shut down from the moment his head touched the feather pillow.

Herr Kleppe had broken out his brightest and best materials for his first overnight guest in perhaps a month. Compared to his tree-stump pillow from the night before, it was the lap of luxury.

Lock already looked forward to breakfast. He could almost pretend that the war was miles away.

That the black masks were indifferent to him.

That all was well with the Lock family.

That his parents would join him for breakfast.

But these dreams were cruel.

As cruel a dream as the return of Pieter Kleppe's son.

- CHAPTER TWELVE -

The breakfast had been hearty, but the travel thereafter had been hard. Lock's legs had ached, and he burned through the food Kleppe provided by the afternoon. A sleepless night by a light stream, with his bag for a pillow, had brought scant rest. The following day though, the pillars of smoke emanating from Manheim's fires could be seen.

Fortune then smiled on him. A trickle of merchant traffic provided the opportunity to hitch a ride on a rough wooden cart. The gruff wagon driver agreed to take him over the Neckar crossing, upstream from Mannheim, for a few shillings of course. The novelty of the bridges, some of them historical relics in their own right, had long since worn off.

With his rested legs, by the afternoon of the second day, Lock was mentally and physically ready for the final phase of his journey – a walk south to Diego de la Barca's camp. Following the wagon driver's advice, Lock bypassed the dark forest on his right, and adhered to the longer, safer route. Two hours of brisk walking brought him to the outskirts of Woodrest camp.

It was a sight to behold. The town had been almost wholly dismantled to make way for the new military installations, which included rows upon rows of tents. These housed the two thousand or so men under de la Barca's command, though Lock noted that a great portion of Spanish soldiers had been drilling outside Mannheim, so his force was likely divided into two main cohorts.

Travel further south was virtually impossible without moving through the camp, as the main road ran right through it. Wooden barricades and palisades had been erected, but these looked somewhat tired, and were likely in need of repair.

Lock wiped his forehead for the umpteenth time. The heat of the early Rhineland summer baked his pale skin, but Lock soldiered forward. Perhaps ten days had passed since the vessel had departed Bristol, and here, hopefully, progress could be made.

Entrance to the camp was relatively straightforward. Soldiers flanked the wide road in large numbers, keeping a watchful eye out for troublemakers, which really meant the local population. The camp's distinguishing feature, aside from the mounds of rubble which suggested the existence of a ruined dwelling, was the command tent. It was larger than all the others, and dyed a shade of faded orange.

Here, Diego de la Barca would surely reside. Here, he could receive the approval he required, to protect himself from the wandering Spanish cavalry that might impede his mission. But the true mission could not be made known to the Spanish.

Lock reminded himself of his surface mission.

He was here on order of His Majesty, to receive the surrender of the Frankenthal garrison.

Much would depend upon the believability of his act, as well as the lax discipline of the Spanish, who would hopefully not look too far into his story. He had prepared his incredulous expressions, just in case.

The soldiers watched him as he approached. He had hoped to wait until a wagon or some other travellers passed by, but these had not materialised. Now their focus was all on him. With his dirty buff coat and dulled boots, he certainly looked the part of the travelling statesman. Father had frequently complained that he wasn't paid enough or provided with sufficient revenue even to purchase better clothing, but the question was whether de la Barca would be fooled.

The soldiers on guard, at least, seemed convinced. The lack of Spanish wouldn't be a problem. All men of importance spoke French, a lesson which his parents had drilled into him from an early age. Lock sometimes even daydreamed in French. The language also granted a degree of precision in diplomacy which, Father insisted, was immensely useful.

It was time to put these claims to the test.

Lock sauntered past the men on guard, being sure to ooze confidence in his stride and expression. A man who looked like he belonged was unlikely to be challenged. The challenge was to find the right balance. Not to swagger, but to glide.

The command tent was perhaps halfway into the camp, perched on a slight hill in an otherwise flat area. Lock made his way past clouds of soldiers tending to small cooking fires, and others nursing minor wounds. It was before noon, and near the time when men would be sent on arranged patrols. In the interim, the soldier embraced the inactivity, and did his best to live.

A few feet from the command tent, the smells of the place surged up his nostrils. Bread and sweat vied for competition with the stench of human waste. Lock maintained his thoroughly unaffected act. A figure out front of the command tent was examining him intently. He looked fairly miserable, and held a long pike upright.

Lock made for him with a cheerful smile, the exact opposite of how he felt. He inhaled deeply, and delivered his introduction in French.

'Good morning Sir. Officer Lock here to see His Excellency, Diego de la Barca. Is your commander present? I wish to speak with him. I am travelling on behalf of His Majesty King James of England, Scotland and Ireland.'

The grim pikeman looked him up and down. He was likely a sergeant, but the rank hadn't served to cheer him up.

'Credentials?' he asked limply.

'Right away Sir,' Lock said, producing the precious document.

The parchment with the heavy seal at its end was presented, and the pikeman took it with surprising delicacy. One imagined the penalty for ruining such a document. Perhaps it had happened before.

Lock watched for his reaction. The morose pikeman didn't smile, but he did gesture at Lock to enter the tent, which was all that was needed. Lock pushed the right flap of the door gently, so that he did not make a sudden entrance, and could fully absorb the sights that greeted him within. The brightness of the late morning gave way to the shade of a forest, but the temperature did not improve.

Lock was immediately struck by the searing heat inside, accompanied by a new pungent smell. Stale wine dominated, and wafted in abundance. It was as though a barrel had been knocked over, and left to evaporate over time. Lock did his best to mask his disgust, and endeavoured to breathe through his mouth.

The tent itself was a simple structure of timber and cloth, erected to provide shade and comfort to the Spanish commander. There was plenty of space inside. Lock thought it equalled his master bedroom, but there was a great deal more activity here.

It had also been reinforced to reflect its martial purpose. Swords were hung on the right and left walls, along with old shields bearing the red cross of Burgundy, the flag of battle for Spanish soldiers.

Three barrels, perhaps containing powder, but more likely containing wine, were dotted haphazardly around the tent. One barrel was directly in Lock's way, and he had to awkwardly veer left to avoid it.

Was he was being watched? Sure enough, as Lock reached the tent's centre, a cough behind him drew his attention to two soldiers guarding each side of the door. The eyes of the two soldiers were fixed forward in an uncompromising stare. Diego de la Barca could not be too careful, but these soldiers were not here for Lock – so long as he played his part effectively.

De la Barca did not seem to have much of a presence. He was seated casually in the back of the tent, and did not even raise his glance as Lock entered. The commander leafed through a set of papers, and sat with his legs crossed. It was a strangely passive aggressive pose.

Here was a man who was confident enough to do things his own way, and this was further demonstrated by the presence of a full glass of red wine, which rested on a barrel at de la Barca's right. Lock was thirsty, but it was barely noon.

Further to de la Barca's right, another door would allow soldiers in and out of the tent. It was quite a system, but the system was somewhat weathered after over a year in the same place. The faded orange colour of the canvas had become grimy and frayed at the bottom, and sunlight poked enthusiastically through small holes which the elements and curious birds had likely created.

Lock realised that it was now time to perform. The onus was on him to draw de la Barca's attention, particularly if the commander was not even willing to glance up from his papers. This was the critical moment.

A mistake made now could cost him his life.

'May God bless you Sir,' Lock began in French, as confidently as he dared, 'I present my humble mission to you, as a servant of His Majesty King James of England. If I may, I wish to travel to Frankenthal and receive its surrender, that our two nations may then enjoy peace that is long lasting.'

Lock held his breath and maintained his bow; the introduction had been quite a mouthful, but the real issue was whether his papers, since taken for inspection, would pass muster. His mouth was dry, and he was aware of how heavily he was sweating. The heat was suffocating.

Lock's eyes darted around the room and he gasped for breath as quietly as he could. *Would he get away with it?* The royal seal of King James graced the top of his credentials, but a closer inspection of the contents would have revealed that a certain Matthew Charles Lock was authorised only as far as Frankfurt, and even then, in a company of far more qualified and experience diplomats than himself. With sufficient prodding, Lock would be completely exposed.

The silence was interrupted when the dour-faced sergeant entered the tent's rear door now lacking his unwieldy pike. He said something quickly in Spanish to de la Barca which Lock didn't quite grasp. Though his bow restricted his gaze to the men's feet, he did notice the moment when his credentials were produced, and accepted by de la Barca.

A palpable tension began to creep into the air. Still, de la Barca had yet to acknowledge his bow. Slowly and steadily, Lock moved his gaze upwards, so as not to attract any attention. To his relief, he saw that de la Barca was flicking through his papers with apparent disinterest.

The commander's skin had been seized by the sun, and a thick black beard covered much of his face. It made his relatively small head appear larger than its true size, and the startling picture was completed with a pair of dark eyebrows that appeared to scrutinise new subjects independent of de la Barca's knowledge.

The Spaniard's bloodshot brown eyes scanned Lock's credentials, as though participating in a tradition which caused great personal boredom. He broke for a moment from his reading, and reached for his cup of wine. For a fleeting moment, Lock's eyes connected with de la Barca's, and the commander offered a weak smile and nod.

Lock exhaled in relief. Perhaps Pieter Kleppe had been wrong about him? De la Barca quickly returned to his papers, and seemed in no particular hurry. Lock took the brief acknowledgment as a signal to release his bow, and he did so as smoothly as he could.

A light breeze ruffled the bottom layer of the tent, briefly lifting the canvas and revealing grass on the other side. Distant laughter mixed with a woman's sobbing could be heard, perhaps from nearby.

Still, de la Barca did not speak. The silence was deafening.

Lock began to suspect that he had made a terrible mistake.

Finally, de la Barca broke the silence by inhaling deeply, before letting out a loud sigh. Two pairs of feet behind Lock scraped the ground, as the two soldiers guarding the door stood to attention, evidently preparing themselves for what would come next.

'You must excuse me, Officer Lock,' de la Barca said in French. His Spanish accent was thick, but his French was smooth and confident, like a native speaker. 'I was just consulting the reports from our scouts. I wish to give you an update. Frankenthal is the final fortress in the Palatinate yet to fly a Spanish flag. It continues to frustrate all attempts to negotiate a surrender. It is my understanding that the garrison commander is *quite mad*.'

Lock smiled. The act was allowed as de la Barca had a similar expression across his own face. The Spaniard's countenance suggested that he respected the commander at Frankenthal, even if he loathed him for causing Spain so many headaches.

If Sir Horace Vere truly was as resourceful as Father had claimed, this would make sense. Because of its resistance, Frankenthal was the asterisk which blighted an otherwise perfect record along the Rhine. More awkwardly still, it was held by Englishmen.

Thanks to the negotiations for the Anglo-Spanish marital alliance, Spanish officials were in a difficult position when interacting with the English. They had orders not to offend or attack any English officials they found, yet when these Englishmen enlisted for war, and occupied an important fortress, how could this fortress be seized without also causing an incident?

This incident could jeopardise the looming marriage between Prince Charles and the Infanta of Spain. Such an incident, Lock believed, was exactly what de la Barca feared. If he played his cards right, Lock could pose as the solution to all of de la Barca's problems, but he had to tread carefully.

'With your permission,' Lock began, 'I would ask that I travel to Frankenthal to receive the surrender of this town, thereby ensuring that our two nations remain in a peaceful coexistence.'

De la Barca nodded his head. 'It would be my honour, Officer Lock. I just have one question.'

Lock body stiffened. Suddenly, a third soldier burst into the tent. Lock did not dare turn around.

'Ah,' de la Barca said, with evident satisfaction, his gaze fixing to a point behind Lock. 'It is about time; I have been waiting.'

As the footsteps behind him grew closer, sweat dripped down Lock's back. The soldier walked past him in a rush, but it was impossible to see what he held, as the contents were placed directly into de la Barca's hands.

As the soldier stepped backward, bowed, and walked out of the tent, only then was it possible to see what de la Barca held. It was a bottle of wine, one for each hand.

'My question,' de la Barca said, 'Do you prefer red or white, Officer Lock?'

Lock regained his composure, 'Red, please, Your Excellency.' Without rising from his large wooden armchair, de la Barca reached with a grunt to a barrel behind him, and grasped two silver goblets which had been resting on top of it.

After a brief flush of activity, de la Barca handed Lock a full cup. It smelt sweet, earthy, and like the last thing Lock wanted to ingest at this moment. The warmth of the wine made itself felt even through the glass.

'Some say I celebrate too often, and with too much gusto,' de la Barca said, his cup held high in the air in the gesture for a toast. Lock quickly reciprocated, and raised his own glass to an equal level. 'But on a day when that wretched blight of a town is no longer Spain's problem, this, I feel, is a day worthy of celebration.'

Lock could barely believe it – was de la Barca *so* desperate to capture Frankenthal that he would believe him so willingly? One of de la Barca's subordinates, perhaps that grim soldier with the pike, had evidently not done their homework when examining his credentials. De la Barca was waiting for Lock to name the toast, so he made the obvious choice.

'To His Most Christian Majesty, King Philip IV,' Lock said, before swallowing as little of the warm, acidic liquid as he thought he could get away with. De la Barca's glass was already empty, and the Spaniard was filling it up again. He gestured towards Lock's glass, but Lock excused himself.

'Forgive me, Excellency,' Lock said, 'I fear I must remain sharp if I am to succeed in this task.'

De la Barca's forehead became furrowed, but he then handed Lock an unopened bottle of white wine which was just behind the leg of his chair.

Was this the commander's secret stash? Either way, it was a gesture Lock could not refuse.

He took the bottle from de la Barca's hairy, outstretched arm with a polite smile. Lock's own palms were sweaty, made sweatier by the warmth of the wine bottle which etiquette required he accept. De la Barca seemed immune both to the heat of the place, and to his soldiers' discomfort.

'Frankenthal is a day's ride away,' the Spaniard said, sipping from his cup. 'If you make haste now you will surely arrive before sunset.'

De la Barca's expression then changed when he realised a problem, just as Lock realised it himself. The commander had likely been informed of this envoy's arrival by foot. Lock possessed no riding gear of any kind. What English diplomat, sent on an official mission, travelled without a horse, if he was not esteemed enough to be granted a carriage?

When caught in a lie, it helped to provide a mix of the truth and additional lies to escape from the predicament. It was also important to show no hesitation. Lock spoke quickly to solve the glaring hole in his plan.

'If I could beg your indulgence, Excellency, and plead for the loan of a mount. I am ashamed to confess that while in transit to this place, I had my horse stolen.'

De la Barca's eyes narrowed. 'What a terrible thing to happen, Officer Lock,' he tutted, 'May God cast his judgement on those that prey upon humble travellers.' De la Barca then sat forward in his large wooden armchair, and stretched so that his gauntlets clinked off his breastplate. Leaning back again, de la Barca paused for a moment before asking 'What horse did you ride?'

The question could be interpreted as a polite conversation among two horse-riding enthusiasts over wine, but Lock knew the Spaniard was testing him. As a member of a privileged noble family, de la Barca would have grown up with horses, would have engaged in regular hunts, and would even have learned which breed of horses suited which rider the best.

If Lock truly was the qualified statesman he claimed to be, his knowledge of equine subjects would have been equally refined and informed. To satisfy this casual interrogation, more than a surface level knowledge of horses was required. Standing at over six feet tall, with broad shoulders and a stocky build, Lock knew from experience that his frame required a larger breed of horse. De la Barca certainly knew this as well; as a soldier he had likely sized

Lock up the moment he saw him.

Lock was careful not to fall into the trap. 'Mine was a black Frisian stallion,' he said, being sure to inject a degree of lament in his voice.

The Spaniard certainly didn't need to know of his struggles with Isabella, nor was de la Barca likely to be impressed with Father's penchant for naming his beasts after Spanish monarchs.

'Ah, what a mount indeed', the Spaniard said. Having finished his glass of red wine, and with the bottle still in Lock's hands, de la Barca greedily opened a different bottle of white.

He swirled the clear liquid around in his glass. Having not cleaned his glass first, the wine was tinted slightly pink, but de la Barca did not seem to care. Its scent wafted over to Lock's nostrils, and Lock knew he had dodged a bullet by selecting the red.

'I remember those Frisian mounts,' de la Barca said fondly, 'a perfect blend of war horse, but also light and nimble enough to save you in a pinch.'

The Spaniard seemed to be enjoying the conversation now. Perhaps he longed for a time when his greatest concern was horse-riding, and no care had to be given to fortresses held by English soldiers on the Rhine. After passing several tests, perhaps de la Barca would now finally give his blessing for the journey ahead.

'I confess, I am quite surprised,' de la Barca said, his eyebrows moving up his forehead. 'A fine steed like that, I do not know how any assailant on his wretched mule could have caught you.'

De la Barca had a point.

Lock's stomach lurched – had he been too clever for his own good? If he truly had ridden such a spectacular mount through this war-torn region, he was likely the fastest man around for several hundred miles. He had hidden the truth of the carriage journey as it still made little sense to him, but now was the time to bring its consequences forward.

'I was ambushed. By bandits... in the forest.'

De la Barca's eyes widened. '*El diablo*. I have heard of these things. Men become crazy like demons when their lands are occupied and their children starve. I have tried to make this war as honourable as possible, but God damn them, not all war can be clean. Please, Officer Lock, tell me what happened to you?'

The lie was now getting out of hand, but he could not turn back from it now. Would he be giving anything away by telling the truth? But how to tell the truth without speaking of the black masks? Lock did not have to feign hurt and trauma, but he did take a deep breath to buy time, aware of the Spaniard's expectant gaze. De la Barca evidently wanted a dramatic story to drink to. Lock had no choice other than to reciprocate.

'It was my own fault, truly,' Lock began, 'In my eagerness, I decided to ride when it was past sundown. Suddenly, as I came to a fork in the road, I lost my bearings. It was then I heard gunshots, and three men accosted me at gunpoint...'

De la Barca slammed his fist on the table in front of him.

The soldiers behind Lock flinched.

'Those damn thieves, *those wretches*! What a terrible thing.'

It was only now that Lock realised something which should have been obvious from the beginning.

De la Barca's impassioned speeches, his thirst for drama, and his inability to smell a rat in Lock's credentials, all served to spell it out. Diego de la Barca was drunk, and as the time was a little before noon, it was a safe bet that he was something of a regular partaker of wine. That explained why the Spaniard had not stood up since Lock had entered the tent – if he didn't wish to commit a shameful tumble, he would have to stay seated.

De la Barca then embarked on an extensive rant about the peasantry, about the godless heathens who ambushed several of his men in the forest, and the horrific methods they used to torture their victims. The Spaniard accused the dispossessed Elector Palatine of sedition against his liege, the Emperor, and all the other reproves which Lock had heard read by those sympathetic to the Habsburg cause.

Lock found he had little sympathy for the plight of de la Barca or his men. Even to see the remains of Woodrest served as a stark reminder of the ruin they had inflicted on the innocents of the Palatinate. Had de la Barca arrived in England with similar aims, Lock did not doubt that England's peasantry would have given him just as hostile a reception.

'Your Excellency,' Lock interrupted, 'I must apologise for burdening you with my troubles. The experience was a traumatic one and I do not wish to revisit it. My only wish is to redeem my honour by succeeding in my mission, and acquiring the surrender of Frankenthal for my King. I would be most indebted to you if you could facilitate this.'

De la Barca initially appeared annoyed that his rant had been ended. He emptied his glass, and prepared to refill it, but then put the bottle down and looked at one of the soldiers by the tent door.

He uttered a command in Spanish, and the two soldiers marched forward to stand at Lock's right and left side. 'Officer Lock, if it pleases you, please accept my escort to the outer limits of Frankenthal. Under such company, no devils will dare to ambush you again.'

Lock glanced briefly at the soldier on his left. The man's face was sunburnt and expressionless, and his dark eyes focused directly forward through whisps of black hair. His other companion had blond hair, and that, Lock decided, was how he would tell them apart. De la Barca smiled fondly at the blond-haired Spaniard, who nodded in response.

Both soldiers wore a cloth uniform with a polished iron breastplate. Each had swords in their scabbards, and each had their hand on the sword hilt. Both were impressively equipped and supplied, the key criteria for any successful army, and Spain boasted many such armies. Lock couldn't help but wonder about their prowess with the musket, though they did not carry firearms – there was hardly any point in firing a musket in the tent after all.

De la Barca's offer of an escort made Lock's journey more complicated, and would draw more attention to him, but it could also be a blessing in disguise. As the experience with the carriage had made clear, the region *was* dangerous, and Lock had been fortunate not to caught by any bandits, yet.

'Your generosity is surely legendary, Excellency, I thank you,' Lock said. De la Barca nodded, and bowed slightly in his chair. The commander then proceeded to refill his glass, before grunting mid-sip as though something had suddenly occurred to him. Lock paused in expectation.

'Officer Lock, I hope to see you this time tomorrow, having completed your mission, and released Frankenthal of its burdens. The quickest route is through the forest, then onto Mannheim where the Rhine can be crossed. I have ensured you will meet no trouble, and your important business will not be delayed. Good day.'

De la Barca did not move from his chair, he simply fixed his gaze elsewhere, satisfied that this would communicate to Lock that the conversation was over. The pikeman handed Lock his credentials, with a Spanish wax seal now attached to the end. Lock did not ask about the seal; as an ambassador, it was surely assumed that he would know what it all meant.

The art of the bluff was confidence. Where confidence was not naturally present, the man must act.

With that, Lock appeared to have been dismissed. He moved carefully to the door of the tent and pushed it open. Had he truly managed it? For a brief moment, the sun blinded him, and his vision then returned, capturing the drudgery of the camp like before. The two soldiers were already close behind him, and no wonder – who would wish to remain in a miserable camp like this, with a commander who drank all the wine rations?

The black-haired Spaniard said something to the blond Spaniard, and both men giggled, as they shared a private joke. Lock held the bottle of warm wine tightly in his hands before putting it carefully in his bag – this would be of invaluable use in the near future.

The two Spanish soldiers gestured to Lock in broken French that they needed to retrieve their muskets from the gunsmith, who was based a few feet away. Lock walked with them.

An essential ingredient in every successful camp was a bakery. This would guarantee fresh bread every day, a vital source of nourishment, and an effective morale boost. The morale was found in the smell, which wafted, so it seemed, through Lock's entire being. His stomach grumbled. In his haste to reach Woodrest, Lock had uncharacteristically skipped breakfast. Thirst also gnawed at his throat.

If he was to play the role of official envoy, then he should surely act with the sense of entitlement familiar to all men of the Crown. After all, the Spanish had given him an escort, would squeezing the King of Spain for some lunch be so difficult? Surely feeding a visiting ambassador was the honourable thing to do?

It was becoming apparent that communicating with his Spanish escort would be harder than Lock had expected. The two men were glued to Spanish and Spanish only when they spoke, though it seemed that sometimes, the black-haired Spaniard showed signs of absorbing and understanding French.

With this in mind, as they walked along the dirt track, Lock tried the French for lunch, and then for food. Both men looked at Lock blankly. He gave up, and made the universal gesture for eating, and in response, the black-haired Spaniard then nodded and grinned. The language barrier would at least make things interesting.

After sitting muted and eating as much as he could from a collection of bread, cheese and mutton, Lock prepared for the trek ahead. He finished his cup of beer, and filled his canteen with more.

He could make it to Frankenthal before dark, but he was less confident about what would happen when he arrived.

What if Vere didn't wish to acknowledge his godson?

For so many years, Father had spoken of Vere's resourcefulness, his grit, his intelligence, and his calm state of mind even when under fire. Navigating the prejudices of an alcoholic Spanish commander was one thing, persuading a veteran soldier-statesman to see things his way was quite another. Still, he had to try. This was his only lead.

The two Spaniards carried food with them, and the black-haired Spaniard wrapped up the food in cloth, handing it to Lock as he did so.

'For me?' Lock asked, pointing to his chest. The Spaniard seemed offended, and gestured to the three of them. 'Great,' Lock sighed, 'now I'm the greedy one.'

The last thing he could afford was to be disliked by his escort; they'd be more likely to run away at the first sign of trouble than actually help.

Lock turned to the rough direction of the Rhine, and began to walk. One of the Spaniards called out, and uttered some words in Spanish. Lock had no idea what he had said, and cursed himself for the umpteenth time that day for avoiding Spanish lessons.

The black-haired Spaniard grinned again, and made the gesture of riding a horse, the blond Spaniard played a supporting role, even replicating the sound of a braying mare with remarkable accuracy.

'I get it', Lock said, rolling his eyes, 'horses, we need horses.'

After a brief detour to the stables, where three horses considerably smaller and slower than Isabella were signed out, the party of three trotted their way due West towards the Rhine. They followed a path which had been borne into the countryside, and which centuries of wheels had ironed into a flat track. Limited efforts had been made to scatter stones on the track to increase traction when the rains came. In the heat of summer these multi-coloured stones could only partially be seen below the cloud of dust that seemed to hover above the road.

Under his breath, Lock cursed his inferior riding skills once again, and wished he had listened when Arthur had tried to teach him. The long path stretched into the distance, forking left, into the forest, or right, through the longer route he had recently travelled. The blond-haired Spaniard seemed hesitant to ride towards the forest, but after a brief pep talk, or perhaps some jeering, his black-haired companion seemed to convince him.

After a short ride, they entered this forest, and in the process, it seemed, entered a whole new world. Trees stretched to the skies, as if yearning to touch the sun, and the canopy provided a cooling shade. Birds chirped and insects buzzed around the pools which remained. The contrast was remarkable, like riding from day into night.

Could an ambush be launched here? Was this not the perfect place, in the cool of the forest, using the dark trunk of the trees for cover?

His escorts did not seem concerned. The black-haired Spaniard still rode in front. His musket was packed away. It would have been hopeless to attempt the cumbersome matchlock routine while on horseback – it was challenging enough while on foot. These soldiers, if confronted, would charge with their swords. They also had pistoles tucked alongside their muskets, though Lock doubted their proficiency with such a specialist weapon.

Several minutes passed, and as the rhythm of the journey became familiar, and the scenery remained calm and unchanging, Lock began daydreaming.

His mind returned to that happy scene. Christmas Day, 1621, the last time the Lock family had been together. The Lockville family estate was fully kitted out with sumptuous decorations, and then, in the grand dining room, a table laden with food of all kinds.

Lamb and mutton were supplied by ragged shepherds, who Father sent away with a gift of wine. There was also plentiful beef, pork and even venison from the contracted farmers and hunters Father employed. Sprigs of holly quite literally decked the halls, and Mother grumbled out of the side of her mouth that Charles had spent too much.

Had he known that Christmas Day 1621 would be the last with his parents, Lock would have eaten even more, unashamed of the gluttony, desperate to taste, to enjoy, to relish as much as he could.

The memory was too warming to escape from for long. There was Mother, sitting next to Arthur by the fire, the two of them chatting and laughing, while Father explained the history of the Bohemian Crown to the older son, and Lock listened in rapture. Lock had recently graduated Oxford with honours. History and law, Mother had tutted, *just like your Father*, but on Christmas Day even she was all smiles. The room was warmed by the fire and by the wine in his glass. He and Arthur later got drunk, and sang some of Father's soldiering songs, before Father gleefully joined in.

Not for the first time, and likely not the last either, Lock had to remind himself that it was all gone.

He would never have Christmas with Mother and Father again.

A twig snapped nearby in the woods, and suddenly he was back.

Lock's eyes followed a bird fly through a clearing, and then another, and then another. The black-haired Spaniard in front of him began to call out behind him. Lock was just about to suggest the two should ride side by side when he heard the sickening crack of a musket, and several shouts.

The language was German.

Lock cursed his folly.

Would de la Barca truly believe that this English envoy was such a magnet for ambushes?

In return for his false pretences, God was now determined to send the Germans upon him for a second time.

- CHAPTER THIRTEEN -

Angry German shouts permeated the forest.

The three horses broke into a gallop. Lock looked behind him for as long as he dared. Another bend in the road loomed before them, and Lock called out in French that the ambushers would surely try again there.

Lock caught a glimpse of the black-haired Spaniard in front. The jovial expressions had long since left his face, and the Spaniard appeared consumed with a grim determination as he drove his horse forward. He cursed in a language that wasn't Spanish, but sounded somehow familiar.

Was it Basque? Perhaps Catalan?

The black-haired Spaniard had cut his neck while shaving, and his nose was badly scorched by the sun. He gestured at Lock to hurry up.

Lock noticed his escort had picked up speed, and he also pushed his mount as much as he dared.

As a child, he had feared that horses could see through him, and could sense his fear as he rode on top of them. Lock's mind turned to that disaster where he really had ridden a Frisian stallion as a child, and it had bucked him off with what seemed like a light flick of its rump. '*My poor boy*', Mother had said, in one of the rare moments of tenderness she shared with him.

Once again, Lock forced himself to concentrate. At last, an end to the forest presented itself ahead.

Were they going to make it after all?

The musket shots ceased, and the smell of powder became increasingly distant. They broke out of the forest into an enormous clearing.

Having ridden in the dim light of the forest for nearly an hour, Lock's eyes took some time to adjust, but as they did, his heart sank.

The road they had pounded on now trailed off to the right, but directly in front was an enormous moss-covered rock with trees behind, where four men were perched. Each man lay almost prone, and propped his musket on a rock, aimed directly at the intruders.

Lock's mind leapt into the process of making calculations. The most professional musketeers could fire and reload twice in one minute, but at their distance, these Germans would only need one shot. Three more men stood behind an upturned wooden wagon, blocking the conventional route. These Germans also possessed firearms.

It was then that Lock's senses caught up to the overwhelming noise – a river surged and gurgled down below. This river, preceded by a steep slope of dense trees, blocked the only other exit, to the left. The blond Spaniard behind Lock was now on his left, and without saying anything, sighed a hopeless sigh that perfectly captured their predicament. They had, after all, ridden straight into an ambush.

A tense sense of anticipation hung in the air. The four Germans in front and three on the right remained still and silent, as if waiting for something. And then, from behind them, a bearded figure with scraggly hair, sitting on a grey horse, trotted into the clearing.

There was enough space in the clearing for the man to ride around his three prisoners, and so he did, as if sizing them up. Lock's mind raced. The unkempt looking man dismounted in front of them, and made his way towards Lock. As he walked closer, Lock could see that the short man's clothes were equally ragged, as though he had been living rough for months.

There was nothing ragged about the man's sword, however. It was brand new, and gleamed as he unsheathed it with a deft flick of his wrist. It was worse than Lock thought – an army of forest bandits, commanded by what appeared to be a war veteran. The man continued to walk towards Lock until he was barely a foot away.

Strands of hair moved away from the man's face, and a whole new aspect of his appearance drew Lock's gaze. A grey patch of cloth was held over his mouth, secured from the other side. And then, at about arm's length, he stood beside Lock and looked up at him on his horse. The two escorts did nothing.

The short grey man stared at Lock over the cloth, with steel blue eyes that gleamed with anger.

Lock stared back, agape, at the man's covered face. It was the height of impetuosity, but Lock couldn't help himself. Perhaps the cloth hid the removal of a tongue, or something worse? Lock shifted uncomfortably in the saddle under the man's piercing gaze, before he remembered his mission and snapped to attention.

'*Stop!*' Lock yelled in German.

The man's eyes widened in surprise, and he paused for a moment. Now was Lock's chance, perhaps the only chance he and the two Spaniards had.

'Who are you? What do you want?'

He cocked his head to the side for a few seconds, before replying in a raspy, pained voice 'I am Georg von Salm. These are my people. You are trespassing.'

'*Trespassing?*'

Von Salm nodded with satisfaction. 'The crime can be redeemed with a contribution.'

Lock's mind turned to the food and wine in his bag, but before he could access it, von Salm spoke again.

'I want your horses.'

Lock's heart sank. It was robbery, potentially fatal robbery. The two Spaniards on his left and right were becoming restless, whispering in increasingly anxious tones. Lock had never wished so desperately to have learned Spanish as now.

Who could have imagined the scene – threatened at gunpoint in a forest, with your only allies unable to understand you?

The horses had sensed the tension, and wished to rid themselves of their riders. Lock could hardly blame them, but he needed to bide his time. The exit on the left which led swiftly down to the river was unguarded still, and it tempted him. Even without a horse, a man running downhill in a forest would be hard to hit, and if the seven Germans each missed their shots, he would be free.

But what about the bottom of the hill? Was he happy to run headlong into a river? Lock knew nothing about its depth, but the current was strong – it churned loudly through the valley with immense force.

But even if the risk was worth it, how could he communicate to his Spanish escort what he intended to do?

Would they follow him?

Their faces were drawn, and they were surely imagining a wide range of horror stories being visited upon them. Lock had to soothe his horse's nerves more than once.

Georg von Salm pushed the tip of his sword into the ground. 'I won't ask you again,' he said calmly, 'Dismount, or we take the horses with corpses.'

Lock ran through his options, but none were of much use.

His eyes moved to the four men aiming menacingly towards his party, on a raised position atop the large mossy rock.

It was difficult to see at first – the dust roused by the activity clouded the air, and a faint mist also did not help – but as Lock focused on each of the Germans in turn, he noticed something.

None of the Germans had a lit match cord attached to their musket.

Without the match, the powder could not be lit, and the weapon could not fire. It was possible that they had other firearms. Wheellocks fired without a match cord, but those weapons were expensive, and he doubted these Germans had much money to spare.

'Get off your horse *now!*' von Salm hissed.

Was the theory sound enough to call the Germans' bluff?

Von Salm's sword was a problem, but if he could be subdued, Lock's party would be safe. Granted, as soon as he made his move, the Germans could produce some kind of lantern to light their match cord. That process could take several seconds though, and it could mean the difference between life and death.

But then what?

'*I will start counting to three,*' von Salm hissed. He balanced the heavy sword with clear dexterity.

Perhaps it was all a bluff after all? Lock hesitated, again weighing up whether a rush down the slope into the murkiness of the Rhine would be possible, or even survivable. It was impossible to know. True to his word, von Salm began to count.

'*One...*'

Would he even survive the act of abandoning three horses to the enemy? Surely Diego de la Barca could only be pushed so far.

'*Two...,*' the man rasped.

Time was running out.

And that was when Lock saw it. As von Salm had threatened him, the black-haired Spaniard had begun to slowly detach himself from his horse.

Did he plan to send his beast into the teeth of the Germans as a distraction?

Just as Lock tried to imagine the scene, in a single fluid motion the black-haired Spaniard moved from a seated to a crouched position on his horse, and then with the use of his legs, propelled himself off his horse and onto the German.

Von Salm never managed to reach three.

What happened next was a blur. As the Spaniard struggled with von Salm over the sword, his blond friend dismounted, scrambled for his musket, and began shouting at the Germans, what Lock could only assume were curses.

Lock's suspicions were then confirmed. The Germans appeared visibly panicked, as though suddenly forced off script in theatre. There were urgent, increasingly shrill requests for a lantern to light their matches, closely followed by another voice which cursed the fact that they had no lanterns.

Lock's momentary satisfaction was replaced with dread when the Germans threw down their muskets, drew knives, farm tools and rusty swords, and began to move menacingly towards Lock and his party of Spaniards.

The black-haired Spaniard continued to struggle on the ground with von Salm. Lock snapped himself out of his trance, dismounted as quickly as he could, and within a few seconds, had joined the fray.

Already, the two men were filthy from the dust, but the Spaniard had managed to keep the sword out of the man's hands.

Lock grasped the sword. It was much heavier than he had expected, and must have belonged to a cavalry officer. That would also explain how the German leader managed to secure such a sophisticated mount for himself. With the Spaniard weighing him down, and lacking his sword, Georg von Salm was defenceless. Now it was time to parley.

'*Stop*!' Lock shouted at the Germans, 'We have your leader. You move any closer and we will kill him.'

Lock swung the sword for effect, and the weight of it nearly pulled him down. Von Salm snarled and squirmed in the Spaniard's grip.

'Tell your men to stand down. We mean them no harm,' Lock said.

Von Salm was wide-eyed. He raised his chin in defiance at Lock's demand.

Lock twisted his face into a grimace as he pointed the sword at the Germans. His arm shook slightly with the effort.

After von Salm's eyes darted back and forth a few times, he nodded.

'*Woodrest! Enough!*' von Salm shouted. The words seemed to permeate the whole forest. A flock of birds evacuated a nearby tree, drawing the blond Spaniard's attention.

Von Salm's command had done the trick. The Germans stopped where they stood, the wind having left their sails. Only now could Lock get a better look at each of the enemy. There was not a well-fed fellow among them. They were all thin and wiry, and all possessed with a desperation that made them both weak and dangerous at once.

Lock now understood how the smaller Spaniard was able to keep their leader down – the bread, cheese and mutton which he and his party had eaten a few hours before were likely just vague memories to them now. Their hunger made them weak – could this be used against them?

The memory of Father's gift, the leatherbound volume of wisdom and wit, returned again to Lock. One phrase had stood out to Lock in an earlier section, and Lock had memorised it off by heart.

'The ceasefire is the moment to make new allies,' Lock whispered, as though spurring himself on, 'always be seen to make the first move.' He exhaled heavily, and nodded at the Spaniard who weighed von Salm down. The Spaniard raised his eyebrows at him, likely unsure of what his charge had planned, as was Lock himself.

Lock cleared his throat, and turned to the startled Germans. 'Gentlemen. Our quarrel is not with you. We wish to go to the fortress of Frankenthal. I am English, and an agent of His Majesty the King, the Father-in-law of your unlawfully dispossessed Elector and the true King of Bohemia.'

Lock saw some of the Germans turn to another, perhaps unsure if it was all a trick. Lock then tried the harder sell: saving his Spanish companions, whom these Germans despised.

'The gentlemen with me have travelled here only to ensure my safe passage. I ask that, please, you do not harm them.'

There was a pause, and some murmuring in German tones. None of them spoke up. Lock looked back at von Salm, and his eyes fixed on the cloth covering his mouth. The cloth was now stained and damp, likely from the commotion.

Von Salm's tongue had almost certainly been cut out, at least partially, or surely, he would be mute. Whatever the circumstances, von Salm's wound hadn't healed, and blood seeped out of his mouth and into the cloth.

It must have caused him immense pain even to breathe.

Perhaps, von Salm was a veteran of wars fought far away, only for war to be visited on his home. Notwithstanding his horrific wounds, the Germans still respected him as their leader, and perhaps more than that.

Pained whispers of *Vater*, the German for Father, emerged from their ranks.

Georg von Salm began to speak, using a mud-caked right hand to hold the cloth over his mouth as he did so, which partially masked the sound of his speech. He was breathing and wheezing heavily, but an anger still possessed him.

He continued to direct all his venom towards the blond Spaniard, not through his words, but with his eyes. Even as he addressed Lock, von Salm's gaze bore a hole in the blond Spaniard, who was unable to look him in the eye.

'You leave us... the blond Spaniard... and one horse,' von Salm said, pausing after each trio of words for a laboured breath.

Lock couldn't help but stare at von Salm again. The iron will which underpinned him; the sheer spectacle of his appearance; the innumerable questions about his past.

But what struck Lock the most was the sense that this man's anger was righteous, and that his quest for revenge did not come from nowhere.

Lock was now occupied with a very different question: *what had this blond Spaniard done?*

Notwithstanding these concerns, it wasn't in him to simply feed the blond Spaniard to the Germans. Lock could not do such a thing.

'Either you allow us all to go now,' Lock said, 'or set your men upon us, and permit them to murder innocent servants of the Crown in cold blood.'

'*Innocent?*' von Salm spat, his whole frame seemingly possessed by the sheer audacity of the word.

He attempted to rise, but the black-haired Spaniard warned him against it. Seated against a tree, the German lifted his mud-caked right arm to point at the blond Spaniard, as though counting his every breath. As he did so, the cloth moved away from his face, momentarily revealing a dark, toothless mouth and a shiny stump of red flesh where his tongue had been.

Georg von Salm hadn't revealed his wounds deliberately, and he self-consciously covered them up as soon as he realised his exposure, but those few milliseconds were all that was required to sear the image into Lock's brain.

'Ask *him* if he is innocent,' von Salm said, this time wheezing after every second word, '*Ask him what he has done.*' He shook a left arm at the blond Spaniard.

The blond-haired Spaniard stood with his back to the horses, his own sword drawn, at a standoff with the Germans who remained behind their upturned wagon. With their leader hostage, the Germans had become more docile, aware perhaps that talks were underway.

They remained in their positions, and had given up the act of aiming their useless muskets towards Lock's party. The firearms had been mostly discarded. With this lapse in danger, Lock had an idea.

Perhaps von Salm could be negotiated with. Perhaps a deal could be reached. His horse now beside him, Lock reached into its saddle bags. He pulled one of the cloth bags free, set it on a tree stump nearby, and produced some bread, mutton and cheese. He held it in his hand.

'Now look here,' Lock shouted, 'I offer you food, a day with a full belly, in exchange for our freedom.'

Even as he spoke the words, Lock knew his offer was not a good one, but it could be sold. He walked a few paces to where von Salm sat.

The piercing gaze now redirected itself like an arrow at Lock. Lock struggled now to maintain eye contact, but he forced himself to. He met von Salm's gaze. He showed von Salm he was not afraid. At least, not visibly. And then Lock spoke.

'You must be starving,' Lock said, and dropped a chunk of bread on the man's lap.

Lock gambled that the smell of bread, freshly baked that morning, would do its job on a starving former soldier. Desperate, starving men were less likely to be generous or merciful men. It might make a difference, perhaps raise spirits and encourage cooperation.

What else could be done?

Von Salm picked up the bread, and began the difficult process of trying to eat with half a tongue. He maintained his stare with the blond Spaniard as he did so, and under the glare of his gaze, Lock saw the chastened Spaniard walk behind the horses, out of his sight.

Lock noticed that the German voices became softer, and more excited, as the men began to negotiate in whispers among themselves. Having watched their leader eat, it was only natural that the subordinates would wish to eat next. Now was the moment to sell the food, so Lock turned to his left, cleared his throat, and prepared to make an offer above the roar of the river.

'I am sure you are all hungry. I have here cheese, bread and mutton, enough for all of us, and I also have a bottle of wine which we should share. I wish to release your leader, on your honour, that you will do us no harm, and on your oath that we may eat together, and then freely pass on. What say you all?'

'*What if it's poisoned?*

Did you poison our Vater?'

'There's no poison, it is not a trap,' Lock said, before eating some of the bread himself as a demonstration. Some of the braver Germans began to descend from their mossy rock, and move towards the food. Lock could smell the rosemary which had been cooked into the mutton, and he did not doubt that the Germans could smell it too.

A firm hand on grasped Lock's right shoulder, and Lock prepared a German word of caution. But it was the hand of the blond Spaniard, whose face twitched in anger. Another life lesson from his Father's book suddenly sprung into Lock's mind:

'*Learn quickly how to recognise the critical signs, of when your enemy intends to negotiate, and when he means to attack.*'

There was no doubt, the blond Spaniard meant to attack, and to take back the food which his charge was giving to his enemies. Lock did attempt to reason with him, but the language barrier made diplomacy impossible.

After mere seconds, the blond Spaniard turned to the right, before launching forward with a hard strike, connecting with Lock's jaw.

Up until the last moment, Lock did not believe the Spaniard would hit him.

To strike your charge was the most heinous of crimes that an honourable man could commit. The Spanish Court would never tolerate such a violation of oath and service. If the fear of being hanged by Diego de la Barca didn't dissuade his act, then the blond Spaniard must have believed death was close either way.

Either that, or he believed himself untouchable.

Lock could hear some German voices telling the Spaniard to stop. He then heard a Spanish voice say the same thing. Only then did it occur to Lock that he was on the ground, and that the blond Spaniard was on top of him, adding more strikes.

Lock's thick, bulky arms provided quality protection, and the Spaniard's wiry frame could not maintain the stiff attack for long. A shout, perhaps from his comrade, caused the attacking Spaniard to turn his gaze from Lock. In this brief reprieve, Lock lunged forward with his hands, reaching up to grab his enemy's throat.

Lock had never used his arms in this manner before. It was slightly disturbing how easy it was to inflict suffering. The blond Spaniard's face reddened, and he gasped.

As he was still sitting on Lock's thighs, he retained some semblance of control. He tried to rake Lock's eyes, and fingernails scratched at his eyelids, which Lock kept tightly closed. Lock increased his grip, fighting against horrific visions of blindness, and a life of darkness.

A sick feeling surged in Lock's stomach, reminding him how precarious it all was.

But the air was coming out of the Spaniard, and the venom of his attacks decreased as it did. With his hands still grasped around the Spaniard's throat, Lock rolled to the right. He was now on top of his foe. In the background, he heard the distinctive sounds of a loading musket. He no longer heard Spanish voices, only German ones. Lock didn't have time to check on his black-haired Spanish companion, though he certainly was willing to admit that the black-haired Spaniard was his favourite of the two.

The life escaped the blond Spaniard, and Lock's muscles screamed. Yet, he remained strangely composed, and then slightly sick. Sick at how easy it was to take a life. *Thou shalt not kill*, Mother had said, when Lock had been caught trying to shoot one of the family chickens for target practice. Lock had always thought it a strange time to recite the commandment, since their estate killed and ate tens of chickens annually.

Father had later clarified what she meant – *do not wantonly destroy things of value*. A chicken shot with a .48 calibre musket ball would be blown to smithereens. It'd be no good for eating. It'd be a waste of something potentially good. Lock knew that there was nothing good, potentially or otherwise, in this blond Spaniard.

And then his whole world was cracked apart.

A loud, piercing sound filled Lock's left ear. In the corner of his eye, he saw the source of his problem. Lock had loosened his grip. In this brief window of opportunity, the blond Spaniard had scrabbled desperately on the ground and found a large stone to embed in Lock's head.

Lock knew his inexperience had cost him, but now he was in a crisis. His body rebelled against him, as though frozen in ice, doomed to watch helplessly as the blond Spaniard, with a twisted, predatory grin, crawled over to finish the job.

Lock fumbled with his right arm, and the use of his legs returned to him, but his vision was blurred.

The Spaniard stood in front of Lock, his hands clasped around a giant rock he had since found.

The rock would kill him. Lock knew it. He imagined it collide with his skull. Then it would all be over before it even began.

Arthur would have to bury another family member.

Arthur would be all alone in the world.

The moment was interrupted by another crack. This was a different sound. Before he turned his head, Lock recognised powder.

A musket had been fired, and just in time.

The distinctive eggy smell permeated, and a cloud of smoke obscured his vision. As it dissipated, Lock's eyes fixed on the incredible scene.

The blond Spaniard's black-haired comrade, presumably no longer a comrade, stood with a pained expression and a discharged musket.

This black-haired Spaniard had saved his life, though the shot had not been a particularly direct one. The greater the distance, the more likely the lead musket ball would miss the target. The closer the range, the more horrific the injury, and the black-haired Spaniard was standing barely three feet away.

The musket ball had hit the blond Spaniard just below the right shoulder. In the time it took to blink, the ball had taken much of the shoulder and the arm, leaving behind a sinewy red mass that poured dark blood.

It was a horrific injury, and out in the depths of the forest, certainly fatal.

There was barely time to register the damage.

The blond Spaniard first let out a cry of pain, followed by a haunting, despairing groan. He dropped to his knees, and then, with the extent of the injury dawning on him, panic set in. As the blond Spaniard lay on the ground, writhing in agony, the Germans now took the opportunity to glorify in the gruesome moment.

On the cue of Georg von Salm, who led the initiative, several Germans fell upon the downed Spaniard.

After a few seconds of screams, there was some gurgling, and then silence.

A scythe had ripped out his throat.

The crude farm implement dripped steadily onto the leaf litter.

Von Salm, now standing upright, held the blooded scythe, and wiped it carefully on the grass. His comrades cheered at the gruesome scene.

Dazed and prone, Lock saw spots, but he had still seen enough. In the space of ten seconds, a life had been extinguished, and now everything was different.

And then, as if out of nowhere, a hand was suddenly in front of his face.

It was the black-haired Spaniard, who pulled Lock to his feet with a grimace.

'You're alright lad,' the black-haired man said, in disarmingly perfect English.

Lock picked up the twang in his accent instantly – this Spaniard was surely an Irishman.

Lock took a few steps forward to regain his composure before stumbling slightly. He could barely hear anything between the sound of the river and the ringing in his ears.

In the aftermath of their butchery, the Germans had made a gesture to the Irishman. Georg von Salm nodded at Lock, and one of his comrades held up the bottle of wine which Diego de la Barca had given him. Lock smiled weakly back at them. He heard the Irishman mumble something, and saw he was holding a bandage.

'You're bleeding,' the Irishman said.

Lock took the bandage absent-mindedly, unsure of where he was bleeding or what to do about it. He just stared at his rescuer and tried not to sway too violently. The Irishman made a quick scan of the area. To remove the need to raise his voice, he walked closer to Lock. Whoever he was, this Irishman finally seemed willing to offer Lock an explanation.

'The name is Flynn O'Toole,' the Irishman said, 'and don't you lose a moment of sleep about our friend, Officer Lock. Believe me when I tell you, that bastard more than deserved it.'

'What did he do?'

Flynn sighed, and after scanning the area once again, beckoned Lock to come closer. The Irishman probably thought it best to have Lock sit for a moment, so the two men sat side by side on the tree stump, where Lock had once placed the bag of food.

The food, wine and even the improvised cloth bag had all been taken.

'My companion, who you were recently choking,' Flynn began. 'He was Gaston Phillipe.'

Lock stared blankly at Flynn.

Flynn squinted back, which caused the weathered skin on his face to be scrunched against his burnt nose. Cold blue eyes that gave nothing away were framed with slight eyebrows, a snub nose and blunt chin. Dry skin flaked where the sun had scorched him.

'Diego de la Barca, the thoroughly steamed commander of the camp,' Flynn said, 'You know him?'

'Of course I know him,' Lock said, pressing his hand to his temple, 'You were there in the tent as I talked to him.'

'Indeed, I was,' Flynn said, 'As was his illegitimate son, Gaston Phillipe.'

- CHAPTER FOURTEEN -

The soldier must be prepared for pain when the rush of battle wears off. That was what father had said, and now Lock finally understood what he meant. Adrenaline had worn off, and his head pounded in step with his ringing ears.

'Mr O'Toole –' Lock began, as he pressed a cloth bandage against his temple.

'Call me Flynn,' the Irishman replied. 'I also go by Sergeant, Captain and sometimes even Lieutenant.'

'What do you mean?'

Flynn scoffed as if it were obvious. 'I arrived in the army of the King of Spain in 1620, Officer Lock. Before that time I had served in many armies and fought in many wars.' Lock prepared to respond, but Flynn interrupted, holding up his index finger for effect. 'Let me show you something.'

Flynn crouched onto his hands and knees and removed the knapsack on his back. Rooting through its contents to the base of the bag, Flynn opened an inner pocket to reveal a piece of parchment. Carefully unfolding it, Flynn beckoned Lock to stand up, and he then laid the outstretched parchment on the tree stump. With the faded yellow parchment fully unfurled, it took some time for Lock's eyes to focus on their contents, apparently too long for Flynn's liking.

'*It is a map of Ireland*,' Flynn said. 'It was commissioned nearly fifty years ago for my Father, and now it is mine.'

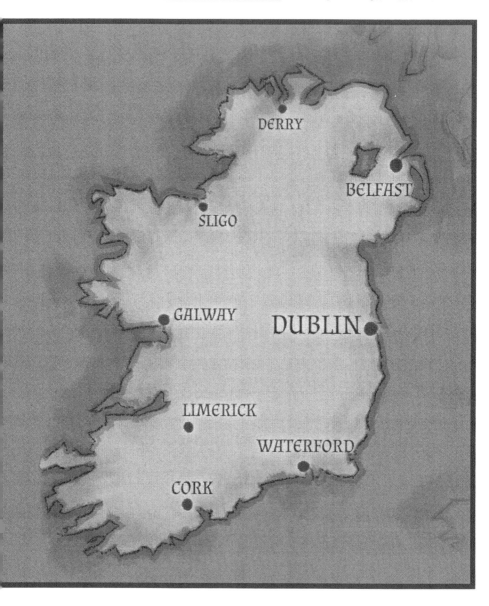

'Why do you have a map of Ireland in your bag?' Lock asked, as neutrally as he could.

Flynn scoffed again. He moved to within inches of Lock's face. A smell of sweet, potent alcohol was carried on his breath.

'Ask your bloody King,' Flynn said, a finger pointed a Lock's chest. 'Your

Majesty King James is the reason I'm here'. Flynn's sarcastic emphasis on *Your Majesty* provoked Lock, even though Father had rarely said anything good about the King.

And Flynn was not yet finished. He returned to the stump where the map rested, and sighed before speaking.

'Do you know of the Ulster Plantations, Officer Lock?'

'They sound familiar.'

'First, they took my job, then they took my farm, and finally, they took my home. And not just any home. Do you know how powerful the O'Toole clan used to be? We ruled over Wicklow like Kings.'

'Officer Lock, they took my job, then they took my farm, and finally, they took my home. And not just *any* home. Do you know how powerful the O'Toole clan used to be? We ruled over Wicklow like Kings.'

'Wicklow? You mean the Pale?'

Flynn snorted. 'I recognise no Pale. And Your Majesty's writ extends scarcely an hour's ride from Dublin.'

'If you hail from Wicklow, why go to Ulster?'

'Because my Father was a second son, Officer Lock. With few prospects, he set down roots in Ulster and sought to make a new name for himself in Hugh O'Neill's service.'

'O'Neill?'

'You've heard of him, I suspect.'

Father's lessons on Queen Elizabeth's ruinous war in Ireland, which was followed by the Ulster Plantation, returned to Lock with surprising clarity. Lock regurgitated Father's observation. 'O'Neill had the English on the backfoot for many years. And then his Spanish ally failed him.'

Flynn's eyebrows raised, though he did not avert his gaze from the map. Had the Irishman not expected such knowledge? 'Yes, Officer Lock. But you should know, O'Neill himself bowed before the might of the O'Toole clan. My Father brought many men to his army. I watched them fight many times, and win.'

'Your Father sounds like a formidable man.'

'He was, and before you English arrived, everything was well. I used to be a wealthy man, Officer Lock, and an heir to a great fortune. The Black Castle in Wicklow Bay will be mine, someday.'

'Is that so?'

Flynn nodded, and looked up from the map, before folding it carefully away. 'It will, Officer Lock. In the meantime, it seems I am instead to save bumbling Englishmen from themselves.'

With that, Flynn started walking towards the path once blocked by the German ambushers and their wagon. Flynn checked the ruined wagon. As he surveyed it, he looked up inquisitively at Lock, as if challenging him to answer.

'*Your Majesty* has nothing to say?'

Lock's fingernails dug into palms. He unclenched his fists and exhaled. The vision of his hands around Gaston Phillipe's throat returned. Flynn scoffed and resumed his wagon inspection.

The Irishman was several inches shorter than Lock, but there was something more to Flynn's unassuming profile than met the eye. Lock rehearsed a list of questions. This was no time to look a fool.

Flynn walked a few paces ahead. After barely a minute, the path turned a corner, and as he rounded the bend, Flynn cried out in jubilation. As if by magic, two of their horses stood grazing lazily.

True to his word, Georg von Salm had only taken one horse.

'I knew I could rely on the bastard,' Flynn said as he whisked himself onto his horse in a seemingly effortless motion. Flynn had also taken the easier mount. Lock's designated horse had multiple wounds in its side where the spurs had attacked its flesh.

As he tackled the task of scrambling onto the saddle, Flynn's eyes bore into him. Lock had little energy left to care. His head was throbbing. His mission was doomed. With one foot in the stirrup, Lock hoisted himself, clumsily misjudging the effort needed, so that he nearly fell off on the other side.

'Officer Lock, you *do* have a way with animals.'

Lock swallowed his retort. He needed this abrasive Irishman on his side if he was to survive out here. He changed the subject.

'I need to get to Frankenthal. Can you still bring me or not?'

Flynn seemed disappointed with the directness of the question, but he nodded. 'I can, but you have to keep this incident between ourselves. If anyone asks, Gaston Phillipe fell foul of the Germans on his own accord.'

'Will de la Barca believe that?'

'His soldiers will. That's what matters. Phillipe was universally loathed.'

Lock didn't doubt it. The whoops and shouts of glee from the Germans at the mere opportunity to end his life had provided more than enough proof. But there was one matter which required clarification.

'Those Germans,' Lock began. 'Why did they have no match cord for their muskets?'

'I did warn them about that,' Flynn said, patting the horse's neck. 'I told them it was a foolish bluff, but understandable. Not one of those men had ever fired a musket before. I doubt they had even raised a pointed object in anger.'

'What do you mean you *warned them*? Do you know these people?'

Flynn had trotted a few steps ahead, but the path was wide enough to ride side by side. Flynn nodded at him to catch up, and Lock obliged.

'I did not know the Germans by name, Officer Lock, but in the last few months, we have developed what you might call a *mutually beneficial relationship*.' Flynn appeared very proud of the term, and he emphasised each word deliberately.

Lock just stared at Flynn blankly. It seemed the best way to deal with him.

Flynn took the hint. 'I know what it means to be forced out of your home, Officer Lock, and for nobody to speak up for you.'

'Is that what happened to them? And their leader with half a tongue, von Salm?' Lock asked. He was careful not to put his heels anywhere near the horses' wounds. The two men maintained a slow trot.

Flynn nodded. 'De la Barca's camp, that was once their village. Woodrest, it's called. They refuse to say the name of the place until the Spanish leave. They're a superstitious bunch. And Georg von Salm...'

'Yes...'

'He was the commander of the militia for the town. A former soldier if the gossip is correct. He was tortured first, and forced to reveal the location of the treasure. When he couldn't, Gaston Phillipe ordered his tongue removed.'

'What *treasure*?'

'Anything, Officer Lock. Anything that could be seized, or attacked, or eaten, or destroyed or...' Flynn took a deep breath. 'The things that de la Barca's son has done... I had never imagined them being done to anyone before he brought that terror to life.' Flynn crossed himself, as though the gesture would ward away the very memory of Gaston Phillipe.

'That would explain why von Salm stared so many holes in Phillipe,' Lock said.

'They weren't very effective at cutting out his tongue. But that didn't matter. Phillipe also had von Salm's two daughters... defiled, and then ordered them strung them up from a tree.'

'Good God,' Lock whispered. '*Such barbarity.*'

'That is who Gaston Phillipe was, Officer Lock. This camp needed to get rid of the monster that lived within it. If it wasn't done soon, there would be a full uprising on de la Barca's hands.'

'So you conspired to murder him?'

Flynn paused before answering, as if weighing up whether his answer might implicate him at some point. Lock's stomach growled in the interim. It was late in the afternoon. Perhaps time for dinner soon enough.

'Actually, the plan had been to deliver him to the Germans in the forest,' Flynn said, his tone tinged with nostalgia. 'But then, you arrived in the camp, on the very morning when I was due to take Phillipe for his final patrol. Two months I spent planning this, but the bastard's dead, so I suppose it doesn't matter much either way.'

After he spat the words out, Flynn held up a hand and stopped. Lock followed his lead. A squirrel leapt across from one tree branch to the next, and Lock watched it with satisfaction. He could almost pretend that they were riding through the grounds of the Lockville estate.

'If you had an agreement with von Salm, why did you leap on him?'

Flynn nodded. 'He was breaking our deal. Our deal was for him to take Phillipe and his horse, but when he saw you, I suppose he decided to change the deal.'

'Yet, he let us go?'

'As I said, Officer Lock, these people are not animals. What good would it do them to kill a stranger, particularly one who offers them food? Or to down a man who has helped them all these months?' Flynn shook his head. 'No, I knew we were in safe hands. I just suspect von Salm got a bit overzealous with his sword, so I had to remind him of our agreement.'

'He could have killed you.'

'As could Phillipe. But I would not allow it, Officer Lock. Enough good men have already died in this war. I would not see another.'

Was this a compliment, or was Flynn merely emphasising his own virtue? Lock did not ask for clarification, and the two men continued their trot.

Lock had a legion of questions he wished to ask the Irishman, but one could not ignore etiquette. There was also the danger of saying too much.

'Not long now. We should be clear of this forest soon, Officer Lock,' Flynn said.

Lock paused before speaking. 'Even if I take the truth to my grave, Flynn, do you really think de la Barca will never learn of the truth? He will surely suspect that you killed his son?'

'*Illegitimate* son,' Flynn corrected, glancing left and right.

'Regardless, what if you are interrogated? Surely you will be, if you return?'

'Perhaps, assuming I do return,' Flynn said, a smirk playing across his face.

'You'll leave de la Barca's service?'

'It seems I may have no choice.'

'Will you travel with me?'

Flynn laughed loudly in an outburst that startled his horse. 'If Father could see me now, leading a blind Englishman to his destination.'

'Will you accompany me to Frankenthal, at least? There is strength in numbers.'

Flynn held up a reassuring hand. 'Yes, Officer Lock. Until we must go our separate ways, escorting you will ensure I retain my cover. This cover will be important if we encounter any of de la Barca's patrols.'

'Thank you.'

'But no mention of Philippe, I must insist.'

'Mannheim will be an issue.'

'We will cross that bridge when we come to it, Officer Lock.'

'You could run for the hills?'

'An innocent man does not run. Spanish patrols are crawling around these parts. If de la Barca's men find us, we will explain that Gaston Phillipe wished to return to camp. They would have no reason to suspect otherwise.'

The path turned another corner and descended slightly. The trees had now become sparser and shorter, and the rays of sunlight more common.

'I would be more concerned about *your* mission, Officer Lock. After all, since you must report back to de la Barca after receiving the surrender of Frankenthal, you will have to let it be known what happened to your escorts. You strike me as an honest man. Will you be able to lie to de la Barca?'

This presented another problem. Flynn still expected him to ask for Frankenthal's surrender. How could this lie be maintained? For now, it had to be.

'I will tell him the truth. We were ambushed.'

'Ambushed *again*, Officer Lock?' Flynn was grinning ear to ear.

'So you *do* understand French!'

'Indeed, Officer Lock, even *your version* of French,' Flynn quipped, before trotting ahead.

Lock rolled his eyes and paused to give some reassuring pats to his horse. At least, the ringing in his ears had finally stopped, and the roar of the river was behind them. There was a tranquil peace to this forest. Perhaps he would reach Frankenthal after all. At least he could take solace from the fact that he would never have to see de la Barca or his sweaty tent ever again.

Flynn looked back impatiently. 'Onwards, *Your Majesty*.' Flynn pointed a few hundred feet ahead. 'Just there, we'll come to a raised position overlooking Mannheim. A lovely town, I'm sure you'll agree, and recently blessed to enjoy the protection of our benevolent and noble Lord, His Most Christian Majesty, the King of Spain.' Flynn gesticulated widely as he finished his description. 'Then, Officer Lock, it's just a few hours to Frankenthal.'

'Where will you go, Flynn?' The prospect of being alone in a land he knew little about filled Lock with dread.

'Well, Officer Lock, it is probably time I enlist with the King of France once again. Perhaps I will put in a good word for you while I'm there?'

'You'll fight for the King of France?'

'I'll fight for whoever wishes to pay me, Officer Lock. A landless refugee cannot afford to be choosy, though I swear I'd rather lose *my* tongue than serve *Your* blessed Majesty.'

'May God forgive me, but I do hope the Prince of Wales will be a touch more sensible.'

'Makes no difference to me, whether it's the Prince of Wales or the King of the Isles, the Stuarts can rot.' Flynn said. He then gestured to his own chest. 'Do your part for Ireland, Officer Lock. Get me through Mannheim and across the Rhine with your pass. Then to Frankenthal. Then I will get out of your hair.'

Lock nodded. Hopefully, the Spanish of Mannheim would be as laid-back as de la Barca had been when checking credentials. As they moved into a slow trot, Flynn made the most of the time by taking the opportunity to reload his musket. The familiar movements were comforting, and Lock watched them with satisfaction.

The five-foot-long piece had only recently been used to liberate Gaston Phillipe from his right arm. Had it been in his hands, Lock knew the Spaniard would have lost his head instead, and the horrific scene would have been over in an instant. Or perhaps that was the point – perhaps Flynn had deliberately maimed Gaston Phillipe, as recompense for the career he had spent maiming others.

Lock allowed himself a moment of pride when he guessed Flynn's rate of fire. If Flynn O'Toole was an exceptional soldier, he would be able to manage one, perhaps two shots in a minute. Most soldiers fell between one and one and a half shots fired in the sixty second test.

Lock smiled to himself. Arthur had always demanded ninety seconds for the same reload test as his older brother. Lock had always let him away with it. He sighed through his nose. Lock had never longed for his brother's company as much as he did now.

- CHAPTER FIFTEEN -

On many occasions, father had talked of a remarkable network known as the Spanish Road, before tracing it on a map of Europe. Lock had been amazed at its scale ever since. For sure, it would have been quicker to sail from Madrid to Brussels, but Dutch sailors had prevented that, so the Spanish had improvised.

A continuous road ran from Spanish held-Milan all the way to Brussels, a feat made possible by the creeping expansion of the Spanish King's realm. The route passed by narrow Swiss passes, treacherous Italian mountains and much of the Rhine's course. Any place the Spanish seized, they fortified immediately.

So it was with Mannheim.

The Spanish could not allow such a commanding strategic position to go to waste. With control over this confluence of the two rivers, Spanish men and materiel could pour into France or into Germany at King Philip IV's will.

'*Your Majesty, are you still with me*?' Flynn called, before laughing at his own joke. Lock was still not fond of the nickname, but he realised he had been daydreaming again. It seemed that every moment of the journey could remind him of Father in some way.

Perhaps Charles Lock had prepared his son for these events better than he had thought, or perhaps seeing his parents everywhere was merely a symptom of grief.

Lock sighed and willed himself onwards. He trotted up to Flynn's horse. They were still far from the town, but it was possible to make out details, such as the walls, bridges, and church spires that characterised many German towns like it.

They had followed a dirt track which snaked out of the woods and towards the main road. As soon as they left the comparative wilderness and used the more common routes though, they would be more visible.

Flynn moved his horse back a few paces behind a large bush. Lock followed. Flynn dismounted, and pointed towards the main road which bypassed the forest.

Lock scanned the road for a moment. Had he truly plodded along this road that morning, before meeting de la Barca, Gaston Philippe or Flynn O'Toole? It seemed impossible that so much could fit into a day. Gone were the lazy afternoons of reading and cards. At least for now.

If they wished to ride to Mannheim's southern gate without arousing suspicion, they would have to adhere to that road from now on. But there was a problem.

'It's worse than I thought,' Flynn said. 'Look.'

To the right of the entrance to Mannheim, in a field, Lock could barely make out several tiny shapes clustered together. It seemed that a regiment of Spaniards were engaging in the drill. Practice was, after all, the best way to stop the men losing the run of themselves.

'I saw them on my travels here. You know them?'

'Yes I know them,' Flynn hissed, 'That's the other half of the regiment under de la Barca's command.'

Lock squinted. As he focused, the distant sounds became more vivid. The familiar roar of the river was already audible, and would become louder as they descended from the hills.

'Will they recognise you?'

'It depends, Officer Lock. De la Barca had been waiting for these men to return for a few days. He said that once they returned, they would make for the forest and smoke those Germans out.' Flynn glanced back at Lock. 'That was another reason I had to improvise earlier on. I did not know if I'd get another chance to bring Phillipe to justice.'

'If they're still here, they cannot know what we've just done. News does not travel that fast.'

'That's true Officer Lock, but they will still wonder where Phillipe has gone. Spanish soldiers do not travel alone out here. If people see me, they will expect to see Phillipe.'

'So they will not see you,' Lock said. 'We wait until they have gone.'

'Or perhaps they are lodging here, and because their bastard captain doesn't wish to return to de la Barca, they have been waiting at Mannheim for as long as they can.'

'How long have they been here?'

'About three days. Their mission had been to reconnoitre with the Mannheim garrison, to make sure they had all they needed.'

'And they are still here?'

Flynn nodded. 'De la Barca's lost control of himself and his men. I doubt Cordoba will tolerate his failures for much longer.'

That explained why the surrender of Frankenthal had been such an exciting prospect for the de la Barca. A pang of guilt followed – Lock would not be able to redeem de la Barca's career after all. Condemning a man to dishonour was no small thing.

'Have you been to Mannheim before?'

Flynn nodded. 'Last time I was there the garrison was having troubles. Most of the English soldiers that had defended it left and raced to Frankenthal, but Cordoba needs more soldiers to fight the Dutch, so he's denuded any available garrisons of men.'

'So Cordoba charged de la Barca with holding the land, with not enough soldiers to get the job done?'

'Indeed, Officer Lock. In truth, the Palatine garrison did not put up much resistance. The only danger to a Spaniard here is a German peasant. We don't expect any armies to come over the hills.'

'Except for the English.' Lock said.

Flynn nodded with a smirk. 'The bloody English. As if England and Ireland aren't enough, they have to land in Germany as well. De la Barca's fear is that the Frankenthal garrison will launch a sortie, so he's making sure they know of Spain's intentions to defend Mannheim.' Flynn scratched the points of stubble breaking through his chin, deep in thought.

Lock was also in thought, though his mind turned to the scene where he would be reunited with his godfather for the first time since he had been a child. Though he had been above Father's station, Lock recalled that Vere had been immensely flattered to be his godfather.

He had always treated the Lock family affectionately, and once gifted young Matthew a model toy soldier for his birthday. Surely that fondness would still be present? Lock sighed. How exciting and easy it had been to play war. The reality was much more difficult.

'We could swim across?' Lock suggested, jerking his left shoulder towards the river.

Flynn scoffed. 'That can be our final option, when all others fail. We should find a way to retain our horses and to restock our supplies. I am not sure how far I'll be going, but in my experience, engaging in diplomacy is much easier when one can offer food.'

Lock smiled. Perhaps Flynn had learned something from his earlier performance in the woods?

A shout rang out from a short distance away. Flynn shushed Lock's response. He gestured to the large bush, and crouched lower, delicately parting back some leaves so he could peer through the shrubbery to the other side. Flynn jerked his head towards the commotion.

'Bandits, three of them,' he whispered.

Lock dared a peek of his own. It was a curious sight. A farming couple with a wagon stacked with barrels and meat had clambered dismounted to confront three ruffians in simple clothing.

'Our German friends from earlier, who wouldn't harm anyone?'

Flynn grunted. 'If you'll recall, Officer Lock, I said they would not harm *us*.' Flynn checked again. 'That's not the Germans.'

'How can you tell?'

'Well Officer Lock, those bandits are wearing clothes. Those forest Germans were hungry enough to eat clothes. Indeed, I have seen them doing so.'

'Are they armed?'

'I saw the glint of a knife I think,' Flynn said, 'but no firearms that I can see.'

'How brazen of them, the Spanish are only a short distance away.' Lock said.

'Officer Lock, the Spanish couldn't care less about these domestic matters. The Spanish soldier is after all, a professional, not a mere policeman.' Flynn delivered the lines in a tone that suggested the message had been drilled into him.

'So the Spanish arrive, seize what they can get their hands on, remove the old administration, and then stand idly by as the chaos they caused consumes the country?'

'Well, if the problem becomes truly dire, they will act, but they have enough to do as it is,' Flynn said with a grin. 'That wine isn't going to drink itself you know.'

The bandits took what they could from the farmer, who was swiftly attacked when he protested. The farmer's wife received a hard slap, and she screamed.

Flynn winced and looked away, but Lock fixed his gaze on the crime. Anger rose within him.

It was not fair.

Was he angrier at the Spanish for causing this chaos, or the bandits for taking advantage? Lock was unsure, but he began to stir beside Flynn.

'Just what do you think you're doing?' Flynn asked, his face turned in an expression of horror, as Lock rose to his feet and unsheathed his sword.

'Good God Officer Lock, remember your rank. You're a statesman, not a soldier. Those ruffians will make short work of you.'

Lock ignored Flynn's protests. The Irishman might think him a mere ambassador with an overactive moral complex, but Lock knew something the Irishman did not.

Lock was trained by one of France's greatest exports, Jean le Renne, a master swordsman. Lock was also taller, stronger and a great deal angrier than the bandits that threatened the elderly couple.

The bandits had become arrogant, and one sat mockingly on the farmer's wagon. Another landed some kicks on the farmer's prone body. In desperation, the farmer's wife threw herself at the swine, but she was dealt with mercilessly. She stumbled to the ground, clutching her stomach in agony.

Lock could not watch the crime unfold any longer.

While checking his sword for sharpness, he turned to Flynn.

'Flynn, I cannot stand any more of this spectacle. Join me if you wish, but I must act now.' Lock began jogging towards the bandits, as Flynn's vain protests reached his ears.

'Shite and God damn ye,' he heard Flynn grunt, as the Irishman forced himself to his feet. He scrambled to keep up with Lock's brisk pace, before reaching his side. The two men were closing in on the bandits, and would soon be seen.

'I'm not saving your life again, you mad bastard,' Flynn yelled.

- CHAPTER SIXTEEN -

The first time Lock practiced with a dummy sword, Jean le Renne laughed in his face.

'Why do you stand scared like a sheep? Do you wait for me to come to you?' the Frenchman had challenged.

He had then introduced his three favourite words. Three words which would be Jean le Renne's motto for as long as Lock continued to practice with him.

Posture. Guard. Attack.

The three words, le Renne claimed, could be used in any order, but the attack was the most critical element of the process. In spite of his decorative clothing, his diminutive size, and his general extravagance in conversation, Jean le Renne was the most serious swordsman Lock had ever known.

'You are not making art, Master Lock. You are making war,' le Renne said. Father had watched approvingly nearby. He clapped or groaned on occasion, when he had the spare time to watch. Once, Lock even caught Father sparring with le Renne, and it was that sight, more than any other, that compelled him to practice. Three hours a day, five days a week.

To appease Mother, le Renne doubled as his French teacher. He taught Lock the breadth and flow of the language as effectively as he taught swordsmanship. Although his French improved, it was the external change that was most palpable in Lock.

Callouses built up on his fingers. His sword arm ached. Blisters appeared on the balls of his feet from standing consistently on edge. But Lock persevered. He trained in the rain. He trained in the relentless sun. He trained even in the snow. Eventually, he won le Renne's respect.

Fencing, Jean le Renne said, was the one good thing the Spanish invented.

What he had neglected to mention was that fencing could also be the cause and solution of all brotherly quarrels.

Again and again, Arthur had used his speed and dexterity to triumph. To compensate for these advantages, Lock had leaned into his larger size. He had perfected his attack. More specifically, the overwhelming attack which harnessed every aspect of his larger frame.

The outcome was certainly not glamorous, but it had evened the odds. No longer concerned with style, Lock dominated at close range. Unsurprisingly, Arthur never went down quietly. One particularly bitter encounter saw both brothers descend into a fistfight, and Lock had to be pulled off his smaller brother, to the abject horror of his Mother.

'*Look at what you've done to my poor boy!*' she had wailed, as Arthur forced linen against his bleeding nose.

When he returned from Oxford, the competitive element seemed to matter less. Now the aim was not to beat his brother, but to strengthen him. As they cooperated, Lock's movements became quicker, and Arthur taught him flurries and combinations which added to his formidable repertoire.

Jean le Renne never showed much emotion, but the sight of his two greatest pupils making amends brought a tear even to his eye. Their fencing contests became leisurely; a moment to catch up, to engage in conversation, or share secrets. Winning had lost much of its appeal.

But these bandits were different.

The fury, the rage and the malice which Lock had supressed in favour of a brother's friendship could now be safely unleashed, without heed for the consequences.

As he closed on the three bandits, Lock whispered his lesson. *Posture. Guard. Attack.*

The three bandits spotted Lock when he was perhaps fifty feet from them, engrossed as they were in the ignoble act. One bandit, with a black pencil moustache on his upper lip, first regarded the sight of the six-foot juggernaut with curiosity. Armed with a sword, a musket over his shoulder, and a bandolier across his chest, Lock had all the markings of a soldier. Yet, something, perhaps the experience of a major battle, suggested he was more civilian than warrior.

Three sets of eyes now fixed upon him. The moustachioed bandit's accomplices gathered to his side, marking him as their leader. Lock had practiced fighting several opponents at once. The farm hands used to be encouraged to partake in fencing practice, despite Mother's objections. It would encourage the rabble to take up arms, she had said, but le Renne had insisted.

Such practice was of great use; it inculcated the art of juggling multiple foes at once, an art which demanded swift, devastating strikes and scant hesitation. Lock prepared to relive these lessons, measuring the bandits with his eyes.

Yet, as Flynn drew nearer, the three bandits appeared to freeze.

'Flynn O'Toole,' one of them said, in what was surely an Italian accent.

Lock paused, and half turned to his Irish companion.

Flynn was as confused as Lock, until he managed to properly examine the three men.

'What the bloody hell are you doing, you cruel bastards?' Flynn challenged. 'You should be back in camp, bringing de la Barca another drink!' The challenge was communicated in French, which one of the men appeared to understand better than the others.

'We're looking for *you*, Irishman,' one of them said. He was overweight, short, and suffering in the heat. 'You and your ambassador friend.'

Flynn stood steadily by Lock's right side. His back was arched. His sweating forehead was angled against them. 'What is this? You always were the worst Christians, but I see that none of you can claim to be men either.'

Flynn's intelligence had not been accurate. The three men held their swords by their sides. Yet for now they remained stationary, their curiosity captured by Lock's silhouette, as the sun shone behind him.

They were perhaps five feet away.

Lock could hear Jean le Renne screaming at him to strike, and to strike at the man in the centre, which would scatter them, but his curiosity had also been piqued.

The man with the pencil moustache grinned, as his friend translated from French. 'Captain Ricardo will hear about this, Irish bastard,' the man said.

'I'm sure Ricardo would like to know why you three are content to wet your blades on these farmers,' Flynn hissed, his voice low and menacing.

'We were sent to find you, Irishman, and we happened across this perfect store of meat. I grow tired of mutton, as you know. Haven't had me some salted pork in the longest time.' The overweight soldier then licked sweat from his upper lip, and rotated his sword in his right hand. 'These two pigs were just about to... sell us some.'

Flynn seemed content to stall, and Lock realised why.

The farmer's wife.

She had risen slowly to her knees, and seemed to understand the situation. Lock did his best to avoid looking at her for too long. He made a show of darting his eyes and his sword point between each of the three men. But she continued moving.

She went to her downed husband, and retrieved a small knife. Lock held his breath, as in three or four short steps, she rushed and plunged the knife into the nape of the overweight soldier's neck. The act made a terrific impression, but it cost her dearly. As the overweight soldier choked and fell to his knees, his moustachioed leader slashed her across the throat before either Lock or Flynn could move.

The farmer wailed and reached out as the act occurred. The odds were now even, and there was no time to waste.

Surging forward, Lock parried one strike, and closed in on the moustachioed figure, who had not expected the act. Flynn emulated the charge, and engaged the other soldier, while Lock focused on his man.

His enemy spoke in a language Lock did not understand. Italian, perhaps. He levelled curse after curse against Lock, and probably against Lock's family, but Lock ignored the vitriol.

He maintained eye contact, and an unsettling smile.

The soldier's expression shifted, as Lock eased into his stance.

Posture, Lock whispered to himself.

Barely a foot of space existed between them, and Lock began to move forward. The Italian walked back, still trying to decipher his movements, still trying to understand how much danger he was in. But he withdrew too far.

His heels cracked against the wheel of the farmer's wagon. The Italian gasped. His legs veered awkwardly to the left, bringing him to more open ground. With his feet then firmly planted, the Italian lunged forward with his short sword.

'*Guard*,' Lock said, as he swiped his weapon in a downward slash. The enemy's blade was shorter than Lock's, but it was also wider, and the hilt contained an elaborate hand guard.

Arrogance and energy reverberated from each of the Italian's attacks. For a few frantic seconds he threw everything he had at Lock, who absorbed it all. As his blows repeatedly failed to land, parried uselessly away, there was something else.

Desperation.

The Italian gasped at his impenetrable target. Now it was time.

Attack.

Lock made deliberately for the left, but at the last moment, he curled his large frame heavily to the right. He stepped forward into a thrust, aimed directly at the Italian's sword hand. The Italian cursed, but had enough room to avoid the main force of the attack. Steel clinked off steel, but the hand-guard served its purpose. A satisfied grin appeared on the Italian's face.

But he erred again. Lock had expected the thrust to be parried. He hadn't intended it to fully land, just to force the Italian off balance. The size difference told Lock that he was stronger than his opponent, so he attacked more directly. In a fluid movement, Lock grasped the Italian's sword under his left arm.

The Italian's grin had long since vanished, and he struggled in vain to free his blade. Panicked breaths carried the smell of stolen meat into Lock's nostrils. The time for comeuppance had arrived. Lock arched his right arm, before delivering the final blow with his pommel.

It landed on the Italian's right temple, and his knees buckled beneath him. As he crumpled to the grass, flailing slightly, Lock kicked him onto his back and bound his hands and feet.

It was certainly worth knowing why these three men were on the lookout for Flynn and himself.

Lock then turned, divorced from his private war, and noted Flynn's peril.

The Irishman was outmatched.

Without realising it, Lock had selected by far the easier target.

Flynn was deflecting, but a wound on his right arm reduced his effectiveness. The soldier could sense victory. He kicked Flynn below the belt, and the Irishman staggered backwards, leaning against the wagon.

Lock sprinted towards the soldier and shouted a curse. The enemy turned, to see a new adversary barrelling in his direction. The momentary distraction was all Flynn had needed.

He grasped the enemy's right arm with his own left, pulling his body down as he did so, while he thrust his sword through his neck. The blade was forced clean through the other side of his body, so that it protruded grotesquely just above the shoulder blades. As quickly as he shoved the foreign object into the depths of his enemy's mass, Flynn then withdrew it, evoking a sickly sliding sound.

The soldier spluttered and gurgled, reaching for the gash in his neck, and taken aback by his sudden, unexpected loss. Within seconds, his gaping wounds had forced him to the ground.

Flynn took a couple of steps forward, before falling to his own knees. Lock rushed to his side.

'Next time... I take the Italian,' the Irishman spat. He panted, and began to chuckle as he caught sight of Lock's grave expression. 'Just what kind of envoy are you, Officer Lock?'

- CHAPTER SEVENTEEN -

The Italian took only a few minutes to wake. He pulled in frustration and shame at his restraints. He seemed wholly unsure of what had occurred.

Lock only wished Jean le Renne could have witnessed his first victory outside of the Locksville estate. The triumph was greater than any victory against his brother. Blood and energy surged through his body. He was alive, no, better than that, he was invincible.

The Irishman was similarly taken aback by the showing.

'Where did you learn to fight like that?' he had asked, while aiding the farmer to his feet.

But Lock had ignored the question. He sat a few feet from the Italian on the grass, staring at his resentful face.

The farmer had armed himself with a scythe from his wagon. The crude farming implement was razor sharp, he had insisted, and had demonstrated by slicing through a swathe of knee-high grass just off the road.

He plainly intended to use it for more nefarious purposes.

The Italian seemed to understand his predicament, but the odds had not reduced his arrogance. A new problem, the language barrier, now confronted Lock.

'He speaks Spanish, Flynn,' Lock called. 'You should talk to him.'

Flynn eased the farmer onto the edge of his wagon, and then walked to the prisoner. Standing above the Italian, he unleashed his best scowl for a time, before unsheathing his sword once again.

'Why are you looking for us?' Flynn asked in Spanish, his body stiffening.

The Italian prisoner smiled. His pencil thin moustache wriggled on his upper lip. His forehead was pumping sweat, his mouth was bleeding and a tooth was missing, yet he was still grinning from ear to ear.

He knew something they did not.

Flynn's sword was still drawn, and he pointed it at the Italian prisoner's groin. His grin began to recede, replaced by a fierce expression of defiance.

The Italian puffed out his chest. '*I will not say*,' he hissed in broken French. Flynn sighed. He moved on the seated soldier, and forced him to his feet. It was an awkward stance. With his feet tied, and his hands tied behind his back, the soldier was quite defenceless, which was the whole point.

'*I... will not say*,' the Italian said again, a little less steady, this time angling his chin at Lock.

Flynn's back arched. '*You won't say*? Don't worry, we'll loosen your tongue.'

With a swift, unhesitating slash, Flynn raked his sword's edge across the prisoner's kneecaps. With a shriek of pain, the Italian collapsed forward. With his hands bound behind his back, there was nothing to stop his fall, and he landed with a grunt on the side of his face.

Lock winced, but Flynn continued the interrogation with a determined, detached calmness.

'Next time I take your legs off. I will ask you again, why are you looking for us? What does de la Barca know?'

The Italian prisoner looked up at Flynn with a grimace, and after a few seconds of painful effort, he struggled back to his feet. He beckoned Flynn to come closer, a forlorn expression etched on his face. Flynn approached cautiously, leaving some space between them.

This was all the Italian needed. He hawked and spat a large globule onto the Irishman's left cheek.

Flynn was stunned for a split second, before launching himself at the Italian, his right hook leading the way. Flynn landed a succession of blows on his face and neck, each strike producing a louder yelp. Lock rushed forward as if carried by the wind.

'Flynn, Flynn... *stop!*' Lock grabbed the Irishman's left arm and jerked back, nearly toppling him over.

The Italian tried to rise to his feet again, and worked his lips produce another globule. Lock reprimanded the Italian, but he did not retreat. He ignored Lock's warnings and Flynn's curses, and half-limped, half-shuffled towards his enemies, determined to show his bravery.

Lock reached for his sword, and prepared to strike another blow, when he was drawn to a sudden rush of activity behind the Italian.

In a flash of gruesome violence, the elderly farmer, now recovered, carved off the Italian's left leg with his scythe. The act was so quick and clean, it took several seconds for the Italian to register why he had toppled over. Once the horrid truth was known, Lock's ears were filled with a shattering screech, followed by a haunting wail that could carry for miles.

'*Shite*,' Flynn said, and he winced as the wailing continued. Blood pumped forth from his stump like a spring. The Irishman turned his back on the traumatic scene.

But Lock could not take his eyes off the one-legged Italian.

The tone of horror in the man's voice as he garbled curses or prayers in his native tongue. The sense of despair which gripped his face. The fruitless attempts to summon the lost limb by looking away and looking back at the stump.

The opportunity that now presented itself.

The elderly farmer moved on the prone Italian with his scythe, and was preparing to sever the right leg when the Italian called for help. He signalled desperately with his shoulders for Lock to intervene.

Lock swallowed his horror.

This man had been violent, he had been ruthless and merciless, and he now cowered when at a disadvantage. Guilt flickered in the man's eyes. A sense of shame. A sense that perhaps, he had allowed the war to warp his true nature.

Then Lock remembered what this man had done, how he had brutalised the civilians, stolen their food, and abused his power. The farmer would surely have been killed, for the crime of being in the wrong place at the wrong time.

Lock tried to let his conscience drift to the back of his head, where it would not see what he knew he now had to do.

This man was a monster.

Like Gaston Phillipe, like Diego de la Barca, and surely also, like the Black Prince.

'Tell us what you know,' Lock began, 'Or my friend will remove your other leg.'

For the benefit of the farmer, Lock then repeated the request in German.

The farmer, as if realising his new role, nodded at Lock with satisfaction, his hunger for swift revenge momentarily satiated as he saw how he could be of use.

Though not a German speaker, the Italian seemed to sense that his other leg was on the line. Still speaking Italian, and in between wails, he wriggled towards Lock in desperation. Lock supressed the urge to vomit.

The ground was wet with a sticky shade of crimson that poured from the Italian's stump. Blood pooled and spread relentlessly, sinking into the earth as it did so. The Italian's white buff coat was covered in his own blood, adding to the horror. The blood loss seemed to wear the Italian down. His ashen face suggested he had not got long left.

'We have to put him out of his misery,' Flynn barked, 'his wailing will bring de la Barca's whole army on top of us.'

The soldier attempted to worm his way along the ground in vain. Lock approached and pushed him onto his back. The Italian groaned, his slightly swollen face now ashen grey, his eyes staring vacantly, but he moved his pleading glance to Lock for a brief moment. Lock switched to French.

'I hope you can understand me,' Lock began. 'You can keep your other leg, once you tell us what we need to know. I will ask one more time. Why is Diego de la Barca looking for us?'

The Italian nodded in recognition of his hopeless situation, lifting his stump slightly off the ground. He was sweating and breathing heavily, the pain consuming his mind, the adrenaline insufficient to hide it. He sighed and inhaled greedily, before looking at Lock and saying in broken French:

'The Germans... The forest Germans... The forest Germans put his son... Put his son's body on the camp.'

'*The body*,' Lock said. 'We never thought about Gaston Phillipe's body.' He turned to Flynn. 'Did the Germans hate Phillipe enough to cut up his body and display the pieces in front of the camp?'

Flynn nodded. 'That's what I would do if someone defiled my daughters,' he said in a low voice. His expression darkened as he stared a hole in the Italian.

Lock tried to scrape the blood off his boots, but it was a fruitless exercise. 'De la Barca knows we were the only ones to travel with Phillipe. He'll be looking for us, the fake diplomat and the Irish Spaniard. It'll be impossible to get into Mannheim.'

'We need to know more,' Flynn said, as he turned to the Italian.

Groans escaped endlessly from his bleeding mouth. He was a picture of pitiful misery. He rotated his throbbing red stump of a leg, as if on a swivel, and he wailed as it touched off the grass.

'How many men does de la Barca have looking for us?' Lock asked, unable to take his eyes off the stump.

The Italian submitted.

Between tears, he spat out a number. 'One hundred. Ten, ten, ten...' Flynn ignored the Italian's garbled speech. He was likely descending into delirium and shock.

'That's a lot of men to send after us Lock, he must think we killed his son.'

'Or, perhaps he worries for the welfare of an English envoy?'

'Horse,' the Italian groaned in French. 'Sir sent horse to Mannheim.'

Flynn cursed. 'De la Barca must have sent a rider to Mannheim as soon as it happened. They'll be looking out for us. We'll be stopped at the gates.'

A few feet away, the greying farmer spoke briskly to Lock.

'I can get you into Mannheim.' He then gestured to his partially damaged cart. 'You can hide in the back, in a special compartment. You can lie flat under the meat.'

'Thank you,' Lock said, and sighed.

'In return, I want that bastard's life.'

'He's yours,' Flynn said in German, before Lock had a chance to respond.

Lock glanced frantically between Flynn and the farmer, but there was nothing that could be done. Nor did the task of saving a one-legged criminal fill him with much inspiration. It was easier, and likely more just, to let revenge take its course.

Though he spoke not a word of German, the Italian sensed his fate was on the line. He met the farmer's gaze. The farmer held his filthy, blooded scythe in front of his body like a sword, and walked gradually towards the Italian.

Once he registered the farmer's mission, the Italian recoiled in horror, and began shuffling backwards on his rump.

'*Non non non non...*' the Italian pleaded, as he waved frantically at Lock to intervene one more.

'May God have mercy,' Flynn said in a low voice. Lock took the message. There was nothing he could do for the Italian now.

The farmer caught up with the whimpering Italian, and angled his scythe to cut the rope which bound his hands. Lock half expected a reprieve, perhaps even mercy, but Flynn's stony expression told him that the Italian was lost.

The farmer then shouted at the doomed soldier in German, demanding that he pray. The wide-eyed Italian took a moment to understand. Once the farmer demonstrated, the Italian tried to follow suit. He leant on his remaining knee, and pleaded earnestly with the farmer. The Italian had clasped his hands so tightly that his knuckles had whitened, but the urgency of the act made no difference.

'Non...non... non...' he whispered, as if unable to believe his ordeal.

'This is for Anna,' the farmer said.

The rage had consumed him. He pushed the Italian backward with his right foot, and took aim at the Italian's remaining leg. The first blow landed, and flicked up dirt and blood as the scythe plunged through flesh, earth and bone.

The victim tried desperately to crawl away, but in vain. Before each strike, the farmer shouted his wife's name at the Italian, until the other leg was removed.

Lock was transfixed.

Deliriously, the prone Italian raised his hands again in prayer, but this was a grave mistake. The farmer took this as an invitation to sever more limbs. He struck again, with a wide swipe at the Italian's wrists, before arching his weapon on a backswing which cleaved his left hand off.

There was a shriek, and the Italian stared in disbelief at his predicament. With a grunt, the farmer completed the hideous act by severing the right hand in one fluid motion. Flynn turned away in disgust, but Lock forced himself to watch it all.

Blood gushed from the Italian's stumps, and the farmer nearly slipped several times on the crimson grass. Somehow, the Italian sat up, before he broke down, sobbing uncontrollably and clutching his knees with his bloody wrists. He passed out in the position, and the farmer glared at his work.

The Italian's blood coated him, but his work was not finished.

The Italian began coughing, blood spurting out of his wrists with each convulsion. His body drooped backwards, and his eyes flittered as his head rested on the grass. He exhaled and groaned one final time, before apparently consumed by a rush of agonising pain. His body convulsed, and with his right stump he attempted to access a knife by his side.

Perhaps an hour before, the Italian had absent-mindedly used this knife to cut the mutton for his lunch. Now he intended the knife to solve another problem, and put an end to the pain in the most obvious way. But the task was futile, and his stump rubbed roughly off the knife's handle, which produced several yelps of agony.

The farmer had seen enough. He held back his scythe and surged downwards, striking with all his might on the Italian's chest. A large rip opened in the Italian's clothes, and the farmer struck furiously for a second, third and fourth time. Blood was flicked and thrown in all directions, and the farmer roared curses at his doomed foe.

The Italian blinked in astonishment, and then the life seemed finally, mercifully, to go out of him.

'Mother Mary,' Flynn whispered.

Lock allowed a momentary silence to creep in, interrupted only by the farmer's heavy breathing and the residual spurting of the Italian's arteries. Blood had been cast liberally around the area, and streaks of it were plastered on the farmer's body and face. The eruption of crimson had not stopped there. Lock wiped at the flecks which dotted his family dolman.

'We need to go,' Flynn said, gesturing to the distant edge of the forest, where they had earlier emerged. Soldiers dressed similar to these men could be seen, and it was only a matter of time before they were caught up with.

Lock turned to see the farmer kneeling at his wife's corpse.

He glanced up at Lock. His eyes vacant. His purpose achieved. His villain slain. 'My name is Herman,' the farmer said. 'If you climb onto my wagon, I will take you into Mannheim.' He then sighed and shook his head. 'Help me bury poor Anna's body.'

- CHAPTER EIGHTEEN -

Herman's wagon was surprisingly sturdy. The false bottom, he said, was invaluable for concealing items which had been obtained in a not necessarily legal fashion, which Flynn explained meant poaching.

If Herman was a poacher, Lock was not about to hold that against him. The wagon was filled with carcasses and haunches of meet of varying size, but the appearance was deceptive.

The wagon used only half of its depth. The other half was given to a secret compartment, which could only be accessed through a trapdoor in the upper left corner of the wagon. It had taken Flynn and Lock several minutes first to manoeuvre themselves into the trap door, and then to crawl into position and lie perfectly flat and still. The Irishman was uncharacteristically quiet throughout the ordeal.

There were barely a few inches of space between Lock's nose and the wagon. He lay on his back beneath a smorgasbord of protein. It was a claustrophobic journey. Herman had assured them both that the process would take an hour from beginning to end. There was less than a mile of road to travel, followed by the procedure for entering Mannheim. The fortress town guarded the only crossing over the Rhine for many miles, so venturing through it was essential.

Spanish soldiers should not have reason to be suspicious of a butcher's cart, but Lock and Flynn had bargained that news of Gaston Phillipe's death would have rendered the Spanish distracted. All would have known that the death of a commander's son – illegitimate or otherwise – could compel de la Barca to depend more heavily on the bottle or, potentially, to resort to greater cruelties.

Lock found the sound of the wagon's wheels comforting. Perhaps it was the consistency of the sound, and the way the wheels seemed to glide, untroubled, along the road. Herman was certainly a steady pair of hands.

Was it unsettling that Herman appeared so unaffected by the murder of his wife and the butchery of the Italian? Or was it reassuring that the farmer could have such steel nerves?

It was difficult to say.

Either way, Lock was happy for the hour of respite. The ringing in his ears was beginning to return, and he was worn out from the intensity of the day. His undershirt was pulled tightly against his skin by a profuse day of sweating. It had been a day of sweat, blood, dirt and meat. Lock yearned for a bath.

There seemed little to do but sleep. The darkness of the compartment was broken by several small holes in the side of the wagon. To guard against a nosy Spaniard investigating, the compartment had been partially filled with more meat, so the untrained eye would not notice the scheme. This deception also meant that Lock was surrounded by the most intense fragrances he had absorbed all day.

Herman had been generous in his provisions, but the hurried picnic of pork and bread did not prevent Lock's nose from honing in on the garlic sausages. On Lock's left, several large hams were wrapped and prepared for sale.

The fragrance persuaded Lock that he was in fact still hungry. Would Herman part with more of his produce? The Irishman suddenly broke the silence.

'I know you are no envoy, Officer Lock.' Flynn said.

The words had been said so calmly, so matter-of-fact, that the very act of denial appeared hopeless, perhaps even shameful. Nonetheless, Lock did try.

'I will have you know, I studied for many years for this very mission. I have worked many years before that. I do not know why you would second guess my integrity after the day we have had.'

The words had been said with force and emotion, but not much conviction. Pretending to be the envoy was a tiring act. The act was also inconsistently portrayed; Lock knew of few envoys that engaged with bandits. He had repeatedly strayed outside of his job description.

The Irishman had good grounds to challenge his story, but why Flynn had waited until now – when they were side by side, surrounded by meat – to have this conversation?

Lock shivered – perhaps the crafty Irishman had been waiting for just such a situation as this, where his English charge would be unable to escape the interrogation.

'I know you are not an envoy.' Flynn said again, 'because you are utterly unlike any envoy I have ever known.'

'I do not know about that...'

'Do you know, Lock, how many envoys would risk life and limb for a farmer they do not even know?'

'I knew we needed his wagon to get into Mannheim.'

'I am afraid I do not believe you, *Officer Lock*.' The Irishman replied. Lock's title had returned, but Flynn had now turned it into something of a taunt. It sounded remarkably similar to the '*Your Majesty*' jest of before.

Lock stayed silent. The last thing he had expected was to defend his story at a time like this.

'You rose to your feet and charged those men because you wanted to help that farmer, not because you wanted to ride his wagon into Mannheim.'

Lock had been surprised at how his emotions had taken over.

The anger. The overwhelming sense of burning anger, which was itself caused by the sight of rank injustice which he could not abide by.

Flynn was correct. The Irishman had figured him out, yet still the dance went on.

'His wasn't the first life I tried to save. I defended those Germans in the forest. I could have let them die.'

'Those Germans would have killed us. I thought your improvisation was impressive, though I do not know what you would have done if Phillipe had not dropped you with one.'

'He hardly dropped me. I was merely stunned.'

Flynn snorted in the dark. 'He dropped you like a sack of potatoes.'

'I had him right where I wanted him.'

'If I had not blown off his arm, he would have caved your sweaty face in.'

'What do you want from me Irishman? Do you want me to admit I am afraid? Do you want me to admit that I do not know what I am doing? Is that what you want?'

The wagon interrupted the conversation with a large creak, as a left wheel struck a stone on the road. Lock wished he was that stone.

'I want you to be *honest*, Lock. I want to know who this man really is before I trust him with my life for any more steps. I have a family, do you understand? I must protect them.'

Even this wayward Irishman was allowed to have a family? The wagon's thin wooden walls seemed to be closing in. After far too long a pause, Lock sighed.

The game was up. On his honour, Lock could not lead the Irishman any further on the basis of a lie.

'I had a family once.' Lock said. As the words fell out of his mouth, they rested in the close confines of the compartment, and Lock could almost believe that he could hear Flynn thinking how to react.

'What happened to them?' Flynn turned on his side to face Lock, and the wagon murmured as several planks of wood creaked a slight sigh of relief. There was barely enough light to see a hand in front of one's face, but Lock took the gesture to mean that the Irishman cared.

'They were murdered Flynn. They were brutally murdered.'

'As brutally as that Italian we just took apart?'

The reply surprised Lock. He projected his disappointment into an outburst of anger.

'That swine deserved it. He preyed on innocent farmers, and betrayed his oaths as a man. I perhaps would not have dealt with him... quite so brutally as Herman, but the thing is done.'

'You had a look in your eyes Matthew. It is a look I have seen many times before. My priest used to say to me that a man balances on a knife edge between good and evil. My Father, God rest him, used to say that this knife edge vanishes during war.'

'What is your point?'

'My point, is that you must be careful not to lose your true self as you search for vengeance.'

Lock scoffed.

'It is only gentlemanly to warn you of such things.'

'*Gentlemanly?*' Lock turned to face Flynn, attempting as he did so to ignore the absurdity of their situation. Trapped in a dark, meaty cart, blundering into enemy Terrytory, without a fragment of a plan between them. 'Was it gentlemanly to ignore Herman's plight, as you willingly did?'

'In my experience Lock, you will quickly lose your life if you attempt to save everyone else's.'

'And what *experience* is that? I know as little about you as you do about me, yet I am willing to follow you to Frankenthal.'

'You need me. You've never been around these parts like I have.'

'And, Flynn, it seems that you need me. Otherwise, we'd be swimming over the Rhine right now.'

'I would have found another way.'

'I told you that my parents were brutally murdered. What kind of gentleman refrains from offering condolences upon receiving such information?'

'Where were they killed?'

Lock rolled his eyes in perfect safety. 'What does it matter where they were killed?'

'Because I might know who was responsible.'

Lock froze. A sharp chill ran down his spine, as did several beads of sweat. Could he find his answer here, of all places?

Visions of resolution flashed before Lock's eyes. A cooperative Dutch magistrate. Compensation. Apologies. Justice. Something he could bring back to Arthur and feel proud of. Once again, the Irishman left him consumed with questions. Once again, Lock had to pretend that he had no questions.

'You would not know.'

'Was it in Brussels? Vienna? Paris? Constantinople? *The recently discovered planet of Mars?*'

Lock was in no mood for teasing. He rolled onto his back again and ranted at the compartment ceiling.

'You imagine that you are some fountain of information? That you know the answers to any and all questions, and that I am a helpless sheep wandering to its slaughter?'

'For over ten years I have been at war Lock, and in that time I have amassed a considerable catalogue of friends and information.'

'How lovely for you.'

'It is indeed, particularly when I am in a position to help a friend.'

'A *friend*?' Lock was caught off guard once again.

The Irishman sighed, and rolled onto his own back to speak to the ceiling. 'It pains me immensely to know that an Englishman has saved my life, but this is the truth. I would not have bested that Italian. It is the closest I have come in the last ten years to meeting My Saviour, but you were there to stop that meeting.'

'I fear I may have only delayed it, the way you wield your sword.'

'So, I will take charge of the punching, and you can take control of the swordsmanship. Fair enough?'

'Fair enough.'

'Very good then Lock. Now tell me, *where* did this tragedy occur?'

Lock sighed. There was hardly any point in keeping this secret.

'They were murdered in The Hague, by men wearing black masks.'

Silence suddenly engulfed the compartment. The Irishman paused before taking a breath. 'That sounds... most curious, but I'm afraid it doesn't ring a bell.'

All the visions of justice faded. Lock regretted saying anything. The silence was punctured by the sound of several barking dogs, which grew louder in intensity. Above them, Herman tapped on the wagon with his stick. Dust and small pieces of meat slipped through the cracks in the wooden planks as he did so. Perhaps the wagon was not so sturdy after all. They could just make out Herman's muffled explanation. Lock nodded to himself.

'What did he say?' the Irishman whispered.

'He says that the dogs are barking because they hate the smell of Ireland.'

Flynn laughed heartily. 'Ireland is certainly not a smell loved by all.'

Lock offered the truth. 'Herman says the dogs bark when they smell the meat because they get excited. They have learned that their masters occasionally get meat for them.'

'Herman said all that?'

'He also said we will be at Mannheim's gates in fifteen minutes.'

'God's guts, I must tend to my German.'

'We make another pact then,' Lock said. 'You handle the Spanish, I will handle the German.'

Flynn laughed out loud once again. 'While we are at it, best keep clear of the horses.'

'I can shoot.' Lock said.

'Many men can shoot.'

'Not many can shoot like me.'

Flynn tut tutted and sucked his teeth to make a loud smacking sound. 'Perhaps if we ever leave the confines of this stinking cart, you will have occasion to prove such a boast.'

There was a loud chomping sound, followed by a sigh of relief.

'Are you *eating*?'

'Please, Officer Lock, Herman must provide his share of contributions.'

'I was hoping to bargain with him for the garlic sausages. I won't be in much of a position to bargain if you eat all of his ham.'

'There are garlic sausages?' there was a brief rustling sound. 'Never mind, I found them.'

'*Flynn...*' A string of meat suddenly struck Lock in the face.

'A fair trade, I think. We saved his life and gave him his vengeance. Surely, Lock, that is more than worthy of a sausage.'

Lock found that he was subconsciously drawing the sausages towards his bag. They would certainly raise spirits once he was forced to travel alone.

'I hear footsteps,' Flynn said quietly. Lock's body froze. A curious storm of sounds swirled outside the wagon. Herman's voice could be heard. Lock could not imagine how that traumatised farmer could now make a sale.

A chuckle was heard, and more barking dogs, closer this time. Snouts pressed themselves against the sides of the wagon, until an angry call forced them away. The voices began to fade. Lock exhaled. He realised he had been holding his breath.

'If your parents were murdered in The Hague, why are you going to Frankenthal?'

It was a reasonable question. Lock had wondered it himself. It was possible that Vere would know something of the matter, but so might the authorities. Why could he not wait in The Hague for more information? Perhaps the assailants would strike again?

In truth he knew why.

Lock was afraid. He was afraid of being alone against such odds again. He was afraid of the pain of defeat. Most of all, he was afraid of dying before he could learn the truth. There was no need to tell Flynn all of this.

'Sir Horace Vere is in Frankenthal. He is my godfather, and might know something of the crime.'

Flynn gave a low whistle. 'Now there's a man I would want on my side.'

'You know of Vere?'

Flynn scoffed. 'Lock, I fought with Vere. I also fought against Vere, a less enjoyable experience. The man is a professional. Fearsome in war, devious in letters, but a treasure of a friend.'

'You two are *friends?*' Lock was irritated to feel jealous.

'Friends? I suspect he does not even know my name. Much too busy for the likes of me, on the King's business and all that.'

And then a tragic thought occurred to Lock. What if Vere was also *much too busy* for his godson? What was to stop the distinguished statesman from resting on ceremony, and ushering Lock away?

'You believe Vere may know something about your parents?'

'He has to, and if he does not, he may know something about my Father that can help.'

'Why is that?'

'The two men were comrades, Flynn, brothers in arms, so my Father says. Barely a day passed without my Father reminiscing about some great feat that Vere accomplished, with Charles Lock by his side.'

'So this performance for de la Barca, when you swear you intentions to negotiate the surrender of Frankenthal... This was all a façade.'

'Yes. I needed to get past Spanish patrols with the required seal.'

'I own, it's not a bad plan Lock.'

'Nor particularly honourable.'

'Nonetheless, you have convinced me.'

'Convinced you?'

'Envoy or not Lock, I will accompany you to Frankenthal after all. Safety in numbers, don't the merchants say?'

'I cannot pay you, Flynn.'

'Perhaps you can contribute some information. Did Charles Lock have enemies?'

Lock paused. It was odd to hear the Irishman say his Father's name. Lock was unsure how he felt about it.

'Certainly not. My Father was a man of virtue.'

Flynn scoffed. 'Virtuous men make virtuous enemies.'

'It is possible to engage in war and adventure without gathering enemies, Flynn. Not all races hold a grudge like the Irish.'

'I will try not to hold that against them.'

The wagon stopped. Lock's body stiffened. Spanish voices could be heard. Footsteps plodded lazily around the left side of the wagon. Herman could be heard lowering himself gingerly onto the ground. The farmer had explained that this part of the process would take a few minutes if the Spaniards were in a good mood, but much longer if they decided to be tiresome.

Lock hoped they would not be tiresome. He also hoped that Herman could keep his composure, as he negotiated with the comrades of those men who had butchered his wife. Lock was now decided, the German farmer's nerves of steel did unsettle him.

'*Shite*,' Flynn said under his breath. Several footsteps now seemed to circle the wagon. They crossed past the small holes in the wagon's side, momentarily obstructing the beams of light and darkening the meaty compartment still further. A bargain seemed to be taking place, judging by Herman's tone. A Spaniard made an exasperated sound and called for his comrade.

Lock's heart thumped in his ears. His hands had been clasped tightly on the garlic sausages, which had quietly burst from the pressure, and now oozed raw meat all over his torso. Lock focused on his breathing, an exercise his Father had taught him when, as a child, reciting poetry before a small audience had paralysed him with fear. Flynn was deathly silent.

'*You wish to take all my ham*?' Herman asked. German voices had finally returned to Lock's ears. Herman was negotiating, and the Spaniard had evidently fetched a German-speaking friend to improve the deal.

'We wish merely to take our share, noble farmer. Times such as these are tough indeed. What say you?'

'I say I will turn this wagon around if you do not let me through with all of my produce. I have a very specific order straight from the Archduchess herself.'

Archduchess? *What was Herman on about*? Brussels was a week away. Was Herman gambling that the Spaniards would not know that? Flynn sniggered at the mention of the Archduchess. The conversation stopped, and Herman returned to his seat atop the wagon. The next phase of the plan appeared, miraculously, to be now in motion.

'And... we're in,' Flynn whispered.

The reassurance had been for the Irishman's benefit as well as Lock's. He would need Flynn's help for what would come next.

- CHAPTER NINETEEN -

The wagon trundled over the bridge. The unsteadiness of the dirt road gave way to the city streets. Herman had made it, but this was as far as he would go. He would park his wagon outside his brother's house, where the butchery was based. Then it was a matter of unloading all the meats for sale.

Once unloaded, Herman would leave his wagon, and his two stowaways would have to clamber out of it. The afternoon had given way to dusk, so the waiting game would not be a long one. Darkness would soon fall over Mannheim.

Lock was startled by several loud knocks. Herman's muffled voice could be heard once again. Lock could sense Flynn's impatience as he waited for a translation. There was no room for jesting this time.

'Herman said the men at the gate were all conscripts, barely armed with a few chin hairs.'

'De la Barca must be more overstretched than I thought,' Flynn said.

'Herman also says that Mannheim's streets appear deserted.'

'I am not surprised; the people here are caught between Frankenthal and de la Barca's fury.'

'You know de la Barca, what do you think he'll do?'

'It depends, Lock, on whether he thinks we killed his son, or whether he thinks we were also unfortunate victims.'

'And if he learns that we did kill his son?'

'Then we should be wary of Diego de la Barca's vengeance.'

The wagon stopped, and Herman put his sales voice on once again. In the dark, Lock attempted to delicately rub some of the sausage off his coat. He was immensely thankful for the decision to retrieve their bags from the horses. A change of clothes, perhaps even a bath, would do wonders.

The wagon began rolling forward again. Its right wheel hit a stone, which shook the whole structure, and drew a swear from Flynn.

After fifteen minutes, following a winding set of turns, the wagon finally came to a complete stop. Herman then set to work unloading it. Another couple of voices entered the picture. What would Herman say about what had happened to him? Would he tell his extended family about the stowaways?

Herman's process was brisk and thorough. Within twenty minutes, much of the weight of the wagon appeared to have gone, and the structure seemed to groan in thanks.

Lock and Flynn still lay in darkness. The two were startled when the trapdoor was suddenly wrenched open. A weak light was enough to illuminate much of the compartment, and the outline of Herman's face was vaguely visible. Lock turned towards the farmer, but became embarrassed when he realised how filthy he truly was. Herman either did not notice or did not care.

'Gentlemen, thank you for your help earlier. I will not forget it. Please pass me out those three large hams, but you can keep whatever is left.'

'Thank you,' Lock whispered, as he regretfully slid the three appealing pieces of meat towards the farmer.

Herman nodded, and appeared to think something over. Conflict was written all over his weathered face, which had been browned by days under the sun.

'If you return,' Herman began, 'You should know that there are men here who wish to take their homes back. At least one hundred men,' Herman said.

Flynn sighed in frustration. 'Tell him we don't want to kick the Spanish out of Mannheim.'

Lock was not certain what he wanted. It was at least useful to know that an improvised militia would be on hand if needed. Herman's expression suggested that he did not hold out much hope, but as a gesture against the Spanish, it was the best he could do.

'We will let you know,' Lock said.

Herman nodded. 'Three hours,' he said. 'You eat and sleep. I will bang on the wagon when it is time, then I will leave you.'

Lock was about to question how wise it would be to eat raw meat, when the farmer handed another cloth bag into the compartment. As Lock's face lit up, Herman gave a satisfied smile, before closing the trapdoor.

'He's lucky I don't need to piss.' Flynn said, reaching for the cloth bag as he did so. The Irishman gasped as the bag was unfurled. It contained cooked meat, breads and even cheeses.

Without saying a word, the food was grabbed, and transferred quickly from hand to mouth. Lock propped himself on his left elbow while he polished off several cuts of ham with slices of hard cheese.

'Like manna from heaven,' Flynn said, out of the corner of his mouth.

Within a few minutes, their furious fit of eating had denuded the bag of its contents. Only a few pieces of bread remained. Flynn sensibly began packing the remaining food into his bag, and he passed some to Lock so he would do the same.

'Check your musket,' the Irishman said, rummaging for his firearm, and securing the unlit match chord. The exercise was immensely difficult while prone and in darkness, but there was hardly much else to do.

Lock did not need to check. He knew exactly where it was, exactly how many cartridges he had on his bandolier, and exactly how long it would take him to burn through his ammunition. He had detached his sword from his belt while prone, but he had rarely kept his hand away from the weapon. It had been a comfort to not be totally defenceless. Lock's eyes grew heavy, and he recalled the intensive day.

'We should aim for as many hours of sleep as we can get, I reckon.' Flynn said, as if sensing Lock's exhaustion. 'Don't know when we'll be able to sleep again.'

With his bag as a pillow, Lock rolled onto his side. His eyes were heavy, but his brain seemed unable or unwilling to switch off and allow the sleep. After a few frustrated sighs, Flynn offered some advice.

'Stop thinking about today,' the Irishman said. 'You must *will* yourself to sleep.' He said so proudly, as if revealing some great and complex discovery.

Lock would have asked for clarity, but within a few minutes, light, consistent breaths told Lock that his companion had fallen asleep. Lock allowed his mind to wander. He was back to that moment in 1613, when he let his family down. Lock exhaled and tried again.

Now he was back in Locksville. It was Christmas Day 1621, and all was right with the world. Lock leapt willingly into this escape.

He must have slept, because what seemed like a few minutes later, Herman was knocking gently on the wagon. The trapdoor opened. Herman had since changed out of his farmer's clothes, and wore an all-black ensemble.

'You gentlemen are in luck. The moon is young and covered with cloud. You should have a dark night.'

Flynn muttered something under his breath, before crawling over to the trapdoor, dragging his weapons and supplies behind him. A few grunts followed, as Flynn lay on his back and then shimmied to the opening. With one final grunt and an exhale, Flynn pulled himself over the edge, leaving Lock alone in the compartment.

The Irishman was out, and whispered a small prayer of thanks. Lock's urge to escape this wooden prison caused him nearly to forget his sword. He pushed his belongings out of the trapdoor first, and Flynn took them in his hands. Lock then manoeuvred himself forward, before sitting up for the first time in hours.

He was hit by a blast of warm air. The smells of a city invaded his nostrils. It was still a drastic improvement on previous conditions. Lock rose up from the wagon, straightened his back, and looked around.

Herman's cart was parked outside a butchery. A few feet from the wagon was the building where Herman had stored all his produce. 'Strasser Brothers, Fine Meats Company' was emblazoned on the building's front.

Herman was now in conversation with another man, slightly shorter than he was, and also dressed in black. Lock assumed the man to be Herman's brother. Flynn was sat in the corner of the wagon, sorting through his belongings.

'Welcome back to civilisation,' the Irishman whispered, his eyes trailing to the rough wooden fence that bordered Herman's garden.

Lock nodded in acknowledgement. He stepped out of the trapdoor, onto the wagon, and then onto the ground.

Herman, no longer alone, walked to the two men. 'The other gate is in that direction,' Herman said, gesturing to his left. 'My brother has drawn you a rough map of the city, but as he confesses, he is no artist, so do be careful.'

Lock nodded in thanks at the Strasser brothers. Flynn stepped gingerly off the wagon behind him, his bags packed and sorted, his musket slung over his shoulder, his hand on his scabbard. Herman and his brother winced.

'You two stink to high heaven,' Herman said, before stroking his chin. He turned to his brother, and spoke in quick German. Initially his brother seemed hesitant, but Herman seemed to win him over.

'Come inside,' Herman said. 'You must bathe. You'll set the dogs off if you walk around smelling like a butcher's cart.'

Lock could have embraced the man. Flynn appeared hesitant to enter a mysterious building at night, but the farmer had a point. Walking a few paces towards the premises, Herman and his brother whispered a few quick words, before Herman opened the door and signalled to his charges to enter.

It was time to rely on the kindness of strangers once more.

- CHAPTER TWENTY -

The premises was an old building, inherited from family members over the course of several decades. The Strasser brothers had a good arrangement in place – Herman would rear and slaughter the livestock, and his brother Theo would handle the business end of things. The partnership had been lucrative, and had netted the brothers a thriving business in a well-to-do part of town.

They were shown the impressive facilities, which included numerous rooms and an extensive basement area, which they were 'strictly not allow in,' Herman had said with a wink. Both Herman and Theo discussed Mannheim's situation openly and honestly in front of their guests, decrying all manner of atrocities, and swearing revenge.

These were the conversations that Diego de la Barca should fear. They demonstrated that the inhabitants of the Rhine were not content to let the Spanish rampage across their homeland. Theo offered his commiserations for Herman's wife. Herman insisted she would not die in vain.

When the tour was over, it was time to bathe, rest and regroup. Lock also made time for a small morsel of meat and cheese. It was supper time after all.

The bath was a dreamlike experience, by far the most luxurious experience he had enjoyed since leaving England nearly a fortnight before. Numerous servants tended to every whim which he might have. Lock was sure to stretch the bath out for as long as possible. It was likely he wouldn't see another for quite some time.

An hour before midnight, Lock was led by a servant to a small, sparsely furnished room with off-white stone walls, the same colour as virtually all the walls in the house. The use of lime on the walls, the servant proudly said, was an Ancient Roman technique used to prevent plague. Such precautions were essential in a crowded city. It suggested that the Strassers had travelled, or at the very least read, very widely.

Now was the time to rest and regroup; to mentally prepare for the task ahead. Lock sat heavily on a wicker chair, and with little else to do, he ensured that his sword was sharp and his musket was several steps ahead in the drill. Firing his weapon would draw the town guard, so it was only to be used in an absolute emergency.

The servants had taken their dirty clothes, and promised they would be ready for collection by the morning. Lock had never been so thankful for an act of foolish impetuosity. Herman seemed to trust him implicitly, and had not asked their intentions or their allegiances. It was good enough for the farmer that Lock and Flynn had helped him exact vengeance and restore justice.

Herman's footsteps grew closer. His approach was easy to recognise thanks to its more plodding, gradual placement of feet. Perhaps Herman Strasser believed he had all the time in the world.

Lock ran a whetstone over his sword.

'My friend,' Herman said, entering the room with a smile. 'I trust you feel refreshed?'

Lock chuckled, 'Herman, I have never lived so well, I feel like a new man.'

The German's expression grew serious for a moment. 'I know Lock, that you may question why I would feed you rare cheese while others starve. It is because I owe you, Officer Lock. I owe you and I will not forget it.'

Lock smiled and shook his head. 'I only did what any man would have done.'

'Sadly, Officer Lock, you are mistaken. Today is not the first day those scoundrels took something from me.' The farmer spat on his own tiled floor, with the speed of a reflex, as though Spain itself was caught in his mouth.

Herman Strasser then sighed, and sat on a wooden chair beside Lock. Without saying another word, the farmer handed Lock something hard, wrapped in linen. Lock looked at Herman's face, which was now drawn with pride.

'This was for my son,' Herman said. 'The Spanish killed him too. I want you to have it.'

The news was delivered so stoically that Lock was unable to refuse. He unwrapped the linen, and his hand rested on a small, cold blade. Lock had never seen anything like it. He ran his fingers over the exemplary craftmanship. It had to be Italian, and very valuable.

'A *stiletto*,' Herman marvelled, as though still in awe.

It was indeed a polished stiletto dagger. Long, thin and very fine. It was perhaps ten inches in length, with *Milan* engraved in delicate letters on the pommel. Herman gestured to Lock to pick the weapon up. As he did so, he noticed additional engravings he could not decipher on the hand guard.

'A stiletto is the assassin's weapon,' Herman said.

'Do you know many assassins?' Lock asked, without looking up from the weapon to see Herman's reaction. The farmer did not answer the question.

'You know what to do?' Herman asked, pointing at the stiletto, before gesturing to his eyes, neck and groin with a stabbing motion.

'I reckon so.'

'Show no mercy Herr Lock. With this in your hand, you are the angel of death.'

The *angel of death*? What did Herman see in his future?

The stiletto came with its own small scabbard, which was itself a silver ornament adorned with several red rubies that had been dulled with time. Lock wondered if the weapon had ever seen war, or if it had spent its life on a mantlepiece. He liked how it felt in his hand. If he had been armed with this blade before, Gaston Phillipe would never have been able to get so close.

'Are we evicted yet?' Flynn had emerged from his nap, and stood with his bags fully packed, his weapons systemised and prepared. The Irishman's eye landed on the stiletto, and Lock thought he saw a flash of jealousy, though perhaps it was just confusion.

'Beautiful knife,' Flynn said, and Herman nodded with evident pride.

'A *stiletto*,' he corrected.

'How long will it take to get to Frankenthal?' Lock asked, as he pressed his finger against the point of the stiletto before carefully sheathing it. The needle was still as sharp as any weapon of war. Jean le Renne used to say that a blunt sword was worse than wet powder, and Lock was sure that his teacher would have been impressed, if a little perturbed, by the danger this tiny weapon posed.

'On foot? You should make Frankenthal before sunrise, if you keep a consistent pace.'

Flynn was now beside Lock, and stuck out his hand to request the stiletto. Lock was reluctant to trust him, and then he was ashamed of himself when Flynn gave a confused glance at his hesitation. Lock handed it to his left.

'A fearsome blade,' the Irishman said, as he turned it over in his hand. With a flick of the wrist, the stiletto seemed to slice through the air. Herman's eyebrows raised in surprise.

'Italian made, I suspect,' Lock contributed.

Flynn whistled. 'Mother Mary, I would've liked this in my hand earlier. Could do real damage with this.' Flynn placed the hilt of the blade in Lock's hand with a respectful nod.

'It is near midnight, gentlemen. You will both be dead if you do not make haste,' Theo Strasser said, emerging from the doorway. He was slightly shorter than his brother, though his thick grey hair was longer. Unlike his brother, Theo's skin had not seen much sun. He was paler, but not quite pasty. Lock knew Father would say that Theo Strasser had the look of a man of letters – someone who would rather write you into prison than engage you in a duel.

'I told them both, wait for the changing of the guard,' Herman said.

'They should, but they should also look for any opening to land a strike,' Theo said, pushing his fist into his palm as he did so. 'These Spaniards are not the Spaniards I once knew. These men are impatient, reckless, and easily frightened. I only wish my old bones did not stop me meeting them on the battlefield. I would smash their tercio. I would break their precious squares.'

'You think Spain is weak?' Flynn snorted.

Theo glanced sideways at Flynn. 'Spain *is* weak.'

'Spain has Germany in the palm of its hand,' Flynn said, this time in English, and with a scoff that both German brothers flinched at.

'Have either of you been to Frankenthal?' Lock asked, interjecting before the conversation became too intense.

'I last saw Frankenthal... hmm... three months ago,' Herman replied. 'Sir Horace Vere had them in good spirits, but they knew they had a tough mission.'

'Are they still there? How do you know the place hasn't surrendered yet?' Lock asked, with a tone of urgency that caused Theo to raise his bushy eyebrows.

'My dear boy,' Theo began. 'If Frankenthal had surrendered, you will believe me when I tell you that we would know all about it. Drunken Spaniards would litter Mannheim's streets, and we would be inundated with wretches and sin.' He adjusted his shirt collar as he said the final word.

'Frankenthal's garrison may not have long,' Herman interjected. 'Farmers have been prohibited upon pain of death from delivering food to their ranks.'

Theo clapped his hands twice, and two servants entered the room to carry bags. 'Forgive us, gentleman, my brother and I talk too much. We rarely have such distinguished guests.' Theo handed Lock a folded piece of parchment. 'Here's your map of Mannheim, I hope it is of use. Take care when travelling to Frankenthal. Spanish patrols control the roads.'

Lock nodded, and walked into a room with polished wood floors. Animal heads were mounted at periodic intervals, and a roaring fire had been set up. One servant dusted a dark wood chest of drawers, and another gingerly slotted flowers into a vase. Herman walked ahead of them, and clasped both his hands on the large copper doorhandle. The hardwood door groaned on its hinges, before swinging gradually open. Herman walked outside and Lock followed.

'My dear brother is sometimes rough around the edges, but he is right. Be on your guard tonight gentlemen. If you get into trouble, jump into the river. Better that than be captured and tortured. I have it on good authority that the Inquisitor is doing his rounds in the area.'

Lock squinted at the name, but Flynn ushered him away from the farmer. 'Thank you, Herman, for everything,' the Irishman said. Lock went obediently. There was no time for more German horror stories now.

Strasser Brothers Fine Meat Company was a brisk twenty-minute walk from the city's walls. Lock could see the walls in the near distance, low and thick, as he waited for Flynn relieve himself down an ally. A haphazard collection of lanterns provided a weak glow of light. The signature smells of human waste, baked bread and sweat formed a potent, familiar cocktail.

The streets were deserted, as Herman had claimed, but they proceeded cautiously in the corner of the street all the same. Flynn had the map in his hand, and walked as he scanned it for guidance. 'Down here, to the left, then a right... There, there's the barracks Lock.'

And what a barracks it was.

Mannheim's barracks had been its prized possession. It was one of the largest buildings in the city, and had been intended to serve as the main armoury for the Elector Palatine, Frederick V. Frederick had approved the finishing touches on the building just before he left for Bohemia. Then the Spanish moved in. Burgundian banners were now draped over its front-facing walls. The building's location had also been deliberate. It was barely twenty yards from the western gate.

Per the instructions of the Strasser brothers, at midnight, the guard standing to attention at the western gate would be relieved. A one-minute window, perhaps less, would then exist. Lock and Flynn would be required to sprint through the gate and over the bridge before anyone noticed what was happening. All they had to do was pinpoint the guard's location.

Sure enough, a shaky guard stood in front of the barracks, no doubt impatient for relief. A weak lantern held above his head outlined his dishevelled stance, and bored expression.

'We should hide somewhere,' Flynn whispered. 'Wait for our opportunity to run. We'll only get one shot at this Lock.'

A side passage, cutting between two houses, provided the solution. They squeezed past ornate hedges and dilapidated fences, to emerge opposite the gate. Lock gasped when he saw how easy it all appeared. The only obstacle to running clean through the gate and over the bridge was a tired soldier. If all went according to plan, then within five minutes, this obstacle would be gone.

At one point, the garden probably served as a pleasant place to eat breakfast, and watch the town go by. It was likely that a well-to-do merchant family owned it. But the dwelling was boarded up now, its inhabitants forced to flee from the threat of war. It presented an eerie backdrop, and was reminiscent of the dilapidated houses Father had occasionally been forced to level on his own land.

Lock crouched behind an opulent granite birdbath, his eyes on the gate. Flynn watched in the opposite direction, to ensure they were not surprised by a guard on patrol. Lock swore he could hear the distant sound of gunfire.

Despite himself, his eyes had become heavy again. His stomach grumbled incessantly, to the extent that Flynn turned his head inquisitively, the hint of a grin on his face, before Lock waved him back.

'Three minutes,' Flynn whispered.

The guard started to become more restless. He shifted on his feet, and drooped his shoulders off the position of attention. This was the posture of a man who believed nobody was watching. A man who believed nobody cared about his job.

This was grunt work, guard duty. Nobody's passion. The one element of the profession that all soldiers universally loathed, whether by a city gate or at the entrance to a fortified camp.

A slight light followed the guard as he stepped nonchalantly in a small circle. Lock recalled Father complain that guards could burn through miles of match cord while on duty. The cord could be wasted on standing still, instead of advancing forward in battle. The standing still, the boredom; Lock knew by looking at this guard that it had consumed him.

'Two minutes,' Flynn said.

The guard looked directly at them, his match cord leaving a whisp of transparent grey mist in the air every time he turned his head. He scratched his moustache, then his crotch. Lock maintained his stare, keeping perfectly still, but the guard was too apathetic to notice.

Clouds moved lazily across the sky, as if bored by a night watch of their own. The overcast blackness granted additional protection, but it also made sudden activities potentially dangerous.

Lock was sweating, even in the cool of the summer night. At least he no longer stank of meat. Distant dog barks emerged at inconsistent intervals from the different corners of the city, like an impromptu chorus.

'Ninety seconds, get ready to run,' Flynn said.

The guard knew his time was virtually up, and as expected, he anticipated the relief by walking towards the barracks. The Strasser brothers had said that if this happened, they would have at least an extra ten seconds. The key was to wait until the guards were just far enough away.

The guard stopped abruptly, and walked briskly back a few paces, to retrieve something which he had dropped on the hard ground.

'Tobacco pipe,' Flynn whispered.

The guard moved the pipe to his lips, and used the match cord to light a small collection of dark material which he'd placed in the pipe's bowl. It was an efficient act, albeit completely inappropriate. Puffs of smoke erupted from his face as he walked, with increasing urgency, towards the barracks, where he could finally turn in for the night.

'*Now*!' Flynn said, and without any hesitation, he began to bound towards the gate. The length of the bridge, and the left bank of the Rhine, could be seen. Even in the dark, its rudimentary nature stood out against the recently modernised city.

It was really a drawbridge, though it hadn't been withdrawn in some time. The bridge's unprotected sides would make jumping into the river easier, if the worst did happen.

Lock leapt to his feet and followed. The guard had his back to them and had made quick progress, nearly reaching the door to the barracks where his relief should emerge.

Within seconds, they had reached the gate itself, and Flynn continued forward. Lock struggled to keep up, and glanced down to ensure he would not trip on an errant stone.

His eyes caught sight of the river, surging powerfully forward in the dark. The sound soon eclipsed all other background noise, as it raged under the bridge. Torrents of white-water swirled northwards, where the Rhine would eventually empty into the North Sea.

When he looked up, Lock's stomach lurched.

Flynn had stopped dead in his tracks.

Just starting towards the bridge on the other side of the river was a company of four Spaniards, their pikes raised, chattering among themselves.

Lock swore. The crisis was plain.

There was a matter of seconds before the Spaniards saw the Irishman on the bridge, and then the entire city would be awakened. Retreating back into Mannheim would lead to the exact same result.

The grim, intimidating solution was the only possible one.

If you get into trouble, jump in the river.

Would Flynn jump?

If he did, Lock had to follow. He did not want to meet the Inquisitor, judging by how the Strasser brothers had spoken of him.

'*Shite*,' Flynn gasped, his glance shifting in different directions.

'Can you swim?' Lock whispered, as loud as he dared.

Flynn faced Lock, nodded, exhaled and then grimaced.

'Keep the sausages dry,' he hissed, before turning and taking three large steps off the bridge's edge.

Lock watched him. Even as he saw the splash into the black water, and Flynn's body bob to the surface, a shiver ran down his shoulders.

'*It is only water,*' Lock whispered.

The four Spaniards would hear the splash. Lock did not dare to look in their direction. A shout was bellowed behind him. The new guard would now be on duty.

If you get into trouble, jump in the river.

Lock drowned out the shouts, and ran for the edge of the bridge. He forced himself not to think, and with a push off his legs, moved into the air.

The fall was higher than a house, but within a breath, Lock was lost beneath the surface. The freezing cold of the water snatched the air from his lungs.

Lock tried to pull his arms up from by his side, but the weight of the current forced them down. His shoulder grated against a rock, and he lost a boot when attempting to kick his legs. He coughed, clouding the darkness with bubbles. Somehow, the musket's sling became tangled around his neck, and it jerked Lock backwards. Following a considerable struggle, Lock released the musket. He watched through blurred vision, as the current snatched it greedily away.

Pieter Kleppe would hopefully understand his decision to save his life, rather than the family heirloom.

After some time scrambling with his feet, Lock found traction on the riverbed, and pushed up with his legs. As he crested the surface, Lock threw back his head and gasped desperately.

He turned to glance back at the bridge, which was now far behind him. He had surged far downriver. Trees and unfamiliar riverbanks went on for miles ahead, snaking and skirting through different bends.

The darkness made the scene more terrifying, and the river seemed determined to carry him indefinitely. There was no sign of Flynn, but then a white hand flashed in front of Lock's face. The Irishman had been on his left. Flynn gasped something at him, but the roar of the river stole the words away.

It was hard to breathe. Lock realised he was also gasping, and his mouth filled repeatedly with water. His sodden clothes desired nothing less than to pull him to the bottom and hold him there, and he wore out his legs kicking against their pull.

Lock was reminded of his grim fascination when he had first watched a fish out of water. Lock had begged his Father to let him put the trout back in the lake, but Father had insisted: '*Nonsense boy, if you want to eat, the fish must die.*'

The fish could have their revenge now. It was his turn to gasp.

Was it exhaustion that pulled him back under, or the sheer strength of the current? Lock did not know. He had lost track of his struggle. He knew everything seemed calmer going under for the second time.

The cold had seeped quickly into his unsuspecting bones. It was quieter, peaceful, even. A jerking moved Lock's shoulder, but he craved the peace and quiet.

Lock took the Irishman's advice. He exhaled, and willed himself to sleep.

- CHAPTER TWENTY-ONE -

Lock's first sensation was that of being supported.

His legs were unsteady, like they'd been afflicted with pins and needles, and had yet to fully wake up. As his eyes opened, he saw grass flash by, and lifted his heavy legs one after the other.

Then there was the coughing. Several times, he pulled down his support, as he crashed to the ground and coughed up large volumes of water. Eventually, when the water left his ears, he could begin to hear Flynn's voice.

Water streamed from his clothes and hair, which caused him to slip on the grass time and time again. He groaned, and Flynn cursed at him, sometimes in a language he didn't understand, all for the sake of pulling him ever onward. Flynn seemed intent on dragging him up a hill.

'Come on ya bastard, heave up, move now... come on.'

'Flynn, I...' and then more coughing. Lock was forced to his hands and knees as his legs gave away. Then, with one final, wretched cough, clarity returned to him. He stretched out his palm to Flynn, to indicate that he was able to walk on his own power.

'You're alright lad,' the Irishman urged. It was part question, part statement.

Lock looked up to him and nodded. 'Thank you, I'm fine.'

The Irishman's black hair was slicked against his face. His blue eyes were bloodshot and wide open in anger. He had lost many of his belongings, and was still checking his pockets and bags, a curse escaping when another item appeared lost.

'All the food's gone. The powder's wet. Our muskets are on their way to the North Sea.' He stood with his hands on his hips, and faced away from Lock as he spat out several more curses.

Lock reached for his side, where his blades had been. His sword had been seized by the current, and wrenched from his side. His boots had also been sucked off his feet. Lock allowed a curse of his own when he imagined how Captain Frank would react. His stiletto, miraculously, remained in place. Lock grasped it and said a brief prayer. At least they would not be defenceless.

'We need to move Lock, we can't stay here.'

Lock heaved himself to his feet and scanned the area quickly. It was still dark, but to the south, the faint glow of Mannheim was still visible. They had been swept quite a distance from the city, which was surely a blessing considering the fuss they had left behind.

The riverbank had been lined with reeds, scrub and plenty of human detritus. A wet trail led perhaps fifty yards downhill to gap in the bank, where the Irishman had presumably started dragging his sodden carcass.

'Thank you...'

'You said so already Lock, come on.' Flynn fumbled through his bag's remaining contents, and tossed Lock a pair of squashed old leather boots. 'You're about my size. They'll have to do for now.'

Lock nodded and took the gift gratefully. 'Where do we go?'

Flynn gestured vaguely to the west. 'We're headed to Frankenthal. Although, perhaps, we'll see if we can find a pit stop along the way to dry our clothes.'

'Any taverns along the way?'

Flynn laughed out loud. '*Taverns?* We'll be lucky if we find a cottage intact along here. The Spanish have raided. If you're not inside Frankenthal's walls, you're not safe.'

Lock's stomach growled, and he shivered. In the pitch black of night, and in soaked clothes, the wind bit into his skin and through to his bones. Flynn began walking up the remainder of the incline, and Lock sighed before following.

'We were *this* close, so naturally the bastards decided at that moment to wander across the bridge.' Flynn hawked and spat twice, and Lock did his best to hide his disgust.

'How far are we?' Lock called ahead. The Irishman was several paces in front of him.

'From Frankenthal? At least a day's walk. More, being weighed down like this.' Flynn pulled himself up the hill, and reached its crest. He scanned the horizon, before nodding at Lock.

'I see a row of cottages,' Flynn whispered, pointing towards a road that stretched several miles into the distance. A row of shapes was all that Lock could make out, but he trusted Flynn's senses.

'Not a tavern, but it'll do,' Lock said.

Flynn held up his hand as he whispered again. 'Careful. If they are looking for us, we have to be wary. You see anyone approach, you let me know. Keep your ears open.'

Lock nodded. The Irishman had snapped into soldier mode, and Lock wasn't about to snap him out of it. He would need all his wits about him for this next act.

The landscape represented a fugitive's nightmare. Once the riverbank's trees and scrub had been cleared, a wide-open grassy space stretched as far as the eye could see. Nowhere to hide, and with the exception of the cottages and the road that snaked past them, nothing to break up the featureless landscape.

'We'll be caught in the open,' Lock whispered, almost to himself.

'We don't have a choice Lock. Either we stay here and the Spanish find us, or we keep moving, and they might find us. Keep an eye out for a fortress. Frankenthal sticks out like a sore thumb, you can't miss it.'

The trek began, and the minutes passed by. Clouds of flies appeared, seemingly at random, to hound the damp intruders, but other than that, there were few signs of activity.

Fields of long grass, wet with dew, surrounded their feet. Lock paused to empty riverbed from his left boot, and as he did so, Flynn kept his eyes on the cottages.

'I think one has a fire going. If we're lucky, they won't turn us away.'

'Let me do the talking,' Lock said, as he tipped a handful of grit out of his borrowed boot.

'*You?*' Flynn snorted.

Lock pulled the boot back on with a squelch. 'Unless your German has improved in the last few hours.'

Flynn grunted. 'I can understand the language. It's just when they talk too quickly I can't keep up.'

'What of that other language you keep cursing in?'

Flynn smirked. 'Irish? Or *Gaelic* as the Scots call it.'

'It doesn't sound like any tongue I've ever heard.'

'It's Celtic. Comes from a great family of languages, like Welsh, or Cornish. Have you ever been to Britany?'

Lock shook his head.

'They speak a fascinating dialect there too. I stayed there a while with my Father, after your King sent us into exile.'

'Just think, if you hadn't been exiled, you never would have pulled me out of the river.'

'If I hadn't been exiled, perhaps I'd own my own river. I'd even settle for a small corner of the Shannon, or the Liffey.'

'There's still time. You could make your fortune, purchase some land.'

'I can't set foot in that place. There's a bounty on my head, Lock. As soon as I'm recognised, I'll be swinging from a rope.'

'Maybe Vere could put in a good word for you?'

'*Vere?*' Flynn was dubious. 'You think Vere would help me?'

'Why not? At this stage, you've saved his godson's skin many times. It's only right.'

'If our world turned according to what was right, Lock, I'd still be in Ulster, and we wouldn't even be having this conversation.'

'Well, it's worth thinking about. I hear he has many friends in high places.'

Flynn sucked his teeth as he turned back to Lock. 'I wish I could have lived before. Before the Romans, and the Saxons, and the Vikings and the Normans, there were just Celts. That was back when our two islands were actually at peace.'

'I highly doubt that.'

'Well, the Celts weren't overly fond of writing things down, so I guess we'll never know.'

Lock jumped a few inches, as a small flock of birds emerged from the grass. Flynn said nothing, but Lock felt his judgement all the same. The Irishman reached into a satchel on his left side.

'See this?' Flynn held a container a few inches from Lock's face. It was a costrel, made of black leather, and ideal for carrying a day's worth of liquid, generally of the alcoholic kind. 'Those Celtic markings there, they don't make them like that anymore Lock. Irish craftmanship. God's guts, if you could see my homeland back in its golden age.'

'Wait,' Lock pointed to a light in the distance.

Flynn abruptly dropped to his knees, and Lock copied him.

'Looks like a small figure. Could be a short Spaniard, we won't know until we get closer. Let's move away from the road. Go further into the grass. We'll approach the cottages from the west.'

Lock nodded. His eyes had adjusted, but it was still difficult to see any detail more than a few feet ahead. The cottages were definitely getting closer. Already it was possible to discern the habitable from the uninhabitable. The dwelling nearest to them had had much of its south-facing wall pulled down. Its neighbouring cottage lacked a roof of any kind. There were perhaps two more cottages beyond them.

Flynn shuffled quickly through the grass. Moisture flicked back at Lock, and he held a cautious hand in front of his face. The grass nearly reached his thighs, and he feared he might tread on a wasp's nest. That would certainly blow their cover.

He could still recall James' sobbing, swollen face when a nest's contents had been unleashed on him. The dogs had run yelping in several directions, while he and Arthur had thrown themselves into a shallow river nearby. Mother had made such a fuss of her youngest and eldest sons, sparing only a glare for him, and Father had permitted James to fire a musket directly at the offending nest the following day.

Lock had marvelled at James' bravery and boldness in firing the weapon. There had been no hesitation, and no fear. He made it look so easy. But it was not easy, as Lock learned a month later, when the family holiday to the Frisian countryside had been so cruelly interrupted, and everything had changed.

'*There*,' the Irishman gestured at the figure, which opened a door into the furthest cottage, the one with a working fireplace. 'I think it's a child, or maybe a youth. Probably German, but let's be careful anyway.'

The building was only a few yards away now. No lights were visible on the building's east side, which meant no windows, so it was safe to approach. Flynn picked up his pace slightly, until he was a few feet from the cottage's wall.

It was indeed the only dwelling of value out of the four. The third cottage appeared inhabited by a particularly noisy collection of animals, and a large hole was visible in its thatched roof.

'What do we do?' Lock whispered.

Flynn appeared to weigh up his options. He glanced left and right, before deciding to move to the cottage's north facing side. Lock followed. The chimney continued to billow thick clouds of smoke, and Lock smelt meat, perhaps mutton. A small clump of birch trees, several yards in the distance, was the most likely source of firewood. He looked at Flynn, who appeared similarly transfixed.

Nearly drowning was an unorthodox way to build up an appetite.

'We should knock on the door, perhaps throw a stone, and hide.'

'Hide *where*?'

'In the grass, Lock, we'll lie down in the grass, and position ourselves so that we can see inside. Then we'll know what we're dealing with.'

Lock grimaced at the thought of lying prone on nature's floor in the dark, but he had no better ideas. 'Alright, lead the way.'

The two men stepped gingerly towards an ideal lookout post. An outline of light surrounded the cottage doorway, and the smell of mutton grew more intense. Lock inhaled deeply, and Flynn glared at him.

Finally, after a few steps, giving perhaps ten feet of distance, the two men lay down. Lock tried his best not to think about the life that teemed and buzzed below him. Once he began to think about it, he knew he would convince himself that centipedes, ticks and all manner of creatures had made their home in his skin. He needed to stay focused.

'Throw your stone,' Lock whispered.

While prone, Flynn arched his right arm, and hurled a stone large enough to fit in his palm. After a brief journey, it struck the upper right corner of the door with a slight crack, before hitting the dirt with a light thud.

'Now we wait,' Flynn whispered.

After less than ten seconds, the door creaked open slightly, and a cautious voice called out. The door opened wider, to reveal a small room, and several children. After a few seconds, the door was then shut.

'Don't see any adults,' Flynn whispered. 'Should be easy enough.'

'*Easy enough*?' Lock pulled on his arm. 'Just what do you plan on doing? Storm in there and steal food from children?'

Flynn sighed. 'Of course not. I mean it should be easy enough to persuade those children to... part with some of their food, and perhaps let us dry our clothes.'

'Have you ever seen anything like it? A cottage full of children?'

Flynn paused, before sighing quietly. 'This war is only a few years old, Lock, but I suspect it's made many orphans already.'

'How do they live like this?'

'As best as they can, Lock. They get the occasional bit of help from *Vater*, or Georg von Salm as we know him.'

Lock nodded. Von Salm's nickname was evidently widely known along the Rhine.

The Irishman rose only as high as a crouch. He nodded at Lock to follow him.

What would they find inside? Could it be a trap? The experience in the forest had made him wary of any plan that appeared straightforward on the surface, but not even Flynn seemed entirely certain.

Flynn exhaled quietly, and rapped his knuckles on the door.

'*Who's there?*' the gruff voice of an adult called from inside.

'Shite,' Flynn hesitated.

Lock used the most respectful tone he could muster. 'We're weary travellers. We escaped the Spanish, Sir, and we would really appreciate a moment to dry our clothes.' The Irishman raised an eyebrow at him, and Lock shrugged.

There was activity within the cottage, including whispers and sprinting children. A pot dropped, and curses followed. A baby cried. Then the door was flung open.

'What do you...' the gruff German stopped. He eyed up the two men outside his door. '*You?* What are you two doing here?'

It was one of Georg von Salm's men. This one had been instrumental in emptying the bottle of wine, Lock recalled that much, but he hadn't got his name. Lock hesitated for a moment, but the German's challenge was softened by the appearance of a child, perhaps no older than four and clothed in a single dark grey garment, who emerged by his right knee.

'Stay inside Lena,' the German urged, pushing her back gently with his meaty right hand.

'They look wet,' Lena said, as she looked up at the man.

'We are wet, young lady,' Lock said, and cursed himself internally for being so formal. Captain Frank's German lessons had skipped the proper means for addressing children.

The German eyed them up and down, his eyebrows crawling across his forehead as he did so. 'We don't need trouble, I have enough to do.' A baby cried behind him and the German grimaced.

'I'm pretty good with kids, Walter, now are you going to let us in or not?' Flynn said, his arms crossed.

Walter shook his head and muttered something under his breath as he withdrew from the doorway, but he did indicate that the two could come inside.

'You might have mentioned that you knew the man before we stood there gawking at him,' Lock hissed.

Flynn smirked. 'I just wanted to give you a chance to practice speaking to children, but I think I've seen enough.' The Irishman walked through the doorway, and patted Lena on the head as he did so.

Lock followed, and the door closed behind him. A wave of warmth hit him instantly. The cottage was a single room, not large, but the space had been economically used. Five straw beds, two of them occupied, lined the left side of the room, which was dominated by a crackling fireplace. A small boy tended the fire with an iron rod, and didn't turn around.

A table and chairs made up the rest of the furniture, and a large steaming pot lay on the table, which was stirred by another boy. Lena ran to him, and held his hand. The boy turned and smiled at Lock, and he awkwardly waved back.

'I am *not* good with kids,' he whispered to Flynn.

'Make yourself at home,' Walter said with a shrug.

'You've certainly been... busy,' Flynn said with an approving nod. There had to be at least eight children in the room.

'Only Lena is mine, the rest are...' Walter's voice trailed off, and he walked to the right, where Lena still held the boy's hand. 'Reminds her of her brother, I think...' the German said with a weak smile.

Now even Flynn found it difficult to know where to look. 'They... they all look well fed, so, you are taking good care of them.' It wasn't a bad complement, and Walter nodded in thanks at Flynn's remark.

'Uncle Walter,' one of the children called from the bed. Lock noticed now that this other girl was cradling the baby. 'They're my sister's,' Walter said quickly, as he walked to them.

Flynn gave Lock a knowing look. The cottage was the epicentre of family tragedy. Perhaps of several family tragedies.

'Need more wood,' the boy tending the fire said, still not turning around.

'No matter Leo, I'm sure our Irish friend would love to fetch us some. When your uncle Flynn returns, he's going to tell you a story all about Ireland,' Walter beamed at Flynn, and not even the Irishman could resist the excited looks of several young children. 'God knows I've heard the story enough times.'

Flynn sighed. Lock nodded at him to go, uncomfortable though he was.

'Walk fifty paces straight ahead, you'll find an axe and a clump of birch trees,' Walter said with a smirk. 'Thank God you arrived when you did, I was dreading heading out there again.'

Flynn rolled his eyes and headed for the door. He closed it quietly, noting one of the children was still asleep in their bed.

Lock was now alone with Walter's enormous adopted family. 'Is there... is there anything I can do to help?' He knew nothing of tending fires, stirring pots or talking to children, but perhaps Walter wouldn't need help with any of that.

Walter smiled. 'I remember you. You gave us food in the forest. You had our *Vater* in the palm of your hand, and you let him go. Thank you.'

Lock smiled. 'The last thing I wanted to do was harm him, or any of you. I had no idea you had so many... depending on you.' Lock found he was desperately curious to know Walter's story.

Walter sat with care on a rough wooden chair, and before long had Lena on his knee. He half turned his head towards the boy that continued to stir. 'That's plenty of stirring, Max, you can rest now.' The boy nodded and climbed down from the table, and went to the boy by the fire, who now just stared into the flames.

Walter shook his head. 'Max is alright, but Leo was here when the Spanish came, when they torched everything. I wanted to keep him away from the fire, but he won't sit anywhere else.' He handed Lena a grubby knitted rabbit, no bigger than her arm. It had clearly been handmade, but was no less adored for it. Lock's eyes fixed on the toy, and Lena turned her face into it shyly.

'Won't go anywhere without it, bless her. It's the only thing left from her Mother.' Walter shook his head. 'This is the last house standing. I used to live next door but... well.'

Lock couldn't hide his horror. 'The *Spanish* did this? They destroyed the other houses?'

'That's not all they destroyed,' Walter said quietly, as he rocked Lena back and forth on his knee. She began to doze before long. 'I don't even know where a couple of these kids came from. They just followed me home one day. What was I going to do, turn them away?'

Lock stared at the sleeping child. 'How could they do this? To *children?*'

Walter scoffed sadly. 'War does this, friend. War has always done this. I just hoped I wouldn't see it again in my lifetime. I thought His Grace would protect us.'

'You fight for Frederick, the Elector Palatine?'

Walter shook his head. '*Fought* for him. At one time, before the knavish bas–' Walter looked around at the room of young eavesdroppers and stopped himself. He cleared his throat quietly. 'Before the *silly Princely man* decided he would rather have the Bohemians than us Rhinelanders.'

'And now?'

'*Vater* has been good to us. He brings us food. We can normally make it last for a week. A few months ago he even had linen we could cut into clothes for them.' Walter shook his head again, and in the light of the fire, Lock saw decades' worth of worry etched into his face. 'In return, I fight for him sometimes. He understands when I can't make it.'

'Do the English help you?'

Walter scoffed with more energy this time. 'Only time I saw them was when one of them knocked on my door in the middle of the night –'

'...Sorry about that.'

'Not you, friend, some Gage fellow.'

'*Gage?*' the name didn't ring a bell. Perhaps he was one of Vere's subordinates?

'Anyway, he wanted food, and supplies. I told him he could take four kids and a babe.'

Lock allowed a laugh, and Walter seemed to appreciate it. 'The English must be desperate if they come to you for help.'

Walter nodded, as he turned his gaze towards the row of beds. Lena stirred on his knee, and he stood up, lifting her carefully to the bed in the corner.

He placed her down ever so gradually on the bed, and carefully loosened her tiny arms from around his neck. Walter turned back to Lock and gestured to the north-west. 'The English are about two miles that way, they don't give us much trouble anymore. I think they got the message.'

'And the Spanish?'

'If they call, I just tell them the truth. Most of the time, you get a respectful bow and even an apology.'

'They can't all be brutes, I suppose.'

'Shame that the brutes have a way of finding us though, eh?'

'It would unfortunately seem so.'

Walter tutted. 'Gaston Phillipe. Bastard deserved what he got. He was here, you know. Him and his ilk. Hopefully you'll get Captain Ricardo next. The truly vile men always seem backed by the powerful.'

'What did Phillipe do here? How was he connected to this Ricardo fellow?'

The door was suddenly wrenched open, and Lock nearly jumped out of his chair. Flynn entered, carrying an armful of wood.

For the first time since they had entered, Leo turned away from the fire, and pointed at the new supply of kindling with glee. The hair on Lock's neck stood up when he saw the boy's face. It had been terribly burned, and half the boy's head lacked hair of any kind, including eyebrows. The skin looked waxy and monstrous, like partially melted candle.

Lock's eyes moistened at the sight.

'Thank you, Irishman,' Walter said with a smile, and he clasped Flynn's hand. Without saying a word, Flynn brought the wood to near where Max and Leo sat. He handed the disfigured boy a hand-sized chunk of wood, and Leo took it with both hands, before carefully placing it near the back of the embers.

Flynn turned back to Lock.

'Don't mean to break up the party, Walter, but I saw a cavalry patrol on my way back here.'

'How many?' Walter asked, his tone suddenly icy.

'Two horses, but there's bound to be more,' Flynn said, 'Our packs are outside. We should get them and move on. I don't want any trouble to come to Walter.'

'Of course,' Lock said, and as he looked back to Walter, it was obvious that the last thing the man wanted was to be left alone. 'I will send you something,' Lock said. 'I will find a way to send you something. I promise.'

Walter nodded. 'Don't worry about it, friend. It was good enough to have some conversation with an adult.' He smiled at a boy who turned to glare at him.

Lock stood up, and took one last look around the room. Flynn placed his hand on his right shoulder, hurrying him along.

'Take care,' Lock whispered. 'And God bless.'

The door was opened slightly, and the two men squeezed out, gently closing it behind them.

- CHAPTER TWENTY-TWO -

'You shouldn't make promises you can't keep Lock.' Flynn said, after about ten minutes of walking.

'I didn't. I fully intend to honour that promise.'

'You don't know what might happen. What if you've no spoils of war to share?'

'Then I'll still have more than he does. God, I can't even imagine how hard it must be.'

Flynn shook his head, before turning and glancing behind him, almost out of habit. 'This is war, Lock. The part they don't write songs about. There's nothing glorious about orphans.'

'Maybe if more monarchs lived with Walter for a time, they'd wage war less often.' The idea was futile, but Lock still believed it. He shivered, perhaps involuntarily.

Flynn frowned. 'I did manage to find something in my travels. It's not much, but it's better than your wet undershirt.' The Irishman handed Lock a rough shirt. 'It's wool. I apologise in advance.'

'*Wool*?'

'At least it's dry. You could wear it until your undershirt dries at least.'

Lock looked Flynn up and down. 'Where's yours?'

The Irishman smiled. 'I'm already wearing it. That reminds me, here.' Flynn handed Lock two wool socks.

'Where did you get all this?'

'That cavalry patrol. I didn't exactly... get out of its way.'

'So it's Spanish wool, then?'

'They don't need it anymore,' the Irishman said, as he walked slightly ahead of Lock.

Lock paused, emptied his hands and began to swap the clothes. An initial sense of relief to be dry in his core was soon replaced by an incessant desire to itch, but it was at least better than shivering. For the moment.

'Thank you. For everything, Flynn. I was wrong about you. I fear I... misjudged you.'

Flynn held up a hand as he walked. 'Let's not forget why I'm here. As soon as I get my pardon I'll be free of these people for good. Let's get to Vere.'

Lock smiled, and gestured at a distant structure. Its details were difficult to make out in the dark, but the presence of faint light hanging above it suggested that it was a moderate sized fortress town.

'Frankenthal,' Flynn said with a sigh of relief. 'At long last.' He looked behind them once again, and nodded at the largely empty landscape. 'The Spanish came through here about a year ago. I was with them at the time.'

'Is that when you met Walter?' Lock found that his skin had already begun to complain at the shirt. Flynn smirked when he saw him scratch.

'We stopped at that row of cottages. It was already afire. Walter was pleading with a soldier, saying his family were still inside, but the soldier couldn't understand him. With my bare bones of German, I was able to figure out what was happening.'

The Irishman paused for a moment, and glanced to a clump of trees. Their full limbs moved slightly in the gentle breeze. A rat scuttled somewhere behind them, but Lock didn't jump. He knew Flynn had the area scouted. He waited for the Irishman to finish the tale.

'We were too late to save his wife, but we did save Leo, just about.' Flynn exhaled. 'I later learned that she'd only been in that cottage because a Spanish captain had been raping her.'

'Captain Ricardo?'

Flynn winced, and then nodded, repelled by the thought. 'By that stage, I'd already started turning against the King of Spain. This was God's way of telling me I made the correct choice.'

'And that's when you found the men in the forest?'

Flynn glanced up at the sky. Much of the cloud cover had dissipated, and the shine of the young moon glinted off his moist eyes. 'Aye. Walter joined them soon after. He remembered me from saving Leo. Put a good word in for me. Helped me bring justice.'

'Why didn't you tell me, before we started throwing stones at their door?'

'I wasn't sure he still lived there, and I didn't recognise the kid who went in.'

'What of Walter's son, he mentioned him?'

Flynn shook his head. 'He was just a boy. He spat at an Italian officer, who decided to make an example of him. I wasn't there for that. Probably for the best. I would have blown my cover for sure.'

Lock didn't need to ask what happened next. 'Georg von Salm. He seemed really to respect you.'

Flynn adjusted his belt as he walked. 'I don't know about that. I never understood how these men keep going when they lose everything. A desire for revenge is probably the most potent force outside of the divine.'

'He has much to want revenge for?'

Flynn paused. 'Look at me, giving away the man's secrets. You can ask him yourself, I'm sure you'll have cause to meet again.'

'I hope not,' Lock said, with a speed that caused Flynn to grin.

'He's not so bad. A bit prickly, granted. If he didn't like you, you wouldn't have left that forest in one piece.'

'We made a deal. We broke bread. Surely they must honour such things?'

Flynn scoffed. 'Honour loses some of its lustre when the other side has none.'

'The Spanish? Father always taught me that the King of Spain was a devout, honourable monarch. A bit wasteful and indolent, perhaps, but not dishonourable.'

The Irishman turned and then side-stepped a rabbit hole. 'Your Father was likely right, but the Kings of Spain don't have eyes everywhere, Lock. Nor does Diego de la Barca. That swine drank the discipline of his army away. You saw him in action. He's like that all day and all night. Some of his own officers even contemplated a coup as a last resort.'

'I confess I was surprised by his state.'

Flynn squinted dead ahead, to check the distance of Frankenthal's looming walls. Another few hundred feet still remained. 'The worst part of his command was the Inquisitor.'

'The Inquisitor?'

'You heard the Strassers mention him? Balding man, a foot shorter than you. Stinks like death, or so they claim.'

'You've never seen him?'

'Oh, I've seen him Lock. But I haven't smelled him. Was too far away.'

'What did he do to build such a reputation?'

'Torture, mostly. He'd take Germans that had been acting out, or were just in the wrong place at the wrong time. Their screams and shrieks would echo throughout the camp, and all the way to the forest, I'm sure.'

'Gracious. What was the purpose of such barbarity?'

'To instil fear, Lock. Fear is the Inquisitor's weapon, though one hears rumours that he's also fearsomely well-connected man. I knew an Italian who swore that the Inquisitor took confession from the King of Spain himself.'

'So he's ordained? He's not just a brute?'

Flynn snorted. 'Don't let the cap and gown fool you, Lock. The Inquisition may be less common now, but plenty of demons remain in the wings, just waiting for an order to revert to their old methods.'

'Someone must give him orders. Where did he come from?'

'Depends whom you ask. I reckon he started his career in the Netherlands. The Spanish liked to send in the Inquisition many generations ago. That was part of the reason the Dutch rebelled.'

Lock snorted at the claim. '*Generations* ago? That is fantasy, Flynn. Such lengthy service would make the Inquisitor a ludicrously old man.' Lock pictured his grandfather in the throes of his life, hobbling around the Locksville estate at the ripe age of seventy-eight.

Flynn turned and looked Lock dead in the eye. 'They also say that he stays so youthful by absorbing the life force of his victims. They never do find their bodies.' He let the words hang in the air for a moment, before shrugging. 'But surely, that is fantasy as well.'

A shiver run over Lock's shoulders. 'Why would the Spanish engage with such evil forces?'

Flynn glanced ahead and nodded with satisfaction at the progress made. 'Never underestimate what a man will do to preserve or further his House, Lock. Remember, the Habsburgs were a family, same as you or I, at one stage. Now they own most of the known world. I can't fathom how they would rise so high without the aid of black magic.'

'Perhaps they're just fortunate in their marriages?'

'Perhaps. Though I've yet to meet a fortunate highborn spouse.'

'*Halt!*' a voice boomed in the darkness. 'Identify yourselves. Come no closer.'

At first Lock thought it could be the Spanish behind them, but Flynn's calm demeanour confirmed that, instead, it was a challenge from Frankenthal's gate. Perhaps one hundred feet ahead, the fortress loomed, like a stone mountain.

'We are here to see the commander.' Flynn said.

'You are... Spanish?' the guard replied.

'English,' Flynn yelled, wincing visibly. This was no time to be a stickler for details, though the claim was still wounding.

'And why should we let open the gates?'

'We have intelligence that will be of use.'

Lock glared at the Irishman, and he shrugged. In their conversation, the proper address for the guard at the gate had not been decided upon. What intelligence could they offer Sir Horace Vere? The commander would surely be interested in the existence of rebel forces in the forest, and of a militia in Mannheim, ready to set upon the Spanish garrison.

A curious silence followed.

'What if they don't let us in?' Lock whispered harshly.

'If the worst happens, we'll just tell him you're Vere's godson. That should send him running.'

'I don't particularly want that advertised. The garrison will think me privileged.'

'I hope they do, Lock. Your sense of privilege is part of the reason we've got this far.'

Lock decided to take that as a compliment, and, sure enough, activity could be heard on the gatehouse.

Some shouts rang out, and the turning of gears could be heard, followed by the grinding of steel on stone.

'Hands front, no sudden moves. You'll be watched at all times.' The announcement was accompanied by more mechanical grinding. Flynn beckoned at Lock, and the two resumed their walk, closing the gap between them and the gate. The area around the walls consisted of dead ground, which appeared to have been recently charred.

Lock squinted, and could just make out small dots of light atop the walls. Those were lit lines of match cord. Unlike the forest Germans, these English were not bluffing. They were willing to burn through as much of this cord as was necessary to drive their point home.

'Alright,' Flynn whispered. 'We're in. Let's see if your godfather is all he's cracked up to be.'

- CHAPTER TWENTY-THREE -

The assailant unfortunate enough to attack Frankenthal head on would have to pass three iron gates, with innumerable daunting kill slits awaiting them. Stains of black pitch could be seen where the searing hot substance had once been poured from above onto an attacker's scalp, and then burnt into the ground.

The night had given way to day, and in the beginnings of the sunrise, bright rays glinted off iron breastplates. As they walked closer, the sun crowned the top of its battlements, and Lock could see two men on a distant wall to the east. One appeared to be smoking a pipe. After a few more tentative steps, they were through the gateway and in Frankenthal's courtyard.

Lock half-jumped at an atrocious sound behind him. The final gate slid down three quarters of the way closed, before catching and screeching to a halt. The guard sighed and swore. He strolled to the problematic gate, and glared at the flaw.

Standing back a few paces, the guard then unsheathed a large hammer, and rehearsed an uppercut motion. After three rehearsals, the guard exhaled and struck forcefully against his iron foe. The gateway groaned, but the gate itself did not budge. The sound made Lock wince.

The Irishman whistled behind him, and Lock turned to take in the fortress town for the first time. It was dirty, shabby, and positively teeming with life.

'Well Gus, I made it this far,' Lock whispered, ignoring Flynn's quizzical expression.

'It's well bigger than I remembered, Lock.'

'Do you think Sir Horace Vere will see us?' Lock directed the question at the guard, who was preparing to strike his iron nemesis again. The guard turned his head to Lock as he rehearsed the familiar motion.

'Difficult to say lad, he hasn't seen many visitors in a while.' The vague answer seemed good enough for the guard, and he returned to his work, apparently forgetting his guests were even present.

Lock sighed in exasperation.

Flynn cleared his throat and pointed to a structure in the near distance, which rose above the other buildings on the skyline. This was surely the citadel, the town's only real building of note aside from the church.

'That's where Vere will be, Lock.'

Lock's eyes met the citadel, the last bastion of defence for Frankenthal. If the walls were breached, the citadel would be a final refuge against the invaders. The Englishmen in Frankenthal had not had to resort to these tactics yet, but they were still surrounded.

Flynn smirked. 'The guard did say we could come and go as we please.'

'I don't recall –'

'Doesn't matter Lock. All that matters is that we can *claim* we were given free reign of the place. By the time they find the right soldier to ask, we'll be out of sight. We only need to walk around long enough to put your plan into action anyway.'

'*A plan?*' Lock's stomach lurched when he recalled that he had indeed made the claim. But that plan had been formulated long before, when Lock had departed in haste from Frankfurt. After all he had seen, it now no longer seemed particularly viable, or sensible.

Flynn shook his head. 'You think nobody will wonder why two ratty looking urchins are wandering around? You said you had a plan.'

The stern challenge compelled Lock to swallow, before relenting. 'My plan was to ask Sir Horace Vere to open the gate.'

Flynn turned abruptly to face Lock, his mouth half agape. 'Why would the commander of the fortress greet you at its gate? Have you been to many fortresses that make use of that practice, Lock?'

Lock went quiet. He had not been to any fortresses, but he had expected Vere to meet him. The commander always met his guests at the gate. That was what always happened in Father's war stories, at least.

Lock blushed and turned away.

The Irishman looked at him expectantly, and then shook his head in exasperation. He rubbed the corners of his eyes with his right hand and sighed through his nose.

'Tell me, Lock. How well do you know this Vere character? Would he recognise you? Could we simply ask to be taken to him?'

Lock did not know. If Vere was not waiting at the gates of Frankenthal, then perhaps the upper echelons of fortress command were more exclusive than Father had implied.

'We could ask, I suppose, but all it takes is a soldier in a bad mood, and we will have no access to Vere at all.'

'God's guts, there's not a hope of me getting my pardon, is there?'

'I didn't say that.'

'Your whole body says it, Lock.'

'We will have to blend in if we wish to meet Vere.'

'And how do we do that?'

Lock stretched out his arms for dramatic effect. 'It is all about the act, Flynn. No doors are closed in a confident man's face.'

'And what if we're stopped?'

'We will simply say that we are here on the business of the King of England.'

Flynn winced again. 'Oof, Lock, I wouldn't mention his name within these walls. His Majesty isn't very popular for sending these men here and then abandoning them to their fate.'

'It worked for de la Barca,' Lock said weakly.

'Do you see any drunkards around here Lock? These men have been under siege for weeks. If Vere was as attached to the bottle as de la Barca, Frankenthal would be in Spanish hands by now.'

'Would you prefer that?'

'I must confess, after spending a few years in their ranks, I feel I understand the Spanish better than the English.'

'Being around all these Englishmen cannot be good for you then,' Lock said with a smile.

Flynn snorted. 'I haven't stayed alive this long by being honest. These louts don't have to know I wish them ill.'

Lock turned his gaze away from Flynn and back towards the citadel. The

Irishman hawked and spat on the ground. He was brainstorming in his own unique way.

'I've got it,' Flynn said. 'My name is Armand du Plessis, the Duc of Richelieu, and *you* are Alexandre François.'

'What is a *Duc of Richelieu*?' Lock turned the strange name over in his mouth, suspecting that the Irishman had probably invented it.

'That's *Richelieu*,' Flynn said, rolling his eyes, '*Rish-el-you*. I met him in France a few years ago. A remarkable man, and a man of God no less. Most in France have not heard his name, so I do doubt these Englishmen will know it. Today, *I* am Richelieu, and *I* am leading this Embassy into Frankenthal on behalf of His Majesty the King.'

'What Embassy?'

Flynn paused. 'A... fact-finding Embassy. In the name of King Louis XIII of France. We wish to inquire whether the fortress of Frankenthal is secure, and if not, whether its inhabitants wish to bargain for supplies.'

'Can I play the Duke?'

'Not with those boots, *Monsieur Francois*.'

Lock looked at his feet, and recalled sadly that his expensive leather hunting boots had been lost in the Rhine. His feet still chafed against the tight, unfamiliar footwear, but the sensation had been lost in a sea of other concerns.

The Irishman had a point. A Duke would never allow it to be said that his subordinate was better dressed than he. Flynn's attire may have been a bit rough around the edges, but it was still better than the garments Lock had begged and borrowed a few hours before. The wool shirt was itchy and abrasive on his skin.

Lock gestured to the guard, still working on the gate. 'Will he not think it odd that we suddenly change our allegiance?'

Flynn started walking and beckoned Lock to follow him. 'If we move quickly, we should be able to lose him. Remember, keep to your character. You speak *only* French, and you are proud of it.'

'And what of Vere? Once we reach his quarters, if your plan works, then what? Do we suddenly change character in his presence? Will Vere not take offence at our deception?' Lock genuinely did not know the answer. Depending on Vere's disposition, his godfather could either see the act as humorous or a grave insult.

'That's when you turn on the charm Lock,' Flynn grinned. 'That's when you play the helpless godson card.'

'*Helpless godson?*'

'I think it is a reasonable position. After all, does Vere know about your parents?'

His parents. Lock had momentarily forgotten, as though his heart and mind had yet to fully accept and internalise his new status. Lock shook his head. As far as he was aware, Vere did not know of his parents' demise.

'Well, there you go then. What godfather would turn his kin away when he hears such news? We will simply plead the urgency of our case.'

'It is a strong case,' Lock said hopefully.

'From what you have told me of Vere, and from what I know of the man myself, he will be perfectly willing to provide you with assistance, information, whatever you need, including...'

'Including the pardon for yourself, yes of course.'

'It is the only honourable thing to do, and Sir Horace Vere *is* an honourable man.'

Lock was not sure if Flynn had said so because it was true, or to reassure himself, but either way, it made him feel better. He was more concerned that his own shameful flight from The Hague might be learned of, but that was a crisis for another day.

He had to see Vere. The man was the only lead he had. If he ever wished to learn the truth of his parents' death and get justice, he would have to start somewhere.

It was time to change the subject.

'I dare say this Richelieu character is the closest you will get to a Dukedom,' Lock said, checking his belt to ensure his stiletto was still there.

'Let's hope so,' the Irishman replied with a scoff.

They turned a corner around a dilapidated house with peeling green paint. A dirt track continued steadily, before beginning an incline, and making for the outskirts of the citadel.

Flynn pointed to its upper levels, and Lock nodded, as the two men began the half mile walk to their destination. The familiar smells of soldiers and habitation filled Lock's nostrils as they moved closer to the bailey.

'So,' Flynn said in French. 'How do you like it, Monsieur Francois? This is the first German-made fortress you have seen in your many years serving France. What is your verdict on its structure and design?'

Lock grinned, but was quickly distracted.

A few paces ahead of them, a young girl with straggly blond hair pushed a small wagon with a loose wheel. Her younger sister, presumably, sat on the wagon, her face scrunched into a grimace to display the universal expression of pain.

The loose wheel predicably caught on a stone, and the straggly haired girl sighed, as her sister began to wail. Lock's eyes fixed on the pitiful sight. The two children were all bones, their bodies covered in rags.

Lock had seen poverty and starvation before, in some of the beggars that had darkened his Father's door, but not to this extent. He stopped to stare at them for a moment, before Flynn turned to wave at him, a glare building on his face.

'I want to help them,' Lock said in French, still staring at the backs of the girls' heads.

'Alexandre Francois does not help little girls,' Flynn said. 'He cares only for his King, and for... poetry.'

'*Poetry?*'

'Yes, Monsieur François, did I hear incorrectly, or did you attend that snooty school north of Paris?'

Lock flinched at the barb. 'Only as snooty as the school of entitlement you appear to have graduated from, *Your Excellency.*'

'Ah, but Monsieur, there is no education quite like being run out of your home, no?'

'I heard your home was a rundown shack of a thing, *Your Excellency*. Indeed, I heard you owed many years' worth of rent, and that your new tenants were more than entitled to evict you then and there.'

'All being well, Monsieur, we will be with your godfather shortly. Then, perhaps, Vere will be able to reveal something of the truth.'

Walking behind him, Lock only caught the corner of his expression. The Irishman seemed suddenly weary. Perhaps the reminder of home had been a low blow.

Lock sped up to walk beside him. Now they had passed the girls, but he could still hear them, the older sister trying to comfort the younger by promising they would find food soon. The tone of desperation in her

German revealed her lie. He half expected to see Lena, or for Walter to return, but in vain.

Here was another couple of orphans with empty bellies – a sight so common no one batted an eye.

Lock's attention was caught by a sudden cough to the left, and he turned to see a one-legged soldier glare at him from his front garden, if indeed it was his. A scantily dressed woman brushed past Lock with a giggle, and made for the one-legged soldier's house. Flynn whistled quietly.

'Monsieur, this Duke wishes to remind you that locals are strictly off limits. You must maintain your professionalism, your reputation and your honour, at all times. Recall, Monsieur, you are a married man.'

Lock shoved the Irishman's shoulder.

'*Oy!*'

'Just making sure it's still you in there,' Lock said, a smile playing across his mouth.

'It is most ignobly done to push a Duke, but Monsieur, I understand, it has been a long journey and tempers flare on occasion.' Flynn looked ahead, and sighed when he realised they had several yards to go. Frankenthal appeared to make him nervous.

'What if everything goes horribly wrong, *Your Excellency*?' Lock asked.

'Now, now Monsieur Francois, I was told you were an optimistic fellow. Where is your positive spirit?'

Lock knew where it had gone. He had abandoned it in The Hague when he had fled from his obligations. Flynn could never be allowed to know that.

They were only a few feet from the main gate of the citadel now. Flynn had really settled into his role as the Duc of Richelieu, but his confident swagger was drawing attention. Perhaps that was the whole point. Now within touching distance of the gate, with no guard in sight, Flynn cleared his throat before letting out an almighty volume of speech.

'Hello?' Flynn rapped his knuckles on the citadel's gate. 'I am here on the business of the King of France. Pray tell, gentlemen, do you abandon all your guests when they arrive? I wished to experience some famous English hospitality. Where is your commander, hmm? I wish to speak with him?'

The challenge echoed off the thick stone walls, turning several heads. Whispers of disgust reached them. Curses for the King of France were even offered. Perhaps all royalty was unpopular here. Lock scratched instinctively at the shirt.

Their plan was surely doomed.

Vere would condemn them for their deception, and curse Lock personally for his dishonour. Flynn dug an elbow into his ribs, as a soldier's silhouette loomed into view a few paces behind the closed citadel gate. Lock now cleared his throat and made an attempt of his own.

'Good morning gentlemen, His Excellency wishes to speak to your commander on the King's business. Please, open the gate and let us in.'

The soldier, bleary eyed and dressed in a ragtag combination of civilian and military garments, made his way to the gate.

'Pardon Sirs, do you speak English?' the soldier asked.

Lock was about to reply in the negative, when Flynn suddenly erupted into a rant.

'*English*? By God's holy relics, but who would speak such a vulgar tongue? I am a servant of the King of *France*! That is France, you fool, of the *French*! Why would I lower myself to your dialect? Do you treat all such servants so poorly in England? Let us in, and let us speak to your superior now.'

The soldier had been taken aback by the outburst, as had Lock, but it seemed to do the trick. He looked at Flynn sideways for a moment, and the Irishman raised his chin towards him in a fearless act of defiance.

'What is your name?' the soldier attempted to ask in broken French.

'You stand honoured in the presence of the Duke of Richelieu,' Flynn boomed, still adhering rigorously to French. He gestured to Lock, 'This is my servant, Monsieur Francois. He carries my notes and occasionally, he even makes himself useful.'

The soldier nodded, almost certainly clueless of what had just been said.

'*Well*?' Flynn said, and began tapping his foot.

The soldier began to shift on his feet. He looked at Lock, who forced himself to maintain a stoic composure. The soldier then looked to the left and right, before shrugging, and unlocking the gate.

The bulky mechanism swung slowly open, and Lock bowed slightly before walking in, with Flynn behind him. The soldier closed and locked the gate behind them.

'Thank... you,' Lock said the expression in English, feigning difficulty as he did so.

The soldier then nodded, and beckoned them to follow him. The courtyard of the citadel was small, and was crowded with barrels of various stocks. A large wagon overflowing with what appeared to be potatoes dominated one corner. Curiously, several piles of linen were balanced on a wooden crate. It appeared far too clean and new for the place it was in, almost gleaming white.

A stench hung over the place.

'Urgh!' Flynn exclaimed, 'such filth, this is no place for a Duke!' He dramatically pinched his nose.

The soldier winced as he walked, unsure of what the problem was, but certain that he was being blamed.

Flynn had not lied. The citadel was filthy. Lock's nostrils were filled with the smell of fresh blood. Three horses, their heads severed, lay unceremoniously to his left. The soldier made a sound of apology, though acknowledging it was a futile gesture. He then tried again with more gusto.

'Sorry for the state of the place... er... Excellency, we're down to our last rations. Forced to eat our own horses, such a terrible thing.'

Flynn scoffed at the English words.

It did not take long to reach the first door of importance. 'The commander is upstairs,' the soldier said, before turning to Lock and making the gesture of a man walking upstairs. Lock turned to Flynn and pretended to translate.

Flynn stood with his chest out and his eyes closed, as if taking in any more of Frankenthal's sights would do him permanent damage.

After Lock translated, the Irishman nodded and let out a spectacular sigh. He opened his eyes, and turned his whole body to the soldier, looking him straight in the eye.

Flynn held out his hand to the soldier. The soldier stayed still, so Flynn wriggled his hand and glared at him.

Now the soldier panicked.

Was this some new protocol?

He scanned the courtyard, and then got on his knees to kiss Flynn's knuckles.

Flynn grunted to himself with satisfaction. The soldier awkwardly rose back to his feet, and then scarpered back to the gate, eager to be clear of the arrogant Duke's presence.

'Poor lad.'

Flynn grinned at Lock. 'I would rather all of England kiss my feet, but I will settle for that gesture for now.'

'I suppose we go upstairs then?' Lock asked, though he wished the moment of truth could be delayed for a while longer.

Flynn nodded. 'This is it Lock, let's hope your godfather is a forgiving and friendly man.'

Lock grasped the brass handle and pulled open the heavy wood door. Its hinges creaked, and a winding grey stone staircase greeted them. The two walked in and closed the door behind them.

'How many steps did he say?' Flynn asked wearily.

'He didn't say, because you scared him away!'

Flynn chuckled, before walking to the first step and beginning the climb. 'Remember,' he said, turning his head to Lock, 'no English.'

- CHAPTER TWENTY-FOUR -

The staircase contained forty-two stone steps. Lock had counted as he climbed, a step behind Flynn. It was his least favourite number. One digit short of the forty-three steps necessary to complete the musket drill. It was the forty-third step, firing the weapon, that had sealed his fate.

'You ready?' Flynn asked, as they made their way down a featureless corridor, the odd candle flickering in a desperate quest to bring some warmth to the place.

'Yes,' Lock simply said.

'Let me do the talking. I have met Vere before, I may be able to find common ground with him.'

'And then what?'

'Well, Lock, if he seems amenable enough, then I will plead our case. If not, you interrupt the proceedings, bow low, and humbly present yourself as his godson. That is, if he does not recognise you first.'

Lock exhaled and touched his neck. *Sweating, again.*

The wool shirt felt as though it was pulling on his skin. Individual wool fibres poked into his armpits and lower back.

They rounded a corner, and there, before a large wood door, was a visibly bored looking guard.

'Time to go to work again,' Flynn whispered, before capturing the soldier's attention by outstretching his arms. The soldier snapped out of his daze and stood promptly to attention.

'Who goes there?'

Flynn feigned offence, and began his French language bombardment.

'I beg your pardon? I am the Duke of Richelieu, here on a mission from the King of France. Let us in, so we may speak to your commander.'

The soldier was taken aback by the French reply, but was less unsure of himself than the guard at the citadel's gate. He looked at the two men up and down for a moment, before sucking his teeth.

'Don't know what you're saying Sir, but I can't just let any old Frenchie in. Commander's busy.'

Flynn pretended not to understand, calling the soldier's bluff, and raising the stakes as he did so.

'In all my years of service, I have never been less impressed than with this reception. Soldiers like you deserve a good flogging. I have encountered *peasants* less insolent than you.'

The soldier stared blankly at Flynn, as if trying to work him out. The language barrier made him nervous, but he also weighed up the consequences of allowing an unauthorised visitor into the commander's quarters.

'How did you get in here?' the soldier challenged.

Flynn was about to launch another tirade, when Lock put his hand on the Irishman's shoulder. He stepped forward, and the soldier's gaze fell onto him.

Lock tried with all his might to resist the urge to itch, an urge which seemed to grow increasingly urgent with pressure. Lock pretended to meet the soldier halfway, and gave an imitation of broken English.

'My sorry... for my... master,' Lock began. The soldier's countenance changed to relief as some English words reached his ears. 'Authorisation... King Louis of France... Need to see your... superior.'

The soldier nodded in acknowledgement, but indicated that he was still not convinced.

'God's guts and God damn ye!' Flynn yelled in French, his deep tone reverberating off the stone walls. 'So help me, if you do not open this door...'

The wooden door was suddenly opened from the other side. A blond-haired head poked through the doorframe.

'What's all the bloody racket for Teddy?'

The soldier gestured in protest at the two false Frenchmen standing in front of him. The blond-haired man looked the two visitors up and down a few times.

'And who are they?'

'Frenchies, Sir, sent by the King himself,' the soldier called Teddy replied.

His eyes narrowed, and then he scoffed. 'Ah... let them in Ted.'

'Yes sir,' Teddy said. He offered a word of apology to Flynn, but the Irishman simply held up a hand in feigned disgust. Lock shrugged his shoulders at the soldier in apology, and followed Flynn in. The door closed behind them.

The two now stood in a sparsely equipped room with stone walls, a roaring fireplace, and some simple furniture. A plate of dark, charred meat rested on the table, but it was untouched.

Seated at the table with his back to them was a grey-haired figure, who scribbled furiously on a piece of parchment.

The blond-haired man walked to his side and whispered something in his ear. The grey-haired man sighed, before pushing out his chair, standing, and turning to face the two guests.

'*Shite,*' Flynn swore under his breath. '*That's not Vere.*'

It was a scenario which had not even occurred to Lock.

Father had said that Vere would lead the defence of the Elector Palatine's fortresses, and deny them to the Spanish. What he had not told Lock was that sometimes, command could be messy. Commanders became ill, or fatigued, or dead, and could be reassigned to a new posting.

'Gentlemen,' the blond-haired soldier said in French, 'You stand in the presence of our commander, Sir John Burroughs. I am Joseph Gage, his second in command. How may we assist?'

Flynn offered their names in return, and then did his best to appear unfazed. 'I was told,' he began in French, 'that the commander of Frankenthal was Sir Horace Vere. Is he dead?'

Lock held his breath in anticipation of the answer.

It did not help that the two men spoke only sparse French.

They looked at one another, before latching onto the name.

'One moment please,' Gage said.

He walked a few paces away, and began to engage in loud whispers with General Burroughs.

Lock now attempted to master the art of eavesdropping, while appearing to be confused at the language barrier. It was not an easy act. He glanced at Flynn, who had closed his eyes and stood fully erect, with his chin raised to the room once again.

The two soldiers were surprisingly careless with their conversation, though they had been assured that their guests could not understand a word they said.

'Should we send for a translator Sir?' Gage asked.

'Our translators are all dead Joseph,' Burroughs said. 'We will have to do our best with what we have. Perhaps they speak German?'

'What should we tell them about Vere?'

The hair on the back of Lock's neck rose up to meet the news.

Burroughs sighed. 'Tell them only what they need to know. Vere should be safe enough now.'

Lock resisted the urge to sigh in relief.

So Vere was alive?

Gage turned to the two guests, an apologetic expression on his face. Lock could not contain himself any longer.

'In German, if you prefer?' Lock said.

Sir John Burroughs' ears perked up and he turned to face Lock. Now he could get a good look at him. Burroughs was the shortest man in the room, probably late-forties, and in possession of a rough beard that had long outgrown its respectability.

This was a soldier concerned with more pressing matters though. Judging by the lines on his forehead and in the corners of his eyes, Lock suspected that Burroughs had been landed in it when Vere had decided to leave, although Vere's reasons for leaving remained unclear.

'You are very tall to be a diplomat, if you do not mind me saying,' Burroughs said, while maintaining eye contact with Lock. The commander's comment had not contained any hint of suspicion, just curiosity.

'I was told I was too tall to be a soldier,' Lock said with a bow, 'Too great a target behind the battlements, so they said.'

'I have many friends in France,' Burroughs said, turning his gaze now to Flynn, before walking a few paces back towards his desk. 'Never could master the language though. Remarkable that you Frenchmen can master both French and German at once. Now, pray tell, what can *I* do for the King of France?'

Lock hesitated when he realised that he did not know. By now, they were supposed to have made a judgement call about Vere's state of mind.

Lock did his best to play for time.

'It is His Majesty's... understanding that the English hold on Frankenthal is in a perilous state.'

Burroughs rankled at the suggestion, sufficiently veiled though it was, that he would not be able to discharge his duty and defend Frankenthal from the Spanish.

'You may assure His Majesty that although we are battered and abandoned by our own King, we will not give up the fight, nor will we allow the King of Bohemia's possessions to be stolen by Spain.'

The King of Bohemia.

Lock was suddenly transported to a conversation many years old. Then, Father had told him with a mixture of fascination and horror how a German Prince from the Rhine had decided to make a bid for the Bohemian Crown. This, Father explained, was an act of incendiary defiance against the Habsburg dynasty, who traditionally had made the Bohemian Crown their plaything.

Lock's mind had wandered, but he had recalled one important detail. Whoever wore the Bohemian Crown got to offer one of seven votes in support of the next candidate for Holy Roman Emperor.

The Holy Roman Emperor, or *Kaiser* to his German subjects, laid claim to a vast swathe of Western Europe. His authority stretched over all of Germany, portions of North Italy, the Netherlands, and even some principalities in the Balkans.

And so, Father explained, Emperor Ferdinand II of the House of Habsburg had gone to war to oppose Frederick's audacious act, and reclaim the Bohemian Crown. But Ferdinand had not marched alone.

The Spanish Habsburgs had surged up the Rhine and seized Frederick's possessions in support of their Austrian Habsburg cousins. Lock recalled Father's sparkling explanation like it had been yesterday, though much had changed since that conversation in Christmas 1619.

The Habsburgs had clearly triumphed in the interim, but Frederick had escaped, and remained a thorn in the Emperor's side. It was up to Sir John Burroughs, so it seemed, to ensure that Frederick's homeland did not entirely fall to the Spanish, and it was a responsibility which the commander evidently took incredibly seriously.

Sir John Burroughs cleared his throat in expectation. Lock snapped to attention and tried to add to the small talk.

'The Duke and I saw the horsemeat in the courtyard. Do tell, Sir, how many more weeks of food do you have?' Lock said. He surprised himself with his directness of speech.

Burroughs titled his head to the right, and scratched at his itchy greying beard.

'Six weeks, if we're lucky, Monsieur François.'

'Will Vere be returning before that time with reinforcements, or with more supplies?'

'Word must have gotten out about Vere, or these two wouldn't keep asking questions,' Gage said in English.

Burroughs looked at his blond-haired subordinate, and exhaled.

'Sir Horace Vere commanded this garrison for several months,' Burroughs offered, 'but he has since become engaged with a private errand. I am in command now, have been for a week.'

A private errand?

This only made Lock more curious. Why did Burroughs and Gage insist on being so cagey? Had Vere made them swear an oath of secrecy?

'Very well,' Lock began.

What could he offer Sir John Burroughs?

And then, the thought arrived. It was not a plan, it was barely an idea, but it was something. Lock had seen the Spanish camp. He had met with Diego de la Barca, Burroughs' counterpart. He had real experience of the dilapidated Spanish defences at Mannheim. He had learned of de la Barca's scattered and divided army, and their difficulties in searching for he and Flynn.

What Lock could offer was not the vague promise of reinforcements or supplies, but somewhat far greater. Accurate, actionable intelligence about an opportunity to restore English honour and fortunes on the Rhine, push the Spanish back, and fill the soldiers' bellies in the process.

Sir John Burroughs' gaze now shifted, and he now paced slowly around the room. Etiquette required that the commander give his guests some time to speak, particularly when a language barrier made matters difficult. As soon as Lock shattered the illusion though, he and the Irishman would be on trial. The only thing that would save them was Burrough's sense of honour, and the fact that Lock knew details which the commander would find useful.

'Before I speak any further,' Lock began, 'I must request your cooperation and patience. What I am about to tell you is incredibly sensitive information, not to be given lightly.'

Burroughs turned back to face Lock. Gage also turned to face him. Flynn turned his head slightly. Somehow, the Irishman managed to glare at him out of the corner of his eye. It was as though he could sense that Lock had determined to blow their cover. Lock exhaled, before switching abruptly to English.

'Gentlemen, I am afraid my companion and I have not been completely honest.'

The faces of the two soldiers darkened.

Lock dared not look at Flynn. He did his utmost not to panic.

'My name is Matthew Lock. With me is Flynn O'Toole. I came to Frankenthal to find Vere, as he was a friend of my parents, who were recently... brutally murdered... in The Hague.'

Burroughs and Gage looked at one another, their expressions now slightly lightened. A look of bewilderment had begun to set in, and into this silence, Lock spoke again.

'Please, gentlemen, I wish to speak with Vere, to see if he knows anything about what happened to my parents. He is my godfather, you understand. If you can tell me where Vere went, then in return, I will tell you all I have learned about Spanish defences at Mannheim, and the state of Diego de la Barca's army.'

The offer hung in the air.

'So you *do* speak English,' Gage said at last, before gesturing to the door. 'Poor Teddy will never live this down.'

Lock nodded slowly.

Flynn remained silent.

Burroughs had resumed pacing, though the room was so small that he only took a handful of strides before turning about on his heel and starting again. He had yet to look Lock in the eye since the news had been delivered.

'Do we have a deal, Sir?' Lock asked. The itch had now peaked, and Lock's eyes watered slightly.

'No, we do not have a *deal*, Matthew Lock,' Burroughs hissed. The commander now abandoned his pacing, and marched to within a few inches of his guests. His face was full of venom.

'You come into *my* home, you lie and deceive your way past *my* men – each of whom will be disciplined, by the way – and now, you stand here as if I *owe* you something.'

Gage coughed, and gave his commander a knowing look. Despite the outburst and anger, something Lock said had resonated with them. There was something the two were not saying.

'Are you Matthew Lock? *Are you really?*' Gage asked, a solemn expression on his face.

'Yes... I am Matthew Lock, son of Charles Lock and Catherine Lock, recently murdered in The Hague.'

Gage's eyes narrowed. Burroughs whispered something in his ear, and Gage nodded knowingly.

A rage began rising in Lock's blood. How could they leave him guessing like this? The mystery had become intolerable.

'Listen to me, the bastards that did this had masks, *black masks*. The same black masks I saw when they came to my home and killed my brother nine years ago.' Lock heaved in a deep breath before staring Burroughs dead in the eyes. '*Is that good enough for you gentlemen?*'

Flynn's head turned abruptly towards Lock. This was new information. Lock had not told the Irishman about James' fate when in the dark of Herman's cart. Flynn now seemed deep in thought.

Burroughs' face remained contorted, but the fact that he had yet to call for Teddy suggested he had been convinced.

'It *is* him,' Gage whispered.

Burroughs nodded, exhaled, and then gestured at two basic looking chairs that were tucked into the table. He then walked a few paces over to the window, a small hole in the wall with a few bars laden across. A light breeze lifted a portion of Burroughs' overgrown hair, and he swept it aggressively behind his ear. He turned back to face his two guests, a smile now playing across his face.

'Alright,' Burroughs said, before turning to face his guests. 'Vere is never going to believe this. Sit down gentlemen. First, we eat.'

- CHAPTER TWENTY-FIVE -

H orsemeat and potatoes made an unorthodox breakfast, but Lock did not dare reveal his fussy side.

Perhaps Burroughs longed for conversations that did not concern the fate of Frankenthal, the state of his men, or the shortages of food. The meagre meal of horsemeat and potatoes, Burroughs said, had been the only thing available for the last week.

'When Vere left, he seemed to take all the good food with him,' Gage had joked.

Lock was eager to bring the conversation back to Vere, and back to the possibility of making some arrangement, but it took nearly half an hour for the two soldiers to properly attend to the subject.

Burroughs exhaled. 'Lock, I will make you a deal, but you must first hear *my* terms.'

Lock sat upright in attention, and slyly scratched at his woollen shirt. 'What terms?'

The commander cleared his throat. 'Listen to my proposal. If you agree, then, and only then, will I tell you what I know to be true about Sir Horace Vere.' There was a strange glint in Burroughs' eye that Lock picked up on.

'Forgive me, commander, does Vere know something about my parents?'

Burroughs sighed. 'I will tell you this much for free, Lock. Since last week, Vere has been looking for you, and his need to find you was powerful enough that it took him away from his duties here.'

Lock's eyes widened.

So his godfather *did* know about him. He was not alone after all. There was hope for his mission. He was not going to fail again. Lock eyes moistened, and he looked down at the table to cover his shame.

Burroughs did not wait for a response. He continued with his pitch. 'From what we know about de la Barca, he has about two thousand men in the area. He also stands ready to receive reinforcements from General Cordoba.'

'Eighteen hundred,' Flynn corrected. 'A few have deserted or died from disease. And don't worry about Cordoba. The two Spaniards despise each other. De la Barca's pride will prevent him from asking for help, unless he's in a truly desperate state.'

Burroughs' greyed eyebrows raised with curiosity. 'Interesting, it seems the Spaniard is in an even more perilous position than I had imagined.' The commander's eyes then narrowed at Flynn. 'But why would you tell us this, Irishman. They told me that Flynn O'Toole does not like us English.'

Lock glanced inquisitively at Flynn, who ignored him.

Flynn scooped up a piece of undercooked potato with his knife, before taking a piece of charred horsemeat between his fingers. He slipped both morsels into his mouth at once, and chewed leisurely. He was the only one of the four still eating.

'I see my reputation precedes me,' Flynn said, a smile playing in the left corner of his mouth.

'I was told to send you straight to the gallows when I found you,' Burroughs replied, his smile a shade darker.

'But?'

'But... I would be a fool to follow such orders, particularly when we have an opportunity to shatter de la Barca, and achieve honour and glory for ourselves.'

'And plunder, and food...' Gage reminded him.

'Yes, yes of course,' Burroughs said. 'Do you have some kind of connection to Matthew Lock? What is a wanted Irishman doing in such company?'

Lock jumped slightly in his seat and glared at Flynn. *Wanted*? How long did Flynn intend on keeping *that* a secret? And wanted *by whom*?

'He saved my life twice,' Flynn said. 'I have only saved his once, so I owe Mr Lock one more life.'

'You are bound by honour then,' Burroughs said, matter-of-factly.

'Yes Sir, I am.'

This was not true, but Lock did not say so. Flynn had rescued him once before when he had massacred Gaston Phillipe, and then again from the river when Lock had nearly drowned.

The two men were even on that score, and Flynn was not bound by any oaths or obligations. He could have gone to France, as he had originally intended to, but instead he had followed Lock to Frankenthal after all.

But why? Why had Flynn stayed behind?

There had been the hope of a pardon, but this was never guaranteed. Had the Irishman stayed because he wanted to help, or because their close scrapes had caused an unspoken bond to develop?

But why not verbalise this bond to Burroughs now? The commander, of all people, would surely understand how men grew closer during wartime.

Lock's face now itched in tandem with his wool shirt. He was not used to stubble, though he was now surrounded by dirty beards of varying length. Flynn glanced at Lock, who pretended not to notice. It was time to return to the matter at hand.

'De la Barca's defences are vulnerable,' Lock said. 'If you tell me what I want to know, I can share my intel.'

Burroughs leaned back in his rough wooden chair. 'We need to recon the area. We need more information before we plan any attack.'

As if on cue, Lock produced the sketch of the inside of Mannheim that the Strassers had provided. He placed it on the table. 'This will help you plan your attack on Mannheim,' Lock said. 'Do we have a deal, Sir?'

Burroughs shook his head. 'I am sorry Lock, but if I act on this intelligence, you must be there when I do. Otherwise, you could have brought me a sketch of your own home for all I know.'

Lock scoffed. It was impossible to believe he had come all this way for nothing. Something – whether it was his itchy woollen shirt, Flynn's deception, or the rubbish food – made him abruptly stand up out of his chair. Its legs scraped off the stone floor. He then snatched the map back from the table. The other three men sat back in surprise.

'Sir John, I do not appreciate the suggestion that I would deliberately mislead one of the King's men. If my word is not sufficient to finalise the agreement, then perhaps Mr O'Toole and I should take our leave.'

Flynn looked at Lock sideways, unsure of what to make of the act.

'Please, Lock, let's not get too hasty. You have not heard my full offer quite yet,' Burroughs said, as he held up a hand to calm the tension. Burroughs' lazy tone suggested that his two guests would not leave without his express permission.

Lock paused, before walking to the wall and leaning against it. It was important to display some semblance of independence. 'Very well, I am all ears. *Sir.*'

Burroughs clasped his hands together. 'Excellent. You see gentlemen, my problem is a lack of security. Even if we seize Mannheim in a blaze of glory, and send Englishmen back over the Rhine, we would be in danger.'

'Because half of de la Barca's army isn't in Mannheim, it's encamped on the other side of the forest,' Flynn said.

'Exactly,' Burroughs clicked his fingers. 'So long as de la Barca's army remains encamped on the other side of the forest, my men will never truly be safe. We would lose men taking Mannheim, and then be in no fit state to defend ourselves when de la Barca returned for vengeance. We would lose Mannheim and Frankenthal, and I would be disgraced.'

'I understand.'

'Therefore, my terms are as follows. First, you will hand over that map of yours Lock. You have my word that it will be put to very good use.'

Lock looked askance at Flynn, who nodded. Lock walked forward and placed the little map on the table.

'Ah, most excellent,' Burroughs said, as he reached for the map with his right hand. He turned it over, and traced some of the details with his index finger. 'This is the handiwork of Theo Strasser, if I am not mistaken.'

Lock could not resist an uneasy glance at Flynn.

'Oh, come now gentlemen,' Burroughs said, 'it is *my job* to know everyone in Mannheim that could be of use. The Strasser brothers have been the most useful of all. True German patriots those two, and they make excellent garlic sausage as well.'

Gage coughed, and Burroughs acknowledged the hint to get to the point.

'In any case, they are master sausage makers, but they are also master smugglers. As usual, Herman Strasser will make his rounds later this afternoon. When he drives that wagon back into Mannheim, it will, shall we say, be a good deal heavier than when he left.'

Lock felt a sense of dread at being in that dark, sweaty, meaty space again. Burroughs nodded at Gage, who suddenly called for the soldier outside the door to enter. The door opened, and the soldier, his expression now a scowl, entered the room.

'Ah, Teddy, thank you,' Gage said. He picked up the map and held it towards the soldier with an outstretched hand. Harry obediently walked over, took the map, and looked at it briefly.

'Memorise that map if you have to lad,' Gage said. 'And find yourself a partner. You're going to Mannheim, courtesy of our favourite butchers.'

Teddy saluted. 'Will I actually get some sausage this time Sir?' he asked with a slight grin.

'There'll be as much sausage as you could ever eat if this works. Go find a mate you can trust, and I will come find you in an hour. We'll talk more then.'

Teddy did not acknowledge the two guests who had once been French. He turned on his heels and marched out of the room, the door closing behind him.

'Sorry about the intrusion lads,' Gage said. 'My nephew has been nagging me for weeks to send him away from this place. Now he finally has his wish!'

Lock sighed in relief.

But if they were not to be smuggled into Mannheim again, what did Burroughs need them for?

'This is a plan we have been waiting to put into motion for quite some time now gentlemen,' Burroughs said. 'In the last few days, matters have become more, shall we say, urgent. And then you both arrive, and I would say that Our Lord is watching over me now.'

Flynn scoffed, and Gage shot him a weak glare.

'We know the Spanish are stretched thin, but we are thinner still. Our walls keep the Spanish out, but they also keep us in. Without any advancement, we are all bound to be forced out of here eventually. But what if it was possible to hold on, and even be resupplied? What if it was possible to take Mannheim back, and to destroy what remained of de la Barca's army?'

'If you did that, I'd knight you again myself,' Flynn said.

Gage gave him a stronger glare this time, but Burroughs just chuckled.

'Indeed Flynn, had you told me such a thing was possible, I would have ordered you burned at the stake. Witchcraft, surely! There could be no other explanation. But then you two came along...'

'This one isn't a soldier,' Flynn said, gesturing to Lock.

Lock's face reddened, and he pretended not to notice.

'Oh, we are aware of that,' Burroughs said. 'But we need you two to fight a battle of a different kind.'

Flynn now scoffed. 'Sir, with respect, we are only two men. What difference could we make when de la Barca returns?'

Burroughs held up a hand. 'You are correct, O'Toole, two men would not make a substantial difference. But, I have it on good authority that you have made some allies of your own.'

Flynn titled his head back. He was clearly caught by surprise. Gage in particular seemed to relish the sight.

'*How do you know about that?*' the Irishman asked.

Gage did not wait long to dispel the mystery. 'We regularly send men out to treat with the Germans in the forest. They give us information on the Spanish, and we give them weapons.'

'I see.'

'We learned that there was a major disturbance in the forest yesterday afternoon. Bloody business. I believe a certain Gaston Phillipe met his end in the encounter, apparently at the hands of an Irishman and his tall English friend,' Gage turned to Lock as he finished the sentence.

Flynn smiled wryly.

'We were not *certain* it was you, considering your reported company. You had us quite fooled with your French act, most impressive. However, now that you have presented yourselves before me, I cannot help but feel God to be at work.' Burroughs' tired face seemed energised, as though the veteran commander finally saw a way out of his predicament.

'I do not understand Sir,' Lock said, 'Are you asking us to meet those Germans, to fight with them? You want us to meet with that German, von Salm? Even with him and his six or so friends, we would still not be a match for the Spanish.'

Burroughs scoffed. 'I am not suggesting you meet the Spaniards outside Mannheim's walls. I do not intend to ever let de la Barca get that far. Instead, you will liaise with your German friends, and ambush the Spanish column in the forest. Flynn is the only one those Germans will trust. Georg von Salm is a hard man to get on your side, but the Irishman has managed it.'

Flynn said nothing.

'Von Salm owes you, and now is the time to collect, Irishman,' Burroughs said sternly.

'You want us eight men to launch an ambush against a group hundreds of times our number?' Lock could hardly believe what he was hearing, and then Flynn cleared his throat.

'There's more than eight men,' Flynn said. He shook his head briskly, as though embarrassed by Lock's confusion. 'I *did* tell you that de la Barca displaced a whole village to make way for his camp.'

Lock's eyes widened. *'There's a whole village living in that forest?'* The deduction was obvious, but he'd been unable to imagine it before.

Flynn nodded. 'About five hundred people, including the ones you saw. I would say about half that would be fighters, but more will fight if you explain the stakes.'

'Could two hundred and fifty men really hope to achieve anything by ambushing a thousand men in a forest?' Lock asked.

Burroughs smiled. 'Well Lock, if your friend's calculations are correct, then you will only be facing nine hundred of de la Barca's men. I will also supply some of my best men for the task.'

Gage made an enthusiastic contribution. 'That puts you at three hundred men. A third of de la Barca's number. A perfect ratio for an effective ambush, I would think.'

'Do you really believe de la Barca would march into the forest? Drunkard though he is, he is no fool.'

A crooked smile grew on Gage's thin lips. 'According to my sources, O'Toole, de la Barca struggles with the tragedy that befell his son, and has taken to the bottle with a renewed enthusiasm.'

Lock was sorry for the grieving Father, but still daydreamed about choking the son. That act of violence had been one of the most satisfying outbursts he'd had in recent memory. That, and outmatching the arrogant Italian with his sword.

His arms ached from the sudden surge of energy which had rushed through his body. Pain had been only temporary, and the sense of power made it more than worth it.

Is this what war felt like? Perhaps he had misjudged its allure.

Burroughs then intervened. 'We may have to play some mind games to send him truly over the edge.'

'Go on,' Flynn said, leaning back in his chair.

'We know his son's dismembered body was safely packed away before the Father could see it. However, we also know where the coffin now rests.'

'Fascinating,' Flynn said with a smirk.

The three men smiled knowingly at one another and Lock just stared at them. Either he had gotten completely the wrong end of the stick in that conversation, or he and Flynn had just agreed to scatter Gaston Phillipe's body parts around the camp.

Lock looked at Flynn.

There was a new sparkle in the Irishman's eye.

'So, we are settled then, gentlemen?' Burroughs said.

Lock was still speechless. He prepared to protest, when the Irishman surprised him by speaking first.

'What if we said no?' Flynn asked.

Burroughs' expression grew more serious. For the first time, the hint of a short white scar began to appear under his left eye. The commander's stare pierced through Flynn, although the Irishman maintained his composure. Droplets of sweat ran down Lock's back, and he offered another sly scratch.

'Flynn O'Toole, you have two choices. You can agree, and you will receive the information that you seek. Or, you can enjoy the finest hospitality Frankenthal has to offer.'

Flynn scoffed. 'So, it's suicide or the dungeon, then?'

'Well, you have travelled under false pretences. You have forged and taken advantage of the King's documents. You have also been identified as a suspect in Gaston Phillipe's murder, and we must concede what our *Spanish allies* wish, must we not?'

The hint of the white scar grew more prominent as the commander spat out the words. A fierceness possessed Burroughs' face. Thanks to Father's wine-fuelled ramblings over Locksville's roaring fire, Lock understood why. Sir John Burroughs was a victim of his King's indecision.

Although it had sent many thousands of soldiers to Germany, England had not technically declared war on Spain. King James maintained this awkward balancing act so that the façade of Anglo-Spanish friendship, and even the possibility of an Anglo-Spanish marital alliance, could both be preserved.

Fulfilling the role of honourable peacemaker of Europe was the King's dream. On occasion, his subjects benefited from it. In 1609, Charles Lock had helped mediate peace between the Spanish and Dutch. It was only a twelve years' truce, but it still covered the Stuart King in sufficient glory for him to gift the Locksville estate to Lock's Father. Indeed, the King's fondness for peacemaking had effectively made the Lock family name, yet that same fondness now cast Sir John Burroughs aside.

'His Majesty has decided that this venture on the Rhine is no longer worthy of his time or money. But, as surely as honour moved him to send me here two years ago, honour now compels me to stay.'

'Why did you come here in the first place?' Flynn challenged. 'Were you not aware His Majesty lacked the stomach to fight?'

Burroughs tilted his chin at Flynn, and the white scar burned brightly, the eye above it suddenly bloodshot. 'I was. To a degree. Who could have imagined that he would abandon his men so quickly? He surpassed even my cynical expectations, I am afraid to say.'

'Yet you serve him.'

'I am one of the King's men, Flynn. I have a reputation to uphold. I also have men to protect. Now that you're here, I finally have the opportunity to fix some of our immediate problems, and to cover the endeavour in glory.'

Flynn seemed to weigh up the commander's stance, but after a few seconds he shook his head. 'You pull on my heartstrings, commander, but I'll take the dungeon. I'll only be there about a month, before the Spanish take this place, and then I'll be free.'

'You'll be marched from this dungeon to the gallows if they find you. It won't be difficult to make your guilt stick for Phillipe's death.'

But Flynn just shrugged. 'I'll take my chances. Better that than to save His Majesty's doomed honour from itself.'

Lock exhaled and leant his back against the rough-cut stone wall. It was the perfect cover for scratching another wave of itching, but the gesture also drew Gage's attention.

'What do you think, Lock?' Gage asked.

Lock sighed. 'I am no soldier. I am, to be sure, not even officially a diplomat.'

Burroughs nodded. 'You have the training Lock, you even have the qualifications. What you need is the experience. This is how you get it.'

Lock could not hide his disgust. '*This is how*, is it? By scattering a man's body parts around so his Father can see them?'

'Sometimes God calls on us to do remarkable things,' Burroughs said.

'What if you underestimate de la Barca? What if he marches his men straight for Mannheim through the longer route, and ignores the forest altogether?'

'Well then, Lock, you will ride through that forest and ensure you reach us first to let us know. Marching that many men would take hours, many hours. Those Germans know the forest, they'll beat de la Barca to Mannheim, and we can dare the Spaniard to come and take the town again.'

'That's assuming your nephew doesn't die in his duty,' Flynn said acidly. The tone turned Gage's' mouth into a scowl, and the Irishman smiled at his work.

'Perhaps, we should just send you into de la Barca's camp?' Burroughs said, 'One look at you is enough to get any man's blood boiling.'

'And perhaps *I* should just ask around Frankenthal for Vere's whereabouts,' Flynn replied, 'I'm sure someone else knows where he's off to.'

Burroughs shook his head with satisfaction. 'That would be a stellar idea, O'Toole, except that Vere left in the dead of night, and made myself and Gage swear oaths to not tell a soul.'

'But you will break that oath for us?'

'You did not let me finish. Vere made us both swear an oath not to tell any man his location, unless that man was Matthew Lock himself.'

Lock's ears suddenly perked up. The conversation had run away from him again, yet here he was, inserted right back into it.

'Vere... he said those words? Truly?' Lock asked.

The itch seemed to have finally gone.

'Indeed, he did lad, by God I swear he did,' Burroughs' steely expression suggested it would be suicide to question his integrity.

Flynn shook his head. 'Regardless, I will not risk *my* neck for His Majesty's honour.'

Lock scowled at the back of Flynn's head. He did not come all this way for the resentful Irishman to deny him his mission.

Gage cleared his throat and nodded at Flynn. Burroughs paused, but then Gage's gaze intensified, and Burroughs sighed.

'My subordinate wishes you to know, O'Toole, that I have been authorised to grant you a pardon if you help us.'

'Authorised... by whom?' Flynn asked, his voice laced with a mixture of curiosity and, Lock though, hope.

'His Majesty is not a brave man,' Burroughs said daringly, 'But... he is sometimes a clever man.'

'What are you talking about?'

'Before sending us on our honourable expedition to the Rhine, His Majesty thought it wise to issue us with several letters of pardon. It seems he expected that certain... vagabonds would be attracted to enlist in our ranks.'

'Like moths to a flame,' Gage added unhelpfully.

'We have already welcomed several men, some of them were an even lower calibre of gentleman than yourself. In return for their enlistment, the letter of pardon absolves them of their past crimes, and entitles them to move freely in Britain.'

'And what of Ireland, Burroughs, what does His Majesty say of that?'

'Yes, yes, O'Toole, Ireland as well, so long as you leave those Scotsmen in Ulster alone.'

'So, what do you say Irishman?' Gage asked, evidently satisfied to possess some leverage.

Flynn put his chin in his hand, turning his gaze from Burroughs, to Gage and back to Burroughs again. Finally, in a surprisingly quiet voice, the Irishman spoke.

'If your bastard King says I can go home, then we will have a deal.'

Gage interjected, leading with his left index finger. 'No, not *your home*, Flynn, somewhere else in Ireland, perhaps?'

Flynn scoffed. 'That's what you don't get about us. Anywhere in Ireland is an Irishman's home.'

Gage rolled his eyes at the response. A smug smile spread across Burroughs' face.

'One more thing, Sir John,' Lock said. The interruption moved the three men to turn towards him. 'That pile of fresh linen that we saw in the courtyard.'

'Surplus. Perfectly useless,' Burroughs hissed. 'A donation from the Duke of Buckingham. Bastard knows how to toy with me.'

'I want it. I want it as part of our deal.'

Gage and Burroughs glanced sideways at each other. 'For what purpose, lad?'

'There's a family of Germans, roughly two miles south of this fortress. While your soldiers do not need the material, they have desperate want of it.'

Gage shook his head. 'Lock, your bleeding heart –'

'Sirs, I will not consent to the deal without the material.'

Burroughs made a gesture at Gage, who rolled his eyes and nodded. 'This is a curious hill to die upon Lock, but... as it is of no use to us now, we will send the linen down south if you wish.'

'You swear it?'

'Yes, I swear it. The Germans will... receive the linen, is that what you want?'

Lock smiled. 'Thank you General. The children thank you.'

Flynn then cleared his throat to speak. 'Since we are all agreed, let's discuss the bloody business then. How many men will you give me for the ambush?'

Burroughs suddenly let out a brief, but boisterous laugh. '*Give you*? Oh, my dear boy, you do not imagine I would allow an Irishman, or a self-professed non-soldier, to command such an important mission, do you?'

It was clear that Flynn *had* expected as much.

Burroughs shook his head. 'No, no, no. *I* will be there for the ambush. *I* will be in command. I have always enjoyed the ambush more than the assault. Much more interesting. This way I can keep track of both of you, and Gage will get to fight the city battle he has always wanted.'

Gage beamed with pride.

'You won't miss the sight of Mannheim falling?'

Burroughs smiled at Lock's ignorance. 'Miss it, Lock? *Miss it*? What makes you think I would miss that sight? Heavens no, I will be there. Once de la Barca's column is destroyed, we march back to Mannheim to watch the spectacle. If Gage requires it, it would also be useful to attack from both sides of the Rhine at once. But, if my calculations are correct, we should be at the outskirts of the forest just as Mannheim is returned to its rightful owners.'

'To the English?' Flynn scoffed.

Burroughs rolled his eyes. 'Such is the price of England's aid. The

Germans will, of course, find us to be better masters.'

'I'm still waiting to hear the outline of a plan, gentlemen.'

Burroughs nodded. 'Very well O'Toole, listen closely. We will head south in two hours. That should give us plenty of time to ride beyond the crossing into Mannheim. We'll hug the Rhine for... twelve miles, until we reach a designated point opposite the forest.'

'How will we get across the Rhine?' Flynn asked, throwing up his arms in protest as he did so.

'Calm down O'Toole, calm down. Do you not think we would have figured that out? Our German friends have promised to set down several ropes and small rafts on our side of the river. Then we cross the river, enter the forest, and look to make some allies.'

'Do they know we're coming?' Flynn asked, crossing his arms again for effect.

'Yes, yes,' Burroughs said. 'Georg von Salm also asked for the one who gave them the speech with the bread.' Burroughs turned to Lock. 'I assume they refer to you, Lock?'

Lock could hardly believe that the whole ordeal in the forest had only taken place the previous day. The hideous image of Georg von Salm's tongueless mouth returned vividly to his mind.

'Yes Sir,' he said.

'Ah, breaking bread and treating. We'll make a statesman out of you yet Lock!' Burroughs said, slapping his thigh as he did so.

'How many men? I want an exact number.'

Burroughs shook his head. 'Patience, Irishman. You may rest assured, we will have enough. Anyway, if all goes according to plan and the Spaniard is successfully provoked, then our numbers will matter less than his blundering.'

'Numbers always matter,' Flynn said warily.

'And that is why we waited for you to come to us, O'Toole,' Gage said. 'We need all the numbers we can get, and you're the only one around here who the Germans will trust.'

Burroughs smiled in the left corner of his mouth. 'Have you seen these Germans fight? That mob would tear those Spanish tercios to shreds.'

'A disorderly mob is no more an army than a heap of building materials is a house,' Lock said, almost to himself.

The three men turned their gaze towards him.

Lock shifted uncomfortably on his feet. 'Socrates said it, not me.'

Burroughs stood up, as if to indicate that the conversation was over. 'Gentlemen, we ride for the Rhine in just under two hours. Ready yourselves.'

Flynn stood up, and walked to the doorway where Lock was standing. He refrained from looking Lock in the eye.

'Flynn...', Lock said, as the Irishman brushed past him and went through the door.

The two English soldiers had seen the moment play out.

Burroughs whistled. 'Be careful with the Irishman, Lock. I would wager that Flynn O'Toole's own Mother doesn't know where he's been.'

- CHAPTER TWENTY-SIX -

The Rhine was a huge beast of a river. It flowed relentlessly from the Swiss mountains, churning millions of gallons of water northwards. It split into several powerful tributaries as it reached the Dutch border, before it finally emptied itself in the North Sea. The river cut a swathe through kingdoms, marking the boundaries of some states, and the first line of defences for others. Millions depended on its constant flow, from minor kingdoms to microstates. Tributaries snaked out from its main course like so many vital arteries, knitting water into the land, and land into life.

Lock had grown up entranced by the huge map of the European kingdoms which had graced Father's study. A favour from one of Charles Lock's cartographer friends, so it was said. It had been too painful to have a last look before he left for the continent. Father was meant to host a refresher course with him. Just one among many things that had to be missed.

How had Spain come to own the Netherlands? A young Matthew had asked.

The same way the Habsburg dynasty came to own the world, Father had replied – *through marriage.*

Father had been most interested in explaining how the Dutch had ingeniously used each of the Rhine's northern tributaries to create a formidable defence against the Spanish.

Father had even used the Rhine as a metaphor: 'Be constant, be unyielding, *be like the Rhine.*' Lock had measured its upper, middle and lower courses. He had even read a dreary pamphlet that had explained the varieties of fish in each section of the river's course. But there was nothing quite like seeing the real thing.

They had ridden south, parallel to the Rhine, always no more than a few feet from the water's edge. Their horses found footing on a dirt track which ran just off the main road, too close to the river for most travellers.

They had passed Mannheim at a distance an hour before, and there was no more than an hour left of the journey. The sheer extent of trunks and slopes revealed the size of the forest on the other side of the river. The place was huge, certainly large enough to fit a whole village.

A hard cough snapped him from his sightseeing.

'*Lock*! Hurry that horse along! Almost there now lad!'

The call had come from Sir John Burroughs. The commander had since been equipped with his military riding gear, and looked like a moving fortress. His polished breastplate harkened back to the medieval knights of yore, but while the armour might protect the commander against lances and swords, it would be easily pierced with a musket ball.

Burroughs claimed he could close on a musketeer before his enemy fired a shot; 'Then,' the commander had roared, 'it will be all over.' But they were unlikely to do much galloping in the forest. A forest ambush was a time for careful concealment, detailed deployment, several interlocking fields of fire, and infinite backup plans. Lock could only hope that Burroughs had read from the same handbook as he and Father.

Burroughs fixed Lock with a slight glare as he approached.

'Sorry Sir,' Lock said. He had been given a horse too small for his large bulk, and both he and the horse were panting as a consequence.

The commander had slowed to a trot, and flicked his wrist at a cloud of flies which he had nearly blundered into.

'You'll need to swap your horse lad,' Burroughs said, matter-of-factly, before chortling, 'Just how many potatoes *did* we feed you?'

'Trust me Sir,' Lock said, 'it wasn't the potatoes that did it. I've got my Father's build you see. He never could find a horse that fit him.'

In truth, Lock had hoped Burroughs had forgotten him.

The commander had engaged in an endless stream of conversation since they had left Frankenthal two hours before. No amount of yawning, or periods of awkward silence, had seemed to communicate the fact that Lock did not wish to talk to anyone. If he was going to go into battle for the first time, he wanted to be of sound mind first, and Burroughs' improbable war stories were far from helpful.

Burroughs did help on this occasion though. He whistled, and several of his riders slowed their horses, before turning to face their commander. The looks on their faces suggested that they also feared falling victim to another of Burroughs' war stories.

'Our envoy needs a bigger horse,' Burroughs said. 'Which one of you gangly lads want to donate to a good cause?' He gestured to Lock. 'This lad will wear poor Lucy out before we get to the crossing.'

The group of riders had mostly all stopped once their commander started talking, and a few now murmured as they decided who would make the trade. Lock had noticed from an early stage that even while they might sigh or grimace when waylaid with a war story, the men adored Burroughs, because he got down in the muck just like they did. He also was not afraid to think outside the box.

Case in point – dragging forty-nine of his best men on horseback twelve miles to the south, where they would, somehow, cross the rushing Rhine, and thereafter, gallop into glory. Gage had questioned whether bringing the horses was wise, since that had left him with barely twenty of the beasts for the assault on Mannheim.

But then, Burroughs had guaranteed that the sight of English cavalry rushing from the forest at the height of the ambush would be worth its weight in gold. '*It's so unexpected. It's brilliant tactics, Joseph, utterly brilliant I say!*' Lock had overheard the commander gush.

Perhaps Burroughs had convinced Joseph Gage, or perhaps he had only convinced himself, but Lock knew that the most dubious of all the men in the company was Flynn O'Toole. The Irishman's entire demeanour towards him had changed since meeting Burroughs and Gage.

Rather than search for the errant Irishman, in the two-hour pause before departing Frankenthal, Lock had taken the opportunity to grab some sleep. The cot he was assigned was even itchier than the woollen jumper he had used as a pillow. In between dozing, Lock had overheard Flynn request scouting duties during the four-hour journey.

Scouting would be a vital duty. Spanish patrols meant that Burroughs' party would have to go the scenic route, which took far longer than twelve miles of riding should. Yet, it was only reasonable to suspect that Flynn's sudden cold shoulder was connected to his desire to separate himself from the group.

Since departing Frankenthal, the Irishman had consistently been far ahead of them, though always still in sight. Lock's puny mount would never catch up with him, not that he really wished to. He did not know what he would ask the Irishman, or even if he should address the previous revelations.

Was it not a dangerous sign that the Irishman was wanted? Was it truly wise to associate with a figure who had such a shady past? This mattered less than the cold shoulder Flynn was suddenly presenting. Ever since the meeting with the two English soldiers, things had been different.

Lock swatted aggressively at the cloud of flies which had become bored with Burroughs.

A short, wiry soldier with red hair dismounted from his horse, and gingerly led his mount to beside Lock. The beast was a large one, perhaps a quarter bigger than Lock's. Burroughs smiled.

'That'll do nicely Benjy,' the commander said, and the soldier smiled and saluted, before gesturing at Lock to dismount.

'Take care of Suzy, Mister Lock,' the soldier said, before leading Lock's smaller mount away.

The soldiers did not seem to know what to make of Lock, but Lock did his best not to burden them. Burroughs had insisted on calling him 'the envoy' at every opportunity. 'They'll take you more seriously if you have a title, lad,' the commander had said.

Lock glanced ahead when dismounting. The Irishman continued to be far in front of them at all times. No matter. When they went on their grisly expedition to retrieve Gaston Phillipe's remains, the Irishman would have to talk to him then.

Lock put the palm of his hand gently against the side of the horse's neck. The whites of the beast's eyes turned abruptly to its new master. A phantom pain surged up the left arm that once been broken by the fall from a mount only slightly bigger than this one.

An irrepressible shudder passed through him. Burroughs either did not see it, or pretended not to notice. Lock performed the now familiar act, and hoisted himself onto the saddle. The horse protested slightly, as though realising it would now have a significantly more difficult journey ahead of it.

'Best horse-trading I've seen all day,' Burroughs said, before emitting a brief, bellowing laugh that startled his mount. The men had all stopped now, and their mounts began nibbling opportunistically at the rare clumps of grass. The area had once been a lush basin of fertile fields and ripe orchards, but it was now stripped bare, but for a few trees with jagged branches. The region was owned by '*some poxy Spaniard*,' according to Burroughs.

As if realising that the party had stopped, up ahead, the Irishman had slowed his mount down. Flynn controlled his horse as Arthur had done. Like he'd been born onto the saddle.

'Gentlemen,' Burroughs announced, 'We will arrive at our destination in less than an hour. From now onward, I want no noise. No talking, no laughing...'

'*What about another war story sir?*' one of the forty-nine men called, to barely audible groans, gasps and some giggles.

A flustered Burroughs turned his horse clumsily, before clearing his throat and riding forward into the mass of the men. They grouped loosely around him and began to trot.

'Very well gentlemen. I will fill you with one more tale of war before we fall silent. This is one of my favourites. The legend of the rebel and the princess. It was, in fact, no legend, as I will testify! Imagine if you will gentlemen, a love story forged in the fires of war...'

In his excitement to share, Burroughs had left Lock behind on his horse. The horse was larger and more agile than the last one, and would certainly be capable of catching up to Flynn. He watched Burroughs ride several paces forward, still spinning his yarn.

'*I deserve answers*,' Lock said, in barely a whisper. His mount seemed to agree. Lock lifted the reins and moved slightly to the right of the group, so that he would have free reign to gallop past them, and as he did so, the horse's muscles whirred into life.

Its hooves pounded onto the grass, then harder and then harder again. The wind began to rush loudly through Lock's hair, and as he passed the group of men, Burroughs called out 'Good lad, that's how you do it!'

But Lock did not look back. His eyes were fixed on the mysterious Irishman.

'*I deserve answers*,' Lock repeated, this time louder. He was closing in on Flynn, and the Irishman had not turned to check the party since their pace had resumed. The speed astonished Lock, and another worry began to creep in – that his overactive mount would gallop all the way to the source of the Rhine if he did not get it under control.

'*Woah, Suzy,*' Lock tugged gently on the reins, and the horse turned its head briefly to the left, before snapping itself out of the rush. His horse stopped just as Flynn turned around to see what the noise had been about. A look of confusion was replaced with one of surprise, and then recognition.

The chase was over. Barely ten feet now separated the two men. They were each well out of earshot of Burroughs' men, yet Lock rode closer. Flynn remained still. Now he was looking Lock in the eye, and Lock forced himself to repeat the phrase.

'I *deserve...* answers,' Lock panted, suddenly realising he was short of breath.

The left corner of the Irishman's mouth began to bunch up, as though Flynn was trying to work out some puzzle. He had definitely heard him, but he remained silent.

'*Flynn?*' Lock urged. 'There is something you are not telling me. I know it.'

The Irishman's face was defiant, as though he had all the time in the world.

'I confessed when you asked, now it is your turn. You owe me the same. It is the only honourable thing to do.'

The Irishman's outburst surprised Lock. '*Honourable?* God's guts Lock, I'd hoped you'd left your bloody honour in Frankenthal. I am not an honourable man, and if you're bothered by that fact, you are welcome to join your bastard friends for another war story.'

The Irishman then paused, and turned his head away, before abruptly turning it back to glare right at Lock. '*I don't owe you anything.*'

Flynn began to turn his horse.

Lock watched the act, as an anger began rising inside of him. The same anger that had driven him towards Gaston Phillipe. The same anger that was only satiated when his arms were around the brute's neck. The same anger that had driven him to rise to his feet and rush those bandits.

Lock aggressively pulled the reins, and the horse protested, but Lock forced it forward. '*Move, Suzy.*' His mount burst into a quick gallop, and Lock cut Flynn off by riding directly in front of him. The Irishman's horse reared slightly in surprise.

Flynn swore.

'It's my parents isn't it,' Lock said, and waited to gauge Flynn's reaction.

The Irishman's confusion told Lock he'd been wrong.

'*What*? I know nothing about that, and I don't like what you're implying.'

'Well then what is it Flynn, why have you been avoiding me? What are you so ashamed of?'

'What makes you think I'm ashamed?'

'I don't know Flynn, because I don't know what you've done.'

'And you never will, *Officer Lock*. Let me tell you something, it is hard enough to stay alive here without having to watch someone else's back. You waited all of five minutes to blow our cover back there, and now you've volunteered us for this scheme.'

'It worked out for you. You get your pardon.'

'But you didn't know that was on offer. And when you attacked those soldiers, you didn't know Herman would bring us into Mannheim. God sakes, must I spell it out? You're a liability, Lock. You let your temper rule you, and I don't want to associate myself with a gentleman who speaks honour one minute, only to be ruled by his fist in the next.'

'But, *Flynn*...'

'It is better this way. You will get your Vere, and I will get my pardon and go home to Ireland.'

'Where will you go?' Lock asked, hoping his voice wouldn't crack in despair.

'Anywhere,' Flynn said. 'Anywhere but the bloody Rhine, and anywhere there isn't bloody Englishmen telling me what to do.' With that, the Irishman flicked his spurs and his mount scrabbled before gaining traction on the dirt.

Lock's eyes fixed on the back of Flynn's horse, as the distance between them grew. Had he really been so inept? He had thought the Irishman ashamed of something in his own past, was it truly the case that he had been ashamed of *him*?

Flynn's tone and speech had been disarmingly cold.

Had the last twenty-four hours meant nothing?

Lock's stomach churned, the same wretched feeling that had stalked him since landing on the continent. A nervous hunger, a bottomless pit of angst. He sighed, then turned to see Burroughs catching up with him, his men behind him.

'I was just asking...' Lock began, but stopped as Burroughs held up a hand, his other hand holding the reins.

'Not to worry lad, we're just a few minutes short of our crossing now.' Burroughs pointed over his shoulder, and Lock turned and focused his eyes to towards the indicated direction. Lock could make out, perhaps half a mile into the distance, a bend in the river, and a few rocks poking through the water's surface.

'That's where we cross,' Burroughs said, and spurred his horse forward excitedly. His men caught up and passed Lock, some of them staring as they did so.

Suzy whinnied impatiently at the sight of her companions surging past, before pawing at the ground.

Lock sighed. 'Alright Suzy. Let's go to war.'

- CHAPTER TWENTY-SEVEN -

The Germans had been true to their word. A network of small wooden rafts, perhaps six in number, had been linked together with a thick rope of grasses made from reeds. The rafts had once enabled the Germans to graze their animals on the other side of the bank, Burroughs had explained. Now, a Spaniard owned the land where the villagers had once lived.

The crossing was bumpy, and Lock's body jerked as Suzy found her footing on the slippery lengths of wood. Finally, with a final lurch, Lock's mount completed the crossing. Lock patted the horse's neck and thanked it profusely. Suzy was more interested in foraging for any clumps of grass that the forest could offer. Lock let her graze for a moment as a reward.

Burroughs' men all crossed in good order, and the commander came last, accompanied by an enormous grin on his face. 'Wait until Joseph hears of this,' Burroughs laughed, 'A cavalry charge from the forest, he'll never believe such a thing!'

A single German waited for them a few paces away from the river's edge, and Burroughs talked with him. English words filtered back to him. Lock smiled. Burroughs lacked translators, so instead arranged to meet with a German who also spoke English. How industrious was this man? Gage's German had been the better of the two, and it was reassuring that Burroughs knew his limits.

The familiar sound of birds filled Lock's ears. A small clearing gave the men room to water their horses, now that the bulk of the danger had passed. Lock no longer heard the river, after hearing it rush beside him for so many hours. On Burroughs' orders, the men moved from the water's edge, and rambled along a narrow dirt track in single-file, before dismounting in a more secluded spot.

They were in a different world now. Once the canopy began to close in, and the sunlight gave way to shade, Lock was transported to yesterday's incident, where he had met the Irishman for the first time. He could not see Flynn, but it was safe to assume the Irishman had been recognised, and was already toasting Georg von Salm.

Burroughs' men milled around in the small space, before some dismounted, and others tended to their firearms. It would certainly be difficult to move horses through this terrain. They rested at the bottom of a steep incline. Lock imagined they were at the bottom of the incline which he had debated hurling himself down only the previous day. An insect buzzed near his ear, and Lock flicked at it without thinking. There was a calming silence to the place, notwithstanding the murder that was soon to transpire here.

Lock heard the German agreeing to take them to the village, and he then heard Burroughs bring his hands together in glee. The commander had a brief word with the German, before signalling to his men to gather around him. Lock now spied Flynn. The Irishman had been watering his horse, and stood a few feet from Burroughs, with his left arm on his mount's saddle. No voices were heard from the men. It was vital that absolute silence was maintained.

'Our friend has agreed to show us the way to his home. Remember, gentlemen, absolutely no sound. Remember also, that we are guests in Herr von Salm's company. Do not do a disservice to your reputations, or I will make sure your disgrace follows you all the way home. Do you all understand?'

The men confirmed their agreement with nods and whispers. The lone German uttered a word of caution to Burroughs about the horses, and the commander replied in a mixture of German and English that the payoff would be worth the initial effort of dragging the horses through the dense forest.

The lone German was on foot, and fifty men could only travel so quickly in single file, but the journey was not far. After half an hour of walking pace, the German signalled for Burroughs' party to stop. He walked three paces forward, before kneeling, and bringing his head level with the ground. The German put his hand up as he did so, before lowering it, as if to indicate that the way forward was safe.

'Checking for traps,' Burroughs muttered behind him. 'I've heard that these Germans can skewer a man with some of the contraptions they build in here. Perhaps they'll let us borrow some.'

The German then sprang back up, and walked to a stump that was as high as his waist. The German felt around the base of the stump, before producing a round stone. The stone was rapped off the side of the tree stump three times, before a few seconds passed, and the German did it again, and then again.

Burroughs' men looked at one another uneasily, but the commander's expression remained flushed with excitement. A few coughs from further down the line could be heard, but the party had maintained silence with remarkable professionalism. Burroughs hadn't lied when he had claimed they were his best. Lock was near the front, a few horses behind Burroughs, and he spied Flynn about ten horses behind him. The Irishman did not make eye contact.

A few seconds passed, and Lock's eyes moved to a bush in the near distance, before a sense of panic gripped him, as the bush began to move. Audible gasps could be heard from Burroughs men, as all along their line, jovial, smiling figures began to emerge from the forest.

'Not to worry gentlemen,' Burroughs offered, a bit louder for those in the rear of the column. 'It seems our German friends wish to show off.'

It was, at least, a brilliant demonstration of how to launch an ambush. Burroughs might claim that he had let the Germans away with it, but the commander's men had been totally at the mercy of these Germans. Just how long had they been watching them for?

The challenge would be to compel de la Barca to enter this killing field. Lock then recalled the grisly errand he would soon be sent on. Squeezing past some of his soldiers, Burroughs' horse sidled up beside Lock. Burroughs used his left hand to batter some branches out of his way as he did so.

'Are you and the Irishman ready?' Burroughs asked.

'I suppose so,' Lock said, 'What do we have to do?'

'You two are the only ones who've been in the inside of the camp, and I reckon Flynn knows it inside out. Getting Phillipe's parts is the main thing. Won't be easy. But it so happens you're in luck lad, the Spanish haven't buried the body yet, so you won't be going gravedigging, just graverobbing.

Well...' the General considered his language. 'Is it graverobbing if the man isn't buried yet?'

Lock looked wearily at Burroughs.

'You're right envoy, it doesn't matter.' Burroughs pointed at Flynn. 'You won't be surprised to learn that the Irishman is good at breaking into places where he's not wanted, so follow him, and when you find the coffin, use this,' the commander handed Lock an empty cloth bag. 'It's gruesome work, but this will cripple de la Barca's army. It might send the drunk over the edge altogether!'

Lock winced at the thought. He had taken Diego de la Barca for a ride from the moment he had entered his camp. He could only hope the Spaniard wouldn't take what happened next personally.

'You'll be going on foot,' Burroughs warned. 'You'll cut right through the forest. The Germans will give you no trouble.'

Lock nearly raised his hands in despair. 'Sir, we're *miles* from the camp, we've gone in the opposite direction.'

'Oh Lock, my dear boy, I haven't told you the best part about this forest village. It seems Herr von Salm was quite the craftsman you see. I'll let him tell you the tale himself.' Burroughs gestured towards the German guide. The guide was now accompanied by another figure, and judging by the cloth covering his mouth, that figure could be none other than Georg von Salm.

Lock gasped, but then steadied himself. If the von Salm had asked for him, then surely, he would be friendlier than he had been on the previous occasion.

Horrific injuries aside, Lock had seen many old men like him on the Locksville estate. Farmers, led into war, and never the same again. After many seasons of killing, these farmers returned to their farms, now accompanied by memories that had been brutally seared into the brain. Lock had spoken to one once. The farmer had been gruff, but harmless. Father said he was a veteran of Ostend. Mother warned her sons to stay away from '*the vulgars.*'

Georg von Salm was very similar to those broken, empty men, Lock had met, except that he was uniquely driven, where those other veterans appeared vacuous and shattered. Lock did not need to ask what drove von Salm onwards. It was written all over his face, and was discernible even under the blood-soaked cloth that covered his mouth.

Revenge.

Killing Gaston Phillipe had not been enough for him. Opening that vile Spaniard's neck onto the leaf litter had only made him thirst for more. Von Salm surely wanted Diego de la Barca's head. The mission was etched into his face, which twitched even as he smiled at one of the jokes the German told him. Burroughs must have known it too.

Did Georg von Salm know that Burroughs had no intention of feeding the Spanish commander to him and his gang of forest ruffians? Burroughs' self-interest, let alone the dictates of honour, required that de la Barca be taken back to Frankenthal as a prisoner. Lock could sense that between these two men, conflict was surely inevitable.

Of course, this was to simplify the issue. The unacknowledged tension between Burroughs and von Salm would only matter if the commander's plan worked. To make de la Barca their prisoner, they would first have to defeat his army.

Lock stole a glance at Burroughs, who still sat beside him on his mount. The commander's gaze was focused on Georg von Salm, as though Burroughs was himself weighing his options.

'You have to tell him Sir,' Lock whispered.

Burroughs' expression took a moment to register the comment, before turning aghast to Lock. 'What on earth do you mean?'

'If you promised von Salm justice, he will expect de la Barca's head.'

Burroughs scoffed. 'Georg von Salm will expect and *accept* what he's given. And besides, we are not here because of a deal I made, but because he likes you two. Do you know how long we've tried to arrange this amongst ourselves? The Germans were never biting, until today.'

Lock was surprised, had his unsuccessful diplomacy of bread and wine really made that much of a mark on the German leader? It was time to find out, as von Salm caught Lock's eye, and waved. Lock's stomach lurched, as Suzy began rambling towards the German. The horse's eye was focused on an apple in von Salm's hand. Lock exhaled, and allowed Suzy to bring him to within touching distance of von Salm. Lock dismounted carefully, and led his horse to von Salm's dirty hand. Suzy's mouth crunched on the apple greedily, and von Salm laughed.

'That's a sight I never grow tired of seeing,' he said. Von Salm now offered his hand to Lock. It had once held the apple, but now it held something of even greater importance: the key to finding out the truth. Somehow, this haunted farmer and his flock had become central to Lock's plans. Lock prepared to switch into German, but first he took von Salm's hand and smiled. Lock did his best to look only at von Salm's forehead, or his eyes – anywhere but his mouth.

Georg von Salm coughed into the cloth piece, before placing his hand on Lock's back and leading him a few paces away from the rest of the men. Lock could feel Burroughs' eyes burrowing into the back of his head, but he had no intention of betraying the General's confidence. Let the lie fester for now – everyone's lives depended on cooperation.

'I am sorry about yesterday,' von Salm said. 'I did not know you were a friend of Flynn O'Toole's. The Irishman has been helping us for some time now.'

'Please, don't apologise,' Lock said eagerly, 'I am sorry for your people. I had no idea that the Spanish had inflicted such horrors upon you.'

Georg von Salm's expression became darker, but he still offered a weak smile in reply. He had now sat himself down on a tree stump, and beckoned for Lock to join him. Lock obliged. Forest hospitality was still hospitality, and Lock knew better than to refuse an offer from a man who had nothing.

'You seemed in a lot of pain yesterday, how are you now?'

Von Salm let out an unexpected belly laugh that startled several men, and drew shushes from other quarters. 'Nobody has asked me how I am in many months, Herr Lock.'

'Please, call me Matthew. That's what my friends call me.'

Von Salm nodded and smiled with his eyes. 'I am better than yesterday. I am sure you have noticed my... wound,' von Salm gestured to his mouth. Lock nodded, and wondered if the German believed his lack of tongue was less noticeable than it was. Or, more likely, Georg von Salm had simply decided to get on with life, tongue or no tongue.

'It is always worse when I get into a scrap,' von Salm said, before winking. 'But that Irishman punches like an Italian, don't you think?'

'Oh, he hasn't hit me, yet.'

'Not to worry, he will!'

A thought suddenly occurred to Lock. 'What did Flynn do for you, exactly?'

Von Salm's face fell visibly, as though it had returned to the void of tragedy. 'My daughters... I had three beautiful daughters before...' The German coughed before starting again. 'I had three daughters before the Spanish came.'

Lock didn't know what to say. 'I heard. I am so sorry.'

Von Salm held up a hand and shook his head. 'It has been two years, but it still cuts like yesterday. At least, I have not lost everything. Carolina... Carolina is still alive, and all because of Flynn.'

Lock gasped, and risked a quick glance away from von Salm towards the Irishman. 'I didn't know that.'

'She said that Flynn told his men he was going to... finish her off, and he brought her into the forest. Flynn told her to find me, and to help him kill evil men.'

'Men like...' Lock hesitated to say his name, 'Gaston Phillipe?'

Georg von Salm's fists were clenched. If he had had any, Lock suspected the German would have gritted his teeth.

'He was the fourth man we arranged to kill. There were others,' von Salm said it so matter-of-factly, that Lock did not dare to doubt him. 'But that doesn't matter now. Soon I'll get the head of the snake. I'll get the man that burned down my village and sent my people into the woods. I will finally get my justice.'

So Burroughs *had* made the arrangement? Or at the very least, Burroughs had yet to inform von Salm that de la Barca's fate rested in very different hands than his own. Sweat dripped down Lock's back. The muggy conditions could be the culprit, but the weather was not to blame. Deceiving von Salm, after he had placed so much trust in him, made Lock feel slightly sick.

Lock could already picture the look on von Salm's face when the German realised Lock had been dishonest. He could already feel that sinking sensation which returned whenever he let someone down. Lock had to get away; he had to go and do this gruesome job. He had to hope that when he came back, Georg von Salm would be far enough from him that he wouldn't have to see his face when the truth became known.

Another figure seemed to have believed so too. The sound of some crunching twigs behind him made Lock turn, to see Flynn's stony expression looking back at him.

Georg von Salm greeted the Irishman again.

Evidently, the two had already caught up. What had Flynn told him?

Flynn's eyes barely seemed willing to waste their energy glancing at Lock.

Lock tried and failed to avoid another round of blushing, but the shame was too much.

'It's time to go,' the Irishman said.

'Very well,' von Salm rose to his feet. 'Follow me gentlemen, it is time I showed you how we managed to turn this forest into a *fortress*.'

- CHAPTER TWENTY-EIGHT -

The three men walked a few metres off the dirt track. The trees lay thickly here, and manoeuvring a horse would have been impossible. Lock had to constantly bat branches away from his face. One could very easily get lost in these parts. A grunt sounded from the man at the front, and Georg von Salm waved limply at Lock to indicate he was about to tell him a story.

'Before the war came, I chased a criminal into these woods with a company of men,' von Salm explained, while walking deliberately towards a disturbed portion of ground. He pointed at one particular portion of raised earth, and indicated for his party to stop. Lock and Flynn obliged. Von Salm cleared his throat and continued.

'Somehow, we lost the bastard. He eluded us for months, until one day, the knave got careless, and I found the secret to his success. He was not hiding in the trees; he had burrowed underground.'

'Did you kill him?'

Von Salm chuckled. 'Kill him? Why, Lock, *not immediately*. First, I made him show me how he did it. I had lived next to this forest for nearly fifty years, and I had never heard of anything like it. Once he had taught me what he knew, then, and only then, did the rogue swing.' Von Salm's described the execution whimsically, as though fondly remembering an old friend.

'And you burrowed underground as well?'

Von Salm's face, or what was visible of it, appeared suddenly drawn. 'To describe what we have done merely as *burrowing* does not do it justice, Lock. I learned from the bastard, yes, but I bettered his techniques and more.'

'You were a quick learner,' Lock suspected a compliment was probably due.

Von Salm nodded. 'Not just me. You see Lock, my village was a humble one, but it was mighty in stature nonetheless. Our woodcraftsmen were renowned across Germany. Our bowls and tables adorned every dwelling for miles around. Emperor Rudolf himself once came here to peruse our wares, did you know that?'

'The Mad Emperor?' Lock whispered.

Von Salm waved the suggestion away. 'This was before he took a turn. He was in the prime of his life, fascinated by artistry, and our village boasted the best wood carvers and carpenters this side of the Rhine.'

'You won't say its name?'

Von Salm shook his head. 'I will not. Not until my people are free.'

'*Free?*'

'Is freedom not what we all seek? I am no Moses, leading the Israelites from Egypt, but I will do all in my power to save what's left of us from bondage, or worse.'

'Naturally, you are bound to them.'

'We were an unoffending town. The militia was barely fifty men strong. Standing and fighting was fruitless. So, when the Spanish arrived, myself and these professionals withdrew to the woods.'

'And, after a time, they put their expertise to good use?'

'*Precisely.* Hmph, they said you were sharp. I am certainly glad we did not mistake you for a servant of Spain.'

A scoff sounded behind Lock's shoulder. Flynn's arms were folded, and his frame leant against a dead tree. It was plain he had heard the story before.

Von Salm did not seem put off by the Irishman's boredom. He sat on a tree stump, but first flicked a small beetle off it with his index finger.

'Just imagine, Matthew, what a village of master woodworkers might be capable of.'

'The craftsman surely outdid themselves, but who was responsible for digging the holes?'

'All of us, Matthew. Everyone who could stand.'

'Everyone agreed to dig?'

'We did not have a choice. This forest is big, but those Spanish would have found us and strung us up sooner or later. To survive, we had to get our hands dirty.' As von Salm said so, he held out his hands, which were just as filthy as they had been the previous day, when Lock had first laid eyes on him.

'How many holes did you dig then?'

Von Salm stood up from his tree stump with intent, as though aching to tell the best part of the story. The words tumbled out with astonishing speed for a man with no tongue.

'Not holes Matthew, *not holes*. Tunnels, caverns, and a set of interconnected warrens to create a new town underground, teeming with life. We've raised *children* here, Lock, can you fathom it? Children, trying to read, in the darkness of a lantern's light, while the Spanish search for them overhead, determined to put them in chains, or worse.' Von Salm seemed to shudder at the thought.

'You made an underground town?' Lock asked, as it dawned on him that he would soon have to see it, and crawl into another dark, damp space.

'It is... quite homely. We have most of the forest covered,' von Salm then chuckled. 'We saw you coming yesterday as soon as you entered.'

The boast was intended in jest, but a slight shiver ran over Lock's shoulders all the same. 'Will it help us against the Spanish?'

Von Salm's cheeks tightened, and Lock could only guess that the German was painfully suppressing a smile. 'Trust me, Matthew, I have been building my forest home for nearly two years. If this does not help us against the Spanish, then I have wasted my time.' Von Salm lifted up a large branch which covered a smooth, flat rock, twice the size of a dinner plate. The German rolled the rock to the side, to reveal a hole in the ground . Von Salm cursed.

'What's wrong?'

'It's the ladder. I told them to have it ready for me. Now we'll have to wait for it.' Von Salm said, sighing as he did so.

'Why not just jump in?' Flynn interjected.

Von Salm rolled his eyes. 'Mister O'Toole, you know that this business cannot be rushed. Or should I tell Mister Lock what happened the first time you went down?'

Lock couldn't help but search the Irishman's face for a hint.

Flynn glared at him. 'I got lost,'.

Von Salm snorted. 'Lost? Lad, you were *terrified*! Screaming to high heaven about the darkness. Said all your prayers faster than I had ever heard them said.'

Flynn switched to another language to swear, and von Salm shook his head and returned to his task. He went down on all fours, dangled his head over the hole, and whistled into it. It was a long, high whistle that was instantly distinctive.

'We have to be careful, of course,' Von Salm cautioned. 'It will only take one careless mistake on our part for all of this to be ruined. That's why we've come prepared. No single German knows all the tunnels. Each man keeps to his own portion, and other Germans keep to theirs. Been that way for nigh on two years now. Even if a man is captured, he can only tell what he knows. There's only one way anyone will find out where all the tunnels lead.'

'You have a map?'

Von Salm turned his head away from the hole to laugh at the very notion. 'Officer Lock, the only way anyone will learn the true extent of the tunnels is if they crack open my head and pull out its secrets.' Von Salm then glanced to the Irishman. 'I suspect Herr O'Toole wouldn't mind such a thing.'

'Just don't let the thing collapse on me again,' Flynn said in broken German.

Lock's stomach lurched. His mind crafted nightmarish visions of being buried alive, accompanied only by a tongueless German and a strangely resentful Irishman.

'It's perfectly safe Herr O'Toole,' von Salm said, as though the question had been asked thousands of times. 'But this may take a minute,' von Salm repeated his whistle. Lock's mind wandered away from the dangling German, and back to the last time he'd spent so long outdoors.

Father used to describe how men would dig enormous trenches, sometimes miles long, to first surround and then destroy an impregnable fortress. When the mood struck them, Lock would sit with Arthur and excitedly discuss the finer points of siege warfare, until the two inevitably grew bored and constructed their own fortress out of firewood and mud.

The forest smelled like that playtime from years before. A potent blend of smells.

The smell of rain on warm wood; of a spring shower on hot stone; of freshly turned earth. The sensation of fingernails clogged with dirt.

Mother's disapproval when her boys scarpered, utterly filthy, back into the house. When they had finally cobbled together a fort they could be proud of, Mother had permitted them to sleep in it overnight, but only after several hours of Arthur's pleading had worn her down.

The following morning, as the sun broke, Father arrived home early, and launched a surprise attack. Despite their best efforts, Charles Lock successfully overwhelmed their defences. As they streamed out of their collapsing bastion, they ran into Mother's arms. She presented them with a soldier's breakfast of bread, meat and cheese.

This they ate while seated on dew covered grass, watched by a chorus of songbirds, as Mother and Father giggled in each other's embrace.

Lock barely registered the details Georg von Salm provided, in between repeated whistles. It was only once the German pulled his head away from the hole, and indicated that he was ready, that Lock snapped out of his childhood.

How had the Germans escaped the Spanish for so long? The question had plagued Diego de la Barca, who would likely never get to the bottom of it. Literally.

Lock had originally prepared himself for a childlike fantasy involving interconnected treehouses, dotted all across the forest, as far as the eye could see. The reality was less romantic but, probably, a great deal safer.

The wooden ladder von Salm had been waiting for had finally emerged. Von Salm ensured it was attached, before nodding at his two charges, and beckoning them to follow him. The German seemed to almost slide down the old wooden ladder, but Lock was more cautious.

He ignored the eye rolling which Flynn offered in response to his hesitation. The hole was wide enough for his frame, just about. He plugged his feet into a lower rung of the ladder, and as his body scraped off the dirt, small clods of earth became detached.

It was suddenly easier to understand Flynn's reported panic.

The light was low, but still persistent. Von Salm had brought a lantern, and bundles of rushlights were stacked all along the way, to be lit as needed. The more important rooms boasted their own lanterns; *courtesy of the Spanish*, von Salm had winked.

Von Salm explained how it had been done in a voice barely above a whisper. The Germans had tunnelled down to begin with, before widening their tunnels into caves, and connecting those caves with additional tunnels.

Before long, a network of underground passages and rooms lined the way.

As he watched his step, careful to adhere to the wooden planks that lined the centre of the floor, Lock was drawn to the sight of ghastly looking tree roots, which occasionally snaked along the walls, or tripped up the unprepared. They came through a narrow tunnel which opened into an enormous, cavernous room several hundred yards in length.

'This is the school room,' von Salm said. 'We moved the children elsewhere in preparation.'

'How does it all stay up?' Lock asked, as he glared at the mud ceiling. Was the earth rippling, or was it merely a trick of the eye?

'Ah, it is the trees, Lock, we are surrounded by trees here,' von Salm gestured to the ceiling of the cave, and noted the tangle of roots which lined a vast portion of it. 'The trees save us, but not how you think. Two years hiding from the best army in the world, and we've never been found. Do you know why? Because we're not hiding *in* a forest, we're hiding *under* a forest. Those roots hold this whole thing together.'

Lock continued to marvel at the sight, as von Salm waved his lantern to ensure Flynn was behind them. In the larger man-made space, one could feel less claustrophobic than before. But could a good night's sleep truly be had under so many tons of trees, roots and earth?

But then, Lock had slept in worse places, and only recently.

'Our Irish friend has seen all this before,' von Salm mused, 'even helped us dig a few holes.'

'Digging never was my forte,' Flynn whispered, and the lantern caught the hint of a grin.

'How many tunnels do you have?' Lock couldn't help but be fascinated, and the German chuckled briefly before turning to face him.

'I'm afraid I cannot show you, or even tell you everything Lock,' von Salm's face was more drawn. He seemed to find it more difficult to breathe underground. 'Can't have you getting captured and showing off our secrets. But what you do need to know, is this.' The German brought his charges around a corner, where a strange sight awaited them.

The underground room was not especially large, but it was uniquely laid out. Ahead of them, the ground remained flat, before giving way to a large ditch. The top of a ladder could be seen at the ditch's edge, and Lock could hear the low conversation of men within it. Even in the poor light, it was possible to see a pile of sharpened stakes, left near the edge of the ditch.

'We have many of these,' von Salm said, gesturing to the ditch. 'I wanted to give you a sample of what to expect later on.' The German coughed as he walked to the edge of the ditch, and then readjusted the cloth over his mouth. He called in a low voice into the ditch, and activity could be heard, as the top of the ladder began to shake slightly. Two men, filthy with mud from head to toe, emerged from the ladder on the ditch's edge. They looked proudly at von Salm, who nodded in acknowledgement at their work.

'Well done lads, make sure you get some air soon,' The men nodded enthusiastically, and Lock guessed they couldn't be much older than Arthur.

Von Salm beckoned Lock to the edge of the ditch. 'Careful Matthew,' he cautioned, holding up a hand, 'don't want to waste this on you.' Lock peered cautiously over the edge, but could not see the bottom of it. 'Do you see them?' von Salm asked.

'It's too dark,' Lock said, with a squint.

George von Salm hovered his lantern over the ditch's edge, and Lock could make out the bare outline of wood, and as his eyes adjusted to the light, he recognised their shape.

Stakes, the Germans were securing sharp wooden stakes to the bottom of this underground ditch. But why?

'It is quite a drop,' von Salm mused. 'I told them to make it ten feet deep, five feet wide and fifteen feet long, but they did their best.'

Lock knew he had to ask the question. 'Why did you dig this ditch here? Do you anticipate the Spanish coming into these caverns?'

Von Salm nodded slightly. 'We hope they won't follow us in here, but all being well, we will have some Spanish in this ditch soon enough.' Von Salm pointed to the ceiling of the cave directly above the ditch. The ceiling was covered with several planks of wood, which were themselves connected to additional reinforcing beams that had been secured into the ground.

'Above this ditch is a portion of the road that runs through the forest. We won't tell you which part. What I will tell you, is that we have many traps just like these. Once I give the order, the wood will be removed, and the Spanish will fall...' von Salm appeared to measure the distance by raising his hand and lowering it '...about twenty feet, into a pit of spikes.'

'How many men can fit in there?' Lock asked, pointing at the ditch, still unable to hide his fascination.

Von Salm appeared to debate whether telling Lock the answer would be wise, but he eventually relented. 'Hard to say, some of my carpenters say fifty men would easily fit.' Von Salm then gestured to the top of the wooden ladder which poked out of the ditch. 'Once you remove the ladder, you've got the enemy trapped. They'll be at our mercy then.'

Lock stopped himself from shuddering at the thought. He doubted whether von Salm had much mercy to spare.

'They've nearly finished with the stakes,' von Salm said. 'If they aren't impaled, and if the fall doesn't kill them, I'm sure we can think of something.' Von Salm used his mouth cloth to dab at some saliva which had dribbled onto his chin. He turned so that his back was to the ditch, and he now faced his two charges.

'We will be happy to show you more after you've gone on your expedition,' von Salm said. 'But you may rest assured, gentlemen, the Spanish *will* pay.'

Lock didn't doubt it. Behind him, the Irishman suddenly spoke up.

'How do we get to the Spanish camp from here?'

Von Salm nodded, before producing two pieces of black cloth from his trouser pocket. 'Put these on,' he said. 'Don't worry, I won't push you in! This is just to keep our secrets safe if the worst happens.'

Von Salm waited for the two men to apply their blindfolds. The cloth smelled like soil and sweat. Lock couldn't help but grimace before tying it at the back of his head. Once the deed was done, von Salm whistled, and the two men from the ditch returned.

'These lads know the tunnels inside and out. They'll guide you to the exit. Once you're there, do not try and come back in. My people are instructed to kill anyone they find down here, so they're understandably skittish.'

'How will we find you?' Flynn asked.

'Don't worry gentlemen,' von Salm said, '*we'll* find *you*.'

With that, a gentle hand touched Lock's right arm, and he obediently walked with his guide. It was a strange experience, to be blind and helpless, in an utterly alien world. Lock tried not to think about it. After a few minutes, he had all but zoned out.

'*Shite!*' Flynn swore, after tripping over an errant tree root. Flynn's German guide whispered apologies.

Another few minutes passed. Lock was amazed at the number of twists and turns, and even more amazed that his guide could remember the route. The Germans walked in complete silence, as though engaged in a sacred duty. Lock longed for conversation, but he still bristled at his shame. Flynn grumbled under his breath.

'Nearly there,' the German whispered to Lock. Lock was himself directed around a sharp bend, and the ground began a slight incline, before the German's hand left his elbow, and he heard his guide working on something above him. Lock was then lifted out of the hole, and the darkness of the tunnels gave way to the shade of the forest.

Lock's blindfold was removed, and he breathed the air greedily. The men were all crouched. His German guide was joined by two other Germans, who were both covered in foliage and dirt. Behind him, Flynn was extracted by these Germans, and the Irishman blinked as his blindfold was removed.

The guide pointed behind Lock, and Lock turned.

He now realised where they were, barely a few yards from the opening of the forest. It was even possible to see the beginning of the track that led through the forest, where Lock had led his horse the previous day.

The Spanish camp could be seen further down the valley. Their tents, rows upon rows of them, could be made out even through the trees. As he took it in, the German guide pointed to a plot of land directly in front of the Spanish camp, where a field had been cleared, and several headstones had been placed into the ground. A tent, slightly larger than the others, sat in the upper corner of the field.

'A graveyard,' Flynn whispered, before rankling at the Germans shushing him.

Lock nodded. The tent in the graveyard would surely be where the unburied bodies resided. On the journey from Frankenthal, Burroughs had told him that Diego de la Barca had wanted to send his son's remains back to Spain, but the combination of logistical complications, the searing heat, and the gruesome state of his son's body, recommended a quick, local burial.

The burial was due to commence the following morning. Even from this position, Lock could see the challenge that awaited them. Dusk was beginning to loom over the camp, and soldiers' voices could be faintly heard. Some soldiers stood in groups, others cleaned their weapons and ate in seated circles.

The sense of calm in the camp reassured Lock. The Spaniards could have no idea that on the other side of the forest, the English were preparing to seize Mannheim. By the time they did realise it, Burroughs hoped, it would be too late, and de la Barca's army would be in pieces.

A German patted Lock on the back, and Lock turned to see his guide signalling at the foliage and dirt which covered his friends. Lock shuddered at the suggestion, but before he could object, one of the Germans crept over to Lock and signalled at him to close his eyes. Muck was smeared across Lock's face, and an errant piece of soil tumbled into his mouth. He spat it out, and one of the Germans giggled.

When Lock opened his eyes, the Germans were now presenting him with foliage, and instructing him on how to attach the branches to his garments. The Germans had certainly been industrious in their search of authentic camouflage. The German then signalled that he and his comrades were about to re-enter the underground.

Lock was relieved not to be joining them. But there was now a different problem to face. It was just himself and Flynn, the situation Lock had feared ever since crossing the Rhine.

'We wait until sundown,' Flynn whispered. The Irishman had evidently done away with the Germans' suggestion that they should not say a word. He indicated to Lock that he intended to catch a quick nap until that time came. It was beyond Lock how the Irishman could sleep at such a time, but he nodded his consent. He would keep watch.

The Irishman rolled over onto his side, and used his dolman as a makeshift blanket. His buff coat, much like Lock's, was ravaged by dirt stains, but the Irishman had more pressing matters on his mind. His decision to sleep was one which Lock found somehow reassuring.

It meant the Irishman did not believe the two were in any immediate danger, and even better, it meant Lock would not have to bear several hours of awkward, shameful silence, as Lock contemplated his many failings. Within minutes, the Irishman's breathing slowed, and Lock knew he was alone.

They had emerged from the tunnels in an ideal position. A plethora of greenery and tree trunks obscured their shapes, and their immediate area was slightly elevated, likely by the mounds of earth that had been excavated.

There could be no doubt that he had been watched from the moment he had entered the forest. It was also clear that Flynn had been well-aware of this, yet had neglected to inform him.

There was, indeed, a great deal that the Irishman had not shared. Lock tried to prevent himself from taking it personally, and he focused on the task at hand.

He turned to watch the Spanish. From this distance, they were like dark, largely featureless figurines. The evening sun cast them as shadows, rather than people. Lock looked back to the graveyard tent where Gaston Phillipe's body surely lay.

It was fortunate that the tent could be reached without entering the camp, but Lock would still have to cross a vast expanse of open ground first. Only a few sympathetic bushes and knee-high grass could be relied upon for protection.

This was why darkness was essential, and darkness was approaching. The birds had begun to deliver their final chorus of the day, and the setting sun hinted at a cooler evening.

Still, sweat trickled down Lock's neck. His hair was smeared with soil, and lumps of earth fell under his collar to meet his skin. Lock exhaled. The business of getting filthy had seemed much more entertaining when he had been a child.

There was little to do now but wait. Sleeping seemed impossible, yet as he sat against a surprisingly comfortable trunk, his eyes became heavy. His shattered frame capitulated, and the filth ceased to matter.

He was awoken from his doze by the distant sounds of hooves pounding along the forest track. How long had he been asleep? Minutes? Hours? It was impossible to tell.

Lock whispered swears to himself as he watched the rider's mount sprint past, within a few yards of their position, before riding unawares out of the forest and towards the camp. The rider was clearly a Spaniard, and Lock watched as the rider's comrades greeted him before returning to their business.

And then the thought hit him. What reason could a Spanish rider have to cut through the forest in such haste, and from such a direction? What if the Spaniard had come from Mannheim, to warn de la Barca that he needed to move?

The possibility had never factored into Burroughs' scheme. A sinking feeling started to set in. The futility of the plan loomed before him. He could not afford to wait and see if the Spaniard had indeed ridden all this way to raise the alarm.

He had to act quickly.

Darkness had virtually enveloped the camp, though the occasional fire cast errant shadows. Lock looked at the route in front of him, and ran over his plan for the umpteenth time. It would take him, perhaps, ten minutes to cover the ground between here and the graveyard tent, then that tent would be searched, and ten more minutes would be required in the return journey.

Did they have thirty minutes?

Lock's heart raced, and a voice in the back of his mind became louder and louder.

'*Go*,' the voice said.

Lock looked back at the Irishman, whose breathing had steadied. He was clearly deep in sleep. There was no time to wake him and explain everything, nor did Lock wish to endure that conversation.

There was also the prospect of Flynn eating his own words.

'A liability?' Lock whispered aloud, the painful rebuke returning to his mind. '*I'll show the bastard.*'

- CHAPTER TWENTY-NINE -

Emerging from the forest had taken mere seconds, and Lock had moved, while crouching, down the slight incline and out into the open ground.

Once there, the combination of the uncut grass and the creeping darkness provided useful cover. Lock moved slowly and deliberately, making sure to not to resort to any sudden, jagged movements which might draw attention. It was like being back in Locksville, when he and Arthur had played the role of assassins, and had crept around the estate's grounds, startling servants, the family pets, and eventually their Mother.

He stopped behind a large shrub, some fifty yards short of the graveyard tent, panting and sweating, but still unseen. He waited to see if any alarms had been raised. So far, no sign of alarm had gripped the camp.

Lock envisioned the Spanish rider deep in conversation with the grief stricken de la Barca, as the commander was told of the full measure of English audacity.

The grass was damp and soft, and some disturbed moths fluttered from the ground, before migrating towards limited sources of light.

Lock knelt, and leaned forward, almost on his toes, in preparation to spring forward when ready. Almost as an instinct, his right hand moved to the scabbard by his left thigh, where the stiletto was safely stored. This would be his sole defence. His bulkier firearm and sword had been left with the sleeping Irishman.

Lock kept his eyes on the tent and closed the distance in another burst of activity. These ten seconds of creeping brought him just outside the graveyard's perimeter.

A low fence marked out the field where the Spanish buried their dead.

The grass was shorter there, and Lock would be more exposed, though he did spy a larger headstone, perhaps provided for a more important Spaniard, which he could take refuge behind.

That was the next logical target.

The distant roar of the Rhine ensured an even level of ambient noise, but Lock confirmed again, as if to reassure himself, that the Spanish didn't seem to be looking for intruders.

With a brief exhale, Lock began to move, creeping slowly first.

Then more quickly.

Stepping gingerly over the fence, he turned towards the larger headstone. Sure enough, it was as high as his waist. Lock nearly threw himself behind it. The safety it promised was too alluring to resist.

Lock was panting. He double checked behind him, to see several clumps of trees, and a small dirt track which led gradually towards the Rhine.

There was no sign of human activity anywhere.

He looked ahead.

The graveyard tent could now be examined in more detail. Its canvas exterior gave nothing away, but its size had certainly been underestimated. It was perhaps twice his height – all the better for stacking coffins within.

Lock would have to get closer, but once he did, he would be completely exposed.

There was no way of knowing what the interior of the tent would be like, or even if any living Spaniards awaited him inside.

Time was running out.

After making one last sweep of the area, Lock exhaled, and resumed his journey, and rapidly closed on the tent.

Much like de la Barca's command tent, the structure contained two doors in the front and back, serviced by a heavy flap that had to be pushed to the side. The dilemma now was which side to enter on.

As he had approached from the end of the graveyard, it made the most sense to choose the door nearest to him.

And then Lock paused, as a shiver ran down his neck.

There was definitely someone inside the tent.

There was the sound of sobbing, followed by hushed whispers of reassurance, perhaps from another figure.

Lock silently prayed that the inhabitants would be less observant than usual.

There was no mistaking it, the voices were coming closer, to the back entrance of the tent where Lock lay flat.

As carefully as he possibly could, Lock rolled to his left, to place himself just around the corner from the entrance.

He was now completely exposed.

If a Spaniard emerged from the forest and marched towards the camp, they would probably see him.

If a Spaniard approached from the camp and made their way towards the graveyard, they would definitely see him.

The tent's back door opened, and two sets of footsteps emerged.

Lock had begun edging further along the length of the tent, away from the men, and towards its front door, when something resonated with him.

Voices. *Familiar* voices.

Lock was sure of it.

His brain began to battle with his body, but Lock urged himself forward, back towards the danger, to confirm his suspicions.

He craned his neck slightly around the corner of the tent.

Lock had been correct.

Diego de la Barca, the source of the sobbing, stood with the morose pikeman from the previous day.

The two men had not seen him.

Both were lost in their conversation. Lock silently cursed himself for failing to learn Spanish. De la Barca was plainly upset, and the pikeman appeared less sullen than the previous day, as he worked with smiles and other gestures to reassure his commander.

Lock remained perfectly still, as de la Barca gestured towards the large headstone where he had only recently been hiding. The subordinate sighed, and walked, arm in arm, with de la Barca.

Of course, the headstone was for Gaston Phillipe.

De la Barca appeared frail, though Lock couldn't see his face from this angle, as the two men walked away from him and the tent, and towards the large headstone.

The subordinate paused halfway there, and stooped to pick up a small branch which looked out of place on the otherwise perfectly manicured lawn.

Lock suppressed a gasp.

The branch had surely fallen from his crude collection of camouflage as he had moved.

Fortunately, the subordinate threw the branch down with a disinterested expression, occupied by his commander's excessive displays of grief.

Both men paused at the gravestone, and de la Barca knelt down to pray. Lock turned away embarrassed, before a slight sense of panic entered his brain.

Had they already buried Phillipe's body after all?

Lock doubted so.

Unlike the other plots of land around the headstones, the ground around Phillipe's designated space was completely flat and undisturbed.

Lock gambled with himself.

Could he enter the tent, grab the body parts, and leave, before de la Barca and his subordinate returned?

Lock wrestled with the idea for a few seconds.

The two Spaniards remained glued to the headstone, and de la Barca appeared deep in a pleading prayer.

Lock resigned himself to his next move.

He slowly rose to his feet, and, holding his breath, he moved around the corner, to the tent's back entrance, before quietly lifting the flap, and shuffling inside.

The air was suddenly heavier, and stank of death.

Lock exhaled shakily, only now realising that his breath had been held since de la Barca had materialised.

But he was in, that was what mattered.

Considering its size, the tent was surprisingly cramped within. Several caskets lined the floor to the left and right, and were piled like crates on top of one another. A sense of panic began setting in.

How does one find a body in a room full of bodies?

'*Where is it,*' he whispered to himself, before his eyes rested on a casket that stood out from the rest.

It was made of a finer wood, and its upper portion was open. Lock crept to it, the grass deadening his steps.

Gaston Phillipe's pallid face was impossible to miss.

The Spanish had done their best to clean and prepare the dead man before burial, and several white sheets lined the casket, covering most of his body.

On Phillipe's chest rested a small gold ring, perhaps placed there mere minutes ago by de la Barca. Lock spurred himself forward. He grabbed the lower lid of the casket, which opened with only a slight creak.

Lock shuddered, as the smell of decaying flesh invaded his nostrils.

He prepared the cloth bag to receive the grisly contents, but the space within it wasn't exactly large. Could the Spaniard's body fit?

And then, overcoming his gag reflex, Lock understood.

Virtually every body part, from Phillipe's head, to his hands, had been severed from the body trunk.

The white sheets had been a last-minute addition, to salve the horror of a Father who couldn't see his son in such a desperate condition.

There was only one thing for it: denial.

He would pretend he was doing anything other than defiling a man's body.

These were not body parts, they were large, ripened tomatoes, which leaked as they placed in the grocery basket.

Lock exhaled to steady his stomach, which rippled with horror.

With a small amount of force, each body part came free with a slight click and squelch.

The hurried burial process aided his grisly task. Lock wound strands of the white cloth around each piece.

The task was taking a while, but he pressed on, the gruesome business catching in his throat several times. The bag became incredibly heavy, and he wrapped it in additional white sheets, before closing the casket's lid.

With luck, the commander would not realise that his son's body was missing.

Lock breathing had become heavy enough to sink.

His hands, filthy from the soil, were also caked with stale blood.

The smell was overpowering.

A dark red patch began to pool at the bottom of the bag, so Lock grabbed one last sheet and wrapped it around, before a sense of urgency began to command him to leave.

But there was another decision to make.

Should he leave through the back door, where, at any moment, the two Spaniards might turn from Phillipe's headstone and see him, or should he exit through the front door of the tent?

The latter option was more uncertain; he could run headlong into an emerging party of Spaniards.

And then, in a flash, the decision was made for him.

A bugle sounded, and Lock's entire body froze to the spot.

He swallowed.

The alarm hadn't been for him – it must be as a result of the Spanish rider. Unable to find de la Barca, perhaps, they had sent out the call instead.

Hooves approached, tearing up the grass, and a call sounded from de la Barca at the headstone. The tent's front door was touched, before the rider evidently thought better of it, and he sprinted around the tent, towards the Spanish commander.

Most men, if given the chance, would avoid walking through a tent filled with coffins.

Lock gasped as quietly as he could, and angled his ears in a vain effort to make out the conversation.

The sprinting Spaniard delivered news in panicked tones, followed by a question from an indignant de la Barca.

Mannheim was mentioned, Lock was sure of it.

He had to think quickly.

There were more distant shouts.

Lock cursed himself for moving without Flynn, though for sure, this dilemma would have happened regardless.

There could be no guarantee that de la Barca was finished grieving.

The moment of truth approached, as de la Barca's voice grew closer.

Lock could barely breathe.

The three men stood just outside the tent's back door, as though debating whether to ruin Lock, or let him escape.

The tent door opened slightly.

Lock's stomach lurched, but then a voice called.

It was de la Barca, and he seemed unwilling to return to the tent. An evening of grieving was enough for the commander, now it was time to go to war.

The three men moved gradually away, and de la Barca's loud voice roused the rest of his men in the near distance.

It was time to go.

With the stuffed bag slung over his back, Lock gently pushed open the tent's back door.

The coast was clear, though this was hardly a surprise.

No one had time to pay attention to the graveyard so long as news of an attack on Mannheim filled the air.

For de la Barca, this was the chance to find a silver lining amidst his grief – to shatter the stubborn English once and for all, and deliver the entirety of the Rhineland to his superiors.

Lock looked at the entrance to the forest, some two hundred feet away.

There could be no alternative with time being of the essence.

Within minutes, the Spanish cavalry could have moved out and begun their journey. It was vital that they, along with de la Barca's entire column, use the forest, rather than the road, if the plan was to work.

Lock exhaled a few times, checked that all was clear one more time, and sprinted, as quickly as his legs would move him, over the dead ground.

He ran slightly stooped.

The weight of Phillipe's remains unsteadied and unbalanced him. In a terrifying moment, the weight of the bag caused Lock to fall hard onto his side.

Lock cursed, and glanced around.

An eerie calm had now descended over the camp, as the oft-rehearsed battle orders were whirring into motion. Lock returned a stray hand to the bloody sack, and then resealed his ghastly package.

Rising to his feet, and looking to where he and Flynn had set themselves up, Lock made quickly for the forest.

The sheets began to rip, so while running, Lock moved the package to his front, where he could support it with both hands.

The rancid smell was directly under his nose, and Lock tried to breathe through his mouth, swallowing repeated urges to gag.

Finally, the forest's dirt track met his feet, and Lock bounded up to where the Irishman had been resting. Hopefully, Flynn wouldn't mistake him for a Spaniard, but he could not afford to wait.

Cradling his bloody package, he trudged up the slight incline, which now seemed far steeper than before.

Breathlessly, he reached the top, to see Flynn staring right at him, sword in hand.

The Irishman deconstructed the incredible sight, as his eyes widened, and his sword hand lowered.

Flynn did not need to ask what the bloody bundle contained.

Lock's own expression revealed the truth.

'God's guts Matthew,' Flynn whispered, before a morbid smile crept across his face. 'Or perhaps I should say, *Gaston's Guts*.'

Lock dropped the bag and threw up beside it.

- CHAPTER THIRTY -

Within minutes, a German had arrived to fetch the bag. Flynn handed it over without hesitation, and the receiving German grimaced at the package's sight and smell. Lock watched the exchange while seated on a low tree stump, surrounded by bluebells. He focused on the calming colours, which helped him pretend that he had not just done it. That he had not just taken pieces of a man and stuffed them into a bag. And yet, he had.

'You did... well,' Flynn said, half turning towards Lock as the German left with the package.

Lock sat bolt upright. He was trying to wash the sour taste out of his mouth with a foul substance Flynn had provided him.

He also wanted to let the Irishman squirm.

'What do you call this?' he asked Flynn, gesturing at the Irishman's costrel.

'*Poitín*,' Flynn said with a mischievous smile. 'Mixed with water, of course. Only the madmen drink it on its own.'

'As you said, it is a... beautiful work of art,' Lock said, running his fingers along the Celtic crosses that were etched into the black leather container.

'It was my Father's,' Flynn said, before extending an arm to retrieve it. The Irishman sipped, wincing slightly as he did so.

'I do prefer wine, but it certainly works quicker than wine,' Lock conceded. His head swam, and he found himself longing for a quiet evening by a roaring fire, where conversation and wine flowed freely. The thought of such leisure moved Mother's refrain to the front of Lock's mind. '*There is nothing less gentlemanly than a drunken brute who cannot control himself,*' she had said, after Lock had clumsily collided with several dinner trays.

Lock smiled grimly to himself. One could only imagine the venom Mother would spew if she saw what he had just done.

'I find poitín does the trick just before a big fight. Calms the nerves. Well, back in...' Flynn stopped himself, and slowly turned away from Lock.

Normally he would have pestered the Irishman for the end of the story, but Lock had gotten what he wanted.

Flynn had been forced to see him.

He had seen for himself that Lock was not just a liability.

Lock stood and walked a few paces, so that he could see the Spanish forming up in de la Barca's camp. He kept his eyes on the distant figures as he spoke. 'I don't think this was part of the script, weren't we supposed to lure them into the forest?'

'I'm sure the Burroughs and von Salm between them can cook up a plan,' Flynn said, sipping from his costrel.

'We could be behind schedule. Will the Germans be able to get into position in time?'

'Trust me Lock, I know I had my blindfold on, but those Germans could be in your privy if they wanted to be, and they could get there in minutes.'

'Have you seen much of the tunnels?' Lock asked.

'*Indeed, there are few sights more repulsive,*' a familiar voice came in a whisper a few feet behind Lock's stump.

'General Burroughs?' Lock called out behind him in a whisper.

'You've done well gentlemen,' Burroughs loomed into view, as he pushed through foliage. 'The Germans are in position.'

'Sir, they're ready? Even with the...' Lock gestured in the direction of the camp. An alarm was trumpeted at ten second intervals. The sound was obnoxious, as was the intention, and it likely carried for many miles. There was a risk it would rouse the garrison at Mannheim to resist.

'They've been ready for two years Lock. Ever since those bastards ran them out of their homes.'

Flynn interjected suddenly. 'Sir, what are you doing so close to the front. Couldn't you send out one of your men to find us?'

Burroughs fired back a grin. 'Reckon I had to see those tunnels for myself O'Toole, after hearing legends for so many years.'

'And what is your verdict Sir?'

'My *verdict*, Irishman, is that I can think of few places where it would be worse to die. You should both make ready. You are to follow me, above ground, in roughly ten minutes.'

Lock looked towards the camp, and then towards Burroughs. 'Where's *our* position General? Will we get to see this battle?'

Burroughs chuckled as quietly as he could manage. '*See it*? Not to worry Lock, I will make sure you see it, hear it, feel it and touch it. You'll be with me.'

'And where will you be sir?' Flynn asked impatiently, as he drowned the last sip of his costrel.

'Well, at the best vantage point in the forest, naturally,' Burroughs said, as he faced de la Barca's camp. 'I reckon the lads are nearly ready now. I'll use the signal.' Burroughs retrieved a stone from his pocket and turned to the tree stump Lock had recently used as a seat.

Lock and Flynn both stared at the General.

'Shush now, I need to get this precisely right, if it's to work.'

Lock held his breath, and kept one eye on the Spanish. They continued to gather in marching formation. This famed military machine was surprisingly sluggish.

The General began tapping the stone on the tree stump. He did three double taps, before raising a finger to Lock and Flynn, as though urging them to wait.

And then, a tapped reply sounded faintly in the distance, which mirrored Burroughs' code.

'What was that?' Lock asked.

The General smiled as he fixed the unlit match cord to his musket. 'I just told them it's time, lads.'

Three minutes passed, before Lock spied a few individuals walking perhaps a hundred feet to the south west. They clogged the road with their activity and unusually slow progress. From their excited shouts, it was clear they were German.

To blend in, they were clad in long, dark green cloaks. And then the sight became even stranger. They pulled a weapon behind them that would not have looked out of place on an ancient battlefield. The General gasped beside Lock, as he spied the Germans and interjected.

'It's a trebuchet, *a bloody trebuchet*,' Burroughs said, hiding none of his awe. 'Von Salm was not lying when he said they were master carpenters.'

'Why would the Germans make a trebuchet?' Lock asked.

He watched as they pushed the machine along the dirt track. Even its wheels looked like a miracle of woodworking, each being fixed with a symbol that was unfamiliar to Lock.

'That's Woodrest's town crest on each of the wheels,' Flynn whispered. 'Von Salm told me about this weapon. He's surrounded by some... truly eccentric men.'

'It looks a shade smaller than the regular trebuchet,' Burroughs said, his right hand shaking as he attempted to focus on the sight.

'It's perhaps a quarter smaller than what the Romans might have used, but it will still pack a great punch.'

'What in heaven's name do they plan on *doing* with it?'

Flynn chuckled. 'Well General, von Salm's original plan was to bombard the Spanish with fire pots, and burn their tents in the night, but I told him that was an insane idea, so he didn't do it.' The Irishman shook his head, his face wearing a wide smile. 'I thought the mad bastard had gotten rid of it. Why am I not surprised he hasn't?'

Lock squinted at the machine, as it trundled towards the opening in the forest, still out of sight from the Spanish, who had just finished forming up. A row of stakes were quickly hammered in front of it, to protect the men from adventurous enemy cavalry.

It was possible to faintly make out the silhouette of de la Barca on horseback, swaying somewhat, and no doubt exhausted from his recent outpouring of grief.

A pang of guilt tugged at Lock's stomach.

De la Barca's night was about to get much worse.

In fact, the Spanish commander was about to have the worst night of his life, and it was all thanks to Matthew Lock.

The Germans began hammering stones under the machine's wheels at breakneck speed. As four Germans set to work, another began winding the machine back.

There was much to be learned from the Ancients, Father had said. And here was living proof.

Lock's lessons in classical warfare reminded him that the trebuchet was a torsion powered siege engine. It was normally constructed from hard wood and ropes, which would be tied and twisted until there was significant pressure in the machine to send a projectile into the enemy's ranks.

This projectile was normally a heavy boulder or rock, and the target was normally a besieged fortress wall.

Lock had glazed over whenever Father had attempted to explain why the contraption worked. It was easier to simply accept that somehow, it did. It seemed likely that on this occasion, the trebuchet would be propelling a very different payload towards the Spanish.

The three men were now transfixed on the machine.

Burroughs in particular seemed positively bursting to gush about the life of the trebuchet. The General pointed in its direction. 'See there, the Germans are putting a rock in its pouch. Ahh, the clever fellows, they must be testing the range!'

One of the five Germans must have done something, because the machine suddenly expended its energy, and with a flick of its long wooden arm, a rock, roughly the size of a cat, was hurled forwards.

Lock held his breath as he watched. The Germans immediately set about refitting the machine to fire again, while a sole German watched to see where the projectile landed.

Lock turned to the camp, to see the stone crash onto the graveyard tent. Nobody was harmed, but a few Spaniards noticed the act.

Increasingly alarmed cries rang out. The Germans ignored them, and were nearly finished winding the machine into the firing position.

Some Spaniards went to inspect the damage, and entered the graveyard tent, before exiting to give an all-clear sign to their superiors.

The Spanish assumed Gaston Phillipe's body to be in the tent.

De la Barca would be reassured that his son's corpse had not been defiled by the projectile, completely ignorant of the horrors that awaited him.

Had the Germans targeted the tent on purpose?

Just how intense was their hatred of de la Barca?

De la Barca gave some form of signal, and at a flash, the gloom of the dark night was suddenly illuminated. Lock's company winced and briefly covered their eyes against the flash of light.

A collection of iron fixtures in front of the assembling Spanish army had been ignited. A handful of these fixtures were also carried nearer to the forest, as figures with torches followed behind.

The cover of darkness was to be denied to the Germans, but they still possessed the cover of the forest.

On the other hand, the sudden influx of light greatly improved German visibility of the Spanish. It had the potential to improve their accuracy as well.

This was tested, as a second rock was flung forward. Lock focused on the Germans by the trebuchet.

Georg von Salm's short frame and slightly hunched silhouette could be made out, as the German worked diligently to direct its operations.

Of course, this was only to be expected.

Von Salm had not gone to all this effort to learn of de la Barca's breakdown second hand.

Notwithstanding the improved visibility, the second rock landed harmlessly in the middle of the graveyard. De la Barca's figure could be seen now, gesticulating wildly at the tent, and then back towards the forest.

The shadows thrown by the fires made all movements appear wildly exaggerated. At one point, the Spaniard pointed directly at the place where Lock was standing.

Even so many hundreds of yards away, the potent mixture of panic and rage in de la Barca's eyes shone brightly.

The Germans scrambled to load one more large stone onto the trebuchet's arm, while de la Barca launched a torrent of abuse at one of his subordinates, who flinched and went to the Spanish cavalry.

Did de la Barca intend to attack with his horse?

Sure enough, a stream of riders loomed into view down by the camp, as they galloped towards de la Barca and awaited orders. They were about one hundred in number, and a constant trickle of latecomers continued to bolster their ranks.

De la Barca's faint shouts drifted back to them.

The commander was likely demanding an attack, and he gestured repeatedly towards the forest.

And then, the third rock flew forward with a loud groan. This time, the effects of the projectile were much more gruesome. The cat-sized boulder collided with the centre of the riders, who had foolishly formed up just in front of the graveyard.

One man's upper body vanished as the boulder cleaved off his head and part of his left shoulder. A cloud of red mist briefly hung in the air, and witnesses cried out in horror and rage.

The stakes had just been raised.

Lock heard Flynn whistle softly beside him. The attack stunned many, but it caused minimal casualties. Limited jeers from the Spaniards suggested that they failed to grasp the German's plan. The miss had been deliberate.

The intention was not to kill, but to incite.

Lock looked back to the Germans, who were now preparing the trebuchet for its fourth shot, this time with very different ammunition.

Lock's stomach lurched.

The familiar bloody white sack was on standby. It was now thoroughly saturated with Gaston Phillipe's blood and stained a dark red.

Georg von Salm had opened it, and was in the process of placing some of its contents into the trebuchet's pouch.

A bugle sounded, and Lock glanced back to the camp to see the cavalry lined up again in battle formation.

De la Barca barked angry instructions, which carried back to Lock in the relative quiet of the night.

'He's ordering them to attack the forest,' Flynn whispered, 'this should be interesting.'

Lock glanced back to the trebuchet. He had been so focused on watching the Germans fire the contraption that his eyes had neglected to pick up several figures dotted at the front of the forest.

'The Germans...' Burroughs whispered, pointing with his sword. 'Look at them gather in position. Marvellous cohesion.'

The Germans had surely emerged from their burrows at the perfect moment, or perhaps they had simply been concealed on the edge of the forest from the beginning.

No more than three hundred yards separated these Germans from the assembling Spanish, and just as de la Barca gave the final order to attack, Lock noted something else. The Germans were accompanied by several tiny lights, and Lock could even note the even tinier trails of smoke, a tell-tale sign that their muskets were primed.

'They've lit their matches,' Lock whispered. 'The Germans aren't bluffing this time.'

From their slightly elevated position, the three men had a remarkable view of the area. One hundred yards ahead of them was the edge of the forest, where the Germans crouched and dug in as they prepared to fire their weapons. Four hundred yards ahead of where Lock was standing, the Spanish unleashed their war cries, and began to advance in hastily joined groups, their swords unsheathed and leading the way.

The night was filled with the sound of pounding hooves, and shrill commands and shouts. A wall of Spanish horses appeared to creep closer and closer to the forest. They would find it difficult to manoeuvre among the thick trees, but this did not deter the Spanish. They were animated by a thirst for glory and a belief in victory. They would locate and destroy the barbaric Germans and their harmless toy, and then, it would be on to Mannheim.

If the Germans had received sufficient training, they would wait until the final moment, when the Spanish cavalry were within touching distance, perhaps ten or twenty feet from the edge of the forest, before they fired their muskets.

If the Germans had *not* received sufficient training, they would discharge their weapons ineffectually, and much too early, which would leave them open to the cavalryman's attack. It all depended on when the Germans fired their weapons.

'*Not yet you bastards, not yet*,' Burroughs hissed, as a few muskets were discharged. Lock saw von Salm call a halt to the firing, and tell his men to wait. It was possible the discharges had been accidental. It was difficult enough to remember the forty-three steps for firing the musket, and the poor visibility hardly made it easier.

The Spanish were making rapid progress. A fearsome collection of sturdy beasts advanced forward, swallowing the distance until Lock could make out Spanish faces, and could see the cold steel of their drawn swords.

And then, perhaps a little less than fifty feet away, von Salm issued an order Lock had not been expecting.

Taking advantage of the slight slope which led up to the forest, von Salm had prepared several wicker balls roughly five feet in height. The German leader was evidently a reader of classical warfare; such tactics would not have been out of place among the tribal Germans from a millennium and a half ago.

Flynn whispered a blessing, and Lock counted at least twelve such flammable balls, which were ignited with remarkable cohesion, before tumbling towards the enemy.

Horses reared at the sight, and angry faces were twisted into panic, as the flaming boulders approached. One careless rider collided head on with the rolling nightmare, and his screams filled the night.

The Spanish ground was illuminated, and there was effectively nowhere to hide. Now was the time to capitalise. Within seconds, another shout was heard from the German lines, and muskets were discharged, only adding to the panic.

Burroughs practically jumped with glee. His knowledge of ancient warfare bursting to emerge. 'Just like the Teutoburg Forest,' he whispered, shaking his head. 'Von Salm has done his homework.'

Some of the wicker balls did not deliver, and rolled limply to a standstill a few feet from the forest's edge. For as long as they burned, the Germans would be able to see the Spanish coming.

A raging fire could overwhelm the senses, not merely with smoke, but with a brightness that cast a glare over darker features in the distance. The Germans, tucked into their forest in the dead of night, would be effectively invisible, though they were far from silent.

The edge of the forest was alive with noise. Smoke seemed to pour from the Germans, as their discharged weapons spewed forth their murderous contents. A steady cloud of smoke was blown by a light wind directly into the cavalry, which confused their advance.

Lock then noted something else.

The Germans hadn't taken the time to reload their cumbersome muskets. They had instead come armed with two weapons apiece. These secondary weapons were now retrieved, and within seconds of the first shots being released, the match cord was lit and attached.

On another command, a second torrent of musket balls was propelled towards the cavalry. The result was two murderous volleys of lead, one after the other, with barely twenty seconds in between.

'*Yes!*' Burroughs exclaimed, punching the air, '*That's how you do it lads!*'

A horrendous carnage followed. A wave of death and awful mutilation swept across the Spanish ranks, annihilating countless men and beasts in a matter of seconds.

Men who had once been so full of life were buried by slain horses. Their limbs were separated from their bodies amidst shrieks of panic and pain.

Or, often, the lead musket ball collided with the human head, and the result was an abrupt, eerie silence and a flash of red mist where the head had once been.

Smoke obscured much of the horror, but hearing the war was no issue.

The knee-high grass quickly became slick with blood and entrails, of human and horse alike, and many men slipped as they attempted to right themselves. Some brave survivors did endure the onslaught.

Perhaps twenty out of the original company of cavalry endured, and these men appeared in some cases to hesitate, before defiantly charging on. Some errant shots were discharged, but the German firepower had plainly been expended. The Spanish seemed to sense the reduction in danger, but the Germans now prepared to participate in a new phase of the fight – the gruesome melee.

The Spanish cavalry had been taught to seek the melee, to confront the infantry in a head-on charge, but not like this. A few guttural shouts could be heard, before several German figures ran from the edge of the forest, pikes in hand, to meet what remained of the Spanish horse.

Some Germans were outmatched or out skilled, but the decimation of Spanish numbers meant that the cavalry's mission was impossible, and this was soon realised.

The air was thick with the sense of struggle.

The smells of powder, blood and soiled breeches wafted back to Lock's nose.

Whoops and cheers from the Germans had to be hushed by von Salm, with only limited success. A piercing, haunting shriek emerged from another burning Spaniard who had been knocked from his horse onto a live wicker ball.

Lock watched as the merciless German crippled the Spanish rider, dooming him to his horrific sentence.

The howls and shouts of pain, the futile pleas of mercy, the harrowing groans of the mutilated and disembowelled, Lock absorbed it all.

De la Barca's profile remained visible. The commander was still seated on his horse, and he appeared to berate the men who had died and the men who had yet to move all at once.

His infantry, unprepared for the spectacle and lacking orders, stood awed at the disaster. The Spanish commander had certainly erred, and in this miscalculation, he had thrown away his cavalry with no returns.

Several mounts milled around behind the lines, some of them lacking riders. One horse, driven mad from a gaping wound in its side, was abruptly executed by a merciful soldier.

Lock half jumped at the suddenness of the act.

Flynn cast him a dubious glance.

An unexpected interlude followed, as von Salm called his Germans back to the forest, and de la Barca took stock of his disaster.

Several burning wicker balls remained, combining with the Spanish fixtures to bath the stark scene in a bright yellow light.

De la Barca moved down his line, and barked orders at his infantry to advance.

Just then, the trebuchet fired, and with a sudden pang of guilt, the machine's original purpose was recalled.

Diego de la Barca's world was about to come crashing down.

A bundle of bloody rags landed with a small bounce a few feet in front of a gathering mass of Spanish infantry.

At first, it seemed, not one of the soldiers was willing to investigate, and they greeted the arrival of the package with some curious turns of their heads. Perhaps they had read of medieval tactics, when trebuchets were used to propel diseased corpses into fortresses. Or perhaps the soldiers simply did not wish to draw attention to themselves.

Then, one officer moved forward to investigate.

Loud shouts followed, and another soldier ran a short distance to where de la Barca still sat on his horse, his eyes burning a hole in the defiant forest.

De la Barca's head turned to greet the approaching soldier, and with a flick of his heels, he made for the bloody package, which several figures now appeared to be examining.

'They sent his legs first,' Flynn whispered. 'De la Barca will recognise his son's boots, but he won't believe his eyes, so he'll send someone to check the graveyard tent.'

The Irishman proved correct.

Dismounting from his horse, de la Barca began walking, then sprinting, as the sight of his son's boots caught his eye.

The splendid black leather boots had been enhanced with gold lace, with Gaston Phillipe's name embroidered into their sides. They had been a gift from father to son, when the son had first determined to join his father on campaign.

Even from nearly half a mile away, de la Barca's despair was as tangible as the wind.

The Spaniard had dropped to his knees, and his arms fumbled with the parcel, before a mixture of horror, rage and sorrow surged through his body.

A quick conversation played out just behind de la Barca, as an officer sprinted to the graveyard tent. Within seconds, he emerged with the news that Phillipe's coffin was empty.

And then de la Barca fall apart.

A loud, unrestrained wail of sorrow reached all the way to where he was standing, and a shiver ran across Lock's shoulders.

The night had become suddenly cold.

How had he done such a monstrous thing?

Had it truly been necessary?

Flynn let out a low whistle as the three men watched in silence.

And then, the trebuchet fired again.

'It's... his arms,' Flynn said, almost apologetically. 'Gaston Phillipe was to be buried with all his finery. I believe one of his rings was quite valuable. He never wore it while on duty.'

The sound of the firing trebuchet caused de la Barca's head to jerk towards its source, before scanning the area.

Once again, the distraught commander looked directly at Lock's position, his face twisted in angst. But his attention was then stolen away once another bloodied package landed, this time a few feet in front of the graveyard tent.

Men shuffled uncomfortably in the Spanish ranks, as they watched their commander come to terms with the horror. One individual, perhaps a subordinate, advanced warily to where the second bundle had landed, and he waved a cautious right arm at a comrade, who hesitated before joining him.

The two men crouched by the package. Their heads began to shake, as the package was opened. One of the men gagged and threw up beside the delivery.

Lock suppressed his own gag reflex.

Even now, the sight still pulled at his stomach.

De la Barca sprinted to its landing place. Some of his subordinates attempted to discourage him from going, but they bowed to their commander. Others were pushed away, and after a brief moment, a limb was produced from the delivery.

Another wail, lower and more constant, followed.

Flynn crossed himself.

The Father removed a ring from his son's hand, kissed it, and placed it on his own hand.

Behind the terrible scene, a subordinate appeared to rally the men, as all suddenly stood to attention, with their eyes projecting forward.

Battle order appeared to be restored, but it was not due to the commands of de la Barca.

At this sudden display, de la Barca appeared to snap out of his grief-stricken trance, he turned his head away from his son's remains, and he shouted some Spanish demands at his subordinate.

'Seems de la Barca wants it to be known that he is still in charge,' Burroughs whispered. 'It will be most fortunate for us if he is.'

And then, the trebuchet fired again. This time, a crack accompanied the familiar sound, and the Germans fumbled around the machine.

Its arm had apparently been exhausted, but it had just about managed to propel its final delivery forward.

'Phillipe's torso,' Flynn said. 'It'd be ravaged by now, but de la Barca will still remember his son's embroidered duff coat.'

The torso landed halfway between the soldiers and the forest. At first, nobody moved. As de la Barca turned his head towards the third package, those around him began pleading with their commander not to investigate. As though driven by a personal mission of grim discovery, de la Barca barked and gesticulated wildly at his subordinates, who all withdrew.

The commander ran before stumbling and falling.

Some of the Germans laughed and pointed.

The trebuchet was broken beyond repair, and its handlers had since taken to watching for the consequences of their actions, while keeping themselves concealed. The Germans that had fired originally had since vanished, likely back into their burrows.

De la Barca picked himself back up, and limped towards the package. A few paces short of it, the commander dropped to his knees. He did not need to open this package; its contents had evidently made themselves known to him already. A subordinate rushed behind him to offer support, and to try and pull him from the sight.

Lock watched, holding his breath, as the commander tried to pull free, before the extent of the trauma seemed to consume him, and he collapsed into his subordinate's embrace. The full measure of grief poured from him.

Loud, uncontrolled sobs gripped de la Barca's shuddering body.

Lock repressed his reflexes once again with deep, deliberate breathing. It was difficult to know if he was sick at the sight, or with his actions.

Behind de la Barca's back, the subordinate seemed to wave at a few more men, who rushed to de la Barca's side. Another figure went to retrieve the package, and the subordinate pulled de la Barca away so he wouldn't see the act.

The Spanish now lined up, before de la Barca, with superhuman discipline, pushed his comforter away, and stood abruptly to attention.

De la Barca bellowed a command.

The commander was imbued with a new venom, a new level of rage, which only more violence could possibly satiate.

De la Barca's subordinates bowed slightly before the display, before turning to their soldiers, and ordering them forward.

There could be no doubt, de la Barca was determined now to burn the whole forest down if that was what was required.

The longer, safter route to Mannheim would be ignored, and the first part of the mission had been accomplished. The only casualty had been a Father's spirit.

Leaves rustled to Lock's right, followed by a snapping of twigs. Lock turned to see Georg von Salm.

It was difficult to tell how the German leader felt. Did he feel better? Or did he merely feel as though order had been restored, now that de la Barca had experienced the visceral horrors which war could visit on one's family?

Von Salm wore a large, dark green piece of cloth which covered his whole face save his eyes, and mud had been rubbed around them so his pale skin did not give his position away.

Burroughs turned to greet von Salm with a nod, and the German leader reciprocated, before nodding at Lock, then at Flynn, and moving off.

Von Salm walked several paces before lifting a branch, and disappearing underground.

'Time to go lads,' Burroughs said.

- CHAPTER THIRTY-ONE -

The underground village had clearly been prepared for war. As Burroughs led the way around an earthy corner, Germans brushed past in the opposite direction. A nervous energy seemed to fill the dark, dust-filled air. By now, everyone had been told of de la Barca's trauma. They had been told of his intention to come this way.

'Where are we going?' Lock asked, just above a whisper.

But Burroughs did not hear him. Thick though the atmosphere of the burrow was, it was also filled with an eerie silence, broken only by the shuffling sounds of men moving to their destinations.

No one stood still. No one engaged in conversation. On some corners, one or two children looked for their parents, and Burroughs swore at the Germans for allowing them to be here.

'*General*, where are we going?' Flynn called from behind Lock, Burroughs stopped abruptly and turned. Dirt covered his face, and his eyes were watering.

'Not far now lads, not far now,' the General simply said, before returning to his quest.

It was difficult to keep track of corners turned, rooms passed, and even time itself. The ultimate nightmare would be to lose oneself in the heart of these tunnels. The air was unusually thin, likely due to the abundance of excited individuals and their deep breaths.

Every now and then, dirt fell from the wall or ceiling of the tunnel. Lock watched a hand-sized clod of earth fall and land heavily in Burroughs' hair, but the General virtually ignored it. He was evidently deep in thought, probably trying to remember how to get to his destination.

After another few minutes of shuffling forward, a corner was turned, and

Burroughs clasped his hands together in prayer.

'*Hallelujah*,' the General exclaimed, in a mixture of excitement and relief. He pushed his way into a narrower passage. The sound of feet on wood followed, and the General rose up a ladder that was set deep into the wall.

Lock looked up, hoping that no clods of earth would land on his face. The night sky beckoned just beyond Burroughs' head. Burroughs disappeared with a grunt out of the tunnel, and Lock clasped the rungs to follow him.

After a few flailing movements, a hand gripped Lock's shoulder and pulled him the rest of the way. A German he had not met grinned widely at Lock, before helping Flynn out of the tunnel, and then climbing back down the ladder himself.

Lock tried to look around and get his bearings, before a sense of recognition began to set in.

He had been here before.

The previous day, when everything had been different, he had come to this clearing in the forest. This time, he was in a more advantageous position. He now stood at the base of the large, mossy rock. From its heights, the Germans had once aimed their unready muskets at him.

Would he have the opportunity to enjoy its advantages now?

It was certainly worth hoping for, as the once humble rock had been utterly transformed. Now, in its place, a true forest fortress loomed fifteen feet high.

It was now a bastion of wood and soil. Mounds of earth had been added to its sides, and wood had been layered to hold the structure together.

Ladders rested against it, and snaked several feet upwards. Burroughs jogged for one of these ladders, and began to climb. Lock followed, and before long had reached the top.

Georg von Salm had plainly mobilised every able-bodied German to pile earth and stack timbers. It was incredible that his army of filthy labourers had constructed such a fortress in a little more than a day.

It may appear generous to label piles of earth, stone and wood a 'fortress.' Lock had also been puzzled, when Father's lessons on siegecraft had paid scant regard to the legendary castles which had towered over England's landscape.

Unable to suppress his yearning for a good castle, Lock had asked why his lessons never addressed them. The answer left him shocked, and a little disappointed. The medieval castle of yore, Father explained, was obsolete – a victim, ultimately, of the advent of gunpowder.

Generalissimos soon learned that cannons would shatter the thin, high walls of stone with minimal effort. It was a bitter lesson to accept, and many a ruler failed to accept it in time. Word soon spread from North Italy, where the discovery was made, that thick, low walls of mud, wood and stone were the future.

Experimentation followed, as Europe's monarchs continued their incessant wars. It was soon learned that the thickest walls could host their own cannons to batter the besiegers. Others angled their bastions, to provide interlocking fields of fire that were virtually impenetrable.

And so, the true war of attrition – between attacker and defender – was invested with new life. Some, naturally, still longed for the old ways.

'Looks ugly as the devil's child, but it's proper secure', Father had said. Now, standing atop this forest bastion, Lock was inclined to agree.

The largely flat platform boasted panoramic views of the forest. Any attackers would be seen in plenty of time. A rough fence of stones and more earth was lumped at the bastion's edges, providing waist-high cover for defenders.

There were also some homely touches. A large rock, slightly smaller than the boulders hurled by the trebuchet, rested in the centre of the bastion. This was the designated dumping ground, and a plethora of war materiel was scattered around it. One German sat on the small boulder, and fiddled with his musket.

Lock walked carefully to the bastion's south-facing edge, and peered over. De la Barca was guaranteed to attack from the south, along the only navigable road through the forest, which Lock had traversed on the previous day.

Provided he did so, they would be ready for him. The clearing was the ideal place for an army to rest while moving through the forest. At least an acre of virtually open land was sprawled out in front of the bastion.

Consequently, it was also the ideal place to launch an ambush.

This was the position Burroughs had referred to. It certainly felt secure. It was also a cut above what Lock had been expecting.

Perhaps the cause was not lost, and the inner cynic would be defeated alongside de la Barca?

A cough sounded behind him, and Lock turned as Georg von Salm's silhouette appeared. The German smiled with his eyes, and waved at Lock.

'You did *very* well earlier,' von Salm said, as he walked briskly towards Lock's perch.

The grisly mission returned vividly to him, and Lock was washed with guilt. After witnessing de la Barca's breakdown, somehow it no longer seemed appropriate to revel in the daring nature of the deed.

Evidently, von Salm felt differently. He was positively joyful.

'It was nothing,' Lock said quietly, before turning his head back to the clearing.

'*Nothing*? Herr Lock, you defeated the commander before he even took to the battlefield. Do you know how many have accomplished such a feat?'

'I can't imagine many would have done what I did.'

Von Salm squinted at Lock. 'Many would have done far worse. It is never a crime to dispense justice, Matthew, remember that.'

Lock searched for another subject. He gestured to the stump where, the previous day, he had placed a bag of food. 'Hard to believe I broke bread with your men down there.'

'For your safety, I wouldn't recommend venturing down there again,' von Salm offered an exaggerated wink.

'Don't worry, I'm staying right here.'

'Remember what I showed you, with the ditches?'

Lock nodded.

Von Salm gestured vaguely to a space just in front of the rock.

Visibility was much poorer away from the fires, but the clouds had departed, providing enough light to see the forest floor. The place was otherworldly in the dark. Yet it was definitely familiar.

The crimson stain where Gaston Phillipe had met his end still shone slightly under the young moon.

'Under the ground, we've got a huge ditch ready for them,' von Salm said, and even in the dark, the glint in his eyes was clear. He had been excited about this moment for some time.

Flynn now walked towards them. In his own struggle, Lock had nearly forgotten about the Irishman.

'When will it happen?' Flynn asked von Salm in his best German, as he pointed at the clearing. Von Salm tilted his head to the right, a gesture which dragged a lock of his matted grey hair across his face. Von Salm flicked it away.

'We have to wait for the perfect moment. I have my men in all the right positions. I say the word, the wood is removed, and the ground will swallow them whole.'

'Will de la Barca die with them?' Lock wasn't quite sure why he had asked such a specific question, but von Salm addressed it quickly.

'I doubt it Herr Lock, I still have one more thing to show him, and then he can go.'

'*Go?*'

'Go to his death. I am sure he will want to make it quick. Once I've broken him, once I've made the bastard feel the pain he made me feel, then I'm finished with him,' von Salm then focused on Lock. 'You can kill him if you like.'

Lock didn't know why he was so opposed to the idea. He didn't have an answer for von Salm. But he did have a question.

'What else is there to show him?'

Von Salm smiled with his eyes once again, before producing a white cloth bag from his left shoulder. There was only one body part left for von Salm to hurl back at de la Barca. Von Salm confirmed as much within seconds, as he pulled Phillipe's severed head from the bag by a clump of hair.

'Not a bad looking man,' von Salm mused, as he rotated the head in an almost complete circle, 'but it didn't do him much good in the end!'

Phillipe's eyes were opened slightly, but his mouth looked as though it had been forced shut. A portion of the ugly gash across Phillipe's neck was still visible from where von Salm's scythe had opened him up. Mercifully, after a few seconds, the head was returned to the bag.

Lock shuddered to think how this latest trauma would be presented to de la Barca.

'Get into position gentlemen,' Burroughs whispered. 'The Spanish have entered the forest, and they'll be with us in less than half an hour.'

'What's the plan Sir?' Lock asked, as the General swept soil out of his hair. Burroughs appeared puzzled that it could get so clogged.

Burroughs glanced up at Lock as pieces of earth fell from his head. 'We had a close call with that bastard rider earlier on. He raised the alarm early, so the timetable has been brought forward.'

A large piece of earth was finally loosened and fell from Burroughs collar, and the General watched it fall with satisfaction. 'You saw that nasty business. Brutal, but necessary I'm afraid. This is how the soldier fights when his back is against the wall.'

'Will de la Barca lead from the front?'

'It's unlikely, but not impossible.'

'If he's so unstable, why does a subordinate not replace de la Barca? Does he not have a second in command?'

Burroughs chuckled. 'Lock, de la Barca is a well-connected man. If he doesn't want to do something, he's not going to do it, and you're not going to stop him if you value your prospects in this life.'

'So his army would follow him off a cliff out of their fear of him?'

'As I said envoy, it's not *him* they fear, but the people he knows. One strongly worded letter sent to the wrong people, you could be on the run for the rest of your life. Unless of course, you know where to hide.' Burroughs was examining his musket, and Lock attempted to pluck up his courage.

'Sir, I can shoot if you need me, just say the word.'

A flash of indignation crossed Burroughs' face, but then he squinted at Lock. 'Vere did tell me you could shoot. I wasn't sure if it was true though, the man did tend to go on.'

'Sir, it is true. I have practiced the drill extensively.'

'We thought you weren't a soldier.'

'I am not Sir,' Lock replied, with a shrug, 'But neither were those Germans, and they still managed.'

Burroughs smiled at a point well made, and he gestured for Lock to come over to him. 'You can take my musket,' the General said. Lock prepared to protest, but Burroughs held up his right hand. 'Relax lad, not everyone carries family heirlooms on their person. This is your standard matchlock. I'll grab another from our German friends. They've got heaps of them after years of hoarding.'

With that, the weapon was placed in Lock's hands, and Burroughs peeled away to pester a German who had several firearms slung over his shoulder.

Flynn glanced at Lock, and Lock met his eyes. The Irishman nodded, and Lock nodded back.

Were they on good terms yet?

Flynn pointed to his costrel, and the memory of the taste returned to Lock's mouth. He hesitated, but then walked the few paces to the Irishman.

'You refilled it?'

'Naturally,' Flynn smiled, 'It's important to prioritise these things Lock. Never know when they might come in handy.'

Lock took the costrel in his right hand, took a large swig, and nearly gagged. He looked accusingly at Flynn, who was suppressing a laugh.

'What *is* this?' Lock spat.

'That's poitín Lock, you met earlier today.'

'This does *not* taste like what I sipped earlier today.'

'Well, it's not mixed with water this time.'

'I thought you said only madmen drank it without water?'

The Irishman chuckled, and gestured vaguely to their position atop the mossy rock. 'Look at us, atop this shite pile, and relying on farmers to defend us. I reckon we qualify as madmen now.'

Lock exhaled. The sudden rush of alcohol made his head swim.

Flynn giggled, and seemed in the midst of another sentence, before restraining himself again.

What was he not saying?

He extended an arm, and Lock hurriedly returned the costrel with a half-hearted thanks.

'I'll see you after,' Flynn said stoically.

Lock nodded, and joined a returning Burroughs, who was now armed with a new musket.

'Ah, good lad. Now about the plan. We destroyed his cavalry, so he's only got a few regiments of foot. The tercio is useless in the forest, so his men will likely be marching...' Burroughs glanced back at the dirt road to the south, as though calculating in his mind, '...four or five abreast I reckon. Eight hundred or so men, marching about four or five abreast...'

'It doesn't sound very precise Sir,' Lock said, mostly thinking out loud.

Burroughs did not disagree, he nodded in acknowledgement and sighed. 'That's war, Lock. Planning is a large part of it, and then you send your men against their men, and hope that the other side loses heart first. Today, we've got the land on our side, but don't underestimate the Spanish. The Dutch did, and now they're fighting for their survival.'

'*Twenty minutes,*' a loud whisper exclaimed.

Burroughs grimaced, and then fumbled for his musket. Sweat glistened on the back of the General's neck, though the air had cooled.

'What did he say to you lad?' Burroughs asked quietly, still with his head down and apparently focused on his musket.

As Lock looked at him, the General dipped his head in the direction of Georg von Salm. The German was standing only a few feet from them, to the rear of the bastion, engaged in conversation with some other filthy Germans.

'About what Sir?'

'De la Barca. Did he say what he planned to do with him?'

'He said he'd break his spirit, and that I could kill him after that for all he cared.'

'You won't though. You won't kill him?'

Lock flinched away from Burroughs. 'Perish the thought Sir! If de la Barca surrenders, I am honour-bound to spare his life.' In truth, honour mattered less than the prospect of adding to the suffocating sense of guilt. The horror of another atrocity on his conscience was almost too much to bear.

Burroughs nodded, but kept his eyes focused on his firearm. 'It is *very* important that de la Barca does not die today. It is a matter of honour, yes, but it is also common sense. He knows much about Spanish armies along the Rhine. He knows where General Cordoba's army is, and how big it is. I hear he even dined with the Archduchess in Brussels last Christmas. If de la Barca dies, this information dies with him.'

'I won't let him die Sir,' Lock said, his body stiffening, before Burroughs waved at him to relax.

The General checked the muzzle of his musket for what must have been the fourth time. He glanced briefly back at von Salm, who was still conversing with the Germans. A thought then occurred to Lock.

'Sir, what happens to them after this?'

'The Germans?'

Lock nodded.

Burroughs sighed and shook his head. 'It depends on what happens today Lock. We can't take them back to England with us, if that's what you're asking.'

'No Sir, I mean, they've lived in the forest for two years. Once the Spanish know of their secrets, where will they hide then?'

Burroughs pushed a strand of greying hair behind his right ear. He turned slightly away from Lock.

'Sir? Will His Majesty send them some aid? They are his daughter's subjects after all.'

Burroughs let a boisterous laugh escape, startling several Germans, who responded with icy glares.

'I will remind you Lock, His Majesty abandoned us here on the Rhine, to surrender, or to fight to the death. We are here now, in this forest, because of you, and because of your Irish friend. We will win honours if we survive, but if we fail, the King will act as though we never existed.'

'But *why* Sir? Can His Majesty not spare even another cohort of reinforcements? Does he not see that failure here will reflect badly on his honour?' Lock's shoulders sagged as the questions were posed.

'Come now Lock, you've heard of the King's dream. He wants to marry his prince to Spain's princess, and craft a match made in heaven.' Burroughs shook his head slowly. 'He arranged peace between Spain and the Dutch, so he thinks he's God's gift to diplomacy.'

'My Father helped arrange that,' Lock said quietly.

'I heard. An impressive man, your Father; as mean with words as he was with weapons.'

'Did you know him?' Lock couldn't help but ask.

Burroughs shook his head. 'No lad, our paths never crossed, but I did hear a lot about him from Vere.'

'*Ten minutes,*' a voice behind them hissed.

'Did you ever –'

Lock was interrupted by Burroughs holding up a hand, and placing a finger on his dry, cracked lips.

'Listen, lad, you can hear the screams.'

But the only sounds that reached Lock were birdsong and the roar of the Rhine beside them. He turned towards the south road, and nearly jumped.

A single figure on horseback approached.

'He's one of ours,' a German to the front of the bastion said.

'Our last scout has come home,' von Salm whispered. 'Positions, gentlemen.'

The figure dismounted, before leading his horse to a small party of Germans, who promptly led the beast deeper into the forest, out of imminent danger.

The figure then made for the bastion, and clambered up the ladder which had yet to be withdrawn. The very act of the climb underlined how high the bastion was.

Once the figure ascended to the top, he made for von Salm. In his haste he nearly tripped over one of the planks which lined the bastion's floor. Before long the two were deep in a conversation of animated whispers, though Lock couldn't quite make out what was said.

'Sir...' Lock began, his eyes still fixed on the conversation between von Salm and his scout. 'Why am I here Sir, on this rock. Should your men not be here instead? Beside you?'

Burroughs was in the midst of checking his bandolier, and did not look up from his task. 'My lads are out in the forest, waiting to eat the Spanish alive. You're staying here, because it's the safest place in this wretched forest. Unless you'd rather be with the children in their hidey hole.'

Lock's face reddened. 'I would rather take my chances here, Sir.'

Burroughs smiled briefly, before gesturing to a point in the centre of the bastion, near to the knee-high boulder. 'You stay *there* lad, you stay next to the rock and you stay low. If Vere learns that I brought you into battle and got you killed, he'd never speak to me again. Now, I do owe him some money, so perhaps there would be a silver lining if –'

'*Sir*? Am I not to fight in the battle?'

Burroughs chuckled while shaking his head, and Lock gasped in frustration.

'I'm to stand here like a decoration?'

'Lock, you are no soldier, you said so yourself. I already risked your neck sending you into the camp. Good haul by the way.'

'I handled myself like any soldier would.'

Burroughs exhaled and turned his head to Lock. 'Have you ever been in battle Lock? A *real* battle?'

Lock maintained eye contact. 'Not yet Sir, but I must start somewhere.'

'You'll still be in the battle, lad, you'll just be safely out of harm's way.'

'What if you *need* me?' Lock asked, looking around the bastion. 'There's only about ten men up here.'

'Don't worry lad, the other Germans will be here shortly.'

'*Five minutes,*' the voice behind them hissed again.

'They had better hurry,' Lock said, as briskly as he dared.

Burroughs glared at him, and then gestured for his charge to go to the centre of the fortress.

Lock sighed before obliging. He took several steps, and it now dawned that he would experience his first battle. Whether at a distance or not, the experience would still count.

Lock tried to settle his breathing, and made for the centre. Regardless of where he was during the encounter, this bastion would likely serve as the main focus of Spanish attacks. It would pay to remain in place, and wait for the General, in his desperation, to untie his ridiculous shackles.

Burroughs certainly behaved like someone who was soon to be in the thick of it. He had not come unprepared, and had seemingly raided Frankenthal's stores in anticipation.

As Lock sat on the rock, the arrangement became clearer. Strewn about were bandages, powder charges and muskets. The firearms were at varying stages of wear and tear; some lacked stocks altogether, and were little more than miniature barrels. This is where the soldiers would come if they needed anything, and Lock could help them find it quickly.

Did Burroughs expect him to do the work of the quartermaster, without the relevant pay or titles?

One German, clad in the familiar dark green coat, crouched beside the haul, perhaps scavenging for spare parts. He grunted at Lock to ask if he had any powder to spare, before moving on.

A few feet to Lock's left, Georg von Salm whispered to some Germans. One was the scout who had recently arrived, and he remained deep in conversation with his leader. His sweating face and anxious eyebrows suggested that he brought bad news. Two other Germans, perfectly still and at attention, stood by and watched.

Lock wondered at the stories these men might have, of living in the forest for two years, of sniping at the Spanish where possible, of cooking up schemes of revenge, and of digging, *lots and lots of digging.* As with all the forest Germans he had seen so far, their hands were caked with dirt, perhaps following some last-minute adjustments to von Salm's horror show.

'Everything alright, Georg?' Lock asked. It felt unnatural to use his first name, but it also felt unnatural to talk to a man with a stump for a tongue.

Georg von Salm glanced at Lock, and gestured for the newly arrived figure to be quiet. 'Herr Lock, I trust you are keeping yourself safe?'

Lock nodded, and prepared to rephrase the question, before von Salm interrupted him. 'We had an issue in one of our tunnels. terrible cave in. Twenty men dead or missing.'

'That's horrible!'

'They knew the risks Herr Lock. And they did not die in vain. While setting their trap, it seems they knocked the wrong plank loose, but the Spanish lost one hundred of their own.'

'Will we have that problem here?' Lock asked, gesturing behind him, where the largest trap of all had been set.

'It is possible, Herr Lock. These things are difficult to get right every time. But my men know it worth their sacrifice. I would swap twenty of my men for one hundred dead Spaniards any day.'

The cold statement took Lock by surprise, but it made sense.

Von Salm had hardly survived this long by being sentimental.

Flynn whistled low, and the sound drew von Salm's attention.

'Your men are here... or what's left of them,' the Irishman said quietly.

Lock shuffled to the bastion's south-facing side, ignoring Burroughs' protest to return to safety. Perhaps twenty Germans walked delicately across the clearing. They were dishevelled and filthy, their dark green coats smeared with mud and, in some cases, blood.

Each man made their way to the bastion's left side, where the ladder had been left. They scaled it, and suddenly the fortress became less spacious.

Von Salm directed traffic, and a boy, perhaps a teenager, pulled the ladders up onto the bastion one by one, before sitting and nodding at von Salm. One of von Salm's subordinates had begun to distribute lit match cords, and the Germans eagerly, but cautiously, snapped the cord onto the musket's serpentine.

The sound of heavy breathing filled the immediate area.

The birds had stopped singing.

The roar of the Rhine even seemed to meekly lower its volume.

Another sound, war, began to fill Lock's ears.

It started slow and small. One or two shouts, a shriek, or a discharged musket. And then another sound could be heard. The distinct sound of the deliberate tapping on wood, most likely a distant tree stump.

As one, the Germans lifted their ears to the sound.

'They're *here*,' von Salm hissed. 'Positions!'

Lock continued to ignore Burroughs urgings, before the General placed a hand on his shoulder. Just before he turned to reach the relative safety of the fortress' centre, Lock spied the enemy, making their way deliberately along the forest road.

They walked five abreast, and moved with a stoic, almost mechanical deliberateness. Some pikes were held upright, but since these were of little use in a forest, it was likely that de la Barca would depend on his musketeers.

Each soldier was bound to be a crack shot and an accomplished professional, which was more than could be said for Burrough's band of ragamuffins.

Lock's stolen glance had confirmed something else.

Something unsettling.

Despite an evening of many tortures, the discipline of the tercio had not been snapped. These Spaniards were focused, and had surely taken the earlier atrocities as a personal insult.

Like de la Barca, they now thirsted for revenge.

- CHAPTER THIRTY-TWO -

The *tercio* is the deadliest weapon in the King of Spain's arsenal. That was what Charles Lock had always said. To make a tercio, as many as three thousand men could be grouped together, and stood in a square formation. The middle of the square was stocked with pikemen, and once they lowered these pointed weapons, a cavalry attack became impossible.

On the outer portion of the square, musketeers watched and waited for an opportunity. These men would fire in volleys, and if reloading, or threatened, retiring behind the pikes was always an option. Charles Lock had noted that swordsmen once filled the ranks of the tercio, but they had since been replaced by even more musketeers. The Spanish had adapted the tercio to deliver more firepower, and the results had been devastating.

This lethal square could fight and destroy any combination the enemy could present. And, when the enemy tried to copy the Spanish tercio, they quickly found that the manoeuvre could be replicated, but not duplicated. No soldiers were as professional or as dogged in their tercio as the Spanish. Their military machine squashed enemy after enemy, and it showed no signs of slowing down.

Nearly a century before, during the 1525 Battle of Pavia, Spanish tercios had ripped a French army to pieces, and even captured its King. In the decades since, the tercio had only become deadlier. It had also become a byword for Spanish professionalism, and Habsburg domination of the battlefield.

King Philip IV of Spain had only succeeded to the throne in 1621, and he had a lot to prove. That same year, the war with the Dutch resumed, following a dozen years of peace. Then, as before, the King of Spain ordered the tercios forward. This time, the Dutch were caught unprepared. Their defences had deteriorated, and the Republic had been riven by internal conflict.

Spanish armies were also led by new men who could refresh the tercio once again. Ambitious Italians like Ambrogio Spinola, whose thirst for command and combat was reinforced by the personal grudge he harboured against the Dutch for slaying his brother. Once he held the reins of command in his hands, there was no limit to what Spinola's tercios could accomplish.

'A formidable man, and a formidable mind,' Charles Lock had said, after meeting the Genoese commander in Milan.

That formidable mind was on full display as Spain prepared to renew its war with the Dutch. On the eve of war, the Spanish moved into the Rhineland, and conquered their way towards the Dutch border.

It certainly helped that the former overlord of the Rhine, the Elector Palatine, had been declared a rebel by the Holy Roman Emperor. It was doubly helpful that the Holy Roman Emperor was a cousin of the King of Spain.

All of these men, the Holy Roman Emperor, the King of Spain, and the Archdukes of the Spanish Netherlands, all hailed from the sprawling Habsburg dynasty. The dynasty had humble origins, perhaps beginning as a family of minor importance in a lowly Swiss castle. But the dynasty didn't remain lowly for long.

Years of scratching and clawing brought them to power in Austria. From this base as Archdukes of that land, they expanded their horizons even further. They had a secret weapon in their arsenal. Not the tercio, but marriage.

So famous was this tactic, that a King of Hungary had once declared 'Let others wage war. You, happy Austria, *marry*!' Habsburg power reached new heights when they did just that, and married into the Kingdom of Spain.

The world outside the Habsburg patrimony did not remain static as that House expanded its reach. England presented particular problems. Following many decades, a Reformation and a Virgin Queen, the subjects of this Habsburg Spanish King engaged in a daring venture: the 1588 Spanish Armada. The plot was simple: to send the might of Spain against puny England, and wipe out the heretical Protestant creed in one great naval assault, followed by an invasion.

As England rallied its militia to meet the invader, Charles Lock, then a seventeen-year-old boy, barely old enough to boast some chin hairs, stood anxiously among their ranks.

He watched the fighting off shore, as fearsome naval cannon punctured several holes in Spanish hulls, and the Spanish commander was eventually forced to withdraw. Once they fled, many Spaniards became shipwrecked on Ireland's western coast. Whisper and rumour told that the wild Irish looted the unfortunate, and boiled alive everyone else.

The story of the Habsburgs, of their unprecedented growth and powers, and then England's humbling of Spain, was Charles Lock's favourite. It quickly became a favourite of his sons.

Lock thirsted for every detail, every juicy piece of gossip concerning who had married whom, which prince had declared what war, and the fascinating, terrifying story of the Spanish Empire's never-ending expansion.

Lock's eyes had widened as his Father told him of Spanish power reaching all the way to new islands in the Pacific, which King Philip had named after himself. But the Philippines was just the beginning for the Spanish Empire. The realm of the Habsburgs became, indeed, an Empire on which the sun never set.

Over time, Charles Lock was forced to begin the story of the Spanish Armada many years before the event, so that his inquisitive son would be fully satisfied, his imagination captured by the sparkling tales of empires, adventure and conquest.

Although some of his countrymen like to claim otherwise, Charles Lock was adamant that the defeat of the Armada in 1588 had been a fluke. Spain was still supremely powerful. Indeed, Father heavily underlined a key lesson which the rise of the Habsburgs had taught him.

Never fight a Spanish tercio on the battlefield.

As Lock watched his German allies stand atop their reinforced bastion, and engage loosely with the instructions of the drill, he said a prayer of thanks out loud that this group of filthy, ragamuffin men would not be fighting the tercio. Calls and shrieks from down below suggested that the Spanish were in a state of panic, but another lesson surged forward into Lock's mind: the cornered rat is often the most dangerous.

By order of General Burroughs, Lock lay virtually prone on the forest fortress. This bastion had taken advantage of the enormous mossy boulder, dropped into the forest by God's own hands, but the Germans had more than improved upon God's minimal design. Weeks of work, most of it in secret and in the dark, had fused wood and mounds of earth to the boulder.

Georg von Salm had wanted to do more, to add additional layers to the fortress, and perhaps add earthen walls to its main level. But there hadn't been time. As a result, the forest fortress was sturdy, and kept men roughly fifteen feet off the ground, but there was little cover to be had when upon it.

With the exception of the fortress' south-facing side, where the boulder naturally curved slightly upwards, the men would be exposed to errant pot-shots from the enemy once they stood up. It was hardly an easy exercise to aim and fire coherently at men who were positioned fifteen feet above you, but the Spanish did have the numerical advantage, and once they overcame their initial shock at the ambush, these numbers would surely tell.

Lock could hear only his breathing.

The roar of the river, the noise of the musket and the screams and shouts of men only occasionally filtered into his consciousness.

Georg von Salm and General Burroughs were both formidable men, and to meet them both at the same time was the height of misfortune for Diego de la Barca's men.

But then, the faces of the Germans who stood, in a row, atop this bastion, told a different story.

Von Salm was attempting to whip them into the musket drill. Forty-three illustrations dictated how the civilian could become the soldier, and these drill manuals had revolutionised how states made war. But Georg von Salm possessed none of these manuals, so the German leader was forced to teach his men virtually from memory.

Eleven Germans had stood, slightly stooped, just in front of Lock. The intention was for them to fire a volley down onto the Spanish, at an angle which ensured they wouldn't hit Flynn, Burroughs, or any other figure who rested their musket at the edge of the bastion. But the request was far too complicated for these Germans.

Though he lay a few feet behind them, Lock caught repeated glimpses of the Germans' faces, as they turned their backs to the enemy to load.

Lock recognised their expressions.

The same mixture of cluelessness, determination, and creeping panic, which Captain Frank had gradually drilled out of him.

It was impossible to say how much practice these Germans had actually been given, but the fact that a couple of the Germans stood still, effectively frozen to the spot, suggested that they had needed much, much more.

A crouching teenager, perhaps having just finished forest school, prepared a lantern to light their match cord, but the Germans were not ready yet, and had not been ready for several minutes.

Flynn eyed these Germans up, as he loaded his own musket for another shot. The Irishman shook his head, and his eyes briefly connected, through a pair of legs, with Lock's. Lock gave Flynn an encouraging smile, and the Irishman tore open a cartridge with his teeth before nodding back at him. Sound erupted from below.

Something was wrong.

The plan had been to lure the Spanish into position in front of the bastion, then to spring the trap, and collapse the ground underneath them. Perhaps fifteen minutes had passed since the Spanish had definitively arrived, but the sound of Spaniards falling to their deaths had not rung out.

Burroughs seemed too preoccupied pointing, waving and occasionally firing his musket, to worry about that aspect of the plan. But von Salm's uneasiness could be read from his face, notwithstanding the cloth that covered most of it. The German leader's eyes continued to dart around the bastion.

He treated his men with increasing impatience, and then, his whitening eyes seemed to connect with Lock's, and Lock's stomach lurched as von Salm, crawling, made his way towards him.

'Something is wrong Herr Lock,' von Salm yelled, as he struggled to maintain his raspy voice above the chorus of noise.

'What has happened?'

The German half slid, half crawled, before he reached Lock's side. 'The ground remains stable. I worry that the Spanish have infiltrated our tunnels.'

'Where's your men? Shouldn't the trap be sprung by now?'

'That is what I mean, Herr Lock, I fear the Spanish may have killed them. Worse, they could be under our feet right now.'

Von Salm delivered this worst-case scenario with the same matter of fact tone as one would use to discuss poor weather. Any panic in his eyes had not yet entered his voice.

It was not hard to imagine why.

The eleven Germans still attempting to fulfil the drill were within earshot. If their leader sounded panicked, what little reserves of calm they had would dry up also.

And then it hit Lock, that feeling of doom and resignation.

A feeling experienced when forgetting to close the chicken coop door, which resulted in twenty-three wandering chickens.

Or when meeting Mother's disappointed face after running mud across her favourite carpet.

Or, most fearsome of all, when the men in the black masks crossed his path for the first time. Lock knew what von Salm was about to ask him, and he knew he wouldn't be able to refuse.

'I need you to get down there,' Von Salm began, and the German held out a hand to point to where the entrance to the tunnel was. 'I need you to find out what happened, and if necessary, activate the trap yourself.'

As he delivered the request, von Salm's piercing blue eyes narrowed, and Lock buckled under the pressure of his gaze. How could he, with honour, stay safely out of harm's way, when his allies risked their necks?

Flynn would never let him live it down. He would always be the liability, the man who needed saving.

Lock looked back at the Irishman, who was then yelling at the eleven Germans to get on with it, with additional curses. With his gaze still fixed on Flynn, Lock sighed through his nose.

'I'll do it.'

'Excellent news. You'll find the trap easy enough. Once you climb down, take several lefts. You'll see a stone with a yellow mark on its side, enter the tunnel beside it. If you see a stone with a blue mark on it, you've gone too far.' Von Salm patted Lock heavily on his right shoulder, before handing him a sword. It was the same heavy sword which Lock had wrestled from him the day before. 'See if you can find a spare lantern before you go down there,' von Salm added, before turning away.

'Wait...' Lock began, before realising he didn't quite know what to ask. 'God bless you,' he said.

Von Salm nodded, and slinked past his eleven fumbling musketeers. As Lock turned towards the rear of the bastion, one of the Germans appeared to get off a shot, followed by three more.

Lock persevered, and made his way to the bastion's back edge. One lone German sat here, barely a teenager.

'I need to go down there,' Lock said to the filthy boy.

'Down, Sir?'

Lock nodded, and the boy reached for one of the ladders which had been pulled from the bastion's side.

'I will have to pull this back up as soon as you're down,' the boy said apologetically.

'Just make sure you lower it down to me later so I can get back up.'

'Where are you going?' the boy asked, turning the ladder and angling it over the bastion's edge.

'I have to fix the trap,' Lock said, gesturing behind him.

The boy grinned. 'You're going underground? You should take my lantern.'

'Thank you!' Lock nearly ripped the lantern from the boy's hands.

He'd already forgotten the one piece of advice von Salm had given him. He had been this close to fumbling around uselessly in the dark.

What else had he said?

Look out for the blue stone?

Or was it the yellow one?

Lock's heart raced, but he tried to keep his composure around the boy.

The ladder reached the ground, and the boy nodded at him.

Lock turned on his hands and knees, and awkwardly twisted his body to scale it.

A fall from this height would surely be fatal, particularly if he landed on one of the many large boulders that dotted the forest floor. His large sword clanked clumsily onto the earth as Lock descended, and it was hard to keep his hand on the lantern and the rungs at the same time. After a pause, Lock removed the musket from his shoulder, and placed it in the boy's eager hands.

There was no sense in bringing a firearm with him – it would be of little use in the dark.

After a brief descent, Lock's feet touched off the leaf litter.

He was suddenly much more exposed.

The noise of battle still seemed distant; the bastion's large size meant that the Spanish had yet to organise themselves to surround it, but they surely would in time.

And there it was, an alternative entrance into von Salm's underground world. From the base of the bastion's right side, a hole with a ladder protruding was barely visible. Lock moved the lantern in front of him and squinted at it, moving gradually over the forest floor as he did so.

Upon reaching it, Lock peered into the depths of the tunnel. No boys guarded this ladder. Although the Spanish didn't seem to have reached it yet, it was entirely possible that an enterprising Spaniard had climbed down into the underground, and waited for his next victim.

Lock longed for some clue of what dangers awaited him below, but darkness was all that stared back. Sheer, black darkness, and the strong smell of earth.

Lock exhaled, before turning to scale the ladder. He lodged his feet onto the fourth and fifth rungs, before exhaling again, and descending.

The light gradually left his eyes.

The lantern clanked off the ladder's wood, and his sword repeatedly caught on the tunnel's narrow sides, but Lock persevered, descending deeper and deeper.

To the last place on earth that he wanted to go.

- CHAPTER THIRTY-THREE -

E ven in the dim light provided by the lantern, Lock knew something had gone wrong underground.

There was a strange silence in the air. The activity he had seen hours before, of Germans all going in different directions, had given way to a stillness. The only sound that could be heard was the groaning and creaking of wooden planks. Lock held the lantern in front of him. He was tempted to call out, but he knew he should wait. If the worst happened, the element of surprise would be his only ally.

What was he doing down here? He should have stayed above. Lock regretted not taking over the training of those eleven Germans. He could have fired all eleven of their muskets in the time it took one of them to cough out some shots. Still, Flynn thought him a liability, and now here he was, fumbling through a fallen civilisation of soil and darkness.

Mercifully, Lock had recalled the instructions to keep to the left. Not that he had much choice. Several tunnels had become clogged with collapsed soil. Every now and then, a distant crack could be heard. Was this the sound of another plank snapping? Another tunnel collapsing?

Lock forced himself forward.

The weak light of the lantern caught the shape of the route, but little else. Lock snatched a bundle of rushlights as he walked. They were slightly damp, but they would suffice if the candle ran out. His foot slid forward on a wet plank of wood. Lock caught himself, and turned another corner. The tunnel was wider now, and additional groans could be heard.

That wasn't wood groaning under the weight of the earth.

It was the sound of groaning men.

Lock flashed the lantern left and right, but could not see the source of the sound. At any moment, an enemy more adjusted to the low light could launch an ambush.

Could they hear his heartbeat?

Straight ahead, the tunnel seemed to widen once again. On his right, rested a stone. It caught his eye because it appeared to be deliberately placed. Lock made out a yellow smudge on its side.

Had he gone too far? Or was this a sign that he had miraculously reached his destination.

Yellow or blue? Lock whispered to himself.

A faint groaning continued. It was muffled, but consistent. He had to bargain with the yellow stone, and hope for the best. A narrow passage led away to the right just beside it. Lock held the lantern in front of him, before pushing forward.

As he rounded the corner, the groaning became louder.

The man was in this room.

But who was he? Friend or foe?

His own breath refused to come quietly.

The air was fleeting and stale.

The lantern still in front of him, Lock moved slowly forward. This was another big cavern, but where was the trap?

Was it in here?

Was the man wounded and groaning at the bottom of that ditch?

Lock's mind crafted gruesome images of men impaled on wooden stakes, reaching vainly out to him with blooded hands.

He shuddered as he stepped, his feet creaking on the soft, sodden planks. The cavernous room continued to open out, and it was impossible to see the end of it.

The more he moved, the louder the groaning became. And then he saw it.

Was it a slumped figure, or was it another stone?

Lock couldn't be sure, but as he edged closer, the lantern caught the features of a man's filthy face.

Involuntary groans escaped from his open mouth, in between wheezing breaths. The man was seated, against what looked like a wooden door, or was perhaps a collection of planks rested against the earthen wall. As Lock closed the space between them, he scanned the wounded man for signs of his allegiance. But the man was too dirty; soil caked his uniform.

He would have to get closer. The groans became more urgent. Then, somewhere in his brain, Lock made the decision to call out in German to the man.

'Hello? Are you injured?'

The question seemed redundant. But it was also the ultimate test of the wounded man's allegiance.

Would he snap to attention and answer him, or would he fire back a reply in garbled Spanish? It was essential to be prepared for the answer.

In the dim light of the lantern, possibly wounded, and far from allies, this man would certainly qualify as a cornered rat.

Lock's hand rested on his sword hilt.

The man's groaning ceased, and for a few seconds, nothing happened.

Suddenly, the man's eyes sprung open, and the lantern caught every flick of his contorted face.

Lock couldn't help but half jump backwards several inches.

The man's blue eyes blinked, the whites around them disarmingly clean.

The eyes darted around, before landing squarely on Lock.

'Are you...' Lock's voice trembled, and he coughed before repeating the question more firmly in German. 'Are you Spanish?'

The man's blank expression created a flutter of panic.

What if he was Spanish, but didn't wish to fight?

Would Lock finish him off here, in the depths of the earth, where nobody but God could see them?

His breathing escalated. Distant sounds rang out.

Screams, shouts, small explosions, evidence of the war above.

Occasional clods of earth and dust fell from the roof, suggesting that the chamber was not long for this world. A clod of earth fell, as if on cue, only inches from the lantern.

'*Shite*!' Lock swore aloud, forgetting himself for a brief moment.

The soldier then coughed and waved a filthy arm at him.

'You... you're the Irishman's friend,' the soldier croaked in English.

Lock sighed in relief.

His imagination had failed to picture an Englishman down here in the depths of von Salm's tunnels. Burroughs had let his party of nearly fifty men have free reign in the forest. But there was a wrinkle.

The English soldiers were on horseback, so what had driven this man underground?

Lock moved closer to the man, and reached to grasp his hand. 'What's your name?' Lock asked, and his tone seemed to compel the man to try to sit upright, which proved a painful task. The man's expression appeared almost offended.

'We... we *met*... Mister Lock,' the soldier rasped. 'You took... my Suzy.'

Lock stared at the man blankly, before the soldier, against all odds, conjured up an impression of a horse. The interaction from earlier in the day returned to Lock.

This was the wiry, red-haired man who had loaned Lock his larger mount.

What had Burroughs called him?

'You're Benjy,' Lock said, unable to hide his satisfaction.

The man coughed as he nodded. Lock tried to discern his age, though the dirt smeared across his face made it difficult to tell. His skin was pale, and flecks of fair stubble glinted under the lantern's glare.

'What happened to you?'

Benjy pointed to his left side. 'Stabbed, Mister Lock. Stabbed in the dark I was. Not sure which bastard did it.'

Lock tried to ignore the nightmarish image of being stabbed in the dark. 'What are you doing down here? You were on horseback last time I saw you?'

Benjy nodded, and reached for his side as he winced. 'Some Italian bastard took my horse, I... I took it back, but then he ran down here, so I followed.' Benjy breathed a heaving breath. 'Had to remove my breastplate to fit. Stupidest idea I ever did have. Bloody idiot I am.'

Lock shook his head, before blurting out. 'I know the way out Benjy, I can get you out of here.'

Benjy's eyes were moistening. Lock suspected the man had already come to terms with his death. 'I won't make it Mister Lock.'

'Call me Matthew my friend.'

'I won't make it Mister Matthew, bastard got me good.'

Lock lowered the lantern towards the man's wound in his left side, a gesture he had hesitated to make until now. The wound had bled through his buff coat.

Benjy groaned and gasped.

And then, that innocuous piece of wisdom from Father returned.

To a confident man, no doors are closed.

'I'm a physician,' Lock blurted out before he could stop himself. 'You will survive this wound Benjy, but we need to get you above ground first.'

Benjy's eyes lit up momentarily, before he suddenly shook his head more abruptly. 'A physician and an envoy? What a mind you must have. But... no, Mister Matthew, I can't leave, even I was well, I couldn't leave.'

'*Why the Devil not?*'

'I swore an oath to a German... that I would set off the trap for him.' Benjy pointed feebly to the corner of the cavern, where Lock had yet to go. 'I cannot fail them.'

'What happened to those Germans?'

'Dead, or gone, I don't know Mister Matthew, I just know...' Benjy groaned urgently while pressing his hand to his side. Benjy exhaled. 'I just know, that I can't leave this hole without knocking those bastards into it.'

'How far is it?'

'The ditch? About twenty paces that way.'

'How do I get it to work?'

'You need... you need to use the stake that's beside it Mister Matthew.'

'If you show me how, I promise to get you out of here, then your task is fulfilled. Can you leave your post then?'

'Mister Matthew, if you can do all that, I'll give you *all* my horses.' Benjy smiled weakly, before pressing a filthy hand back to his wound and failing to suppress a grimace.

Lock glanced to the darkness. Death lingered within it, there could be no doubt. Lock shivered slightly as he rose to his feet. The damp of his undershirt made the underground surprisingly chilly. 'Alright Benjy, I need you to stand up.'

Benjy shook his head and groaned. Lock leant close to him, and wrapped his arm over his shoulder, before standing upright. Benjy let out a mournful cry. Lock held his breath, and forced his way forwards by effectively overpowering the man. Benjy might object, but so long as he still lived, he would thank him later.

With one hand holding the lantern, and another supporting Benjy, Lock pushed gradually forward. Benjy's feet slipped on the muddy planks, but Lock steadied him. Planks squelched into the wetted mud underneath.

As Lock made his way towards the trap, the dim light began to highlight more man-made features, and then Lock stopped.

Georg von Salm had shown them one of these ditches to demonstrate the concept, but this ditch was perhaps four times its length. Lock allowed a few moments to marvel at the sheer scale of the excavation. It seemed to curve around a further corner in a semi-circle, as though mimicking the shape of the clearing directly south of the bastion.

'The size of it...' Lock whispered, half hoping the comment would rouse Benjy. The wounded soldier stirred, seemingly content to doze while balanced on Lock's shoulder. 'Come on Benjy,' Lock whispered, as gently and firmly as he could manage. Benjy groaned, before coughing, and partially steadying himself. Benjy glanced at the huge curving ditch and nodded knowingly.

'This is nothing Mister Matthew, you should see the tunnels Doyle and I dug at Ostend.'

'*Ostend*?' Lock asked, looking back at the face of the man still on his arm. Thanks to his Father's intensive schooling, Lock knew that the siege of Ostend ended in 1604, when the town fell to the Spanish. He also knew that the commander at Ostend was none other than his godfather, Sir Horace Vere.

'*You* were at Ostend?' Lock asked, hiding none of his jealousy as he eyed up the enormous ditch in front of him. Large planks lay in long horizontal rows in the ceiling, supporting the ground and preventing the trap from being sprung.

Lock shook Benjy's shoulder.

He longed to know more about Ostend.

Benjy's service there made him a veteran with at least twenty years under his belt. A rare commodity indeed.

Lock recalled Father's motive for refusing to bless his application for military service.

The rarest English soldier, Charles Lock had said, *was one who lives a long life.*

The statement still produced legions of questions in Lock's mind. When he had challenged Father as to the purpose of his schooling, following a particularly long session in the drill, Lock had been told that he should be educated in war *and* letters, since he should be prepared for anything.

But that answer had always felt unsatisfactory.

Benjy stirred more intently on Lock's shoulder.

'Ostend... Ostend, Mister Matthew? Aye, they said Spinola was digging under Ostend's walls, so Vere sent me and Doyle to meet them halfway underground.'

'What was it like? To serve under Sir Horace Vere?'

'Vere was... Vere was a rare good man, but he always travelled with that rank bastard friend of his. Burned me bad he did. Many times... many times.'

Had Benjy sunk into delirium?

'Benjy, how do I work the trap?'

'That's why I ran after the bugger, see? I knew that even if he was bigger than me, he didn't know the underground like I did. I thought I'd get him first, but he got me. Don't know where he is now...'

'Benjy,' Lock urged, shrugging his shoulder a touch rougher than before.

'*Doyle,*' Benjy stuttered, 'We need Doyle,' he pulled on Lock's shoulder, and nearly destabilised him altogether, but Benjy was too weak to pull down Lock's frame.

'Who is Doyle?' Lock asked, struggling to return Benjy to the matter at hand.

'Doyle came with me down here. He... he left me and said he'd be back. I... I hoped you were Doyle... *Are you Doyle?*'

Lock exhaled. 'Benjy, I need you to focus.'

'Doyle, we have to wait for Doyle,' Benjy said firmly. Once again, Lock found himself ready with a lie.

He exhaled before its delivery.

'Doyle sent me Benjy, he sent me to tell you that he... survived the battle, but that he needs you to help me work this trap.' Lock turned Benjy's weakened body towards him, and he held the declining man's cold face.

Benjy smiled, 'Doyle... Doyle said we should get the long stake and push out... the beam.' Benjy made a vague gesture towards the ditch, before his eyes seemed to glaze over, and his legs began to stutter.

Like a new-born fawn in spring, Benjy's legs simply refused to cooperate.

Benjy capitulated to the pain and exhaustion.

He fell gradually backwards, pulling Lock with him. There was a brief flutter of panic, but they were far from the edge of the ditch.

There was a greater emergency.

The jolt from the fall had knocked the lantern out of his hand. It fell in a mercifully straight angle, landing upright on the edge of a clod of earth, before tumbling towards the direction of the ditch.

Lock watched its movements with his heart in his throat.

The lantern came to a rest beside a large wooden stake, which had been laid flat. Small wooden supports confirmed that the stake had been stored here deliberately for a vital mission – arming the trap, and dooming the enemy. The stake was remarkably long, but not as thick as other stakes Lock had seen.

Lock removed his arm from Benjy's, and carefully laid him on the earth. Another clod fell from the ceiling not far from Benjy's legs. To protect him from additional clods, Lock reluctantly removed his dolman and draped it over Benjy's body. Benjy enthusiastically accepted the makeshift blanket and the chance to sleep. He pulled it greedily over his shivering body.

Lock turned from his charge and lunged for the stake, grabbing it with his hands. He carefully teased one half of it behind him, and balanced it under his right armpit. With his grimy hands wrapped around it, he had little difficulty lifting it off the ground. It was about the length of his own body, slightly damp, but surprisingly light. Lock squinted at the ceiling of the cavern, where the planks seemed to snake across one another.

What had Benjy said?

Push out the beam?

Lock looked around for something resembling a beam in the near darkness. A clod of earth fell behind him, this one sounded larger.

Lock ignored it.

Then, in the ceiling, above the very edge of the ditch, the target became visible. Lock found it by following the planks. They all appeared to rest on a larger slab of wood, which had been jammed into the earth to anchor the trap. Without hesitating, Lock began stabbing at the beam, but it wouldn't budge.

'*Come on,*' Lock urged. He extended the stake's length by sliding it forward in his hands. The rough wooden stake rubbed his hands raw, but

Lock ignored the stinging pain. He was too angry at the ineffectiveness of his tool.

The act was familiar. It was reminiscent of the few times he had helped the maid dust the highest cobwebs, by standing on his tiptoes and reaching as far forward as he dared.

If only Miss Wells could see him now.

The stake pushed harmlessly against the beam. But then, Lock saw it. Beneath the beam, another clod of earth fell into the ditch, and the beam shifted ever so slightly.

Work on the earth, not the beam.

Lock started to dig furiously at the earth below the beam. Pieces of soil fell away, and tumbled into the darkness below. Again and again, he stabbed at it, shouting at it, cursing at it to move. And then, there was a slight groan.

For barely a millisecond, the beam appeared to defy gravity, before its sheer weight pulled it down. The entire thick slab of wood fell, pulling earth with it, and it disappeared into the ditch. More and more planks of wood followed, and Lock stared, transfixed at his vandalism. The commotion even drew a startled yelp from Benjy, a few feet behind him.

Still, the ground seemed to hold.

Lock swore in disbelief.

He spied some roots that snaked across the roof, which the planks had obscured. These few pathetic roots, it seemed, now held the entire roof in place.

Could the secret to von Salm's tunnelling success now also spell its doom? One great attack, one great impression from some heavy object, might rupture this balance, and finally activate the trap. But how?

And then, an idea surged forward, but he would have to return to the surface to bring it about.

Lock turned, and with unconcealed surprise, saw that Benjy was seated upright, watching him.

'You've got the right idea Mister Matthew,' he croaked.

'We need to go Benjy, we need to go *now*.' Lock rushed to his charge. 'Come on,' he reached for Benjy's right shoulder, and the wounded man squealed in pain.

Adrenaline had worn off. Now the body was protesting. Lock was forced to ignore Benjy's protests, and he half carried, half forced the wounded man onto his feet, and back to where Lock had come from.

Lock began sprinting with Benjy.

His caution from before had now vanished, as he rushed to implement his plan. Benjy's protests had given way to slight yelps. Lock allowed the lantern to lead the way. Distant underground voices could be heard for the first time. Had the Spanish truly invaded the tunnels? The sinking feeling it caused only spurred Lock onward.

His breath quickening, he rounded one corner, and then another. And then the yellow stone loomed into view. Lock shouted something calming out loud. He was overwhelmed, panicked, endangered, but also uniquely alive. Distant voices became clearer, and Lock grimaced as Benjy attempted to wriggle free.

'Nearly there,' Lock gasped.

Benjy's leg caught on a plank, and Lock abruptly lurched forwards, before righting himself. Benjy mumbled something in anger, and Lock yelled a garbled reply. He ached to be free of the underground darkness. The lantern creaked as it struck off an occasional corner, and the candle flickered unsettlingly.

Lock pulled round another bend, and there was the ladder, illuminated by the faint light of nature. Lock's eyes adjusted to the sight, and only now did he realise his predicament.

How was he to get Benjy up a ten foot ladder? The soldier groaned in protest again, and leaned back lazily on the ladder's bottom rungs. Lock's temper surged forward, and without thinking or hesitating, he slapped the soldier's face.

'Doyle... *you bastard!*' Benjy swore, swiping at the air with a long sleeve. Benjy still wore his dolman, and the sight made Lock shiver. A stray musket ball would ruin his Father's coat. This was another reason to save Benjy.

For a brief moment, Lock hesitated under Benjy's angry stare, before formulating a new lie. 'Benjy, we need to escape from... Ostend. We have to climb this ladder to get out, *can you manage it?*'

Benjy stared at Lock sheepishly, a weak smile playing across his lips. 'I'll go first Doyle. I'll... I'll show you how it's done I will.'

Benjy removed himself from Lock's support and clasped his hands on the ladder. As he did so, he winced, before turning back briefly to look at Lock with a defiant grin, and then, he began climbing.

As soon as he could fit underneath him, Lock attached himself to the ladder. He looped the lantern around his right hand, and glanced up to see Benjy stall. Benjy's feet seemed to dislodge a small clod of earth, which peppered Lock's face. Lock swore.

He tried not to overthink the act, as he moved under Benjy's legs and, with his head between them, began to climb steadily upwards, as though Lock had climbed the ladder with the soldier on his shoulders. Benjy giggled, but Lock pushed on. The climb seemed eternal. Lock's arms shook with exhaustion.

And then, a slight breeze rushed past his ears.

'Come on Benjy,' Lock urged, as he pushed Benjy's rump to get him out of the tunnel. With a final heave, Lock pulled himself out and onto his hands and knees.

Benjy lay on the ground, panting, but Lock couldn't wait. He turned to where the bastion was, and the sounds of war returned with a startling abruptness.

Lock didn't care.

He was too happy to be free of the underground prison. Pulling on Benjy's shoulder, he brought his charge to the bastion's right side, where he had descended perhaps half an hour before. An anxious young face peered over the edge. Lock waved at him, and the face paused to look at Benjy, before Lock waved more urgently again, and a wooden ladder slinked down the earthen wall.

'One more climb Benjy,' Lock whispered. The air seemed to do Benjy good, but the man was still delirious.

'I can't make it Mister Matthew,' Benjy despaired, before sitting down abruptly beside the ladder.

Lock swallowed his urge to scream. 'We have to climb it Benjy... because... because Doyle is waiting for you at the top. He expects a full briefing.'

Benjy's face lit up, and he scrambled to his feet with a grimace. Lock directed Benjy gently to the ladder, and the soldier began his second climb, this time much quicker. Lock glanced around, before following upwards.

As he climbed, there was a loud sigh of relief, as Benjy's wounded, exhausted body collapsed when he reached the top, and was pulled from the edge of the bastion. With a final push of his legs, Lock heaved himself onto the bastion unaided. The sound of musket, of shouting men, and of the river, had all become deafening.

It was like a blur of indistinguishable noise.

Lock stopped himself from checking on Benjy.

There was simply no time.

He turned on his knees towards the south facing side of the bastion, where the eleven Germans had only recently attempted to return fire. Several lifeless bodies now lay strewn around, untouched, aside from some who boasted large bandages wrapped vainly around their heads.

While crawling, Lock gingerly avoided a man whose stomach had been opened by a musket ball. Lock judged that he had been shot through the back.

He remembered his lessons. If fired at an iron breastplate, a musket ball made a hole roughly one and a half inches in diameter. Upon exiting the body on the other side though, the lead ball would disintegrate, leading to horrific injuries, including wounds that could be as large as a human hand.

The unfortunate German's mouth and eyes lay open, staring emptily at the night sky. Lock stopped himself from dwelling on the grisly scene. He crawled past, as the overpowering pong of sulphur mixed momentarily with the pungent smell of fresh blood.

Shouts and shots still rang out ahead of him, and a clump of men rested at the bastion's edge.

They had not yet seen him, and were too focused on firing the occasional shot down on the Spanish. As far as they were concerned, the teenager watching the rear would shout if there was an issue.

Lock forced himself to adhere to the plan, reckless though it sounded. The large boulder, commandeered as a makeshift stool, still rested in the bastion's centre. Lock made for it.

It was even bigger than he had remembered.

He pushed it, and it budged slightly.

He tried to wrap his arms around it, but couldn't gain any traction.

Lock spat out a mixture of a swear and soil from his mouth.

He foolishly kicked the rock, and it shuddered onto its side.

Lock ignored the pain in his toes.

He pushed the rock again, effectively rolling it towards its destination.

He continued this for a few seconds, ignoring errant musket shots, the shouts of men, and everything else around him, until a hand touched his shoulder.

'*You're alive?*' Burroughs said, unable to hide his surprise. A mixture of blood and mud was smeared on the General's face. He was crouched beside Lock.

'The rock, I know what to do...' Lock managed to say, taken aback by his shortness of breath. Lock then gestured with concern to a clot of blood on Burroughs' head.

'Not mine lad,' Burroughs said, before gesturing towards the unfortunate soul whose stomach had been opened. 'Nasty business, he could have used your support.'

'I was busy, Sir... I can explain.'

'You were supposed to stay behind the line, to stay out of sight, so I could keep an eye on you.'

Burroughs and von Salm clearly weren't in the habit of communicating. 'Sir, von Salm asked me to...'

Burroughs cut him off with a lift of his hand. The General looked back to his shaky frontline, where the shortage of powder had become a serious problem, before shrugging slightly.

'Well, now that you're with us lad, if you could fetch some powder...'

'Sir, trust me, I have a plan that's better than powder. Please, help me get this rock to the edge.'

Burroughs eyed Lock up and down, before looking intently at his eyes. A slight smirk crept across his face.

'Seems you've been busy lad,' the General said, before turning towards the boulder.

He tried to lift it with both arms, ignoring Lock's gesture.

'Christ but she's heavy.'

Lock joined in, and after a few pushes, the two men managed to coordinate their efforts. Within seconds, the boulder was a foot from the bastion's edge.

'God's guts Lock, where have *you* been?' Flynn barked to Lock's left.

Lock ignored the Irishman's question and his tone. Georg von Salm knelt to his right, but was transfixed on his own mission, which appeared to involve the levelling of curses towards the Spanish.

'We're out of powder,' Burroughs gasped, as if in explanation. 'So whatever your plan is Lock, I hope to God it works.'

Behind him, Flynn retrieved a small charge of powder from a dead man's bandolier. The unfortunate man's corpse had been pulled beside the Irishman in the thick of the battle.

'*Shite*! Lock, what are you playing at?'

'Give me a hand Flynn. Trust me, this *will* work!'

Flynn glanced at Lock, then at the General, before swearing and shuffling to them. He and Burroughs then half lifted the boulder into Lock's arms.

A musket ball cracked into the edge of the bastion, throwing up a clod of earth.

Lock exhaled, and prepared to lift the immense load.

It was the heaviest thing he had ever carried.

His fingers dug into its side, and his arms throbbed with the effort, but Lock pushed forward.

He would be more exposed to the Spanish below, so he had to hurry. His eyes absorbed the scene on the forest floor.

Several bodies were strewn across it, but pockets of soldiers were also gathered in clumps, as if aware that the men above them no longer had an answer. Most of the Spaniards didn't bother looking up at him.

There had to be one hundred in all, and to the rear, just before the clearing, Lock could make out Diego de la Barca's silhouette. The Spanish commander appeared deep in conversation with a subordinate.

Now was the time.

Lock exhaled, and with all of his might, he hurled the boulder forward.

It moved barely a few inches away from him, before plummeting relentlessly downwards.

It seemed to fall in slow motion.

Several Spanish heads turned towards Lock.

A multitude of confused expressions watched his act.

It was a strange thing to do when under fire, but its purpose would soon be revealed.

The boulder disappeared through the earth with a dull thud. Lock fell to his knees in thanks.

The ground absorbed the impact, but then it seemed to ripple.

A crack then appeared in the earth, then another.

A group of Spaniards watched a crack leer towards them in frozen confusion.

Suddenly they were gone, and now the ground itself disappeared.

Shouts and screams rang out from the consumed.

De la Barca turn his head, before taken by an expression of horror.

His men tried to run, but had all been placed perfectly in front of the bastion.

They had intended to storm the fortress, to kill the tongueless German, and return honour to Spanish arms, but they had been sitting on a trap the whole time.

Perhaps in the space of seconds, the ground simply ceased to be, and the men that had once walked upon it ceased to be also.

Piercing screams and shrieks filled the night sky.

Men continued to run. Others stayed perfectly still, unable to believe the sight, and unsure of how to escape the terrible fate.

Piece by piece, the ground fell away.

Spaniards lunged and grasped at one another in a frenzy of panic, but the collapse pulled them all in. Shrieks echoed from the gaping hole in the ground.

It was a perfect semi-circle, which ringed the bastion's south-facing side. The trapper's dream result.

'God save us all,' came a voice behind Lock.

It was Georg von Salm, who held his empty musket to his left side. 'You *did* it Matthew Lock, you *actually* did it.'

- CHAPTER THIRTY-FOUR -

The first time Lock had ever been hunting, he had surprised a deer, which had skirted and darted wildly, until running towards a lake and jumping in. The act of desperation had made Lock pause, and he watched his target swim furiously to the other side.

Once safely across, the deer shook the water off itself, before turning back to Lock and staring. The staring had been intense, intense enough to compel Charles Lock to tell his son to lower his weapon.

'Let nature have this one, son,' Father had said.

The deer maintained its stare, a large body of water now between itself and the once dangerous humans, before it pawed the ground, and scampered into the forest.

As he stood on the edge of the bastion, with a chasm of darkness and death between himself and Diego de la Barca, Lock couldn't decide if he was the deer, or if the Spaniard was himself about to scamper off into the forest in retreat.

De la Barca's position was hopeless, Burroughs had insisted, yet the Spaniard refused to see sense.

On the contrary, the Spanish commander stood erect and defiant. With a pale-faced subordinate by his side, he stared at Lock, Burroughs, Flynn and von Salm across the enormous ditch which had swallowed so many of his men.

It was a piercing gaze.

It was the gaze of a Father who had lost everything, and now challenged the enemy to make it worse.

'Come forward, General de la Barca. Come forward and surrender your army to me. I will not ask again,' Burroughs yelled, for what must have been the third time. A curious stalemate had set in. De la Barca's column had been annihilated, but so long as he could not be reached, he seemed unwilling to surrender.

'I don't have time for this,' Burroughs muttered. 'O'Toole, perhaps –'

From behind Burroughs, von Salm emerged, a bloody white sack in hand. Von Salm placed his hand into the bag, without looking first, and with a knowing chuckle, pulled out the head of Gaston Phillipe.

Burroughs' mouth fell open, as von Salm walked to the bastion's edge.

'See *this*, Spaniard? This is your son's head. If you want it, and if you want to bury what's left of him, you will surrender to General Burroughs' army right away. If not, then...' von Salm began to dangle Phillipe's severed head over the enormous ditch which had recently swallowed so many of de la Barca's men. Faint groans, mixed with the occasional sob, wafted up from its depths.

Across the field, a subordinate whispered in de la Barca's ear. The colour drained from the Spaniard's face as the words were translated from German, piece by devastating piece. De la Barca raised a hand towards what was left of his son, and his knees trembled slightly.

Not anger, not a thirst for revenge, just sheer, gutting despair.

The Spaniard let out a wail that seemed to hang in the air.

Lock flinched at the sound.

'God sakes, what is von Salm *doing*?' Burroughs' protests seemed almost half-hearted, and he made no attempt to retrieve the head from von Salm's grasp.

'I thought you had fifty men on horseback,' Flynn hissed at the General. 'Now would be a good moment for them to show themselves, and take de la Barca into custody.'

Burroughs shook his head at the Irishman. 'I don't know where my men are Flynn, but I should remind you that they are professionals.'

'I suspect they went underground Sir, that was where I found one of them,' as soon as Lock shared the news, he regretted it.

Burroughs effectively threw his hands into the air. 'Heavens above envoy, why didn't you mention this sooner?'

'You were... busy, Sir,' Lock replied lamely.

'Well, where is this gentleman now?'

Lock gestured to the rear of the bastion.

Bodies were still strewn where they had fallen in the hours before.

Lock had gone out of his way not to look back there again. He longed for a barber surgeon to come and tidy up the disembowelled corpses.

At the bastion's rear, the filthy teenager on ladder duty tended to a prone Benjy, who was still wrapped in Lock's dolman. Benjy's fingers were moving, but little else.

'Is that Benjy, *wearing your coat?*' Burroughs exclaimed, before taking several large strides towards the wounded soldier.

Burroughs slid in beside Benjy, before cupping his left hand delicately under his head, and offering him a drink.

Even now, Benjy's delirious requests for Doyle continued, the fragments drifting back to Lock.

Hearing a shriek from de la Barca's direction, Lock wheeled around to see von Salm threatening to let go of Phillipe's head.

De la Barca muttered some words to his subordinate, who seemed to hesitate, before de la Barca barked the same words again, and the subordinate exhaled, before moving carefully forward.

If the subordinate had kept walking, he would have experienced the same gruesome fate as so many others, but he halted after a couple of steps.

A small white piece of cloth was produced from the subordinate's hip pouch, which was then waved.

Diego de la Barca's army now belonged to General Burroughs.

'We'll go over,' von Salm said, nodding at Lock.

'*Me?*'

'De la Barca has no reason to distrust you. You can read the terms of the surrender and receive it on Burroughs' behalf.'

'*Distrust me?* I told him I was an English envoy, accredited by King James himself to bring peace to the Rhine,' Lock virtually spat the words out.

Von Salm absorbed the information, then let out a cruel chuckle. 'Perhaps, de la Barca has no reason to suspect your deceit? Perhaps you continue to play along?'

'*Play along?*'

'Is that not what you diplomats do? You play the game?'

'I suppose...'

'You are an intelligent man Lock, I am sure you will think of something.' As he spoke, von Salm bent over to rustle in Burroughs' bag. He retrieved a piece of parchment, and chuckled affirmatively to himself. 'We get him to sign this, and de la Barca's army is no more.'

Lock racked his brain to recall his last conversation with de la Barca. How could he fool the Spaniard for the second time?

Once again, he would be the imposter.

'I want to see this... de la Barca up close when I break him,' von Salm said, standing upright, and folding the parchment into his hip pocket.

'How do you plan to break him?'

Von Salm glanced at Phillipe's head, which he still held by its blond hair.

Lock did not press him further.

Von Salm turned to Flynn. 'Tell Burroughs we will return shortly, with de la Barca's surrender in hand.' Von Salm then made for a ladder on the bastion's left side.

The Irishman nodded, and took a quick sip from his costrel, before offering it to Lock. The memory of the bitter taste returned to his mouth in a flash.

Lock shuddered, before following after von Salm.

'Watch your step Officer Lock,' von Salm called back, as he descended the ladder.

The warning to tread carefully had not been an idle one.

The vast majority of the ground in the forest clearing was now gone. In its place was a truly enormous semi-circle shaped ditch. Lock did not dare peer over the edge. Instead, he followed von Salm's sure footing.

The German was taking the scenic route through the forest. It would certainly take longer, but short of extending several shaky planks across the chasm, this twenty-minute detour was their only option.

Lock's eyes had adjusted to the darkness of the night, but it was still difficult to push through the clumps and tangles of branches in his way.

Von Salm proceeded as though possessed; he walked defiantly forward, regardless of the strength or size of the plants in front of him. His small frame seemed to glide through the foliage, and he despatched any branches which lay in his path with relish.

The German was joyful.

Gaston Phillipe's head had been returned to the bloody white sack, but as von Salm moved, and the head pressed against the material, Lock became transfixed on the outline of the face which seemed to burn through it.

The two men cut deliberately through the forest in relative silence. This was the moment that the German had been waiting for since the Spanish had first arrived.

But what would happen when revenge was secured?

What would Georg von Salm do when his mission was accomplished?

Lock envied von Salm for being at the end of his journey, but the prospect of being in a similar position also filled him with a kind of angst.

'We are here,' von Salm said.

With one more flick of his sword, a branch fell away, and the German pushed onto the main road, where de la Barca and his subordinate were standing.

Lock followed behind.

The rustle of branches had drawn the Spaniards' attention, and they both turned to catch a curious sight.

Lock had feared how de la Barca would react to him, but he had forgotten that he was travelling with the bogeyman of the Spanish camp.

The eyes of de la Barca's subordinate widened in horror, as he levelled a pointing finger at von Salm, and mouthed a curse.

'They think I am the devil,' von Salm scoffed, as he turned towards Lock a few feet from the Spaniards, and waited for Lock to catch up.

'Are they correct?'

'At this moment, Officer Lock, the devil himself fears me.'

- CHAPTER THIRTY-FIVE -

The subordinate did most of the talking, and the reacting. He couldn't take his eyes off of von Salm, but he did offer Lock a hasty introduction.

'I am Luis Romera, the commander's aide and translator,' he had said.

Romera's tone suggested that he neither enjoyed the role, nor had been in it for very long.

'Where's your predecessor, the pikeman with the scowl? He sticks to de la Barca like glue,' von Salm replied.

'Duke Enrique Zuniga vanished in the forest, like so many of our brave soldiers tonight,' Romera said.

The subordinate's fear of von Salm had dissipated somewhat, but his hatred for the German clearly had not. Romera maintained a piercing stare at all times.

Lock was not left out. De la Barca's eyes now rested on him.

'Officer Lock? *Do my eyes deceive me?*' the Spanish commander asked in French.

It was immediately clear from his body language that Romera did not speak French. Lock was the only one who could engage in conversation with all three men.

A sly smirk grew in the corner of Lock's mouth.

It was time to put the semi-rehearsed plan into motion, a plan which required him to feign a mixture of offence and despair from the beginning.

'It is quite unfortunate that we should meet in these circumstances,' Lock began, with a slight bow. 'It is equally unfortunate that I should have trusted one of your soldiers to bring me to my destination unharmed.'

De la Barca made a slight bow in response, and his face was drawn with regret. 'Please accept my sincerest apologies for your troubles Officer Lock. I had no idea that your guard contained that treacherous villain, or that my son...' De la Barca steadied himself, 'Nor did I imagine that my son would come to such grief.'

'Indeed, a terrible tragedy. You have my sincere condolences for the loss,' the words barely escaped Lock's mouth, before a pang of guilt, mixed with visions of choking Gaston Phillipe, returned to him.

De la Barca shook his head in despair. 'Those Germans, those... *barbarians*. They did this. They destroyed my army in the forest. I watched hundreds of men disappear before my eyes. Good men. Men with families. I am... disgraced... by my failures,' the admission clearly pained him. 'I wish only to bury my son.'

Lock had to suppress a rush of sudden anger.

Did de la Barca not think of the German families he had displaced when he had come to the Rhine and burned Woodrest?

The Spaniard thought only of his own failure and disgrace.

Von Salm clear his throat, and Lock nodded in recognition.

'You work for these *Germans* now?' de la Barca's question contained an icy undertone. Clearly the Spaniard's ability to judge others had not diminished, but Lock was ready with an answer.

'You need not condescend to *me*, commander,' Lock enjoyed the riposte, which caused de la Barca to visibly flinch. 'I am a prisoner of these brutes because of a failure of *your* intelligence. Once I do what they ask, so they say, I am free to go.'

De la Barca gripped Lock's right forearm. 'And you *believe* these men? You believe they can be trusted?'

Lock recoiled slightly. 'They would not harm an agent of His Majesty, Excellency. Not when they wish for England to rescue them from their plight.'

De la Barca seemed to weigh the idea up, before von Salm interrupted.

'Cease this conversation. Return to German. Tell de la Barca that he must surrender to Burroughs now. I have the document here.'

Romera sighed at de la Barca's blank expression. He translated from German to Spanish.

De la Barca's face fell when he realised Lock could offer him no sympathy.

Lock shrugged. It was hardly enjoyable watching a man be broken, but the Spaniard's lack of remorse made the task easier.

Von Salm shoved the parchment in Romera's face, and the subordinate snatched it into his hands. As Romera read it, de la Barca also skimmed it over his subordinate's shoulder. De la Barca pointed at one line of the contract and Romera's gasped.

Without thinking, Lock reached for his stiletto.

The feeling of cold steel seemed to jolt him forward.

'Gentlemen, is everything in order?' Lock had to ask the question in German and in French.

'I am afraid it is not, Officer Lock,' Romera began, 'I have an issue with –'

The subordinate's speech was interrupted when von Salm landed a clubbing blow on the back of his head.

Romera crumpled to the ground.

Lock and de la Barca flinched in shock.

'*You utter fiend*!' de la Barca yelled.

'Tell him his friend is still alive, for now,' von Salm instructed. 'And tell him, if he wants to bury his son, *all of his son*, then he will agree to *all* of these terms, without exception. Tell him that the contract is non-negotiable.'

Lock nodded wearily, and sighed in relief when Romera stirred slightly on the ground. Lock looked de la Barca directly in the eye as he communicated the terms.

The Spanish commander nodded. He stooped to pick up the parchment, which Romera had dropped, and as he skimmed it, von Salm reached into the white sack.

Lock's stomach lurched for the umpteenth time.

By the time de la Barca had finished reading, a clump of Gaston Phillipe's blond hair was in von Salm's meaty hand. As soon as the Spaniard's eyes locked on the grisly spectacle, his reserves of restraint appeared to vanish.

His knees trembled, and with a gasp, he fell involuntarily onto all fours.

As if to illustrate the point, von Salm strolled deliberately to the edge of the great ditch. He peered over the edge, shook his head briefly, and then held Gaston Phillipe's head out in front of him. 'Tell him to sign the contract, *now*.'

Lock turned from von Salm back to de la Barca.

The Spaniard was barely holding it together.

A mixture of tears and mucus descended down his dirty face, and all de la Barca could manage was to outstretch a hand in a vain plea.

'*Sign it*,' von Salm barked, 'or else.'

Without taking his eyes off de la Barca, von Salm moved his arm further and further to the right, until the head dangled precariously over the ditch.

The only thing that protected de la Barca's plans for a burial were the strands of Gaston Phillipe's blond hair.

The threat had immediate effect.

De la Barca sprang into action with a shriek.

He crawled to Romera's groaning body, and rummaged through his belongings, until an inkwell and a quill were produced.

De la Barca then frantically ripped the lid of the inkwell open, and as the black substance spilled onto the leaf litter, the commander bathed the quill in it.

He brought the quill, still dripping, towards the document.

De la Barca looked at von Salm one last time, and then to Lock.

'Does the German *swear*, on his... honour, that if I sign this, he will return my son's... remains... to me?'

Lock nodded.

'*Does he swear*?'

Lock sighed, and threw the question at von Salm in German.

Von Salm appeared to laugh at the notion, but then returned several nods. 'He swears.'

De la Barca sighed, and shook off the loose ink, before signing his name on the document. Without speaking, he handed the parchment to Lock.

Lock didn't know what to say.

De la Barca then stood up, and dusted himself off, before making gradually for von Salm.

Lock walked the three or four paces beside him, and the three men then stood at the edge of the ditch.

It was only then that von Salm's promise to break the Spaniard returned to Lock.

Lock swallowed hard.

Von Salm's steely gaze pierced through de la Barca.

He clearly longed for the Spaniard to feel great pain.

With his arm still outstretched over the ditch, von Salm encouraged de la Barca towards him with his eyes.

De la Barca did not show fear. He whispered a prayer to will himself forward. When he was merely fingertips away from his son's head, Georg von Sam released his grip on Gaston Phillipe's hair.

The severed head plummeted out of sight in an instant.

De la Barca barely had time to react, but once his eyes connected the spectacle to his brain, the Spaniard's frame effectively collapsed into von Salm's smaller body with a haunting wail.

A chill ran down Lock's back.

Von Salm pushed the Spaniard roughly.

De la Barca tumbled a few paces backwards and fell on his rear.

Von Salm walked deliberately towards the fallen Spaniard, and crouched in front of him.

In between sobs, de la Barca mumbled Spanish words and curses, the latter of which he lobbed in great number at von Salm.

The German chuckled, and reached to the back of his head.

In a single swift movement, he removed the piece of cloth that covered his mouth.

De la Barca recoiled in horror at the sight.

Lock couldn't help staring.

'Look at me, Spaniard, *look at my face*,' Von Salm hissed.

Lock's ears now picked up the sound of French.

Had von Salm been fluent the entire time?

De la Barca would not look at the German. He covered his eyes with filthy hands, as his body shivered with grief. Von Salm forcibly pried the Spaniard's hands back, and although he sobbed, de la Barca offered no resistance.

Von Salm brought de la Barca's face within inches of his own.

'*I* am your penance. *I* am the punishment for your sins. *I* am the agent of your destruction.'

'*Diablo!*' de la Barca said, in a disbelieving whisper. Von Salm did not require translation.

'*You* are the devil, Diego. You are the devil in command of devils. Those devils burned my village. They slaughtered my neighbours. They raped and murdered my daughters. But that wasn't enough for them. They took my tongue, so that I could never speak of your crimes. Your son made the cut, but he was never particularly good at anything but torturing others, so he did not take my speech.'

Von Salm leaned in even closer to de la Barca, whose wide eyes darted wildly. Von Salm cleared his throat, before speaking in perfect French.

'Your son was a pig. He was a filthy, vile worm. Now his soul will wander forever. He will *never* be at peace, and neither will you.'

The venomous diatribe had its intended effect. De la Barca's entire body capitulated to grief, and the Spaniard became utterly inconsolable.

His frame shuddered with violent, uncontrollable sobs.

De la Barca fell back on the ground, his fine clothes now caked with dirt, as ruined as his reputation, as unsalvageable as his military career.

Georg von Salm rose to his feet with satisfaction. 'Tell the pig that he and his aide are now Burroughs' prisoners, and that they'll be brought to Frankenthal.'

Lock raised an eyebrow at the request, and von Salm sighed.

'I don't normally speak French, Officer Lock, but I have practiced that same speech for the last two years.'

'I think he got the message,' Lock said quietly. De la Barca had curled into a ball, and held his knees, a picture of sorrow. The loud sobs had turned into quiet shivering.

'God sakes, pick him up, and put this on,' von Salm threw a black piece of cloth at de la Barca's feet. 'Wait...', the German hesitated. He knelt at his feet again.

Lock held his breath.

'I want his boots.'

Before de la Barca could process the request, von Salm had removed his right boot, and was working on the other one.

Von Salm's bare feet were momentarily visible. Only three toes remained on each foot, the two outer digits having been removed. Von Salm caught Lock's eyes.

'Yes. He botched the tongue job. He couldn't make me mute, so Gaston Phillipe decided to humiliate me in another way, by forcing me to limp whenever I walked. The better the boots, the less trouble walking I have. It is only right for the Father to contribute.'

There was something darkly poetic about von Salm's vengeance.

The Spaniard didn't protest, and von Salm slid each boot on with a grunt of satisfaction. 'Perfect fit,' he said, as he turned his feet from side to side. He tossed his old patched boots into the ditch without a glance behind him.

'We're done here.' He then turned his back on his fallen foe.

Lock tied a blindfold first around Romera, who had begun to come to, but as he made for de la Barca, the Spaniard leapt to his feet with startling speed.

His lack of boots did not slow him down.

De la Barca was a few strides away from ending the pain for good, and this new goal appeared to consume him.

Lock shouted a panicked protest.

Von Salm had turned at the sound of the commotion, and at just the right time. His large fist landed in de la Barca's gut as the Spaniard tried to move past him. De la Barca doubled over, and von Salm pushed him backwards, as his eyes narrowed. 'Not so fast, Diego,' von Salm hissed in German. 'You are still useful. You do not get to die yet.'

De la Barca was enraged to find himself once more on the ground. Lock came behind him and placed a hand on his shoulder.

The Spaniard turned to Lock, his face a picture of misery.

'Just let me *die*, let me have one final mercy. I am disgraced, I am without family, honour or country. *I am nothing.*'

Lock shook his head slowly, before linking his arm in de la Barca's. 'I cannot let you do that, Sir. Enough men have died today.'

The Spaniard still seemed unconvinced, his eyes shifted back and forth between Lock and von Salm, before settling on the enormous chasm that had swallowed his army.

'Then I will keep trying. You cannot watch me forever. *What have I to live for*, Officer Lock?'

'You are alive, Sir. You must live for Gaston Phillipe's memory. You must restore the de la Barca name.' Lock worried the urging could seem insincere, as all he knew of Phillipe was that the fiend had tried to kill him, and nearly succeeded. But the appeal to redemption did seem to resonate.

'Restore... the de la Barca *name*...' de la Barca whispered. As he did so, von Salm tied a blindfold over the Spaniard's eyes.

Lock gently pulled de la Barca to his feet and away from the edge.

The Spaniard was now malleable and docile in their hands.

Von Salm walked to Romera, and a yelp emerged from the aide as he was jerked to his feet.

The German chuckled heartily, before letting out a whistle. Within a few seconds, several Germans emerged from the forest and onto the main road.

'Bring these men to the crossing,' he said to one of the Germans. A German nodded, before speaking in hushed tones with von Salm, who nodded.

Lock stared at the spectacle, as four filthy Germans, clad in dark green and sporting farm implements, then led the two blindfolded Spaniards away.

Diego de la Barca's whispers could still be heard, as the Spaniard repeated his mission to restore the de la Barca name.

Lock gestured at the Germans indignantly 'They would have been useful earlier, why didn't you call them?'

Von Salm nodded at the idea. 'They were my plan B, Herr Lock. A soldier must have a plan B. But plan A, this is always the more entertaining plan.'

Lock watched them disappear into the forest, only the faint sound of rustling leaves and snapping twigs now palpable.

'Where will they go?'

'To the Rhine crossing. They'll be met by some of Burroughs' men, and then whisked away to Frankenthal.'

'You know of Burroughs men, how they fared tonight?'

Von Salm chuckled. 'My boy, if I told Burroughs all that I knew, there would hardly be any need for me anymore.'

'Where are Burroughs' men?'

Von Salm gestured vaguely towards the forest. 'All over, it would seem. Many lost their horses in the initial fray of the battle. Others decided to chase Spaniards underground, which explains why that trap was so long in being sprung.' Von Salm then tutted. 'Chaos, Officer Lock, chaos is what follows men that do not follow orders.'

Lock nodded slowly. 'Where will you go now? With de la Barca gone, you have had your revenge –'

'No,' von Salm said abruptly. 'I have my revenge when Spain is in ashes, but I will start by taking Mannheim.'

'The English were taking Mannheim,' Lock said, as he imagined Joseph Gage's midnight assault on the city.

'Well, it seems they did a poor job of it. The Spanish are still there. If they were to suffer another attack, perhaps from the south, that would truly spell their doom. Mannheim would be German once again.'

'You want to come with us?' Lock asked, to a vague nod from von Salm. Lock wasn't sure whether Burroughs had factored von Salm into his plans, though apparently, those plans had already gone up in smoke.

De la Barca's army may have been destroyed, but another half of it remained intact. The news was important, and should be delivered to Burroughs as soon as possible.

Lock turned north to stare back across the ditch to the bastion, where he had once held out. The truly intimidating spectacle of the forest fortress now loomed before him.

His eyes then rested on a figure, waving frantically back at him.

Lock waved back in response.

A shout was then heard from deep in Burroughs' belly.

'Matthew Lock, get yourself over here right away. We make for Mannheim post haste. Tell your tongue-tied German friend that he can come too.'

'Yes Sir,' Lock called back, before turning to von Salm.

Now that his grisly mission had been accomplished, Lock found the German's presence increasingly unsettling.

There was something unrefined and unpredictable about a man who had achieved his revenge, yet kept raising the bar.

How many more would have to die before Georg von Salm would be truly satisfied?

Would he *ever* be?

'We go to Mannheim?' von Salm asked. 'Last time I was there, my village was at peace.'

Lock nodded, doing his best to hide his hesitation.

With a low whistle, Von Salm handed the signed contract to Lock, and bowed slightly. 'Your first negotiated surrender. Keep following me Officer Lock, and there'll be plenty more.'

- CHAPTER THIRTY-SIX -

After several minutes listening to Burroughs' curses about Joseph Gage's ineptitude, finally, the party emerged from the forest, and Manheim loomed into view.

The sight was a familiar one.

Lock half expected to see Herman Strasser to his right, struggling with the same bandits from the previous day.

But things were different now.

Lock and Flynn were not alone, and the late-night sky cast a curious shadow over Mannheim's skyline. There was no activity on the roads. There was no activity outside of Mannheim whatsoever. Instead, all the action appeared to be taking place within it. Even from this distance, faint shouts, musket shots, and explosions could be made out.

Lock pulled carefully on Suzy's reins. Benjy had made the transfer official, just before he was carted off to Frankenthal for convalescence – the beast was his now. It was the least he could do, Benjy said, to repay Lock for saving his life.

Burroughs' demeanour had suggested that Benjy was not out of the woods yet, though the commander had seemed positive. 'He's a strong lad, that Benjy. Mad as a box of hats, but strong.'

Lock did not doubt it. Any soldier that endured two decades of service was certainly deserving of respect, and was also likely to be somewhat mad.

The business with de la Barca had been handled smoothly enough. Lock gave the signed contract to Burroughs, who had mumbled a thanks.

Georg von Salm had assured Burroughs that neither de la Barca nor Luis Romera would be giving him trouble any time soon. The statement had barely registered with Burroughs. He had seemed far away, likely imagining how to turn this triumph to the advantage of his reputation.

It was, by any standard of measurement, a remarkable victory.

The process of finding and burying the dead had been extensive, but the forest Germans were given the bulk of the task. There was simply no way to keep track of the men lost, the Spaniards caught or on the run, the tunnels collapsed or inhabited. The honeycomb of passages presented a potential death trap for friend and foe alike, particularly as it was rumoured that many Spaniards had fled into the tunnels blindly.

Von Salm had insisted, though, that their prospects for survival were slim indeed. He claimed that the northern section of tunnels, less advanced but still considerable, remained untouched and unknown to the Spanish. That was where the remaining Germans would hide if the Spanish returned.

Lock was just glad to leave the earthy hell behind him.

And then, they had packed up and moved off. As quickly as the bastion had served as their desperate line of defence, now they abandoned it for a new theatre. The haunting groans which emerged from the depths of the sprung traps would be left to cry out in vain. Burroughs was given more intel about the state of his own small party of men. He had lost twenty out of his original forty-nine, though many of the horses were remarkably intact.

Burroughs greeted the news with a loud curse, followed by an assault with his sword on an innocent tree stump. Nobody had restrained him. Everyone seemed to have been affected by the night's events. It was now plain that the plan to coordinate the destruction of de la Barca's army with the seizure of Mannheim had been an abject failure.

German scouts confirmed it.

Mannheim remained in Spanish hands. Half of it, at least.

Burroughs had indicated that he intended to be engaged in triumphant revelries in one of Mannheim's taverns by now. Instead, he had to finish carrying the ball which Joseph Gage had dropped.

The once jovial relationship between Burroughs and Gage was likely now at an end.

The Irishman made no effort to talk with Lock after the battle.

Every now and then, he caught his eye, but Flynn would always look away.

The day's events had sapped Lock's patience.

If the Irishman did not wish to repair things, or to apologise for his baseless claims, then that was his choice.

Lock considered that he had done well.

A 'liability' could hardly have enjoyed such success in such grisly tasks.

But then, Lock's efforts to explain his exploits had not gone well. Burroughs was greedy in sharing his triumph.

Only Georg von Salm continued to sing his praises, and only to his Germans. Von Salm brought thirty of these Germans with him. The remainder, he claimed, had returned to their families, were nursing their wounds, or had perished.

The Germans may have been impressed with Lock's subterranean exploits, but Burroughs' men seemed to believe that Lock had vanished for much of the battle. The great collapse was attributed to Burroughs' ingenuity, and Lock's role had been airbrushed out.

Some had asked about Benjy's status, yet even that act had been obscured by the fog of war. The men managed only to learn that he was recovering in Frankenthal, and once that became common knowledge, proclaiming himself as the saviour seemed tacky.

To escape this awkwardness, Lock remained with von Salm. Though the German's bloodlust was unsettling, von Salm was loud in his declarations that Lock had saved the battle.

Such praise could do wonders for the psyche. Von Salm also humoured Lock's complaints, no matter how selfish they sounded. They rode on horseback a short distance behind the rest of the group, with the remaining Germans on foot in front of them.

Lock sighed, as he stared at the smoke trails above Mannheim. His mind had not yet moved on from the recent encounter. 'Benjy has my dolman wrapped around him. Do Burroughs' men not notice that? Do they deliberately ignore what I've done?'

'I'm sure, Herr Lock, that is precisely what Burroughs intends to do. He wishes to seize the glory for himself. My Germans know the truth. They will speak to your deeds.'

'I do wish the English soldiers felt the same.'

Von Salm cleared his throat. Evidently, he did not prioritise glory. Revenge was more than enough of a motive for him.

'I think, Herr Lock, it is time to fashion a new coat for yourself, with new materials.'

'A new coat? How would that help me?'

'Perhaps you could harvest the resources of your fallen enemies. They are... many in number, after tonight.'

Lock halted his horse and squinted at von Salm. 'The resources of my enemies?'

'Indeed. Take their coats, their shirts, their skin, anything they do not need.'

'Their *skin*?' Lock nearly choked on the word.

'Perhaps you wish to be respected, or to be honoured, Herr Lock? I have found none of these things as useful as being feared. You must make a nemesis of your name. As I have done. The Spanish fear *El Diablo*, they fear the tongueless man in the forest, and I can use that fear.'

Lock flung himself into a new subject. 'Look at Mannheim. It appears Gage's men have only taken half of the city.'

Von Salm's grey head turned to the new target. 'Indeed. It makes sense. Mannheim is designed to be defended in two halves.'

'The Spanish *planned* for this?'

'They did, Herr Lock. The Spanish have barricaded themselves within the city's eastern side. They've destroyed several footbridges within the city. By my count, only the market bridge is still intact.'

'The Englishmen said they would infiltrate it at night, with help from the Strasser brothers. Do you know them?'

Von Salm clasped his hands together. 'Strasser's Fine Meats! A wonderful place to stock up on glazed hams. Will we be using their tunnels?'

'You know about their tunnels?'

Von Salm scoffed, slightly offended by the idea that other tunnels could exist without him knowing about them. '*Herr Lock*, I taught those boys everything there is to know about tunnels. In return, they've given my people full bellies more times than I can remember.'

'I hid in a sealed compartment, in his meat wagon.'

Von Salm chuckled, and adjusted the cloth on his face. 'That sounds familiar. I've never been myself, but I know many who have taken the journey.'

'It got us into Mannheim.'

'If he'd known that you'd been friends of ours, I'm sure he would have offered a discount lad.'

'He gave me something much more valuable, and useful.' Lock pulled the stiletto from its small scabbard, and von Salm's eyes glittered in recognition.

'The Italian's blade! I wondered if I'd ever see that again!'

Lock turned the small weapon over by twisting his right wrist, keeping his left on the reins. 'You've seen this weapon before?'

'I certainly have, it was I who sold it to the Strassers. This little prick here kept two hundred people fed for a month, I'll have you know.'

Lock narrowed his eyes at the stiletto. The weapon remained an enigma. There was the engraving on the guard which he still could not make out. Then the pommel, which contained the more straightforward engraving, *Milan*. The blade itself was long and thin, and its sharpness still took Lock by surprise.

'Was nearly stuck with that myself when we got it,' von Salm said, shaking his head at the idea that something so small could do so much damage.

'Who did you take this from then?'

'Do you remember I told you that Flynn brought a total of four men into the forest? Well, this stiletto here belonged to the... I believe it was the third man.'

Lock flung his gaze at the German. 'What was his name? What did he do?'

Von Salm cleared his throat and looked around him.

He and Lock were several strides behind the other Germans, and the Englishmen were further in front of them. Von Salm signalled to Lock that he was satisfied, but he beckoned him to move his horse closer. Lock squinted at von Salm, but the German beckoned him again, so Lock obliged. Suzy turned willingly.

'It was a weird one Herr Lock. The other two, we knew a lot about them, and Gaston Phillipe, of course, we have been through all that, but this fellow, I can barely recall his name...'

'Did Flynn explain *why* he wanted him dead?'

'He did, in a way. Well, he said he needed him dead, and asked me to make it more discreet than usual?'

'*More discreet?*'

Von Salm chuckled. 'You saw Phillipe's body, of course. But this was the opposite. There was no display. No message. We just made him... disappear.'

'And he had this dagger?'

'That's a *stiletto*, Officer Lock, Italian made.' Von Salm appeared to relish the weapon's name, even adding an Italian accent for effect. He reached for it, and Lock passed it to the German.

Von Salm examined it fondly in his hand. 'Judging by the hilt, I would say late 1580s.'

'Was it in this gentleman's hand when you...?'

Von Salm nodded, and then handed it back to Lock. 'I had to lie about its origins to poor Strasser, of course.'

Lock pulled Suzy's reins and she whinnied obediently. 'Its origins?'

'Well, I know that the stiletto did not belong to this man originally. It was not an heirloom. It was made for him, as a gift.'

'How do you know that?'

'It was made in Milan, Officer Lock, and the man we took apart could not speak a word of Italian.'

'You heard him speak?'

'Yes. He babbled. Mostly in a language I did not understand. Perhaps it was Dutch? I do not know.'

'What did he say?'

Von Salm paused, checking again on Flynn's location. The party was far in the distance. They would have to catch up soon.

'I didn't hear much of what he said.'

'Why not?'

'I was with my men the entire time.'

'So Flynn talked with him?'

'He didn't just talk, Herr Lock, the two men laughed and joked for nigh on an hour, until Flynn gave us the signal. They seemed to be so enjoying one another's company that I'd begun to think the Irishman had given us the wrong date.'

'Well, maybe they were both soldiers? Maybe Flynn was playing along, like he did with Gaston Phillipe?'

'Maybe,' von Salm said the word, but with a faint trace of disdain.

Lock tried to refocus. 'What was he wearing?'

Von Salm looked at Lock up and down, before nodding. 'He was dressed very similarly to you, I believe. In fact, when you came into our home, I'd thought he was bringing us another one, spontaneously this time.'

Lock shuddered to think at the power the Irishman had had.

All Flynn needed to do was blink, and the Germans would have ripped him apart.

Lock sighed.

Was he onto something? Or had Flynn just taken his role as self-appointed vigilante too seriously?

Von Salm had paused his horse, and was staring down the hill into the rushing Rhine.

Von Salm sighed as he gazed at its course. 'There was one thing I did make out. He mentioned something, just before he died, about a Black Prince. Strangest thing I'd ever –'

'*Stop*', Lock said, more firmly than he had expected to.

His hair stood on end.

Visions of black masks.

Powerlessness. Failure. Crippling, shameful, failure.

And there was that name again, the Black Prince.

The same he had heard on the boat, and in the carriage.

Von Salm had turned back to Lock, his eyebrows raised.

'Georg, do you know who the Black Prince is?'

A boisterous laugh escaped from von Salm's belly. It was a strange, almost whirring sound, followed by a whooping cough. Von Salm shook his head, his eyes were watering as he continued to chuckle. After a laboured exhale, he finally addressed the question.

'Herr Lock, *nobody* knows *who* the Black Prince is, or even *what* the Black Prince is. He is a mystery, a myth, and some would even say, a complete fiction.'

'A fiction?'

'Does a single man have the power to command so many men to do his bidding? And if so, where does this man live? How has his identity not been discovered, and promptly used against him?' Von Salm raised his palms when asking his questions, as though the answers were impossible even to fathom.

'Well, what *do* you know about him?'

'Why this curiosity, Herr Lock?'

'Why this *caginess*, Herr von Salm?'

Von Salm's eyes narrowed, and he looked away from Lock, sighing heavily. 'I know that *some* have claimed to act in the Black Prince's name.'

'*Some*? You encountered many of them?'

Von Salm shook his head. 'My friend, I have not left that forest in many years, you must understand. We don't get much in the way of... exalted guests coming our way.'

'Yet you have heard of the name?'

'Oh Matthew, every German has heard of the Black Prince! Why I used to use his name to make my daughters behave, you...' Von Salm went quiet. He shook himself, perhaps involuntarily. His bloodshot eyes blinked heavily, though there were no tears.

'I am... very sorry, for what you've been through.' Lock briefly placed his hand on von Salm's left shoulder. The German seemed at first taken aback, and then warmed by the gesture. Lock imagined him smiling under his cloth.

'It does not do to dwell on loss, Lock. Such things can drive a man crazy. Revenge is a potent force. But, it can also be a weakness. Remember that.'

'So you say. Yet here you are marching to Mannheim to take revenge on the Spanish.'

Von Salm paused. 'Perhaps, when revenge is what keeps a man alive, wakes him before the sunrise, comforts him to sleep, it is not always a wholly negative force.'

'Or perhaps when the man wants revenge desperately enough, he will say anything to justify it?'

Von Salm turned his horse. 'Hmph. In any case, I would urge you not to follow my lead.'

'Why not? You've had your revenge, and you're out to get more. Your legend is at its height. You're a powerful man.'

'A powerful man can be a weak man. This is the problem with those that work for the Black Prince.'

Lock forced Suzy to a stop. 'How can that be so? Surely a powerful man is *always* powerful?'

Von Salm sighed. 'If you hand a man power and privilege. If you tell him, he is to be feared, and that he answers to neither man nor God, how long will it take before that man is corrupted?'

Lock shook his head.

'This is the Black Prince's problem, Officer Lock. His men are invincible, like demigods, but many years of knowing this has made them reckless.'

'What does it matter if they're reckless?' Lock asked, as visions of his parents' blood splattered across their Hague residence returned to haunt him.

'It evidently matters a great deal to the Black Prince. Else he would not have sent so many men after those agents of his that have gone... rogue, so to speak.' This was too far for von Salm. As soon as the words left his mouth he winced in regret. Or perhaps, he had talked too much for his damaged mouth.

Lock moved Suzy to resume her trot.

After a long night, the light was finally bursting through the darkness. The morning chorus was beginning in the forest behind them. It was like a return to peace. Lock contemplated dropping the matter, but the Black Prince's two signals stuck in his mind.

'So, he has a moral compass, this Black Prince?'

Von Salm sighed in exasperation. 'I really do wish you would drop this matter Lock.'

'*Please*,' Lock pleaded. 'It is really important to me. If you tell me, I swear I will drop it hereafter.'

Von Salm tugged at his shirt collar, as though the conversation was heating his very body. 'Perhaps, the Black Prince has no moral compass, Lock. It is difficult to say. But he certainly has common sense.'

'What do you mean?'

Von Salm gestured at the city of Mannheim, one half belching smoke, the other being warmed by the rising sun. 'What good does it do a man to watch the world descend into chaos? Order is in the Black Prince's interest, but it is order on his terms.'

'Sounds like many German princes I know of.'

'It is true. Perhaps this Black Prince, if he exists, idles his time away in a minor German court somewhere east of the Rhine? Or, perhaps, the Black Prince is an idea, invented to scare children into doing their chores.'

'How do I get in contact with him?' The question was risky, and could send von Salm over the edge. Lock did not meet the German's eyes, but he could sense his demeanour change.

Von Salm halted his horse and made Lock look at him.

'Listen to me, Matthew Lock. You do *not* contact the Black Prince. Understand? You steer as far from the Black Prince's world as you possibly can. And, you thank God that you are not on his list of enemies.'

'What does the Black Prince do to his enemies?'

Von Salm's eyebrows drew together, and the German adjusted the cloth over his mouth. 'Matthew, I am warning you...'

'Please, Georg. *Please.*'

Even with the large space between the two and the party, von Salm's apprehension was palpable. What could make this man, who had just engaged in such grisly pursuits, now hesitate and draw back in fear? Lock maintained eye contact, and von Salm was gradually worn down.

The German sighed.

'The process is shrouded in legend. I do not know anyone who has been on the receiving end of it. If I did, I would cut all ties with them immediately. It is not worth risking the Black Prince's wrath.'

'I don't believe you,' Lock said. The words had tumbled out, but they were true.

Von Salm hadn't danced so long around an issue he knew nothing substantial about. The German tried to maintain his front, but he then sighed. The day's events had sapped his endurance.

Lock shocked himself by his desperation. He ached to know the truth. More importantly, he wanted to know what the Black Prince had planned for him next.

Von Salm moved the cloth aside from his face, exposing his fleshy stump of a tongue. This act meant that he could speak as low as possible, and not have to strain his voice. The German was taking no chances. Lock moved as close to the grotesque sight as he could, and von Salm exhaled.

'That stiletto of yours, it once belonged to a servant of the Black Prince, the man we disappeared.'

'How do you –'

'The Irishman, he said that servants of the Black Prince only receive such weapons after ten successful missions. It is a mark of their seniority in the organisation.'

A chill ran down Lock's spine. 'Good God, you're telling me Flynn conspired to murder an agent of the Black Prince?'

Von Salm shrugged. 'Who can say? It is possible the man we disappeared took that stiletto from someone else. People steal things all the time. Perhaps Flynn took offence to it?'

'And had him murdered in a forest?'

'Do not dwell on it Matthew, I am sure there is a perfectly reasonable explanation.'

'I confess I am not so sure.'

'For Flynn to kill a high-ranking member of the Black Prince's organisation would be the height of folly. He would not last long in the world after such a crime.'

'That explains why he engaged in your services. What better way to hide such a crime from the Black Prince?'

'But why risk the murder in the first place, Matthew? Why risk the Black Prince's wrath, for the sake of a stiletto?'

'I don't think it was about the stiletto Georg, I think it was about something else.'

'You do?'

'This figure you arranged to disappear, did Flynn give any clue as to why he might want him dead?'

'As I said Matthew, he did not, and we did not ask. I thought he'd earned my trust after his past actions.'

'Did you not demand more information once you learned of the man's connection with the Black Prince?'

Von Salm shook his head. 'Matthew, I understand it may be tempting to see conspiracy everywhere, but there's no reason to assume that a man is the Black Prince's servant simply because he holds his stiletto.'

'You said the disappeared man mentioned the Black Prince's name?'

Von Salm paused for a moment, before wiping spittle from his chin. 'He didn't mention it, he cursed it, like he was getting the taste out of his mouth. This disappeared man was no fan of the Black Prince. I dare say, he may have been his enemy.'

'What does the Black Prince do with his enemies, Georg?'

But this had become too much for the German. 'I cannot say anymore, Matthew. I'm sorry.'

Von Salm began to trot away from Lock, and in his desperation, Lock blurted it out.

'He warns them first, with a black mask, a note and black wax seal. Doesn't he?'

Von Salm paused on his horse, and turned back to Lock, his eyes wide and darting. 'Do *not* speak on this Matthew. Do *not*.'

'Georg, I need your help. Tell me what you know and I will never ask for it again, I swear.'

But von Salm was close to apoplectic. He was also aggressive.

'You... brought the Black Prince's wrath to my people?' It was an accusation rather than a question, and Lock steadied himself before replying.

'No, Georg, I have nothing to do with the Black Prince.'

'Well then why...'

'It's... it's my sister, Georg. My sister is in trouble. That's why I'm here. I'm here to find out more about the Black Prince so I can save her.'

The German softened visibly. 'Your *sister*?'

Perhaps it was the adrenaline, perhaps it was the heat of the moment, but for once, Lock's nervous ticks did not expose his lie. The gutting sickness that came with being false to a friend remained in place, but Lock decided he could deal with that if it meant protecting von Salm from the truth.

'She is all I have, Georg, please. You're the first fellow brave enough to provide information of any kind. I have nowhere else to go, and she is in danger.'

Von Salm held up a meaty hand and shook his head. 'I understand, Matthew.' A slight smile, or perhaps angst, now flashed over the German's face. 'What I know is limited, but I will tell you what I know, and we will never speak of it again.'

'Thank you, Georg, thank you.'

'*Never* speak of it again.'

'Never, Georg, I never will.'

'You wish to know what the Black Prince does to his enemies? I only know what I have heard.'

'First, the offending party is left a black mask, with note attached, communicating the Black Prince's displeasure. If this gentle warning is not heeded, and the offending act is not ceased or redeemed, then a group of men will visit, and remind the offending party of his place.'

'And then what happens?'

'If the man is deranged enough to ignore these two warnings?'

'Yes.'

Von Salm shook his head, as though such men could not possibly exist. 'If... the offending party is contacted for the *third* time, then the men will attack. Not necessarily to kill, but certainly to intimidate, and rough up the offending party. This is the final warning.'

'Well –'

Von Salm held up a hand. 'Before you ask, I don't know what happens after. Some say his enemies are simply murdered, others that they are disappeared. Nobody knows for sure. That is what makes it so terrifying.' Von Salm shivered in his saddle.

'*Disappeared?*' the word fascinated Lock.

The German glanced around, perhaps involuntarily, once again. 'They say that the Black Prince's enemies are handed over to the *Inquisitor*.'

There was that name again.

The Inquisitor.

The only name that aroused more fear than the Black Prince.

Von Salm then flashed an insincere smile at him. 'Your sister will be fine, provided she heeds the Black Prince's warning, whatever that warning might be. After all, would not all *sane* people rectify their behaviour after the *first* warning?'

The words landed heavily on Lock's chest.

He kept his hands clasped tightly on the reins, so von Salm could not see them tremble.

The colour drained from his face.

Lock could not unburden himself any further, nor did he have time. A whistle from the front of the column suggested that General Burroughs had a plan.

Von Salm did not hide his relief that the interrogation was over.

But there was another matter. The Irishman.

The list of things Flynn O'Toole had not told him was now long indeed.

Why had he not identified the stiletto when he had seen it? Was he hunting agents of the Black Prince? Was he in danger of incurring the Black Prince's wrath, the longer he stayed in the Irishman's presence?

There was a window of time where Lock might ask the Irishman himself, but the window was closing. If an assault on Mannheim occurred, Flynn could die, and his knowledge would die with him.

The best way to prevent that outcome was to protect Flynn. To do that, Lock would have to persuade Burroughs to put him in danger. In the thick of it.

De la Barca's surrender had presented a new opportunity. Lock pondered his options – could he leverage this act in return for a favour from Burroughs?

It was an appealing plan. It was also the exact tactic Father had used, first to make his name, and then to make the Lock family fortune. Locksville Estate had been a gift from King James, in return for Charles Lock's success in helping mediate the Twelve Years Truce in 1609. The peace between the Spanish and Dutch had long since expired, but the Estate was now Lock's by right.

Von Salm seemed miles away, but he remained just a few feet from Lock's horse. The two men began to trot, neither one acknowledging that the conversation had happened, or that it had finished.

Von Salm didn't ask why Lock wanted so many details, and Lock didn't ask anymore questions. The perfect arrangement.

Burroughs face scrunched into a frown when he caught sight of Lock's ashen complexion. Lock ignored the reaction, and the General began to speak to the sixty or so men assembled in front of him.

'Gentlemen, it has been quite a night, I am sure you will agree.' The statement was greeted with cheerful grunts and nodding heads. Lock picked up on the expressions on the faces of the different men, be they German or English. All stood erect, with smiles either half playing or fully embraced by their faces. These were confident, accomplished men, who wished to finish the job, having come so tantalisingly close.

Burroughs nodded in recognition at the responses, and held up a hand to quell them. 'I need you for one more exertion. In a moment, we will enter

Mannheim. We will enter through the tunnel prepared by our allies, the Strasser Brothers.' A slight cheer emerged from some of the Germans, who recognised the name.

The response caused Burroughs to pause, as though realising that half his audience did not understand him. Lock pounced on the opportunity by shooting up his hand. 'Sir, it would be my honour to translate into German for you Sir.'

Burroughs thought about it for a second, before nodding, and beckoning Lock to move his horse beside him. Lock did his best impression of a confident soldier. The assembled men dug into his back with their eyes.

How many resented him?

How many believed him a coward?

Burroughs cleared his throat and nodded at Lock.

Lock nodded back, and turned to face the Germans, who stood largely separate from the English cavalry. Lock quickly repeated what Burroughs had just said, but in German. Once their allies were up to speed, Burroughs resumed his speech, leaving a pause after each sentence for Lock to translate.

'Our men are in trouble, it would seem. The Spanish within Mannheim wish to become martyrs. Or, perhaps, they wish to shed more of our blood before surrendering with the colours. It does not matter, comrades. What matters is that we take this city, and we return it to the Germans.'

The last sentence was particularly popular with the Germans, as Burroughs surely expected it to be. Lock's attention was briefly seized by an eagle's cry somewhere in the distance, before he nodded at Burroughs to resume.

'The Spanish are many, but we have something they do not. Knowledge. We know that de la Barca's army is not coming to save them. De la Barca languishes now in *our* custody!'

The statemen drew jeers from the English, and many Germans joined in. De la Barca was plainly one of the most unpopular men on the Rhine.

'If these Spaniards are smart, and if they are honourable, they will surrender to us before engaging in any fruitless combat. But until this surrender is heard, you will enter your city, and you will eliminate them.'

The final sentence elicited a cheer from English ranks, which was quickly hushed. Lock did his best to reiterate the command, while maintaining Burroughs' firm tone. The exercise drew a curious look from the General.

Burroughs then pointed to the abandoned hamlet a few feet behind him. 'You will enter this place in an orderly fashion, and you will traverse its depths. One more tunnel, friends, will bring you under Mannheim's walls, and into the cellar of the Bee and Bard.'

Some expressions dipped at the mention of more underground antics, but Burroughs' waved hands were enough to hush the louder protests.

'Once you reach into the cellar, you will find muskets and powder, courtesy of our allies. You will wait in that cellar, and prepare your weapons, in absolute silence. The cellar is large, and largely devoid of drink. However, I warn you now, that any man who drinks will be shot. I won't allow any drunkards to ruin our plan tonight. Are we understood?'

Lock translated the orders, and some shoulders slackened. Burroughs appeared to note this as well, and he allowed final declaration.

'Cheer up, gentlemen. Once Mannheim is our hands, you may return to the Bee and Bard, or any other of the city's taverns, and drink yourselves into a stupor. I will personally purchase the first round for you, though I'm sure our German friends will be on hand with tankards filled. Until then, comrades, maintain your honour, and *fight like men*.'

Cheers had once more to be suppressed, and the men began lining up in preparation to enter the hamlet. Lock remained near Burroughs' side, as the General conversed with two Englishmen.

Lock glanced towards the target in the near distance. Mannheim's walls were perhaps a few hundred feet away, but there was no sign of any defenders on or near the walls. Perhaps the Spanish garrison was even more denuded than had been supposed? The city gates were closed at least, and a Spanish contingency plan was bound to be in place.

Finally, as the men began to enter the hamlet, Burroughs finished his conversation, and Lock moved to his side. Burroughs nodded at him.

'Quick thinking on your part lad, sometimes I forget half my men aren't English, though they do fight like it.'

'Sir, I want to go with the army into Mannheim.'

The General shook his head knowingly, as though the request had been expected long before. 'Lock, you know I cannot do that. I swore an oath...'

'To Vere, yes Sir I know, but surely I have demonstrated my aptitude for survival?'

Lock was disappointed to see the General's bland expression greet him in response. Had Burroughs worked so hard to write Lock out of his triumph that he'd forgotten the key role he played?

Lock swallowed a protest, and tried a different approach. 'Sir, I retrieved the surrender of Diego de la Barca. His surrender now speaks to your honour...'

The General partially raised a hand, indicating he lacked the time for flattery.

'...But how much more honour would it bring to you, Sir, if Mannheim *itself* surrendered to you.'

'Lock, this is precisely the outcome I expect.'

'As you should, Sir, but who among your men possesses the diplomatic experience necessary to retrieve that surrender? Would it not be wise to appoint someone that does? How terrible would it be if the wrong man messed up the arrangement?'

Burroughs shifted in his saddle. 'I have the Irishman on it, envoy. I am sorry.'

Lock did not have to force a scoff. '*Flynn*? You trust your honour with Flynn O'Toole?'

'I trust, Lock, that his yearning for a pardon will be to my advantage.'

'His German is far too substandard for this task.'

'This may be true Lock, but it is the Spanish I wish him to treat with.'

'But the city is *German*, Sir. You must treat with the German city Fathers, as well as the Spanish defenders. Otherwise, the city will be untethered from its Spanish docks, and will drift back into German hands.'

'German hands?'

'Sir, do you imagine the Germans will be pleased to welcome the English back in, after they've been abandoned before? They'll need to be persuaded.'

'I will *persuade* them with the tip of my sword!'

'But you won't, Sir, because you are an honourable man. No, it is more likely, that Mannheim's residents will step into the power vacuum left by Spain, and fill it themselves.'

'They would not *dare*.'

'If you were them, Sir, would you be content to swap one overlord for another, or would you prefer to regain the independence you had lost?'

Burroughs paused in his response, and his head tilted to the left.

Had he found the chink in his armour? Lock cleared his throat and doubled down, by referring to a scenario Burroughs could never stomach.

'Unless, Sir, you wish for Georg von Salm to receive the surrender of Mannheim for himself.'

'That devil could never run a city,' Burroughs hissed, though this very response confirmed that the General did indeed fear it.

'And how do you prevent it, Sir, if the man you send in to negotiate cannot reach the Germans? This would surely place the role of saviour in von Salm's hands. After all your honourable efforts, would it be truly fair if Mannheim's city Fathers ungratefully forced your men out?'

Burroughs remained silent.

'Let me accompany the Irishman, Sir, and you can be guaranteed that the Spanish and German elements will be aligned to your benefit.'

Burroughs shifted in his saddle again, and exhaled. Lock went in for the killer blow.

'Sir, I know the Strasser brothers well. I even saved Herman Strasser's life. He owes me a debt, and would surely repay it by persuading Mannheim's residents to welcome an English garrison.' Lock did not lift his gaze from Burroughs. The General shook his head, not in refusal, but apparent frustration.

'Oh... oh very well lad. Once again, I find you are too valuable to keep away from the battle. But listen to me now. You *do not* engage with the enemy. You do not fire a single musket. You keep away from the heat of the fighting, and once the Spanish request a surrender, you and Flynn go there to meet him. Then, you may work on the Germans.'

Lock knew had no intention of adhering to any of this advice, but he nodded with enthusiasm all the same.

'Then go on, go and find O'Toole. I believe he's already in the cellar.' Burroughs clicked his fingers at a grey-haired man on foot, standing nearby him. The man was certainly a civilian, and was much too thin and unimposing to be a soldier.

The slight man produced a piece of parchment, leaned on the rump of Burroughs' horse, and began writing on it. After a few scribbles, the man nodded, and handed Burroughs the parchment with the quill. Burroughs scribbled something at the end of it, and then handed it to Lock.

'If the Irishman gives you any grief, show him this. It should shut him up.'

Lock nodded gratefully.

'Well, go on then!' Burroughs said, gesturing at the hamlet.

Lock dismounted, attached his pack to his back, checked his sword and stiletto were still in place, and, his heart racing, joined the diminishing queue for the hamlet's front door. At last, he would be able to drill the Irishman for more answers.

He would also have the opportunity to show these men what was he was made of, a prospect which filled his belly with nervous excitement. He would show himself as masterful of the drill as he was of letters, just as Father had intended.

- CHAPTER THIRTY-SEVEN -

Perhaps, in its heyday, the Bee and Bard had been a favoured destination for Manheim's residents. Its weathered chairs and sticky floors proved that at one time, the establishment had welcomed and entertained a myriad of guests. But that time had since passed.

This was a Spanish tavern now, or at least it had been, until Joseph Gage began his attack on Mannheim, and awakened the Spanish garrison from their slumber.

Fortunately, the Spanish guests had stayed above ground, and had not ventured into the cellar since the premises had come into their hands. The dimly lit room had been used for storage in peacetime, and now a different kind of materiel had taken the place of the innumerable barrels which had once occupied so much space.

Stacks of muskets, crude melee weapons, and plentiful stores of power and cartridges filled the cellar. The haul was so extensive that the rustic stone walls were nearly completely obscured by it.

It was the Strasser brothers' favourite secret.

Once one entered the Bee and Bard unseen, and made his way into the cellar, he was effectively safe. He also had a direct, albeit dark and dusty route, to the outside world.

The abandoned hamlet outside Mannheim's south gate was rumoured to be haunted, a rumour which Herman Strasser had played no small role in propagating.

The superstitious Spanish, it was assumed, would not risk damnation to investigate such a grotty, dilapidated building. But if any did, the Stassers had made the hamlet so unpleasant to wade through, and the secret compartments so expertly concealed, that many a Spaniard who had risked his soul had come away with nothing to show for it.

This was the story which filled Lock's ears as he had squelched along damp planks in a waterlogged tunnel, with Theo Strasser by his side. After this small talk, Theo turned to the most pressing matter – Joseph Gage's plan had completely failed.

'Gage underestimated the Spanish. The bloody Englishman thought he could do no wrong, thought Captain Ricardo's men would roll over. Can you fathom it?'

It had been hard to argue with Theo Strasser's cutting analysis, so Lock did not try. The failure, after all, spoke for itself. Gage's plan had succeeded as far as it possibly could, because the Englishman had failed to reconnoitre the Spanish positions beforehand.

Lock had nodded respectfully at each new piece of information, each new condemnation, and each new curse which had flowed from Theo Strasser's mouth. Now was the time to turn the situation around, but it would not be easy.

Once the Spanish realised de la Barca was not on his way to relieve them, it was at least possible that they would surrender after a brief negotiation. As he gazed out of the broken windows of the Bee and Bard's upper story, however, Lock found it hard to agree with that assessment.

The innumerable barricades blocking various streets; the proudly parading Spaniards that had marched tantalisingly close to them, and the poor progress of Joseph Gage, all pointed to a fact which would have been difficult for Burroughs to accept. The Spanish intended to resist for as long as possible, until reinforcements from further afield arrived.

And they were in the ideal position to do so.

In the moment of Gage's attack, as had been the plan, the Spanish had seized foodstuffs from whatever vendors they could, before barricading themselves into a defensible collection of interconnected houses. This row of houses overlooked a river, which separated Mannheim into two halves.

As far as the Spanish were concerned, no Englishmen had breached the river. Mannheim, Theo Strasser complained, was now divided into an English and Spanish half, with its German citizens caught in the middle. There was ample proof of this. Screams and wails drifted towards the Bee and Bard, like an intersection of human suffering.

The sounds agitated the Germans, who wished to act, but the English were anxious to tread carefully. The element of surprise was the most valuable weapon in their possession, and would have to be leveraged as effectively as possible, if the Spanish garrison of nine hundred men could be compelled to give up the fight.

Three English officers, none of whom Lock had interacted with before, had taken effective lead of the Anglo-German army while Burroughs remained outside Mannheim's walls.

After speaking with Theo Strasser and excusing himself, Lock had asked after Flynn, and he had been directed to the Bee and Bard's second floor. Lock now sat on a stool in what had once been the Bee and Bard's VIP area, where town magnates had once been entertained at great expense. Below his feet, in the stony cellar, the English officers debated their next move.

The room stank of sweat and sweet pleasure, despite being out of use for several years. An excessive red leather upholstery lined every piece of furniture in sight, none of it particularly comfortable. Rugs cut from various animals lined the floor. Richly engraved wood panelling adorned the walls, courtesy, one suspected, of Georg von Salm's woodworking friends.

Broken glass littered the floor, and there was a small hole in the corner of the roof, where wind and the occasional nesting bird entered. Perhaps the only benefit to being in the room was the view it granted of the Spanish-held buildings, and the large market square, which once teemed with activity.

Flynn had labelled it a 'shithole', but Lock wasn't yet ready to be so harsh. It was at least a floor above the mess below them, and it separated them from the crowd. Perhaps, finally, he would have a chance to speak with the Irishman.

'That's the third parade in an hour,' Flynn said, his whisper momentarily filling the soulless room. The Irishman knelt on a gaudy red armchair, and peered through a broken window. He had been careful, almost excessively so, to ensure that no Spaniard could see him.

The tattered curtains had been repurposed to provide extra concealment, but the Irishman had remained uncharacteristically quiet just to be safe. He had barely spoken since Lock entered the room.

Lock shifted uncomfortably.

The hardwood stool had clearly been brought upstairs by someone of simpler means, and Lock had been drawn to it, as the most normal piece of furniture in the room. After half an hour seated upon it though, he had come to envy the plush but ostentatious armchair which Flynn now occupied. It was also the only piece of furniture without a gaping hole in the seat.

That act of vandalism fascinated Lock. It would surely have taken several hours to cut a large hole through the leather and padding of each sofa and chair. The same person had likely smashed each of the windows, drained the alcohol, and scattered broken glass on the floor.

The Irishman had claimed that such behaviour was not irregular. When given the chance, and faced with no consequences, man's destruction could know no bounds.

Flynn turned to Lock, as though surprised by his lack of reaction. Lock nodded limply.

What could he say?

How could he even approach the subject?

Why had Flynn targeted men with a specific stiletto?

Why had Flynn said nothing when Lock had been given the weapon in the Strasser residence?

The Irishman gave nothing away.

Rather than launch the interrogation he wanted, Lock just glared at the back of his head.

'*There*', the Irishman whispered, and pointed to a sight far from the building.

Lock shuffled gingerly to the plush red armchair. His hand drifted up the material, before resting on its right arm. He had definitely chosen the wrong seat.

Flynn moved some strands of his black hair from his face before pointing again to the target. The river which divided Mannheim into its English and Spanish halves could be seen, but this was not what had drawn the Irishman's eye.

'They've got three defensive positions on the main parts of the river, do you see? But there's a part in the far-right corner that is almost completely undefended.'

'That's because the river runs fastest and fullest there, and the Spanish destroyed the bridge,' Lock sighed.

Flynn quickly turned his head back to Lock. 'And what if we bring a new bridge of our own?'

'Build our own bridge?'

'Yes, Lock. Those rafts we used to cross the Rhine before, we could use them to cross the river there, and Gage's Englishmen could then get across. The Spanish would have to defend on all sides, not just from the front, where they expect the attack.'

Lock tried to imagine the feat of organisation which would be required to make the Irishman's plan work. His expression moved Flynn to defend his plan.

'Those Germans with us, they could surely whip up some rafts in double quick time. Then all we need is to distract the Spanish from that corner of the city.'

'And how do we do that? This is assuming the Germans are happy with labouring on more rafts.'

Flynn grimaced, and Lock smiled inwardly at the appearance of the Irishman's anxious ticks.

Perhaps Flynn had expected him to be a more amenable audience? Well, he was finished humouring him.

Flynn had blown hot and cold so many times, and he continued to lie. Who could trust such an unreliable companion?

Lock found his anger rising every time Flynn opened his mouth. He could not tolerate such dishonesty for much longer.

But when to confront Flynn, in a crisis moment like this?

'What distraction did you have planned?' Lock asked, being sure to concede nothing in his tone.

The Irishman nodded, before pointing to the opposite end of the river on the far-left. 'There. If we focus our attack there, then the Spanish will move men away from the true target. Classic deception.'

'How would you coordinate with Gage? How would you let him know your plan, and how would you guarantee the Spanish don't find out about it?' Lock knew he was being uncharacteristically negative, as Flynn's second grimace confirmed.

'That's what Theo Strasser is for. His warren of tunnels and interconnected cellars is on par with von Salm's.'

'Von Salm showed him how to tunnel, so this is hardly surprising.'

Flynn bristled at the brisk reply. He then exhaled, before turning his steely blue eyes at Lock.

'You're angry with me, I know.'

The directness was unexpected.

'I am,' was all Lock could muster.

Flynn nodded. He allowed the armchair to absorb his frame, and he crossed his legs while facing Lock.

'I have been unfair to you, Lock. I have misjudged you and I have erred in that. My German is not on par with yours, but even I can tell that the Germans are buzzing about what you did. You saved us in the forest. You are not a liability.'

As quickly as the Irishman delivered the judgement, he turned his head back to surveying the city. Lock stared at the back of Flynn's head in silence.

A smile began to spread, unrestrained, across his face.

But what of the stiletto?

Lock suppressed the dilemma.

It could wait until after the city was delivered. If Englishman and Irishman cooperated, Lock was certain that the enemy would not stand a chance.

'Alright,' Lock whispered, half crawling to another broken window. 'Let's run through your plan again.'

A smile grew in the left corner of Flynn's mouth. 'We need three things. First, we need rafts from the Germans to cross the city's river. Second, we need coordination from the Strassers, so that Gage knows where to attack. Third, and most importantly Lock, we need a distraction, so that the plan can be carried off without a hitch.'

'Can von Salm arrange the rafts?'

'You could ask him. He seems fond of you.'

'I wouldn't be so sure,' Lock said. The more he thought about it, the guiltier he felt about squeezing the German for information about the Black Prince.

The best way to alleviate guilt was through sacrifice, Father had said. Now seemed like the moment for such a gesture. Lock exhaled, and presented his scheme.

'*We* could be the distraction, Flynn. We could lead the English into that empty market square behind the Spanish houses. It should be wide enough for the men to stand in file. If we remain out of range, they'll have to come out to face us.'

Flynn tilted his head to the right. 'It is risky.'

'Do they have cannon?'

Flynn shook his head. 'Plenty of powder, but no cannon, thank God. They were back in de la Barca's camp.'

'We could send for those cannons, and blast them from their houses instead?'

Flynn shook his head. 'It would take too long to drag them here. By then the men will surely have outed themselves, and the surprise will have been lost.'

'So we send von Salm to arrange the rafts, and we provide the distraction which will let Gage's men get into position.'

'But how will Gage know when and where to strike? We could be left to face the Spanish alone. They outnumber us, Lock.'

'Herman Strasser,' Lock whispered. 'He told me that there's a hundred Germans waiting to rise up. Those numbers will help.'

'You said it yourself Lock, rubble doesn't make a house.'

'We don't need to make a house, Flynn. All we need is the appearance of foundations. Think on it. We have the element of surprise, and the Spanish are surrounded, with help far away. The more numbers we appear to have, the lower their morale.'

Flynn's expression grew darker. 'These men are well-led, Lock. They won't flee when the battle goes against them.'

'Then... then we will hold as well. We only need to hold for as long as it takes Gage to be informed, and to bring his men to bear.'

'We'll need to gather these Germans up first, how would we do that?'

'Send out the Germans that von Salm commands. Fan them out across the city, to collect as many able-bodied men as can be found. If the Germans want their city back, they can fight for it.'

Flynn half squinted at Lock. 'Now you're starting to sound like a soldier.'

'In a few hours, we could have a new cohort of German militia by our side, with rafts to bridge the river, which will bring Gage's men to the battle. The Spanish will be surrounded.'

'Lock, you know Burroughs wants you far from the battle.'

Lock winced at the unwelcome truth. 'Burroughs isn't here.'

'And thanks be to God for that. He'd probably suggest a cavalry charge through a rushing river.'

'It will be a nice change to finally fire my musket.'

'Well for God's sake Lock, you better stay alive long enough to receive the surrender.'

Lock nodded, but the prospect churned his stomach. The experience of receiving de la Barca's surrender had not been a pleasant one. This one, hopefully, would be less eventful.

Flynn pointed to a cleared stony area perhaps a hundred feet in the distance, now overrun with weeds. 'That square, it used to host the farmer's market. The Spanish buildings are in front of it, so they'd all have eyes on us, but it's just far enough away so they can't reach us. We could gather the men there.'

Lock exhaled. 'Let's go below and tell the men. It's time to give Mannheim back to the Germans.'

- CHAPTER THIRTY-EIGHT -

Four hours later, the skeleton of the plan which Lock and Flynn had arranged in the Bee and Bard's VIP area had acquired a great deal more meat. Two rafts had been hauled underground and into the cellar at great effort, courtesy of Georg von Salm. A grand total of seventy-seven Germans had been gathered from the dwellings on the Spanish side of the town, once they'd been informed of the looming showdown. Many boys and children, some as young as eight years old, had to be turned away.

There was no denying the enthusiasm of Mannheim's German citizens. The challenge now was harnessing it. There was, at least, a great surplus of powder and firearms – the Strassers' efforts in stockpiling had seen to that. But the muskets varied in quality and condition, variables as formidable as the skill level of the Germans themselves.

It would require considerable organisation to arrange a coherent firing drill among men who had never fired these weapons before. Lock's preview of the Germans' capabilities in the forest had not instilled confidence.

It was a hesitation which was shared. The English officers charged with leading Burroughs' group of thirty or so professionals refused point blank to take command of them.

'Not a chance,' the bald one said. 'What you're asking for cannot be done. It'd be safer to give them pikes and send them to storm the Spanish houses.'

The idea was as equally problematic as Lock's.

The row of three Spanish manor houses that overlooked Mannheim's main river system were virtually impregnable. There was no question of breaking in.

The Spanish would have to be persuaded to come out. That could only be done with deception. Luring the Spanish to an apparently easy victory; luring them towards the opportunity of revenge on Mannheim's rudimentary militia – that was the only sure way to win.

The atmosphere in the Bee and Bard's cellar was muted, but tense. Men were ordered to observe strict silence. The success of what happened next depended on the element of surprise. Lock watched the debate take place as he sat on a barrel which had been laid horizontally on the cellar floor. Flynn stood, arms folded, to his left.

The bald officer's objections threatened to sink the attack before it had even begun. He was far from pleased to see more untrained Germans appear in his midst. Thankfully, the more senior of the three officers, a red-haired, red-faced bear of a Scot named Captain Monro, seemed more on board with the idea. He even provided a twist of his own.

'We should place some of our men among the Germans. The Spanish will think their enemies crack shots.'

'How do we persuade the Spanish to come from their den?' the bald officer challenged.

Monro had alluded to a great collection of Spanish flags. The red cross of Burgundy was well-known. To the citizens of Mannheim, it was a symbol of oppression and occupation. But to the soldiers in Spanish service, it was a symbol of immense pride.

'We gather as many of those flags as we can, and once we're in position, we raise them, and set them *alight.*'

Many in the cellar gasped at the audacity of the idea, but Monro waved the objections away.

'This insult to their honour is the only sure way of angering the Spanish enough to bring them out of their den.'

'If we're playing with fire, then why not just set their dens on fire?' the bald officer asked. His plummy tone suggested that the solution was blindingly obvious.

Monro shook his head with considerable restraint. 'We don't know where their commander is. If we burn the houses down, and he burns with them, how will Officer Lock receive the surrender of the town? It will drift out of Spanish hands, and away from ours.'

Lock's stomach lurched at the mention of his name. Murmurings, whispers, and several glances in his direction all followed. Lock did his best to keep his eyes forward, and pretend not to notice the less flattering whispered comments.

'So we gather in the square, and we wait for the Spanish to see us burn their flags? Even if they emerge from their strongholds, then what? How long do we hold out for? We have at most one hundred and thirty effectives. The Spanish could be as many as nine hundred. We'll be obliterated.'

The objections were not unreasonable. Men glanced at one another in the dim light. Monro seemed to wave the objections away, but his bald subordinate was not backing down. After clearing his throat, Monro addressed the men.

'Listen to me, gentlemen, you know me and my record of service to His Majesty, and to the honour of England. You know I would never rush headlong towards disaster, unless a considerable reward awaited me at the end.'

Chuckles and the occasional grumble followed. Monro then gestured to Lock.

'I've been told by Herr von Salm, that without Officer Lock's efforts in the forest, we would have all been lost. This plan is partially his. And *I* trust him.'

Most of the heads in the cellar now swivelled towards Lock, and under the pressure of so many eyes he could not hide his embarrassment. His face became increasingly flushed.

So Georg von Salm had revealed his role after all? Perhaps this meant he harboured no resentment for the quasi-interrogation? Lock searched for the German's face in the crowd without success.

Monro waved a hand at the rising commotion, and officers shushed their men.

'Remember, gentlemen, *we* are the distraction. We are, perhaps, the sacrifice, so that Gage can bring our compatriots over the river in safety, and thence, to our side. Do you wish to fight with your comrades? I want no words, just a show of hands.'

Hands shot up across the room. The Germans, out of the loop due to the language barrier, sheepishly followed suit.

This reminded Lock of the need for translation once again.

His heart pounded in his ears as he moved off the barrel, and cleared his throat.

'Officer Monro, may I translate for our German comrades?'

Monro's irritation at the source of the request vanished when he saw Lock standing with his right hand in the air. He nodded.

'You may translate, Officer Lock. But I have another idea. You and your Irish friend... there he is. You and O'Toole can also take those Germans under your wing. They can be *your* responsibility.'

Flynn let out a heap of curses in his native tongue. Lock attempted to protest.

'Sir... I have never commanded men in my life, surely there is an Englishman, or even a German, better qualified than I...'

Monro shook his red head briskly. 'I cannot persuade my men to command them. They will stand among them, but they need to tend to their own duties. I need someone who knows the language, and you speak it far better than any of us.'

Lock couldn't believe what he was hearing.

'Sir... Captain Monro... I am not a soldier.'

Monro nodded and smiled. 'I know. And Burroughs will have my head for this, but it is the best way I can see to gather the Germans together. They know you, they respect you, they will follow your commands.'

'My *commands*?' It occurred to Lock that he had not the faintest idea of how to order men around.

'The drill manual, lad? Surely you know the drill? I have been told you learned it from an early age. It's time to pass that knowledge on.'

'Sir... with respect, it took me many years –'

'We only need to buy *time*, Officer Lock, isn't that what you said? If your Germans can fire even a handful of shots among them, then that will keep the Spanish busy. As soon as the flags start burning, the countdown will begin. We'll get those rafts in place, and Gage's Englishmen will be with us.'

Lock was speechless.

His confidence in the plan was being used against him.

The bald officer now had a sickly smile plastered across his face. The bustling activity of the English soldiers confirmed that the discussion was over. But what of von Salm? Would he stand among his men? Would he stand with Lock and Flynn? Would Flynn stand with him?

A hand on Lock's shoulder answered the latter question.

Flynn couldn't suppress a grin. 'Next time, perhaps don't be so willing to share your ideas.'

Lock exhaled, and saw tens of German faces staring back eagerly at him. Was he in command?

A familiar, raspy voice sounded from his right. Lock exhaled once again. It was von Salm.

'My friends,' the German began, adjusting the cloth over his mouth as he did so. 'This is the time to stand for Mannheim, and for Germany. The enemy is there. He is only a few feet from you, and from the barrel of your gun. Will you join with me, and with our friends, Officer Lock, and Captain O'Toole?'

Lock eyed Flynn up and down. Flynn shrugged at his sudden promotion. Captain O'Toole did have a certain appeal.

'They have already done a great deal for us,' von Salm continued. 'It is time we return the favour. It is time we show them how we fight. It is time we show the Spanish how the Germans treat their friends, and what we do to our enemies. March with me now, for those that could not join us. For all our lost loved ones. *For Woodrest.*'

As one, the Germans silently raised their hands in the air.

A shiver ran over Lock's shoulders.

Von Salm nodded at the gesture, and marched to Lock's side. He slapped him on the upper back.

'The rafts are ready. My men are ready. Are *you*?'

Lock couldn't help but hesitate.

Last week, he would have fled from such a challenge. Now, he saw it as an opportunity. The shift in outlook scared him.

Was it a natural outcome of war?

After facing his first battle, in the depths of the forest, did all subsequent battles lose their fearsome quality?

There was something else.

Was it excitement?

Was he excited at the prospect of risking his life?

He turned to check Flynn's expression, but the Irishman was already among the Germans, whispering in hushed, excited tones about the encounter to come.

The men were all smiles, as though preparing for some great celebration.

The fact that many had seen their final sunrise did not seem to register. Or if it did, it was ignored.

- CHAPTER THIRTY-NINE -

Captain Robert Monroe hailed from a long line of warriors in Scotland's remarkably warlike Monroe clan. When the seven-hundred strong clan wasn't fighting in local conflicts, many a Monroe made his name fighting on the continent. There was scarcely a battle in the last century that a Monroe had missed.

Monro was of a similar age to Lock, but from very different means. He had joined Sir Horace Vere's volunteers for a chance at adventure, but it had turned into a passion, and Monro had risen from corporal to captain in the two years since arriving. His rapid rise had made him some bitter rivals, but it had also contributed to his no-nonsense approach. This was no time to suffer fools.

'I suspect many of us will die today,' Monro said to Lock, as they looked down at the square from a cracked window of the Bee and Bard's VIP area.

The observation had been stated without emotion, in the same tone as a mathematician reaching the end of his calculations.

Lock did not argue with him. 'The plan is dangerous, Sir, but it is the best one available. All being well, we will only have to face the full attention of the Spanish for a short period. Then, Gage's men will arrive and take the pressure off.'

But even as he said the words, Lock knew it was asking a lot.

So many variables had the potential to go disastrously wrong. What if the Spanish were not sufficiently distracted, and noticed Gage's men attempting to cross? What if the Spanish obliterated the men in the square before Gage's men even arrived? What if Gage simply refused to move? Tactics, it was said, were not Gage's strongest suit.

'Aye, time is running out for Mannheim. If we don't kick out Captain

Ricardo's men soon, we'll be surrounded by his reinforcements.'

'Who is this Captain Ricardo I've heard so much about?'

'He's a hard bastard Officer Lock. A real nasty piece of work.'

An Irish voice whispered to their right. 'I am familiar with Captain Ricardo, Sir. Permission to travel with Officer Lock to receive his surrender, when this is over?'

Monro smiled grimly at the request. 'I like your enthusiasm. Permission granted. We will have to arrange a location for the –'

'Sir, might I recommend Mannheim's main church? With the great spire?'

Peace in a church made sense. When matters were more sacred, a church was a safe place, which soldiers wouldn't dare to dishonour. The location would hopefully guarantee a modicum of safety, provided Captain Ricardo had honour to spare.

But Monro's mind was on other matters. He shrugged at the request. The location was of little interest to him. 'Host your negotiations wherever you wish, O'Toole. But let's beat the bastards first.'

The bald officer walked almost silently through the door. 'Sir, the Germans are in position with the rafts. They confirm that the Spanish still leave the pass unguarded.'

Monro nodded with satisfaction, and rubbed his filthy palms together. 'Alright lad,' he turned to Lock. 'Let's see if you've taught those Germans anything.'

It had all been pre-arranged.

Lock, Flynn and von Salm would serve as the organisational head of these ragtag Germans. Lock would shout the commands, and with sufficient space between them, the Germans would observe and do their best to copy what von Salm and Flynn did.

Each German was armed with a musket, and three powder charges. This would reduce the risk of large explosions, and limited the demands on the Germans themselves. If they could squeeze out a single shot, Lock told them, they'd be doing well.

He had tried to explain the different steps involved in the drill manual, but after receiving several blank stares, he tried his own approach. There was no time for the forty-three steps. They would learn and fulfil his thirteen steps instead.

Thus began the first leg of the plan – leaving the confines of the Bee and Bard, and heading across open ground, to congregate in the square.

Blood had already been drawn, as a blissfully unaware two-man Spanish patrol was cut down by more than twenty jubilant Germans. There was little sense in keeping the Germans on a leash at all times – the brutality could occasionally be useful.

Now it moved the Spanish to barricade themselves in their reinforced houses, in anticipation of an attack. This granted a degree of cover, and a small window where positions could be reached, and a system prepared.

Men had begun to fill the acre of stony ground that constituted Mannheim's market square. The flat area, peppered with the skeletal remains of rose bushes, had hosted Mannheim's farmers' market at one time or another. Such events had ceased when the Spanish arrived.

As they made for the area, sweat ran down Lock's back in the afternoon sun. He was among the last group to move, but Georg von Salm had gone with the first group, rousing them forward, and shouting blood-curdling songs at regular intervals since. Their chants echoed through the Spanish quarter.

Lock nodded at Captain Monro, who signalled for his men to follow. A few shots from windows would be expected, but if the Spanish wished to engage with their assembling enemy properly, they would have to leave their buildings.

Several Spanish flags being unfurled by the Germans as Lock half-jogged to the square. The area was virtually full with men. A few shots sounded from the windows of the Spanish buildings three hundred feet ahead of them.

They had watched the assembling army for the last half hour, but refused to attack for now.

One shot was heard, but it had little chance of reaching its target. All Germans were strictly instructed not to fire at the enemy until ordered to do so. The English soldiers did not have to be told. They knew an impossible target when they saw it.

A musket's effective range was perhaps two hundred yards, but that was only in the most capable soldier's hands. Most would be happy to strike a target at one hundred yards, but others still would wait until the enemy was fewer than fifty yards away.

The closer the enemy, Lock had told them, the more likely it was that you would hit him, and he would hit you.

But the plan did not rely on statistics alone. It also depended on the emotion of the Spanish soldier, who would be tempted with an opportunity to wipe away the hated German peasantry in one great attack. If that temptation failed, the outrage caused by several burning flags should do the trick.

Wooden frames, the remnants of stalls from the farmer's market, were improvised as a makeshift wall to the front of the square. This would delay the enemy's advance, and give the soldiers something to hide behind. To the left, right and rear of the square, shrivelled trees and shrubs provided some measure of visual cover, but little else.

Spanish flags were now raised on short poles. It was strange to stand so close to the symbol, after skirting around it for so long, but Lock knew the Spanish could see it too. The very sight would draw their attention.

Perhaps, if they were lucky, Gage's men would arrive before the shooting even started. But Lock didn't feel particularly lucky. He was also heavier than usual.

The Strassers' penchant for stockpiling had netted him an iron breastplate, attire normally reserved for the cavalry. All Englishmen had acquired one, which helped them stand out among the hundred or so Germans they stood among. The suggestion had been Monro's. Lock had been impressed at the simple ingenuity of the idea, though some Germans had complained at feeling exposed in comparison.

A bandolier stretched across his chest, and the twelve apostles were near at hand. His musket was partially primed, needing only the match to be lit, and the powder to be checked a final time.

For several hours, as the men had talked and plotted, Lock had worked through the hundreds of muskets in the cellar. He and a handful of quartermasters and volunteers had arranged to prepare these firearms for battle.

Some firearms had become brittle and rusted in storage, others were good as new, but the experience had covered his hands in black powder. He looked like the other English soldiers, though he was an imposter. Nonetheless, Father would certainly be proud, though also likely quite furious.

There was no escaping underground this time. He would be amidst the battle with the rest of them. He would, at long last, have a chance to show Flynn, von Salm and anyone else who watched what he was capable of.

Lock whispered the thirteen steps of the drill to himself for the umpteenth time in the last hour. It was recited like a bible verse. Each step brought a new pang of nostalgia for the life before. But then, he recalled Father's words.

The man that trains without the possibility of action is like the beautiful dress that is made but never worn – a tragic waste.

The simile had always puzzled him, particularly since it was impossible to keep Mother out of her range of expensive, imported dresses. But the message was undeniable. It was time now to dispense with theory, disregard personal records, and focus on sending as many musket balls as possible into the enemy.

The Englishmen got into position, filing among the Germans, who shifted excitedly on their feet. Englishmen were biting cartridges, looking over their shoulders and nodding at their comrades, and in some cases, patting Germans gently on the back.

The sun warmed Lock's neck. The weather was cooperating, and not just in the delay in the expected rain, which would have ruined the powder. With the sun in their eyes, the Spanish would have another disadvantage to overcome. Every disadvantage to the enemy was a mercy to the English and Germans. Their blended force would need all the help it could get.

Men and younger boys wandered through the ranks holding lanterns and lengths of cord. Some of them were very young, far too young. Monro, or perhaps von Salm, had evidently thought it worth the risk.

A shout emerged from his right, and smoke emerged from one of the flags. Monro stood beside it, before shouting at his compatriots to do the same.

Lock bellowed the command in German, and a hundred grinning heads spun around to see the arson first-hand. Smoke poured into the air, cheers rang out, and Lock stared dead ahead at the Spanish-held buildings.

With only a few windows through which their national sacrilege could be witnessed, it was hard to discern the Spanish reaction right away.

A smile crept over Lock's face. Even at this distance, he could see frantic waving and gestures in the windows.

'They're not happy with us!' Lock bellowed in German, and several men cheered and jeered. 'Keep at it!'

Lock eyed von Salm to his left, near the front of the square. It was vital that the men at the front maintained their nerve, or the whole arrangement could break down.

Von Salm did not have to be told this.

The German had removed his cloth face covering. The distinctive red cloth now hung around his neck, his disfigurement now visible to the enemy. Perhaps he had done so to make shouting commands easier.

Perhaps it was a symbolic gesture. Either way, Lock found himself saying a prayer for the man's well-being.

Protests from the Spanish buildings became increasingly loud, as another flag was burned near the front of the men.

'Should we *stop*, gentlemen?' Monro's voice boomed over the square, and jeers and shouts erupted from the men.

Another collection of flags was hoisted and waved at the Spanish, before also being set alight by gleeful children armed with nothing but lanterns.

Lock watched them.

Did they even know what was to come?

Did he?

A bugle sounded from the Spanish buildings, followed by several angry commands. A cloud of figures began to emerge from the buildings ahead.

'It's working,' Flynn shouted. 'They're coming to meet us!'

'*Get ready*!' Monro's thick accent stretched over the soldiers' heads.

Lock exhaled.

His first battle was at hand.

- CHAPTER FORTY -

$\mathbf{M}$uch had changed since Lock had first picked up the dark wooden broom and the piece of string, which served as a surrogate for the musket. Much had also changed since father had first taken an interest in his education, and participated personally in the teaching.

This teaching included many hours of military tales, often joined by Arthur. Lock had listened awestruck to the story of the Battle of Nieuwpoort in summer 1600, when Dutchmen and their allies, trained in the new musket drill, shattered the might of Spain on the battlefield for the first time.

The musket drill, Father had explained, was inspired by the Ancient Romans. The Roman skirmisher had thrown his javelin, wheeled to the left or right, and then returned to the back of the unit. He would then queue up and prepare himself, until it was his turn to fling his javelin at the enemy again. The next rank would then follow his lead.

This, Father said, was the basic premise of the musket drill. What Father had not mentioned was that the more modern iteration was dirtier, louder, smellier and certainly more dangerous. Throwing a javelin took seconds. Muskets had to be tended to, and loaded in a laborious process. This could be done as the man readied himself behind the other ranks.

Only when he reached the front rank, would the musketeer fire his weapon.

Lock did not fire the weapon until his sixteenth birthday.

Instead, he memorised every step, every slight movement of the drill manual, until the forty-three steps had become part of his muscle memory. It had been a gruelling experience. Mother had not approved, insisting he should spend time in learning. But Lock had proved his ability for balancing the arts of war with his letters. It was hard to imagine her reaction to where he now stood.

The mass of men stood in reasonably organised ranks. Lock was in the sixth or seventh rank, it was difficult to tell, even being a head taller than most of the men.

Commands would have to be issued to the front rank, whether he was about to fire or not. Georg von Salm, it was hoped, would be able to assist those that fell hopelessly behind.

The Spanish continued to take the bait. They congregated in a vast group, before arranging themselves into a square. Pikes pointed to the sky. These would be lowered horizontally as the square approached, and the men on the outer rim of the square would begin firing.

This was the tercio in action.

This was exactly the scenario Father warned him to avoid.

Tercios could contain thousands of pikemen and musketeers, but Captain Ricardo did not have thousands of men. He had perhaps nine hundred, and he had divided these men into a miniature tercio. The sun glinted off swords, armour and muskets. There were repeated shouts of Spanish commands.

'They're coming!' Flynn shouted, and Lock repeated the call in German, as did some others.

And it was coming.

The tercio shuffled with very little grace, but it bristled with danger. No enemy could close with them in melee, so long as they faced so many points, and no enemy could hope to match their organisation in the square. This the Dutch had accepted twenty-two years before, in the Battle of Nieuwpoort.

They had decided simply to shoot the tercio to pieces instead.

Lock hoped they could replicate the Dutch success, but the main reason the Spanish marched was to capitalise on the disparity in numbers. If Gage's soldiers from the Frankenthal garrison did not materialise, they would all be sunk. For now, there was no way of knowing that this element of the plan was being carried out.

Lock could only hope that the Spanish had averted their eyes from the broken bridge in the river's left corner. He could only hope that the Germans had acted in this window as ordered. He could only hope that they had reached Gage's command centre, and that the commander would march.

But such hopes would be for naught if the Germans broke as soon as the battle began.

The sight of the tercio would send ripples of panic through the militia. Its imposing silhouette was all too familiar. They had watched this military machine conquer its way up the Rhine. Could they really be expected to stop it in its tracks, when so many others had failed?

As if sensing the fear and apprehension, von Salm had begun calling out reassurances.

Lock reinvigorated himself on a diet of Charles Lock's tales from the Battle of Nieuwpoort.

The fear which came before the battle.

How men lost control over their faculties, and their bowels.

The key role of discipline in the victory.

That discipline and survival were closely connected.

The tercio was closing in. As a distance of one hundred yards, it would pause, and the musketeers on its edges would begin firing.

To defeat it, they would have to overwhelm the enemy with firepower. This required long ranks of men, which they had, and a rotating line of firing muskets, which they also hopefully possessed.

Much depended upon him, a fact that became was driven home to Lock with shattering clarity when the lantern boys began their rounds. These boys would have to remain near the front rank at all times, and presented a perfect target for the Spanish. They could take cover behind the wooden wall which had been cobbled together from the market stalls, but stray splinters presented their own dangers.

'Two-hundred yards. Ready your pieces.' That was Monro. The red-haired Scot was a picture of calm. Others were not so controlled. A German on Lock's right had hands which shook so violently he could hardly remove his firearm from his shoulder. He became partially entangled in the musket's sling, and only his comrade's calming hand on his shoulder prevented a meltdown. There were surely others who would break altogether. But nothing could be done about that.

The tercio had passed the marker which denoted one-hundred and eighty yards. Now, it was safe to begin the musket drill. By the time the drill was completed, in perhaps forty seconds, the first three or four ranks of men would be ready to fire, and the first hail of balls would fly into the tercio.

To maintain momentum, the first rank of men would withdraw to the rear of the order. The next in line would fire their pieces, these men would then withdraw, and so on.

Those that could not fire their piece in time were ordered not to linger, but to follow their comrades to the back. The whole arrangement became a jumbled mess when men ceased behaving like a unit, and acted like self-appointed gladiators, desperate for glory.

All men would have the chance to fire their piece, Monro had assured them. Indeed, some men carried more than one piece over their shoulder. Perhaps to use shortly, or for a souvenir after the event.

The commands would all have to be ordered in German, and he could only pray that the thirteen steps he had developed with the help of Captain Frank and Father could be applied here.

The English, Monro assured him, would operate independently on his orders, but they could certainly pitch in if needed.

Lock cleared his throat, and boomed the first command.

'Germans, friends, take hold of your piece and hold it well in your right hand.'

Muskets clinked and voices muttered, as the act was obeyed. Those unfortunate enough to be left-handed would just have to adapt, Lock could hear Father say. There was no time to dawdle.

'With your left hand, take down your piece, and blow at your pan.'

Each German had received perhaps half an hour of basic training before the battle. They had been shown the names of the different parts, a task which was now put to the test.

Would the Germans recall the location of the pan, or its central importance to the whole process? The pan held the powder, and would be touched by the match to fire the weapon at the end of the process. An error now would cause misfires and even explosions later on. Glances left and right showed the lingering uncertainty, but the process could also be copied.

Muskets were pulled to the left side of the body, so that the mouth could clear any dirt, debris or excess powder which remained on the pan's surface. There was no time for marvelling at the drill, time was of the essence.

'Move your piece to your right hand. Charge your pan with the powder. When full, shut your pan. When shut, shake your pan.'

These four steps were the most complex.

They had been memorised and internalised by Lock, but it was inevitable that some would be left behind. Lock had been sure to dictate them slowly enough, and there were only a handful of confused faces that he could see.

He barked the fourth order.

'Move your piece to your left side, and let the powder sink.'

At varying speeds, a hundred firearms were clinked back to the left side. This was perhaps the simplest step. Its main function was to place the musket in position for the insertion of the musket ball.

'Men, handle your cartridge!'

Now there was scrambling with the right hand, as men worked to extract the musket ball from wherever they had stored it. Lock knew from his own experience what soldiers were meant to do and what they actually did could look very different, and varied according to personal preference. So long as the musket ball was slid into the barrel, he did not care how it got there. Lock allowed five seconds for the act.

'Next, men, charge your piece with your powder.'

The sixth step required some dexterity. The soldier would have to pour powder into the barrel after the ball. He would have to do so quickly, without spilling the powder onto the ground, or all over his weapon, a recipe for total disaster.

'Men, draw out your scouring stick. Shorten it, and ram the powder down the barrel.'

A slick *whoosh* sound followed.

The Germans reached under the musket's barrel, to where a purpose-built stick resided. With a flick and slight pressing of the stick against the body, it could be shortened, and it would then be inserted into the barrel, and pushed. This would ensure that the ball and cartridge were properly gathered together.

'Now, men, retrieve your scouring stick from the barrel, and return it underneath.'

Men did as they were told. Some had issue reinserting it, and dropped it in frustration or panic. Still, they were doing well. It was remarkable progress for men who had scarcely seen such a weapon up so close. But the most difficult and dangerous part of the process hadn't yet been dealt with.

Under normal circumstances, the soldier would balance these commands with the act of blowing on the match cord, which would ensure that it remained lit and ready for ignition. But Lock recognised that this asked too much of his band of novices.

He had a different system prepared.

At the command to store the scouring stick, the figures holding the lanterns rushed between the men, and handed each a piece of lit match cord. This the German then held with his right hand.

Two things were essential when dealing with the match cord, Lock had told them. The first was that the match cord stayed burning, and the second, arguably more important, was that the lit end of the cord did not touch off the weapon. Residual powder could be fatal, and set off a chain of explosions.

'Men, bring forward your piece and hold it well.'

After this ninth step, the firearm was primed and ready.

All that was required for ignition was for the lit end of the cord to touch off the powder in the pan. But this could not happen with all ranks at once. To lay down consistent firepower, the volleys had to be staggered. This was more accurate, and more devastating for the enemy. Lock moved to the tenth step.

'With your right hand, take hold of your match. Blow well on your match.'

Excessive breaths of air followed, with an urgency that sounded as though a large mass of men were seeking to blow some great threat away.

In a sense, they were.

An occasional shout for help brought a lantern to the German's side, armed with a freshly lit match. The system seemed to be working, so far.

Now came the test. The anxious moment when the lit match would be clipped into the musket.

'Men in the first three ranks. Cock your match. Blow one more time on your match. All other ranks, prepare to maintain your match indefinitely.'

The men obediently fixed their march cord to the serpentine. A succession of breaths followed once again. The Spanish were getting closer, but Lock forced them from his mind.

If he timed this right, their proximity would be to his benefit.

Now came arguably the most dangerous step.

Step number twelve. The pan would be opened, and the lit end of the match would be a finger's length away from igniting. There was nothing for it but to proceed. Lock exhaled, before bellowing the command.

'Men in the first rank. Present your piece. Open your pan.'

Three or four explosions erupted from the other side of the square, followed by several shrieks. If the musket had not been adequately prepared or made safe, and it exploded next to a man's face, instant death was the best outcome that could be hoped for.

But Lock could not dwell on those losses.

He had the final step still to order. The most critically important step of the process. The part which he had been unable to complete in 1613.

The Spanish had stopped moving.

Now was the moment. There was no room for quarter.

Lock gave them none.

'When I give the order, men of the first rank will fire, and will wheel to the back of the line. Men of the second rank will then step forward and make ready.'

A brief pause was necessary. The process was slightly more complex for a cohort of men than for an individual, but after explaining his process to Captain Monro, the latter had insisted that it was certainly workable.

Lock exhaled, before he bellowed the essential command.

'First rank, *fire!*'

For perhaps a second, the air seemed still.

And then, an eruption of musketry followed.

The air was clogged with smoke and the stench of eggs.

Screams rang out, as did shouts and whoops of celebration, but these had to be cut short if the next rank were to fire.

Mercifully, Lock spied the first rank wheel left or right and then file quickly to the back of the line.

As far as he could tell, only a portion of the first rank had been struck down. The Spanish fired in uneven intervals into their ranks.

The strength of the drill was its sudden rush of firepower, and its consistency.

It was time for the second rank to step forward.

'Men formerly of the second rank. When I give the order and not before, fire your piece, and withdraw to the back of the line. Men of the third rank will then step forward.'

Again, Lock paused.

'New first rank, *fire!*'

Another hail of musketry followed, and a much more orderly withdrawal took place. The second line had clearly watched their peers carefully, and guessed that they could do it better.

Now it was the third rank's turn.

The smoke made visibility nearly impossible.

The wind was still.

All Lock could do was shout into the swirling grey void and hope for the best.

'Men formerly of the third rank. Prepare to fire. When I give the order and not before, fire your piece, and withdraw to the back of the line.' Germans shuffled near him on the balls of their feet, and all Lock could hear were several breaths forcing the lit match to stay alive.

'New first rank, *fire!*'

And the third eruption rang out, accompanied by more yelps and shrieks, this time audible in Spanish ranks.

Every rank that fired brought Lock closer to the frontline.

He was now four ranks from the front. Soon it would be his turn to fire.

But the next three ranks would go first. A familiar rhythm could now set in. As intended, Lock could now resume the drill from the eleventh step for the next three ranks.

'Men in the first three ranks. Cock your match. Blow one more time on your match. All other ranks, prepare to maintain your match indefinitely.'

The clicking of muskets followed. The Spanish plodded forward in front of him. Several corpses or moaning wounded were peppered among them.

The first three volleys had left their mark. The tercio remained stationary, but it would not do so for long. It seemed a Spanish officer was arguing with his peer about how to proceed. Perhaps they had not expected such resistance? Perhaps Gage's men had arrived? There was no time to hesitate.

'Men in the first rank. Present your piece. Open your pan.'

He was closer now, closer than he ever had been to war.

Lock was consumed by the drill. All other issues ceased to matter. It was like returning to a close personal friend.

Looking around, Lock noted he was perhaps the only one who felt this way. The smell of soiled trousers suggested the Germans were struggling.

So long as they obeyed his commands, this did not matter.

He would squeeze them for as long as he needed to, until the Spanish buckled. Until his peers respected him. Until Flynn O'Toole was honest with him. Until he was redeemed for James' death.

'When I give the order, men of the first rank will fire, and will wheel to the back of the line. Men of the second rank will then step forward and make ready.'

Then came the pause, and the command to fire. With this fourth delivery of coordinated shot, the tercio had begun to move towards them again.

If they wished to avoid being impaled on a pike, it was essential that the drill was pursued to its smoky end.

There was a silver lining to the enemy's advance though.

A tercio that was on the move was a tercio which very rarely, if ever, let loose a volley. Now was the moment to capitalise, without sacrificing efficiency for speed.

The first rank had wheeled around, and the second rank prepared to fire. Lock gave the order. A problem which he had not expected was beginning to plague him. He was losing his voice. If he could not shout above the din of the battle, the Germans would stand helpless.

His next order to fire had to be coughed out, but it did the trick. Lock swore for the first time in the encounter. A hand fell on his right shoulder, and was about to repeat the command, when he stopped.

It was Flynn.

'I think Your Majesty is losing his voice!' he bellowed, as a smile spread across his mouth. 'Tell *me* the order, Lock, I will shout it out. My German is of lesser quality, but we make do with what we have.'

It occurred to Lock then that any other German could fulfil this role, and would probably do it better than the Irishman. But there was something reassuring in watching Flynn pick up the slack.

Lock nodded briskly, and prepared the next three ranks to move forward, with he and the Irishman at the front.

What followed was a blur of volleys and smoke.

The Spanish continued their grim march forward with a stoic detachment. Yet, they were not invincible.

Their soldiers continued to fall.

Spaniards yelped and cursed, or were seized with a grunt, as death struck them instantly in the face.

Red mist mixed with smoke on occasion, as entire heads were ripped apart, and brain splattered onto the man behind.

It was an intense, visceral feast for the eyes.

And then it was Lock's turn to fire.

He now understood the soiled trousers.

The first rank were completely exposed, and the Spanish were closing in, perhaps forty yards from them.

Lock reiterated the orders, and Flynn regurgitated them for the Germans. He fired his piece, aiming for the very heart of the tercio. As Lock began to wheel to the left, he spotted a prone figure.

Georg von Salm.

He was lying next to a portion of the wooden stall that had been adapted for a makeshift defensive line. There was a red stain on his shoulder.

Lock stared at him for too long, to see if he could detect breathing. Some Germans shoved into him and gave their instructor a puzzled look.

Lock made the decision.

He could not leave von Salm to die, or at least not to die alone.

He rushed the few feet to where his body lay, and fell to his rear beside him. He leaned against the wooden barrier with his left side, and as he moved his right hand across von Salm's face.

Lock barked out the next set of commands to the first rank, which was barely a few feet from him. The command was repeated louder by Flynn, still by his side. The Irishman had not left him.

Georg von Salm smiled weakly at Lock, a difficult act with his disfigurement. The horrific sight no longer unsettled Lock as it used to. All he saw was a man. A man who was suffering. Lock could see why.

A large wooden splinter jutted out from his shoulder.

'It's just wood,' Lock assured him with a smile. 'Not from Woodrest, but it will have to do.'

Von Salm smiled in return, and coughed slightly. He took Lock's right hand in his own. He beckoned him closer.

Did the German wish to speak?

Lock obliged, hovering his ear just above von Salm's mouth.

'You...are a bad liar... Matthew Lock.'

Lock flinched from von Salm, and stared at his smiling face.

'A *liar*?'

'I know you are not... blessed with a sister... Matthew.'

'Then why –'

'It was important to you... I owed you.'

'*Georg*,' Lock's voice cracked.

'The debt is paid.'

Lock grasped the German's hand more tightly. 'There was no debt, Georg, you owed me nothing.'

Von Salm smiled weakly at Lock. 'Look after... my Carolina. She... was the best of me.'

'Your daughter? I... I will Georg, I swear it.'

'The best... of...'

Von Salm's body stiffened. His eyes became glassy, his breathing light. This was the moment. When the soul departed from this life and into the next.

Lock called for a physician which he knew would never come. He rubbed tears from his eyes with filthy fingers.

Georg von Salm was gone.

There was no time to grieve for him.

A shout, followed by an explosion, snapped Lock back to his command.

Flynn patted Lock gently on the back. 'Lock, he's gone. We can't stay here. We have to move *now*.'

After putting it off for several minutes, Lock glanced up from von Salm's body and towards the Spanish tercio.

They were closing the distance.

Barely ten yards now remained between the tercio and the wooden defence. Following a barked command, Spanish pikes were lowered.

Lock watched them in awe, the closest he had ever been to a tercio in action.

Even though its men had been pulverised by volleys, it was a fearsome sight. The men who remained at the front seemed transfixed on their own drill, which was barked at them by captains to the rear.

Another rank fired to Lock's right, this time on its own accord. Lock turned to see Monro's Englishmen, now reconciled into two lines. This would give Lock's voice a break.

He turned back to von Salm.

The man's eyes were open, but the soul was gone.

His glassy eyes stared emptily into the flawless sunny sky.

Lock swore viciously.

Flynn's hand rattled Lock's shoulder.

'*Matthew Lock*, get your arse in gear! Let's go!'

It was sensible advice.

But Lock didn't want sensible. He wanted revenge.

Muskets littered the ground around him. As he made for one, Flynn bellowed a warning against the act.

The Spanish were almost on top of them, but due to the length of their lines, they were still a few yards from where Lock sat.

The English line fired off its next volley, a more refined, accurate salvo than the Germans before them.

The tercio absorbed it with grim determination.

Its journey to close with the enemy was littered with dead and dying men, who cried out in English, Spanish, Italian and German for rescue, but none came.

A multinational chorus of misery.

Now that they were within touching distance of the English, the tercio entered the melee. Contrary to Spanish orders, the front ranks of the pikemen began to walk towards the barricade independent of the tercio.

Monro's men rushed forward, swords drawn, to meet them.

'God's guts Lock, we have to get out of here!' Flynn yelled, but Lock waved him away.

He was possessed of a new mission.

He *would* kill a Spaniard. No matter what it cost him.

He would take a life in exchange for Georg von Salm's.

Perhaps as revenge for James as well.

Then Lock spied him, a Spanish official barking orders.

The musket was steady in his sweaty hands.

Lock abbreviated the drill he spent several minutes barking out, and blew on his match to resuscitate it.

He fired with barely a thought for his act, and the ball flew to where Lock knew it would: twenty feet ahead into the Spanish officer's throat.

It was such a simple, natural action, like throwing a ball, or eating with a knife and fork.

Was it wrong that he felt nothing for the target?

The throat was ripped from his body, and the man died before he hit the ground, splattering blood in all directions. The tercio lacked one of its instructors, but order on both sides had deteriorated beyond repair.

Lock found himself far enough from the melee that he had yet to be targeted, but it was surely only a matter of time.

This time could be harnessed to his advantage.

There was no time to cycle through the necessary steps. He grabbed another musket, aware of several Germans behind him who shuffled forward.

'Officer Lock, Sir, what are your orders?' The request had come from a baby-faced German holding a musket without its match. Lock had seen the boy carrying a lantern only a few moments before. Suddenly, such concerns seemed to matter little.

'Get out your sword lad. Get out your sword and ram it into the bastards. Rip out their guts. Do it for *Vater.*'

The boy nodded, and pulled out a pitiful carving knife from his trousers. He made for the Spanish left flank with reckless abandon.

An Irish swear made Lock aware that Flynn was watching him, seated by von Salm's corpse.

Lock grimaced at him, and prepared another weapon to fire. He ignored whatever the Irishman said, and focused on his targets.

As the tercio disintegrated, its soldiers had begun to move, and fan out across the line.

Very soon, surely, they would see him.

But there was still time to take them down.

The first kill had not made the pain go away.

Perhaps two kills would.

Or three kills? Or four?

Lock was consumed by the blood, by the smoke, by the fury.

He lost count of the muskets he picked up or cast aside, or of the balls he sent careening into Spanish throats.

Always the throat. Just like what had befallen James.

Perhaps one of the Spaniards had been there in 1613.

Perhaps one of them had ruined his life.

If so, now the debt had been repaid.

Men fell before him, and Lock bellowed at them in a blur of uncontrolled rage. The Spaniards still outnumbered them, but Lock shouted loud enough for ten men.

A blow struck his face, somewhere from the smoke and noise.

Lock collapsed to his rear, still near von Salm's corpse. It was now riven with additional holes and wounds.

Lock gasped at the act, but there was no time to lament.

He had drawn attention to himself.

Pools of Spanish blood had left a trail of evidence towards him, and his exposed position.

Then there were enemy soldiers to his right, emerging from the smoke, and Lock blew on his match before pulling the trigger once again.

The man's head erupted with blood, and the force threw his headless corpse backwards.

The din of the melee was only vaguely known to him.

He was his own army.

A soldier serving no one but himself.

His hands slicked up and down the muskets, caked in a mixture of blood and powder. He swapped for another when his firearm became too hot.

His head was bleeding. A drip entered his eye as a large Spaniard, sporting a face wound of his own, made towards him.

The large Spaniard cursed and shouted in his native tongue. Lock returned the vitriol in whatever language came first. For whatever reason, it was Dutch.

The Spaniard wheeled around, and with brutal swiftness, impaled a young German's stomach on the end of his pike.

Lock recognised the victim.

The helpless boy he'd sent towards the tercio moments before.

Or had it been hours?

It was impossible to tell.

All he could tell was that the Spaniard was making for him with malicious intent.

The pike head shimmered in the sun, and blood trickled like a stream down its head to the handle.

He was three yards from Lock.

Two yards.

Now just one.

The Spaniard arched back his pike, and Lock moved for him as he did so, having no notion of what he would do next. But Lock had not looked down, and his foot caught on a musket sling.

The trip sent Lock crashing with his left shoulder into the wooden barricade. A flash of pain rushed through Lock's left side, and the Spaniard licked his lips at the opportunity.

Lock prepared his musket to deflect whatever happened next, but the defence was unnecessary.

A musket ball struck the beast in the nose, and Lock's last image of the Spaniard was of his body writhing while upright, as the sun shone clean through the other side of his head.

He was dead before his soul even realised it.

Lock panted breathlessly at the carnage.

He then noted his wound. A large splinter had pierced his buff coat, and embedded itself in the upper part of his left arm.

Lock stared at the wound in fascination.

Somehow, he had come to believe he was invincible.

Flynn crouched beside him.

Perhaps he asked if Lock was alright, but eardrums had been shattered.

All Lock could hear was ringing.

But the danger had not abated. Swords clashes and pikes thrusted, and the Spanish still held the field.

Then there was a ripple, and then a roar.

Calls and shouts behind him were accompanied by whoops of joy to the far-left of the square.

Could it be?

A bugle sounded, and the tercio's men yelped and shrieked in terror, as several horses rode into their right flanks.

Cavalry chased men down, and cut into their backs without mercy. The remaining Spaniards pleaded for quarter, with only limited effect.

The bloodlust seemed to have worn off him.

Lock craned his neck for signs of von Salm, but the ground was a sea of dead and mangled bodies.

Let the barbers do their work first.

There would be plenty of work to do.

In the near distance, Joseph Gage lead a loud, triumphant charge of horse on the Spanish right. The weight of the beasts crushed the unprepared infantry, as men were trampled or hurled backwards.

Following a few more such displays, any Spaniards who had yet to surrender were persuaded to do so.

The tercio had been shattered.

Flynn jumped and punched the air in a mixture of relief and joy, but Lock found it difficult even to move.

A final few shots rang out, and prisoners were seized.

Gage had arrived just in time.

Monro's Englishmen had been severely bloodied, but the captain was himself intact. He jogged carefully to Lock's side.

'God save Scotland! You kept your expertise a tight secret, eh?'

Lock smiled weakly, and reached for the hand Monro extended to him. He winced as the captain hoisted him to his feet.

Monro's eyebrows narrowed at the expanding blood stain on Lock's left arm. 'You look like you've been through the wars Lock, but by God did you take some of the bastards with you. Your arm needs attention. I'll take you to the barbers.'

'Sir, what of Captain Ricardo? Has he declared his intention to surrender?'

Monro half walked, half supported his charge, as they shuffled off the square. The area was awash with blood, bodies and discarded materials.

'He has, Lock. We'll send you and Flynn to receive it tomorrow morning. Captain Ricardo has made a base in the church, just up the road from here.'

'Georg von Salm...'

'Aye lad, I saw him fall. His comrades are on it. They'll give him a proper send off, you need not worry.'

Men shuffled about the square and beyond, toward the reinforced houses. Surrendering Spaniards streamed from the urban bastions, right into captivity.

Some bore horrific wounds, while others had lost entire limbs.

Others clutched arms, their sides or held bandages to their face.

Vacant eyes stared back at Lock from the walking wounded.

Others were jubilant, and had already located drink for themselves and their friends.

The appeal was certainly strong to indulge, and force out the trauma of the day, but his duties were not done. Monro set Lock down gently on a stiff wooden bench, a few feet from where a barber surgeon loudly did his work.

Flynn then appeared beside him.

'Ready for tomorrow, Lock?'

Lock nodded. 'I'll be ready. I've got the credentials on hand.'

'You saw von Salm?'

Lock nodded.

'Had he only been satisfied with his revenge, and not pursued it to Mannheim, he would still be alive.'

'What else could he do, Flynn? After all the Spanish had taken from him? What else did he have other than his revenge?' Lock's throat whirred with strain.

Flynn winced at Lock's left arm. 'Does it hurt?'

'Only my pride. To think, in all that carnage, and I suffer a bloody splinter.'

'Be thankful that's all you got, Lock. I saw you out there. I saw you shoot.'

Lock prepared himself for a compliment.

'You were out of control, Lock. You nearly sank the whole arrangement with your bloodlust. You sent that boy to his death.'

The boy?

His childlike face returned to Lock with a pang of guilt.

Had he truly done it? Had he really lost control of himself?

The last few minutes of the affair were shrouded in smoke and blood.

'I... I don't remember him.'

Flynn's countenance darkened. 'What did von Salm say to you, when we marched on Mannheim?'

Sweat collected on the back of his neck. Lock turned his head to speak to Flynn, but winced. The act seemed to awaken his left arm to its circumstances.

The stiletto, ask him about the stiletto.

But Lock could not.

He lacked the energy for the confrontation.

He wanted just one moment to dwell on his triumph.

Just one moment when the Irishman would be proud of him.

Flynn nodded gravely. He seemed to hesitate before speaking. 'Rest... for now, I'll find you when it's time to go.'

Lock exhaled as Flynn rose from the bench. He gazed into the still cloudless sky. Crows, ravens and other scavenging birds had already begun to accumulate. The barbers would have to work fast to deny them their feast.

'You felled a lot of men today.' The Irishman uttered the words while facing away from Lock, and gazing at the carnage.

'Do you believe me now, when I say I can shoot?'

Flynn chuckled, and turned back to face him. His eyes were moist. Flynn waved his right hand in front of his face. 'Sorry, I... I lost some friends today. I fear that soon I will lose more.'

Lock shifted on the hard bench. 'I think we all did well, given the circumstances. Have you seen Burroughs?'

Flynn shook his head and exhaled. 'No, Lock, he's too busy giving Gage a good hiding. We probably won't see him till after our... meeting with Captain Ricardo.'

'I just want to make sure he knows we did our duty. I want to make sure he fulfils his end of the bargain, gives you your pardons, and tells us about Vere.'

'Don't worry about that Lock. There isn't a man around us who would try and claim you didn't do your duty. Many had never seen a drill like that. It was as though you possessed those Germans.' Flynn offered his costrel with a grin.

'I have my Father to thank for it. And... other important factors.' Lock seized the costrel with his right hand. The left arm was already afire, and limp by his side.

He took a long, greedy swig. The foul liquid burned all the way down his throat. His head swam instantly. His left arm cooled. It was a kind of peace.

With a grimace and a nod, Lock handed the container back.

'Sit tight, Lock. The way legends grow, by tonight it'll be said that you broke a tercio with your bare hands.'

'Do you think?'

Flynn chuckled. 'Just think, the legend of Matt Lock and his matchlock.' After a few seconds of silence, the Irishman gasped, and slapped his right hand to his head. 'God's guts, that's it! *That's* what they'll call you. It's written in your bloody name and all. *Matchlock.*'

Lock rolled his eyes, though the act made his head hurt. 'I don't need a legend, or a nickname, Flynn.'

'As you command... *Matchlock*. Say no more.' The Irishman grinned, before turning on his heels and sauntering towards a group of Englishmen a few yards away.

The men had located some wine, and were passing the bottle around. Flynn slapped one of them on the back, and gestured back to Lock. He heard the men laugh, and then grow suddenly sombre, as though struck with a piece of earth-shattering news.

One of them shouted the nickname with aplomb, raising a bottle to the air, and his comrades followed his lead.

They gestured at Lock, and began making their way towards him.

One of them carried an unopened bottle of wine.

Lock sighed, and forced a smile.

Perhaps cultivating a legend would be worthwhile after all.

.

- CHAPTER FORTY-ONE -

Manheim was eerily quiet by the next morning. No dogs barked. No women wailed. No muskets were discharged. It was a like a preview of how the city had once been, before the war arrived at its gates.

Lock kept his eyes fixed directly ahead, determined to give no impression of anxiety.

Flynn knocked on the church's door and shouted something in Spanish. Flynn's booming voice punctured the silence, and after a brief pause, the hulking wooden door creaked open.

Bleary-eyed Spaniards waited for them inside, no doubt shattered by the recent ordeal. They did not exchange courtesies, but Flynn pressed them to bow all the same.

It was proper, Flynn said, that the surrendering party pay homage to his enemy.

No weapons were seized, and barely a soul seemed to remain in the church's entryway. One Spaniard gestured to a smaller door behind them, which led to a room where the captain was said to be expecting them.

Lock's heart was in his throat, and he tried to regulate his breathing. The strain drew a glare from Flynn, but the sweat on the Irishman's brow suggested that he was also struggling with the effort.

Here in this building, both men were completely exposed. The ultimate irony, as Lock had relished pointing out, was that Flynn now owed his life to the code of honour which he had so loudly lambasted in the past.

Both men shuffled to the smaller door, and Flynn exhaled before pushing it open.

It swung forward with little exertion, and barely a sound.

Before them was a large, open hall, intended for worship.

Pews lined the hall, partitioned by a red carpet aisle in the centre which led to the dais at the back of the room.

The rays of the morning sun poured through the stained-glass windows, highlighting clouds of dust that hung and whirled in the stale air.

Lock began walking forward, his eyes taking in all they could, with Flynn in front of him.

No balconies were visible, meaning they were not in danger from dishonourable types who might snipe at them. Still, the room was not empty.

Two armoured figures stood against each wall, perfectly opposite one another and perfectly still. Each man seemed to be clad in ceremonial armour, and Lock only decided that the figures were real after several stares.

Seated in the back of the hall, on what had once been the pastor's chair, was Captain Ricardo. In comparison to his ragamuffin soldiers, the captain's uniform was immaculate. His breastplate gleamed, and his buff coat was bleached nearly white. Over his left shoulder, a pelisse of brown fur hung to his left knee, partially obscuring his blades.

It was difficult to judge a man's physique while he was seated and in armour, but the captain's hard, bony features and slight facial hair suggested that he was one of those rare things in the Spanish army – a soldier who had risen through the ranks by merit and skill alone. Or, perhaps, he was a well-connected noble with a viable exercise and diet regimen.

It was difficult to miss the captain's high cheekbones, a persistent head of thick dark hair, and blue eyes. The combination was instantly striking, and Lock found himself staring at the spectacle which the captain presented.

Even as they came closer, the captain remained seated, his legs crossed, his gaze never meeting theirs.

They came to a halt perhaps five feet from him. Lock glanced around him one more time. The soldiers by the walls remained perfectly still, and Lock second guessed his initial judgement, so impressive was their act.

Lock quickly returned to the present. The captain's eyes pierced him with an unyielding stare.

Lock's left arm throbbed, even under its dressings, but he suppressed a wince.

The captain's expression did not change, and Lock narrowed his eyebrows. Just as he was inhaling to speak, the captain interrupted him.

'Your friend is injured, Flynn O'Toole,' the captain said in perfect French. His voice was silky and smooth, as though his throat had been bathed in milk and honey before speaking.

'It is only a flesh wound captain, I assure you I will be fine,' Lock spoke quickly, before the Irishman could speak for him. The captain flung his hands up in mock surprise, and a red ruby ring glinted on his right index finger.

'*The prodigal son speaks!* Tell me, Matthew Lock, what do you think of Mannheim? Have you enjoyed your stay?' The question was asked with unsettling enthusiasm, as though they had arrived for a holiday.

Lock nodded respectfully, before moving his feet together. 'Captain Ricardo, I have here the document which requires your signature, and which will transfer this city to the authority of England. Hand Mr O'Toole your sword promptly, and you will be entitled to march out of this place with full honours. You have our word as gentlemen that we will honour this arrangement.'

The captain tilted his head at Lock, a flash of disappointment on his face. Lock waited for the Irishman's verbal support, but it did not come. Flynn had yet to say a word, and Lock hazarded a glance at him.

'It seems your Irish friend is suddenly mute!' the captain laughed, before pushing his polished boots into the stone floor and rising to his feet. His frame emanated power and strength. With these qualities came confidence, but there was something overbearing about this confidence that caused Lock's heart to race.

The captain did not look like a man about to surrender.

Within two steps, the captain stood on the edge of the dais, a few inches away from Lock. Even from this distance, the captain's hard breaths brushed Lock's face.

They smelt of a hearty breakfast. A celebratory breakfast?

Lock swallowed.

He glanced again at Flynn, but the Irishman's gaze remained unchanged, even if his stance had become more rigid.

Flynn clenched and unclenched his fists, and his blinks were long and deeply felt. The Irishman was psyching himself up for something. In a dangerous situation, the diplomat protected himself by reverting to protocol. Lock repeated the challenge.

'Do you surrender your sword to Flynn O'Toole? Do you consent to return the city of Mannheim to its German residents, under the protectorate of General Burroughs?' Even as he said the words, Lock inwardly cursed himself for his unconvincing tone.

The captain ignored the question, and strolled nonchalantly back onto the dais, as though he had all the time in the world. A heavy wood table behind him, where communion was likely performed, appeared to draw his attention. The captain hummed slightly as he turned his back on the two men, and ran a finger over a silver candlestick.

The disrespect was intolerable.

'Sir?' Lock said. '*Do you consent to the terms of surrender?*' he ensured his tone was more appropriate, and the question reverberated off the walls. 'If you do not, then why have you summoned us here?'

The captain held his unaffected stance, with his back to his guests. A chuckle escaped from him, and he shook his head.

'I note you have brought your musket with you, Matthew.'

'I am *Officer Lock*, to you, captain. My friends call me Matthew, and we are not friends.'

'Oh no? Even with all the history we have together?'

Lock stared a hole in the captain's back. He looked not even remotely familiar.

Had this captain *followed* him? For how long?

'I do not know you. We have never met. Dispense with this nonsense and hand Mr O'Toole your sword.'

'*Mr O'Toole,*' the captain repeated, mockingly. 'You have no idea what's going on here, do you Matthew? You have no idea how much danger you are in.'

Lock remained silent. He did not dare take his eyes off the captain's back. Captain Ricardo remained transfixed on the silver goblet.

'Your musket, Matthew. Did you ever master that last stage of the drill? If I recall, you had some trouble with it.'

'I shoot just fine captain, but this is not about me.'

'Oh, indeed Matthew, I jest, you are quite the shot. It satisfies me to see it, since your performance was so... disappointing before.'

'Disappointing?'

Captain Ricardo nodded at the stained-glass window in front of him, still refraining from facing his guests.

'Indeed, Matthew, you have improved a great deal since 1613. Perhaps, James Lock did not die in vain after all.'

The words hung in the air.

Lock's teeth ground together.

His fingernails dug into his palms.

His heartbeat moved into his ears.

Cold beads of sweat gathered on his neck.

The telling, shameful reaction had all been involuntary.

James Lock's name did not belong in this place, or in this captain's mouth.

'Who are you?' Lock screamed.

The captain ceased humming, and his investigation of the altar. He leaned back onto his heels, and stood completely erect. Still, he did not turn around.

Slowly, the captain's hands moved up to his face.

Was he retrieving a deadly weapon?

Lock was just about to shout another challenge, when Captain Ricardo abruptly wheeled around.

He was now clad in a black velvet mask.

'Do you remember me *now*, Matthew Lock?' the captain boomed.

He walked towards Lock in three quick steps, the final one taking him off the dais, and down to Lock's level. Lock instinctively arched his body away from him.

A whimper, so shamefully produced, escaped from his open mouth.

Raspy breaths fell from trembling lips.

'I haven't seen that look on your face in nine years,' the captain whispered. 'You remember the date, I'm sure?'

'11 March... 1613,' Lock managed to say. He wiped cold sweat from his forehead with a shaking hand and suppressed a shiver.

The captain smiled greedily at his suffering.

'Of course, Matthew, as you recall, I was not alone.' The captain slid in beside Flynn, and clasped his hand on the Irishman's right shoulder.

'Your Irish friend was there with me. He made the Black Prince proud that day.'

'*You*...?' was all Lock could manage to say, before the captain turned from Flynn and stepped back onto the dais. Lock searched for a response on the Irishman's face. Flynn did not dare meet his gaze. He stared at the ground. His blue eyes were dulled, his cheeks burned red, and his shoulders were hunched.

Lock had his answer.

'Oh yes, Matthew. I remember the day well. A sumptuously decorated holiday home. Far too many valuables in one place, if you ask me. We had not come for James, of course.'

The captain checked Lock's expression again, and was not disappointed. With feline swiftness, the captain took three quick steps towards Lock, drawing his sword as he did so. The point of the blade shimmered a few inches from Lock's throat, but Lock didn't register the danger. He could focus only on the black mask.

'You promised you would not harm him,' Flynn said quietly. His tone was uncharacteristically distant, and it took Lock a few moments to realise the Irishman was talking about him.

The captain lowered his sword and titled his head towards the Irishman. 'I would never *dream* of harming him, Flynn, not when the Raven has such great plans for him.'

Flynn snapped forward in protest. 'That was not part of our arrangement Ricardo. We agreed not to get the Raven involved.'

A smirk played on the captain's face, and the mask moved slightly on his cheekbones. 'Honestly, Flynn, do you take me for a fool? Did you think Fabio would disappear and I would not learn of it? Not even his stiletto could be found, and you know how fond he was of it. You dishonoured him so.' The captain tutted, and returned his sword to his scabbard in a single fluid movement.

Flynn's tone became steadier, and more direct. 'You dishonoured the Black Prince, you and your Rogues.'

The captain continued his tutting. 'You imagine the Black Prince cares about our... extracurricular activities.'

'You force yourselves on women against their will. You and Phillipe. You are *scum*.'

'Spare me the lecture Flynn. We both know what you've done in your own time. Ah, but you always were his most naïve servant. And where is the

Black Prince now? He cannot save you from me.'

'Fabio was watching me. He was careless. I am surprised you put up with his mediocrity for so long.'

Captain Ricardo scoffed and turned briskly, allowing his pelisse to fall from his left shoulder to the stone floor. For the first time, the scabbard where the stiletto rested became visible.

There could be no doubt.

This was one of the Black Prince's most senior agents. He had successfully fulfilled at least ten missions for his master. And yet, he seemed to disdain the very mention of the Black Prince's name.

'I told you that things were changing, Flynn. I told you to get into the Raven's good books. I told you to stop your pursuit of Rogues. But you didn't listen. The Raven was forced to act, and he honoured me with this mission.'

In the corner of his eye, Lock noticed that the ornate suits of armour had begun to move. Each figure was now itself adorned with its own black mask, and had his longsword drawn.

'*Traitors!*' Flynn hissed at them.

Captain Ricardo grew empowered with each of his enemy's frustrations. His wolfish grin caused the black mask to curve slightly upwards. Lock's eyes were fixed to his face.

'I will *not* hand this man to the Raven,' Flynn declared, his chin angled at the foe.

Captain Ricardo scoffed at the defiance. 'You do not have a choice, Irishman. I will be feeding your English pet to the Raven. In exchange for Fabio's life, I will take your life as well.'

Flynn slowly drew a sword from his left side. 'I warned you never to cross swords with me, Ricardo. Perhaps now that your foot has healed, you've forgotten your deficiencies. It would be my pleasure to remind you.'

Captain Ricardo shook his head dismissively, before gesturing to the four men in armour that were slowly inching towards his guests.

Two moved towards Flynn's right, the others towards Lock's left. Their armour clanked slightly as they walked. The armour appeared medieval, but it was the perfect attire for betrayal in a closed space.

Captain Ricardo addressed the armoured figures. 'Gentlemen, you recall what I told you. Whoever severs the Irishman's head will receive triple his wage.' The captain then pointed his sword at Lock. 'But let's be delicate with our softer friend. Do leave the Englishman alive.'

Before Lock could expel a breath, Flynn dropped his sword to the ground with a sudden clatter, and in the brief window that followed, pulled two pistoles from his back.

With stunning speed, Flynn pointed and fired at each man on his right. The two shots produced an almost deafening sound in such close quarters, and Lock winced reflexively.

With a yelp, each man crumpled, and their armour clanked loudly off the hard stone floor as they fell. Flynn held the two pistoles aloft, as smoke streamed out of them, and he waited for the sight to dawn on Captain Ricardo.

In a final gesture of defiance, Flynn grasped the barrels, and hurled each expended pistol at the captain with considerable force, aiming at the captain's unprotected crotch.

'*Bastard Irishman*!' Captain Ricardo yelled, barely managing to deflect the unorthodox attack, 'I should not have been so naïve as to expect you to fight with honour.'

With great coordination, the captain then retrieved both his longsword and his stiletto from their scabbards. His left hand held the stiletto as though the blade was part of his body. The sinister smile suggested that the captain now felt in his element.

'Three against two,' Flynn said, as he quickly stooped to retrieve his sword. The Irishman caught Lock's eye. '*Wheellocks*,' he said, nodding at the smoking discarded pistols, 'As you said, *very expensive*, but certainly convenient.' Flynn risked a smile, and Lock's facial muscles partially responded in kind, though he felt no happiness. A numbness consumed him.

A few feet separated them from their attackers, but Flynn's expression remained calm, perhaps even jovial.

He placed his right hand on Lock's shoulder. 'I swear, I will explain everything.'

Lock began to speak, but Flynn talked over him.

'You took on the might of Spain and lived to tell the tale. Ricardo is but a man. Don't you think you should kill *him* now, Matchlock?'

And there it was.

The paralysing terror which had ensnared him was gone.

It was replaced with something else.

A warming sensation he had come to recognise, even welcome.

It was a rising, burning anger.

It was sheer, quaking rage.

This time, Lock's hands were not empty.

For nine years, the black mask had haunted his every waking moment, and his sleep. He had fled from it. He had feared nothing else like it. The black mask had resembled failure, shame and disappointment. It had shattered his family and ostracised him within it.

Here was the opportunity to let loose every foul, vengeful thought and every whispered oath. Now was the moment for revenge.

Von Salm's fatal pursuit of the same ends briefly returned, as if a warning. But all sense of caution evaporated when the captain bowed mockingly at him.

This captain was only a man.

His black mask was merely a piece of velvet.

The mask's power over his mind had been sapped.

Lock was suddenly lucid, and certain of what he had to do.

He would conquer the captain, and the black mask.

'Take the men on my left, the captain is *mine*.' Lock hissed, his eyes meeting the Irishman's.

Flynn nodded, and stepped behind Lock's back, his sword pointed at the two figures. As he did so, the Irishman whispered something to the back of Lock's head, which was absorbed.

It was an instruction, regarding the captain's key weakness, and it represented a potential lifeline.

Captain Ricardo had learned to use a sword after a lifetime of combat and war. Lock had learned to use a sword in peacetime, courtesy of one of the greatest swordsmen in France. It was experience versus theory, and, as far as the captain was concerned, two blades against one.

The captain was ignorant of a key fact – Lock had a stiletto. This advantage should be leveraged for all it was worth, but how?

The captain was barely a foot from him, a picture of sheer confidence, notwithstanding the sudden death of his two goons. But, for the captain's mission, there was a complication. How do you keep a man alive, if that man does not wish to come quietly?

The captain would try to immobilise him, perhaps targeting the legs, or Lock's already injured left arm. But he would not be permitted to land the killer blow, and this gave Lock an opportunity.

'You want to fight me one on one, Matthew?' Captain Ricardo scoffed, 'Are you insane?' The question was valid, from the captain's perspective at least. He certainly did not expect this wounded diplomat to be proficient with blades.

The captain had been pleasantly surprised by Lock's proficiency with the musket; it was possible he would be equally surprised by a sudden flurry of unexpected assaults.

But this would have to be perfectly timed.

Lock would not have the luxury of underestimating him.

The captain would have to be lured into a false sense of security, before Lock could strike at his highlighted weakness. That, Lock hoped, would be enough to end the nightmare.

Behind him, a sudden piercing scream rang out, and in panic, Lock wheeled around to see a knife protruding from the left eye slit of an armoured figure, Flynn's hand on the other end of it. The unfortunate figure's armoured partner lay on his back, but was scrambling to his feet.

Just what had Flynn done to them?

Before the prone man could raise himself, Flynn finished off his one-eyed partner by withdrawing the knife from his cornea, and driving it into his neck. Sticky, bubbling blood was spat through the holes in the visor. Flynn then nodded urgently at Lock, and readied himself to face the final armoured figure.

Lock's decision to take in this sight had been a critical mistake.

In the bare second that had passed, the captain closed the distance and cracked Lock in the head with a staggering blow. Lock suddenly stooped onto his right knee, the blow clearly weakening his legs.

Captain Ricardo used the rare half-sword technique.

With his hands clad in heavy linen gloves and clutching the sword blade, the captain plainly intended to batter Lock into submission with his sword's pommel.

It was not a bad strategy, and the first blow certainly stunned him, but

Lock thrusted his blade forward to parry the second blow.

A distinctive clang followed.

Lock was pleased to see a flash of surprise, perhaps even panic, across the captain's face.

Jean le Renne's instructions surged through his ears, as though he were a fresh-faced lad of fourteen once again.

This time, it would be *Parry. Posture. Attack.*

Lock planted his feet firmly on the ground.

It was then that he was made aware of the height advantage which the dais had disguised.

Now was the moment.

Lock surged forward with a relentless determination, leading with his blade. The captain's expression ranged from a grimace, to wide-eyed surprise, but he had certainly ceased mocking him.

So long as you attack, your enemy must defend.

The aggression had thrown the captain's game.

It forced him backwards, onto the dais. The captain winced as his heels cracked against the metallic altar.

Lock almost believed it would be that easy, but from the depths, a blow struck him in the crotch.

The captain had lunged forward with a desperate kick.

It had been a Hail Mary, but it was effective.

Lock's lower body spasmed, and he had to fight with the sickening pain in his gut to avoid doubling over.

And then, there was a smash, and dust clouded around Lock's face.

In his moment of difficulty, the captain had seized a clay plate from the altar, and broke it over his foe's head.

The consequences came in rippling waves which blurred Lock's vision and brought stabbing pain to his temples.

A swear emerged from Lock's mouth as he steadied himself.

Now it was his turn to absorb the captain's flurry.

Feel your enemy's strikes.

Absorb their meaning.

Use this knowledge to your advantage.

The half-sword technique had been abandoned, in favour of the more traditional stance. The sword edge nicked Lock's hand, drawing a smile from the foe. Captain Ricardo seemed content to wound. Perhaps that was all the Raven would allow.

The defence was never an enticing prospect, but as the blows came, and Lock deflected one, and then two, he noted something.

Either the captain worried that he may harm him, or the captain was not as powerful a swordsman as his swagger had implied.

His attacks appeared somewhat half-hearted.

The blade is not your only weapon.

Words, too, can disarm and wound.

Now was the time for taunting.

It was the moment for spelling out to the captain precisely how doomed he was, and how hopeless the prospect of immobilising him would be.

With a grunt and a baring of his teeth, the captain struck forward again, this time with more force, but with both hands controlling his blade Lock struck the thrust down.

The momentum carried the captain forward to within hugging distance, his face barely inches from Lock's.

'This is for James you rat bastard,' Lock hissed.

With his left hand, he seized the captain's throat. Such an underhanded move was normally only taught by desperate, writhing soldiers, but the experience with Gaston Phillipe had left a lasting impression.

The captain's eyes widened as his breathing was suddenly restricted.

Lock squeezed as tightly as he possibly could, digging his nails into the skin on the captain's neck.

Being so close, and unable to use lethal force, Captain Ricardo would have to awkwardly fight out of Lock's grip with both hands full. The surprise could only last a second, before professional instincts kicked in, so Lock returned the captain's low blow with a swift knee to the groin.

Captain Ricardo cried out, but using his elbows to free his throat, he then lunged at Lock's neck with his teeth.

Lock turned, but the captain latched onto his earlobe.

Pain seared through Lock's stretched, bleeding ear.

With a clatter, the captain dropped his longsword, and focused on Lock's wound.

An invasive, forceful finger ripped through the outer bandage, and a churn in Lock's stomach told him that the captain had found his weakness.

The pain was close to crippling, and shot from his shoulder to his fingers. The body rebelled against the invader, forcing Lock to do something. Crucially, it pulled Lock's attention from the critical matter of defence.

And then, a merciful flash of memory returned to him.

The words Flynn had whispered as he'd walked behind him.

'He's missing two toes on his right foot. Stab him there again.'

Lock swayed slightly as he absorbed a fist to his jaw, but when the captain went for a body blow, Lock grasped the right arm with his left.

He tucked it forcibly by his side, and the captain grunted in protest. Lock tightened his hand on his longsword, and glanced down for a brief moment to find the target.

The captain realised too late what Lock was attempting, and he struggled in vain.

As though planting a flag in hard ground, Lock grasped the hilt, pointed the blade downward, and drove it straight through the captain's right boot.

For the first time, the mask of confidence slipped, as the captain squealed aloud.

With scant consideration for the foe, Lock turned the blade in the captain's foot. His enemy staggered, Lock grabbed at the black mask, and wrenched it from the captain's face.

The drawn, sweating face that was revealed helped to confirm an important fact.

Captain Ricardo was just a man, and that man was in trouble.

Indignant at his exposure, the captain was clearly more occupied with the mission to remove the sword point from his foot. With a sick twist, Lock pulled the blade from his foot, before surging downwards once again.

Lock guessed that his strike came closer to the ankle joint, rather than the foot, but the howl of pain which followed confirmed that accuracy did not matter.

Several weaker strikes jabbed at Lock's breastplate, and Lock's right leg was captured with a flash of sudden warmth.

The captain, in desperation, had abandoned the non-lethal parameters of his instructions.

Now it was about survival, the Raven be damned.

Lock released his sword to interrupt the attacks before they could find a home. The weapon pull itself from the captain's foot as it fell, and clattered on the floor.

The captain then dropped to a knee, perhaps a reaction to the blinding pain in his foot.

In fact, it was the beginning of a new attack.

Captain Ricardo dug his right shoulder into Lock's torso, wrapped his arms around Lock's waist, and lifted.

Lock's feet moved off the ground.

The captain let out a roar, and Lock was aware of his sudden powerlessness.

The landing would be worse than the act, and Lock instinctively lifted his arms to protect his head, as the wind rushed by his ears.

The dull thud of the landing winded him, but there was no moment of respite. The captain was on top of him, just as Phillipe had been.

It took a moment to realise that several blows had already been landed.

The captain switched the stiletto to his right hand, and prepared to force its blade onto Lock's face with both hands. He applied all his strength and body weight to the task.

Lock's left arm began buckling under the pressure.

The point of the blade edged ever closer to his throat.

Inches from his Adams apple.

He could not stop it.

A shriek, followed by a loud clatter, came from Flynn's direction.

It seized the captain's attention for a split second.

The uncomfortable lump digging into Lock's left side called out to him. Now was the time to reveal the secret weapon.

Lock arched himself slightly, and reached for the scabbard.

He pulled the stiletto free, and aimed its point towards the sky.

There was no room for hesitation. No time to waste.

Expecting no hidden dangers, the captain had been sloppy.

He had nearly triumphed, but the job was unfinished.

Lock determined to finish the job himself. He plunged the blade deep into the captain's crotch.

Before the assault even registered with the captain's brain, Lock pulled out the blade and thrust it forward into the same area.

The shock of the attack rippled through Captain Ricardo's frame. An involuntary flinch caused the stiletto to be flung from his right hand.

It clattered on the stone ground.

The sound meant the captain was effectively defenceless.

With his left arm, Lock pulled the captain's body close against his own. His height advantage trapped the captain, who squirmed in vain against his enemy's superior strength.

He gasped into Lock's bleeding ear, the pain having not yet fully registered with his brain, and panic existing in its place.

But this wasn't enough.

Lock tightened his hold on the stiletto, before twisting it maliciously. The narrow blade nearly slipped from his sweaty hand, but Lock managed three rotations.

With his left hand, Lock grasped the captain's throat once again. The captain's arms flailed at Lock's face, a trial Lock endured through curses and squinting.

The assault stung, but was mostly ineffective.

Captain Ricardo was caught between tending to his wounds and attacking his foe. The nightmare cocktail of panic and pain was etched on the captain's face.

The greatest pain was uncertainty about the injury's severity.

The mutilation meant the end of many things.

Lock hadn't intended to castrate the captain, at least not initially, but the captain's breastplate had highlighted his nether-regions as the most suitable target.

Perhaps, considering the captain's villainous exploits, the wound was poetic justice.

Besides, the captain had gone low first.

Don't go low if you can't take a low blow, this was the motto he and Arthur had abided by in their impromptu wrestling contests, as the two boys had struggled for an advantage.

He could call on all manner of excuses, but the truth was that Lock enjoyed it.

It was satisfying to plunge the stiletto into such a vile man. It was cathartic to inflict pain upon one of those responsible for the 1613 attack.

It was his first taste of revenge, and Lock thirsted for more.

The captain would have no say in what might happen next.

His strength seemed sapped, perhaps even halved, thanks to his horrific wounds. In vain did he strike Lock's face with his hands. The attacks became weaker and more futile, though some did land.

To the side, Lock spat out blood which had gathered in his mouth. Captain Ricardo whimpered as his predicament dawned on him. Lock held him closer, his damaged left arm screaming in league with the captain's own intermittent yelps.

Unable to rise to his feet, and unable to attack, the captain was seized with panic, and his prospects deteriorated dramatically.

The sweat on the stiletto handle was replaced by something else. The wounds were now pouring blood. They quickly soaked the captain's linen breeches.

The vital red liquid flowed, warm and sticky, onto Lock's right hand. As the stiletto slipped slightly, Lock pulled out the blade, and as the captain gasped, he thrust it deep for a third time.

This strike was filled with the most malicious intent.

For the first time, Lock heard a man scream.

In desperate agony, the captain's fingernails scraped for his stiletto on a distant stone tile.

Lock then leveraged his body to force the captain onto his back. A click sounded in his left arm, but Lock ignored it. There was work to be done. He was rewarded with another sickening sound, that of the captain's head cracking off the stone floor.

Now shorn of his mask, and utterly defeated, the bleeding captain pleaded in mumbles for some semblance of mercy, even decency.

'*11 March 1613*,' Lock hissed at Captain Ricardo, hurling blood and spittle into his face as he did so. 'Why did you do it? Why did you kill James?'

Somehow, the captain smiled. His composure was slipping, but his tone held.

'Who else was there with you? *I want names!*'

The new challenge appeared to reinvigorate the captain. His expression changed, giving way to defiance, and a brave, if fearful grimace seized his lips.

'*Answer me! Bastard!*'

But the captain did not. He shook his head. Despite everything, he was not ready to give in. Lock reared back on his knees, and struck the captain's nose with his clenched fist. He was rewarded with a crack and gasp from the captain, as his knuckles connected under the right nostril.

But Lock did not limit his attack.

Again, he reared back, and again he struck, this time at the captain's eye. Lock's right hand screamed with pain, but he blocked it out. He switched to his left hand, and focused on the captain's face.

Several seconds seemed to pass. Lock lost track of his blows.

He left the stiletto embedded in the captain, and let loose with both his fists. The captain's arms flinched uselessly by his side with each blow.

Lock lost himself again in the carnage and rage.

'*Answer me!*'

Another crack sounded just below the captain's right eye, but Lock couldn't stop now.

'*Who else was there! Names!?*'

Hell poured forth from him. The questions were screamed, rather than spoken, and the interrogation echoed in the church.

A cough from his enemy moved Lock to pause, and look at his handiwork. Captain Ricardo's eyes had swollen shut, and blood bubbled out of his mouth through missing teeth. His limbs were lifeless, and moved only with the rhythm of his body's suffering.

But then Lock remembered how his hesitation with Gaston Philippe had nearly killed him.

There could be no mercy, not with these people.

Lock returned his hand to the stiletto lodged in the captain's crotch. Even touching the blade caused the captain's whole body to flinch.

'*Tell me*,' Lock said, this time in a whisper. He blinked sweat out of his eyes. 'Tell me what you know Ricardo, or I *will* cut it off.'

Lock scarcely believed a shred remained of the captain's manhood, but the threat had its intended effect.

The captain's body capitulated.

Lock stared down at him. '*Well?*'

The captain coughed and spluttered several times. 'I... I don't know, I *swear*.'

Lock mouthed a curse, and tightened his grip on the stiletto.

A gargled scream emerged from the captain's mouth.

'Mer...cy!'

'*Mercy*? What of my brother? Did you give him mercy? *Did you*?'

Lock tightened his hand on the stiletto still further, and felt the captain's body squirm in vain desperation.

'He was not... not supposed to die!' Captain Ricardo wailed.

'You killed my brother by *accident*? *Did you*?' Lock only had to hover his hand over the captain's crotch for the conversation to continue.

An accidental death? The possibility seemed somehow worse than murder. Manslaughter, it was called, but Lock knew it by other terms: pointless, preventable, needless death, caused by nothing but a mistake.

It was also a lie.

James had been struck down with malicious intent.

'It... it was not my doing,' the claim was uttered through quivering lips.

'*You* did not kill him? Then who *did*?' Lock wished to drag out the process, though he had once believed such cruelty to be against his nature. Perhaps his nature had been warped by evil men.

The captain's body was seized by a shiver.

His fat, bruised lips only angered Lock further, and he partially shook the captain. His right eye, slightly less swollen than the left, suddenly opened. The eye darted around in panic, but returned to meet Lock's gaze. A cough followed.

'I swear...', the captain rasped. 'I did not know him. He was...', several coughs pushed more blood out of the right corner of his mouth. 'He was... a replacement... last-minute... replacement... for my friend. The bastard was crazy... he ruined... everything.'

The lament was sincere, but the revelation was gutting.

Lock would not get justice for his brother's killer today.

But his foe still lay at his mercy.

He could be plied for more information.

'What was your friend's name? Who did the killer replace? *Tell me who*!?'

The captain coughed up sobs, and he shut his eyes, as if desperate to hide from the terrible reality of his situation.

But Lock would give him no respite.

Finally, after a fountain of red spittle emerged from his mouth, Ricardo whispered two names. 'Rudolf... Macht.'

Lock ceased punishing his foe.

He stood up from Ricardo's body, only to be forced to his rear with a wave of intense dizziness and pain.

His ear. His left arm. His right leg. His hands. It all ached.

And all he had to show for it was another wretched name.

Rudolf Macht, whoever that bastard was.

The captain raised his head slightly, registering that Lock had moved off him. With a whimper, his right hand felt at the stiletto still deep in his crotch. He appeared to pass out with the pain, but involuntary sobs kept him awake. With each wave of agony, the captain's body shuddered, and the sobbing intensified.

Lock sat beside the captain's prone body, his back against the corner of a hard wood pew.

His hands were soaked in the captain's blood.

Lock tried to focus on the name.

Rudolf Macht.

The man who was supposed to have been there in 1613, but had been replaced.

Would Macht know *why* he had been replaced? Would he know *who* had replaced him? It was more of a lead than he'd had a few minutes ago.

A creak was heard from the end of the pew, and Lock turned his head to see the Irishman standing there, his mouth agape.

Flynn was himself doused in blood, following his private battle with the two armoured figures. A fresh cut had gone through to his right shoulder, and the Irishman flexed his fingers in his right hand, as if checking that they still functioned. He was also missing a boot.

Lock did not need to ask how he had managed it.

That information was irrelevant.

The only information that now mattered was the name he had been given. He turned his gaze from Flynn, and back to the captain's shuddering frame.

Blood now gathered under the captain's pelvis, and the expanding pool inched its way towards Lock's seated frame. Sunlight twinkled off the blades which lay discarded by his side.

'Mother Mary,' Flynn gasped, as he cautiously approached the scene.

Lock blinked at Flynn, and the memory of what had come before then returned to him.

'You... *betrayed* me.' Lock stared at the captain's bubbling mouth, before his steely gaze drifted up to the Irishman.

Flynn's eyes moved from the captain's body to the blood-soaked figure seated next to it, and back again.

'Lock...' Flynn said, creeping ever closer to him. 'I can explain.'

'I don't need you to explain, I need you to *leave*,' Lock winced as a jolt of pain shot through his left arm. Blood dripped from the wound down his forearm and off his pinkie finger. He gingerly placed the left arm by his side, and with his right hand, he gripped the hilt of the sword which rested near him.

'Please, Matthew. Let me explain.'

'Only my *friends* call me Matthew,' Lock said through his teeth.

Flynn nodded. 'I know I have not been honest with you –'

'*Honest*?' Lock spat out the word. 'You filthy knave. You were about to sell me to the Black Prince! After everything I told you! Even worse...' Lock pointed the sword directly at him '...you were *there* in 1613, on the worst night of my life, when James was killed. You were a black mask, just like them.'

Flynn bowed his head. 'I know.'

'You work for the Black Prince, is that it? You're his favourite servant, like Ricardo said?'

'It's hard to explain.'

'That makes us enemies.'

'Lock, stop, you... you won't understand. Let's get out of –'

'*Help* me understand it then, you vague Irish bastard! Have I not been through *enough* with you?' Lock winced and shifted his body weight. The hard stone floor numbed his backside. His head throbbed from the conflict. There was nothing to do but focus on the new enemy before him.

'Maybe it all meant nothing to you. Maybe you always intended to sell me out. Maybe you disdain honour so much because you have none.'

Flynn closed his eyes and slowly shook his head. He took another step forward, leaving only a few feet between himself and Lock.

With difficulty, Lock once again heaved the sword off the ground with his right hand. It scraped off the stone floor. The sound made Flynn wince.

'Stay there Flynn, you... you go no further.'

Flynn raised his palms to indicate he was not armed.

'Alright Lock, then let me explain now. You listen to my explanation, and then you never need see me again if that is what you wish.'

'Wait,' Lock said. 'I wish to stand first.' Lock bent his knees, and while grabbing hold of the pew, he pushed himself back to his feet.

Once upright, his head swam, and the room seemed to sway. Spots flickered before his eyes. A searing pain began to throb from his temples all the way down his back to his calves.

Flynn grimaced. 'You're *hurt*, Lock, your arm looks really bad. I can... help you.'

'*No*,' Lock waved him back. 'First... tell me right now what you did in 1613. You will... explain your betrayal. Then I will leave this place without you.'

The captain coughed and wheezed, and Lock glanced at his mutilated body. Now that he stood over him, the captain seemed an even more pitiful sight than before.

Had he truly done that to him?

The pool of blood continued to grow.

It now lapped at Lock's boots.

Lock watched the blood with fascination.

He moved his hand off the pew, which proved a mistake.

It was his body that was swaying, not the room.

Lock inspected the wound in his left arm. As he did so, the energy drained from his legs. His body had shut itself down on its own accord. He had no say in the matter. All that remained was to give in, and close his weary eyes.

Flynn swore, and scrambled to catch Lock before the stone floor rushed to meet him.

The rescue was only partially successful, as the fall was cushioned, but not stopped.

Flynn's hands fussed over him, but proved unable to prevent Lock's face from landing in the captain's pooled blood.

His eyes focused on the stiletto which still protruded gruesomely from the enemy's crotch.

Captain Ricardo was silent and still.

Herman Strasser had been right.

The angel of death had arrived after all.

Matthew Lock smiled and closed his eyes.

- CHAPTER FORTY-TWO -

Hours passed by, perhaps days. Lock couldn't tell.

It was all a blur. He was grabbed by several hands. He was lifted carefully up steps and around corners. Countless scruffy faces peered into his own.

But it all seemed so intangible.

Pain shot through his frame at regular intervals.

Soldiers, flanked by other soldiers dressed as physicians, spoke in hushed, concerned tones near him.

But where was he?

He was in a bed, that was certain. A rough cot which did not contain the length of his body. The backs of his heels rubbed off the solid iron frame. The cot creaked when he moved, but he stayed largely still.

He shivered. A voice cried out in agony, perhaps his own.

Calls were heard, and more blankets were dumped on top of him. He grabbed blindly, desperately, at as many quilts as he could.

He woke up hours later covered in sweat, desperate to unwrap himself from the bedsheets.

This struggle continued for what felt like an eternity.

Lock swam miserably through it all.

Every now and then, a cold hand was rested on his forehead, which seemed to bring peace. Concerned voices grew louder. Occasionally, they seemed to argue with one another, but the sounds melded together like an incomprehensible blur.

Perhaps they didn't speak a language he knew.

More likely, his brain simply was not willing to cooperate.

His arm ached.

That pain cut through relentlessly. It gnawed at him.

He couldn't escape it.

The stinging, burning, arching pain.

Sometimes it moved from his left arm and seemed to consume the left side of his whole body.

Sleep was the only relief.

But the dreams were worse.

Vivid, fearsome nightmares haunted him.

He was in a church, choking innocent people. He was before the royal court of the King, and he somehow managed to soil himself. He was at home in Locksville, and Mother screamed at him, blaming him for the loss of her favourite son.

When the anguish overwhelmed him, Lock learned to press his hand against the wound on his left arm.

It caused a rush of agony, but it at least pulled him out of his own head.

And then, there were several loud noises in rapid succession.

Muskets being discharged, the sound was unmistakable.

Was it another nightmare?

No. It was reality.

Matthew Lock was awake, but he kept his eyes closed.

He waited for the distinctive, eggy smell of used powder to waft towards him. It did not arrive. This meant, hopefully, that the muskets were not too close.

But was it an English or a Spanish musket? Lock still couldn't tell. Captain Frank used to say that each musket created a distinct sound, and even a different smell. To Lock though, it always sounded the same – like a bag of air being heavily ruptured.

Lock opened his eyes.

The ceiling was rough, grey, and high. He was on a cot, in a room big enough to fit three more patients. His feet hung over the edge, as expected. The four stone walls matched the ceiling, and by the finish, Lock judged that he was within some kind of fort.

One of the far beds was occupied.

His left arm still ached, but the bandage had been replaced and wrapped tighter. It no longer crippled him, and dominated every waking thought, but the tension in the dressings told him he was lucky the arm was still his.

Lock smiled. How Captain Frank would laugh at his left arm beating the odds once again. The smile became a wince.

Moving facial muscles had awakened cuts and welts inflicted by Captain Ricardo.

Lock groaned as he slid his hand towards his throbbing temple.

His hands.

They throbbed, as though the knuckles had been squashed between large stones.

Who knew the captain could have such a hard face?

Captain Ricardo.

Lock sat upright with unwise haste.

He let out an involuntary groan, and saw one of the figures stir in the cot nearest the door.

What had Captain Ricardo said?

That Flynn O'Toole had been there in 1613, the holiday from hell. That he was the Black Prince's favourite servant.

Lock's eyes darted around the room.

Where was the Irishman?

His stomach lurched to think about it, that Flynn had been on the cusp of handing him to the Black Prince. That Flynn had been there in 1613, and taken an active part in James' murder. That for the last three days the bastard had been ducking and dodging the matter, and manipulated him so that he wouldn't ask too many questions.

Lock's cheeks burned, but it was not fever.

The mere thought of Flynn compelled him to clench his fists.

His hands throbbed at the act.

How many times had he struck the captain?

Had he really... ruined him, in that way?

Lock shivered slightly. Perhaps *this* was fever?

The figure in the cot near the door coughed, and began to sit up. The man's face rose above the light sheet, and his eyes met with Lock's.

The man grinned widely.

'*Benjy*!' Lock croaked, with a weak wave.

'So, you made it back after all, Mister Matthew?'

Lock gestured to his frame and smiled weakly.

'This is the first I'm learning of it. Do you know how I got here? Where are we?'

Benjy shifted his legs over the side of his cot, and the structure creaked in protest. Benjy's shirtless state revealed a thick bandage around his waist, and a wad of material was stretched over the wound in his left side.

'Reckon you arrived...' Benjy appeared to access an invisible calendar in front of him. '...Tuesday, definitely Tuesday. And today is... Friday. I would say Friday. If it's not Friday then it's definitely Thursday.'

'Friday? I've been asleep here for *three days*? What is this place?'

'Three days? That should be long enough. Your dolman should be cleaned and by your cot now. Thank you for the loan. Beautiful coat saved my life I reckon.'

'You're welcome Benjy, of course, but...'

Benjy winked at him. 'I was just getting to that part Mister Matthew. I remember that Irish fella. Finn, was it? Or was his name Patrick?'

'Patrick?'

'I swear he went by both but... Yes, *that* lad, he said you had a bad arm, and a fever.'

'Well, that would explain –'

'He also said you weren't used to sleeping anywhere other than a deluxe feather bed, and that you were likely exhausted because of that.'

'The cheeky bastard.'

'He's here, in Frankenthal.'

'*He is?*'

Lock turned rapidly in his cot, again to his cost.

His left arm called out in protest.

Benjy held up a calming hand. 'Easy, now, easy. You must sit still for a week, that's what the warden said to me.'

'*A week*? I don't have a week! I barely have a day!'

'Got somewhere to be, Mister Matthew?'

'Well, yes, actually...' Lock paused. 'How do I find Flynn in this place?'

A frown spread on Benjy's bony face, scrunching his fair eyebrows together. 'I wouldn't put weight on them legs in a hurry, Mister Matthew.

You got to ease into walking when you've been lying for long.'

Lock allowed an eye roll as he forced his feet onto the cold stone floor. His feet were bare, but it was tremendous to have a break from heavy boots.

A cut he hadn't noticed before on his right calf continued to ooze lazily. As he gazed at the surprise wound, a rush of dizziness overtook him.

Lock stumbled to the window, and grasped its sill to steady himself.

Benjy moved gradually towards him. 'See now, Mister Matthew? See what I mean? You must take it slow. Finn isn't going anywhere without you.'

While leaning against the windowsill, Lock turned his head to Benjy. 'And how do you know that?'

'He told me,' Benjy said with a shrug. 'I smelled he was on the poitín, but I saw the gleam in his eye.'

It was time to admit defeat.

His legs were not at all strong enough, even with the support of the sill. He retreated back to bed, and sighed in relief as his body sank into the cot.

Lock caught Benjy smiling back at him.

'I need to speak with Flynn, Benjy, where is he?'

'Don't you want to know my news first?' Benjy's expression lifted slightly. But his eyes were red, and his smile, when examined for a moment, was weak.

'What's wrong? What happened?'

'Oh, it was *terrible* Mister Matthew,' Benjy rose to his feet with barely an effort, and Lock watched anxiously as the bandage shifted and strained with his movements. Benny shook his head, and made his way towards the windowsill.

'My bastard brother, Mister Matthew. Haven't seen him in many years. He was my ticket onto Vere's army in 1601. Been serving longer than me. Always liked to rub it in, but I let him have it.'

'What happened to him Benjy?'

Benjy put crossed arms on the low window sill and stared into the courtyard, without meeting Lock's gaze.

'He died... Mister Matthew. He...' Benjy cleared his throat before continuing. 'It was a cannon. Always hated cannons he did, always told me to stay away from them. Bastard cannon got him at Wimpfen.'

'*Wimpfen?*'

Benjy sighed. 'I forgot you've been away for a while, Mister Matthew. Battle happened about a week ago now, near Heilbronn.'

Lock wracked his brain to picture a map of the Rhine and its Neckar tributary, at the junction of which lay Mannheim.

Lock sat bolt upright. 'That's barely forty miles from here!'

'Thirty-eight miles, by General Burroughs' estimation.'

'What are we doing here, in Frankenthal? Aren't the Spanish on their way?'

Benjy waved the suggestion aside. 'Cordoba is more focused on taking Heidelberg, and he'll want to make a show of force outside Frankfurt as well.'

Lock nodded. The logic made sense.

Heidelberg was the capital of the Palatinate. It was also the cultural, literary capital of Protestantism in the Rhineland. But it was also a punishment, levelled against the Elector Palatine, Frederick. Here, the King of Spain would demonstrate the price for defying the Habsburgs, by seizing Frederick's home.

If the Spanish did seize Frederick's capital, that meant any possibility of a compromise peace between Frederick and the Holy Roman Emperor would vanish. The war in Germany would continue, and possibly escape its German confines.

It was fair to claim, then, that the Spanish had bigger fish to fry than Burroughs' defiant band of ragamuffins, their exploits notwithstanding.

In any event, at some point, the Spanish would have to turn their attentions to the stubborn English positions on the Rhine.

General Burroughs' days were numbered.

Lock snapped back to the present.

Benjy stared absent-mindedly out the window.

'But Benjy, even if we have several more months, you can't fight the Spanish with barely a thousand men.'

Benjy grinned again. 'I don't intend to fight the Spanish, Mister Matthew, I'll be going home.'

'What do you mean?'

'That's the thing about my brother dying, you see. He was supposed to inherit. My Father is in ill health, bless him. This news will surely send him over the edge. Always preferred the bastard to me.'

'When will you depart?'

'Soon. Especially if I want to gather the bastard's mementoes.'

'He had many possessions?'

Benjy scoffed. '*Far* too many. Father always told him he should leave his prize steed in Blarefield's stables, but the bastard never listened. Suzy was a worthy mount, but she wasn't my best. You left her in Mannheim, but she's in the stables below us now. Off the menu, Burroughs swears. Not a good start in your relationship, but she's a forgiving sort...'

Lock tuned out, and his eyes flickered, threatening to close.

How could he still be tired?

'...Horses don't deal well with abandonment Mister Matthew. Nor do dogs. Silly bastard brother brought his hunting dogs with him too. Shame the bastard cannon didn't hit them instead.'

'Benjy... Did you say Blarefield? As in, Blarefield... in Yorkshire?'

Benjy turned on his heels and gave a satirical bow. 'At your service Mister Matthew. Benjamin Blare, soon to be the third Earl of Blarefield, but you can call me Benjy.'

Lock couldn't control the outburst. 'God's guts Benjy! Your family are rich, *really* rich. My Father once fixed a loan from your uncle. He owned a quarter of all viable land in Yorkshire!'

Benjy extended his arms in triumph. 'And now, Mister Matthew, you can consider the debt settled!'

'Well actually, he repaid it several years –'

'The Blares take care of their friends, Mister Matthew, and considering the fact that you saved the last surviving male heir to the Blarefield estate, I reckon you qualify as a friend.'

Lock chuckled to himself, but then his shoulders sagged.

The only person he'd want to share such news with could no longer be considered a friend. The only person who understood what had just happened, could not be trusted under any circumstances.

Anger and rage returned to Lock's veins.

The bastard Irishman had ruined everything.

Benjy filled the silence, evidently eager to talk. 'It will be strange leaving this life. Reckon I should settle down and continue the Blare name.

Thought I'd have more time I suppose.'

'You'll have plenty to do, I'm sure. Plenty of balls and parties and hunting,'

Lock's mind wandered to his first attempt at mastering the steps of a pavane, the only dance he could manage.

He had trampled on his partner's feet and sweated through his undershirt. He still recalled her disappointment when Arthur arrived, and delivered an ambitious volte with perfect grace.

Lock decided long ago that he preferred the travelling life to one stuck in balls and parties. He was old enough now to bow out of the dance, and adhere instead to polite conversation near an open window.

The fact that Mother and Father could no longer order him to stand in step, and 'maintain the family image', returned to him coldly, and moved him to shiver.

Benjy had continued to stare out the crude window. The Yorkshireman's attention seemed far away.

'Stuff the balls Mister Matthew. I confess, I'd sooner keep my brother alive. The bastard drove me to distraction, but he was my brother all the same. He would be better at this, being the head of the family with all those airs and graces, I mean. I hear it can be quite lonely.'

'Not if you surround yourself with the right people. You're an *Earl* now, Benjy, you can invite whoever you want to Blarefield, and they can stay however long *you* want as well.'

'I can't invite Doyle though,' Benjy said quietly, before turning back to the window.

'Benjy...'

'Yes, Mister Matthew.'

'Do you remember, when I found you, the state you were in?'

'The *state* I was in?'

Lock cleared his throat. It was still raw. 'You were delirious, Benjy. You were asking after someone, do you recall whom?'

Benjy's expression changed. 'Asking after someone? I must have been in a dreadful bad way.'

'Benjy... You remember, don't you?'

The smile he had been forcing gradually cracked, first in the left corner, and then, like a curtain falling across the mouth, the lips turned down.

Benjy exhaled. 'I thought it was a *dream*. I thought *you* were a dream until they told me about you.'

'Who told you?'

'One of the quartermasters. A new Irish fellow. Hadn't seen him before. Baldrick Murphy, if memory serves.'

'I see...'

'He told me how you rescued me, Mister Matthew, but you didn't just *rescue* me. You truly are a great man, and I mean it sincerely when I say that I owe you, and your talents, more than I can repay.'

Lock's cheeks reddened, and his head swam.

Flattery was the last thing he expected from the red-headed Yorkshireman. The only escape was to change the subject.

'That Doyle, is he your brother?'

'It would seem so. Such a curious thing. As if I knew he was in danger.'

'Did you receive a letter?'

'I did, Mister Matthew. According to the surgeon on location, Doyle Blare died of his wounds at approximately four in the morning.'

Lock's mind flashed to Arthur, and then to the brother he failed to save. 'Please believe me when I say, Benjy, I really am sorry for your loss.'

'It is a remarkable bond, between brothers, is it not?'

'It is, Benjy, quite remarkable.'

'Do you have a brother, Mister Matthew?' Benjy continued staring out the window, oblivious to Lock's rolling eyes.

Lock sighed. It was best to simplify matters. 'I have a younger brother. Arthur is his name. He's only just nineteen, and he's at home in Locksville, just north of Dorchester.'

Benjy whirled around from the window with open arms.

'You're a Dorset family! How *exciting*! My grandmother's side were Poolers. I even went to Poole once as a young 'un. The weather was *bollocks* though.'

Lock nodded in acknowledgement, though the act made his head throb.

He reached for a drink beside his bed.

His stomach growled, and Lock gasped slightly.

He tried to focus on the conversation.

His throat ached, a consequence of shouting himself hoarse in

Mannheim's square. He tried to stretch his fingers, but his cracked knuckles protested heavily.

Conversation. Focus on the conversation.

'Truth be told Benjy, my Father was always more at home in Scotland. That's where his Mother's family were based. I always intended to go north and visit them.'

'The Lock family *does* like to travel! What brought him so far south in the first place?'

'*Love*,' Lock said, in an incredulous whisper.

It was always what his parents had said, but Charles and Catherine Lock had fought so often, it seemed like a bad joke the more he'd heard it.

Benjy nodded knowingly at the answer. 'My Father was a miserable bastard. Made my brother into one. Didn't get to me though. I left as soon as I could. Had to leave poor Mother behind though. She didn't last long after I left.'

'Did they marry for love as well?'

'Nothing so romantic Mister Matthew. The marriage was arranged. Money was traded. The usual story.' Benjy's gaze returned to Frankenthal's bailey, as though suddenly bored with his family's tale.

'You can't choose your family,' Lock said, wincing again at the throb in his head. Benjy didn't notice his discomfort.

'Aye, but you can choose your friends Mister Matthew. I reckon you've got a good one in the Irishman. Shame he's part-rats most of the time.'

Lock forced himself to breathe.

Could he tell Benjy about what Flynn had done?

The Irishman would deserve it. And his pardon would certainly be withdrawn. That would be sweet revenge for a villainous betrayal, and no soul could accuse him of an unjust wrath.

Lock cleared his throat to begin the tale, but then paused.

Would the sabotage solve anything?

In fact, it would complicate matters.

What if Flynn was held in the dungeon as punishment, but Lock was forced to travel further afield, to meet with Sir Horace Vere?

The mystery of 1613. The events surrounding James' murder. All of that would remain under lock and key.

But if Flynn could be compelled to travel with him to meet Vere, then on the way, the interrogation of the Irishman could begin.

Lock smiled.

This was what Father meant when he spoke of plotting ahead.

The door into the infirmary opened abruptly, jolting Lock out of his smug satisfaction.

Benjy wheeled around, just as startled.

But the visitor was no stranger.

Benjy clasped his hand to a salute. 'General Burroughs, Sir, how good of you to join us.'

The General's face was drawn with concern, and the concern was not for the Yorkshireman.

'Thank God, you're looking better Lock. Despite your deliberate disobeying of orders.' His tone was neutral, but the hint of a smile moved Lock to reciprocate.

'I'll be fine Sir. Made sure to get some shots at the bastards before they nicked me.'

Burroughs walked past Benjy and to the end of Lock's cot. 'So you did. The men won't cease raving about it. Many are convinced you were trained by William Louis himself, with skills like that.'

'William Louis, Sir?' the name was vaguely familiar, but Lock couldn't quite place it.

'The cousin of the Prince of Orange, lad. We have him to thank for inventing a new way to smash those tercios. He liked to think of himself as the Father of the drill, and after what happened in Mannheim, I reckon you two have much in common.'

Lock nodded. A faint memory returned of Father at the dinner table, discussing his admiration for yet another figure his family would never meet.

'My Father met him, Sir. By all accounts he was quite a man.'

'Indeed.' Burroughs said, before placing himself carefully at the end of Lock's bed.

Lock drew his feet closer to his body to make room.

Burroughs chuckled. 'They don't make these cots for well-fed, well-grown men like us, do they?'

Lock might have contested the well-fed part of the comment, but he just smiled and nodded.

Burroughs' expression became more serious. 'You gave me quite a scare there, lad. I didn't want you to leave before I had the chance to thank you.'

Lock winced as he rolled his left shoulder. 'I was proud to do my duty, Sir.'

'And the Irishman? He's been quite cagey about what happened in the church. Said that Captain Ricardo engaged in a double cross, and that you had to put him down. Is that true?'

Now as the test of his resolve.

Lock nodded as neutrally as he could.

Burroughs frowned. 'Such a rank pity to see men abandon their honour in such a way.'

'It is, Sir.'

'You will recall, we had a deal.'

'I know, Sir. Vere.'

'Yes, Vere. The Hague, Lock. That's where Vere is. I sent a letter ahead to him. I even shared with him some detail about your... exploits.'

Lock resisted the urge to swear in frustration.

So it was back to that wretched city again, where he had run so desperately and shamefully from danger.

'Thank you, Sir. The Hague is... is a fine city.'

'It is built by republicans, but they did alright, in my book.'

'Sir, there was another part of our deal.'

Burroughs held up a hand. 'I haven't forgotten about that linen, Lock. It has been sent.'

'It has?'

'Naturally. I uphold my obligations, let it never be said otherwise.'

'Did Walter receive the linen? Were his children alright?'

'I didn't accompany the cloth myself, Lock. But I have it on good authority that Walter will have plenty of material for new clothing. Just in time for the winter as well.'

'Sir, what kind of good authority?'

Burroughs winked at him. 'Let's just say that Joseph Gage has been... demoted, to more menial tasks, one of which included chaperoning these materials to their destination.' Burroughs chuckled, evidently satisfied that his subordinate's failings had been made good.

A wave of relief washed over Lock.

For once, a piece of purely good news.

Burroughs squinted at Lock's expression. 'Are you alright lad? Benjy isn't grilling you too heavily about Doyle I hope?'

'Haven't even mentioned him Sir!' Benjy called from behind Burroughs' frame.

'I wanted to make sure you know, Lock, that if you happen to find yourself near the Rhine again, I would be happy to take you into my service.'

'You do me an honour, Sir. But...' the question was a delicate one. 'Will you remain here long? The Spanish seem to be closing in on your position.'

Burroughs sucked his teeth. 'Yes, it seems not all Germans will fight like Georg von Salm, may God rest him. Soon, the Rhine will be overrun. But we knew this would happen, Lock. My men can still take heart from their performance. They fought with honour. They showed the King of Spain that Englishmen will not roll over.'

Burroughs then turned his head to the side and scowled.

'Whether His Majesty King James likes it or not.'

'You will remain until the end, Sir?'

Burroughs laughed. 'I will, lad. I will probably have to surrender to one of Cordoba's lackeys, but this is nothing to concern yourself with. You'll be in The Hague by then, God willing. Vere can continue to work for English interests in the Dutch capital, and we will hold the line here, just as we always have.'

'Then, if we do not meet again, it was a pleasure serving under you Sir.'

Burroughs rose from Lock's cot, and the structure creaked in relief. 'You stay out of trouble now lad.'

The throbbing in his head had escalated.

Perhaps the fever was not yet done with him. To keep up appearances, it was important Burroughs did not see him like this.

Lock smiled weakly.

'I will do my best, Sir.'

Burroughs turned on his heels, nodded at Benjy, and made for the door. It closed behind him with a slight crunch.

'Thank God,' Lock whispered.

'I suspect you'll be back to causing trouble soon enough Mister Matthew,' Benjy said with a grin. He continued to gaze out the window.

Lock winced in pain. 'Anything exciting happening in the courtyard?'

'Not so far, but there's due to be a parade soon. There's one poor bastard who always gets his drill wrong. Worth a look.'

'Doesn't sound particularly... riveting.' Lock cupped his right hand onto his throbbing left arm, and exhaled heavily as the next wave of pain hit.

'When you're stuck in here for so long Mister Matthew, you can make anything exciting if you try hard enough.' Benjy smiled at his comment, but as he turned his head to Lock, his face fell.

'Mister Matthew, you're awfully pale all of a sudden.'

'I'm perfectly fine Benjy, never better.' The persistent throb in his temples told him otherwise.

'I just need a lie down.' Lock sank into a prone position, and pulled a light sheet over his body.

He suppressed a shiver.

The prospect of facing another battle with his temperature loomed before him. His left arm cried out to be itched, but it pulsed whenever he touched it.

Lock was suddenly aware of Benjy's face in front of his.

He had sat down on his cot, and Lock hadn't even noticed.

The sense of exhaustion was overwhelming.

'Reckon you strained yourself Mister Matthew,' Benjy said with a wry smile.

Lock grabbed his right hand, as a surge of pain passed in a wave. Benjy flinched slightly.

'Not to worry, Mister Matthew. The physician is on his way.'

Lock smiled at Benjy. 'You'll make a great Earl...' but the words barely tumbled out.

'Mister Matthew?'

Lock had no energy to answer.

He capitulated to his affliction's demands, and was rewarded with a deep sleep.

- CHAPTER FORTY-THREE -

Lock was back in Manheim's church, with his hands around Captain Ricardo's throat. The captain's black velvet mask challenged Lock to squeeze as hard as he could.

But Captain Ricardo didn't sound like himself.

His pleas for mercy didn't sound hostile.

He sounded like Arthur, yet Lock couldn't stop choking him.

Or perhaps, he *wouldn't* stop choking him.

His brother's eyes rolled to the back of his head, but Lock clung tenaciously to his throat.

Lock stood up from the grisly deed, and recoiled in horror.

His brother's corpse lay on the church's hard stone floor.

Lock screamed.

He called for help.

He bent to his brother's corpse.

He slapped Arthur's cold face.

Nothing worked.

Murky clouds of dust swirled around him, obscuring visibility more than a few feet into the distance.

The sun's rays no longer shone through the stained-glass windows.

It was dark and cold, just like the church for James' funeral.

And then Lock glanced back to the floor.

Blood, a cascade of blood.

It was gathering on the floor in a pool, and the pool was expanding.

It edged its way ever closer to where Lock stood.

He shouted at the blood to stay back, to leave his brother alone.

But the blood did not stop.

He felt it under his feet. His bare feet.

It worked its way under Arthur's body.

Droplets crawled their way up Arthur's legs, and then his torso, until, reaching his neck, it covered his face.

No matter what he did, Lock couldn't rub the blood off.

It was all over his hands, the warm, sticky liquid.

The blood pooling on the floor had become deeper.

Deeper than his ankles.

It was dripping from the ceiling.

It was pouring through the open door.

The building was filled with blood, submerging Lock under it.

Lock screamed, and was suddenly awoken by a terrible jolt.

He sat bolt upright, and took in his immediate surroundings.

A wooden interior.

A very small room.

Exterior sounds.

And... the Irishman.

Flynn was seated just opposite him, a tan-coloured floppy hat covered his face while he dozed.

Everything seemed to be moving.

There was an intense draught.

Windows, covered with purple curtains that flapped in the wind. They revealed a rush of countryside, and the lure of nature.

Lock exhaled and leaned back into his seat in relief.

He was in some kind of horse-drawn carriage, or perhaps even a stagecoach if he was lucky.

The Irishman was keeping him company.

Lock shifted uncomfortably.

His rear was tired from the journey on the hard wooden bench.

He had evidently spent much of the time lying down, and some generous soul had lined the bench with sheets and a small pillow.

The carriage was wide enough for him to lie down without his feet hanging over the side, a luxury which Lock appreciated.

But how long had he been out?

Where was this carriage heading?

It was fortunate that Flynn remained, but it was unlikely the Irishman intended to answer Lock's questions. He had surely stuck around for another reason. Convenience, most likely.

An abundance of birdsong filled Lock's ears.

Lock stood up gradually, allowing his body to come to terms with the new stance. Obeying the height restrictions, he adhered to a slight crouch.

The window panel – perhaps that would shed some light on what was going on. The two-step journey was an awkward one. Lock took it slowly. He was careful to place as little pressure on the door as he could – falling out of a fast-moving carriage was the last thing he needed.

He poked his head gingerly out the window, to see a world of colour of life.

Wind rushed through his hair and whistled in his ears.

Where were they?

The road ran through wetlands Lock had never seen before, caused by flooding along the Rhine, and the overflow of its various tributaries.

With difficulty, he turned his head to the left and right of the window. The carriage was pulled by four horses, and was fashioned with richly adorned wood.

Was this another product of Woodrest?

It was certainly a stagecoach, and an expensive one at that.

How had the Irishman afforded it?

In a glittering river a few yards away, an eagle swooped to grab a large fish, and the activity startled a group of children that clustered around their parents.

One of the children waved at the coach, and Lock withdrew embarrassed.

He sat down with a slight thud.

Without standing, he could just about make out the scenery outside. This would have to suffice for entertainment, until the Irishman woke up.

Lock couldn't decide if he wanted the Irishman awake or not.

Their confined circumstances meant that Flynn would be forced to give him straight answers, a prospect that filled Lock's stomach with a churning, nervous anxiety.

Or perhaps it was merely hunger.

On the window to the left, a cloud of small birds flocked to an old tree. Lock watched their exodus. He had always enjoyed birdwatching in Locksville, particularly the herons that seemed to tiptoe over shallow water.

'*Matchlock*,' Flynn said, with a chuckle from under his hat.

Lock jumped at the sudden disturbance.

He could no longer be alone with his thoughts.

He stared at the Irishman, and waited for him to remove the hat from his face. Lock was determined to fix a glare at him once he did.

The Irishman caught Lock's expression and held up his hands in mock appeal.

'That's what they're calling you now, honest. Even the really sinewy old bastards have gotten in on the act.'

Lock was unsure what to say, or even where to begin.

A slight draught caused him to shiver, and he closed his dolman with a fold of his arms.

'We're going to The Hague, Lock. I'm going to leave you to do your business with Vere, then I will be out of your hair.'

The meeting with his godfather – it was *finally* happening.

It was difficult to focus on one's parents, when 1613 was so fresh in the mind.

Lock despaired about locating a solution for either case, but if Vere was as good as Father had claimed, surely a lead of some form would be gleaned from the encounter.

The Irishman was still talking.

'I know you're angry, Lock. You have every right to be, but look, we're in this fast coach, courtesy of the Strasser brothers by the way, so unless you want to sit in a dull silence for the next two days, we'd better get through this.'

'*Get through this*?' Lock turned over the words out loud. His throat crackled slightly as it warmed up to speech. 'By *get through this*, do you mean explaining to me why you tried to hand me over to the Black Prince? Or perhaps you'd prefer to describe how you happened to arrive with a band of knaves in 1613 and murder my brother?'

The Irishman shifted uneasily in his bench.

He turned the hat over in his hands, folding it in half, then unfolding it, then starting again.

'Or, or maybe you don't wish to speak of any of that. Maybe you'd prefer to explain why you all but shunned me, or why you treated me like a pariah.'

The hat folding continued.

Lock folded his throbbing fingers into his palms.

'Perhaps you would like to look me in the eye and explain why you *really* told me I was a liability?'

'I did apologise for –'

'You can shove your base apologies. You were never truly vexed about my temper at all, were you? You were just worried I'd figure out what you really were, so you concocted this front to capitalise on my guilt.'

'I think you may be taking this too much to heart.'

'I scarcely know whether to throw you out that door, or jump out of it myself.'

'You still haven't let me explain the –'

'*Explain*? Let me guess. It was easier to lay the blame on me, the bullfinch from Dorset, than it was to gaze into the looking glass, and confront the blackguard staring back.'

There came no reply, just more hat folding.

'Is that about the sum of your situation, *Irishman*?'

Flynn's back arched defensively and his mouth, normally hosting the hint of a smile, flattened. He exhaled, and Lock raised his eyebrows at him.

The stagecoach wheel then struck an errant stone, jolting Lock suddenly forward, and nearly onto Flynn's knees. Lock steadied himself, and lowered his frame back into the bench with a wince.

'You couldn't have found a less comfortable stagecoach to travel in, could you?'

Flynn rolled his eyes. 'Excuse me for taking up Herman Strasser on his very generous offer of five day's travel to The Hague. We could have walked if you preferred.'

'What's this *we* business. I thought you were bound for Ireland, now that they don't want your head.'

'Someone always wants my head.'

'Right now, I think it'd look pretty good on a spike.'

'Or perhaps you'd just castrate me, like you did to Captain Ricardo?'

Lock's face fell when reminded of the horror.

He glanced at his hands. Dried blood still lay under the fingernails. The captain's blood most likely.

'I didn't mean to deal with him... in that dishonourable manner. I just... I panicked.'

Flynn waved a hand as he sipped from his costrel. 'Far be it from me to criticise. Truth be told, the bastard deserved far worse.'

'That's what you said about Gaston Phillipe.'

'One was as bad as the other.'

'I see.'

'I could tell you about a dishonourable arrangement they had going. *The Business*, they called it, but really it was just a way for vile men to pay for services from unwilling women.'

'Good grief.'

'Believe me, Lock, there's a long line of women who wish they could've done exactly what you did to Captain Ricardo.'

'Well, I suppose that makes me feel a little better.'

Flynn then smiled knowingly. 'Fortunately, he also expected very little from you.'

'What do you mean?'

Flynn crossed his legs and rested his folded hands on the right knee.

Lock couldn't fathom such a flamboyant posture, but the Irishman pulled it off. He made it look somehow classy and refined.

'I knew Captain Ricardo was up to something, but I didn't know he was the Rogue I was looking for. So, I left information for them to come upon, which could... influence their approach in a certain way.'

'Information? Of what kind?'

'The kind that painted you as a snivelling, helpless worm, and the kind that portrayed me as in way over my head.'

'He knows I'm no worm now,' Lock said quietly. 'Though that would explain why he was so surprised when I fought back.'

Flynn nodded. 'Captain Ricardo wanted to make an example out of you. He died shortly after our encounter. Likely better that way.'

'I *killed* him,' Lock said with a gasp.

There was something chilling in hearing it confirmed aloud.

Father's warning returned to his mind: *A life taken is a line crossed. Once crossed, the man does not return to the life he used to know.*

This pearl of wisdom had always been followed by his bright-eyed boys asking if their Father had ever killed someone.

Father had always found a way not to answer.

'Yes, Lock, you did. Him and many others in Mannheim's square. Such is the nature of war. I suspect, it was in your nature all along.'

'You know nothing of me or my nature.'

'Don't be thinking about it now, you had no choice.'

'I wasn't supposed to kill people, I was just supposed to find answers.'

'You took the scenic route. Hardly your fault, with blockheads like Burroughs and Gage in command. Idiots managed to waste their advantages with constant mistakes. If you hadn't intervened in the forest, Lock, de la Barca's men would have destroyed us then and there.'

'Burroughs made many mistakes?'

'Lock, he tried to use cavalry in a forest. He relied on German farmers to hold the line. He's lucky, not skilled. I'd advise you to steer clear of him if you can help it. One day he'll get someone important killed.'

Lock felt strangely defensive of Burroughs' reputation. 'I think you're more than capable of killing them yourself Flynn.'

'In Mannheim's church, do you mean? Daft bastards deserved it for their shoddy preparations if nothing else. Didn't even search us for weapons when we walked in. Good thing too, else they would have found my wheellocks.'

Lock recalled the sudden murder that had flowed from Flynn's hands. The Irishman had fired, without match cord, and had taken his foes utterly by surprise. In another time, perhaps, he would have jumped at the chance to learn more about such elusive firearms, but there were more pressing matters to tend to.

Lock cleared his throat. 'What Captain Ricardo said –'

'About me being present in 1613? It is true.'

Lock's breathing accelerated. Hot rage flowed from his head to his fingertips. His eyes settled on Flynn's frame.

Striking the Irishman.

Bludgeoning him.

Leaving him to suffer and die by the roadside.

All were possibilities. Could he do such a thing?

He could not.

At least not so long as he needed information.

'What did you do?'

'In 1613?'

'Yes in 1613! You think I'd rather hear what you did for breakfast?'

'Two eggs and a piece of –'

'*Enough*, Flynn. I've had enough of your lies and your tricks. I've certainly had enough of your jokes. Just tell me the truth.'

Flynn exhaled.

He had surely known an explanation would be required. He hesitated, and turned the hat over a few more times in his hands.

Lock bit his tongue.

The arm throbbed. His head was still ringing. His hands ached and stung. A knot in his stomach refused to be quenched.

He was in no mood for this.

He glanced at the hat and then the handle of the coach door several times, before taking one more glance at Flynn and rising carefully to a crouch.

Flynn mouthed a question at him, which Lock ignored.

He shuffled forward, and grabbed the hat out of Flynn's hands.

Lock then seized the door handle with his left hand, and as the heavy door swung open, Lock flung the hat outside with all of his might.

It sailed enthusiastically, captured by the wind, until it landed irretrievably in a fast-flowing river mirrored by the road.

'God's guts Lock –'

'Don't you dare, you cheeky bastard,' Lock spat, as he grasped the door handle and swung it closed with a jerk. 'You're humming and hawing in your chair, wondering what to tell me or what not to tell me. You don't *get* to choose. I'll boot you out of here right now, in the middle of... in the middle of...'

'Cologne.'

'Cologne, I'll boot you out and you can walk to the North Sea coast from the Archbishopric of Cologne,' Lock sat down with a grunt. 'Or, for *once*, you can be honest with me. You can confess your crimes, and then, *maybe* then, I'll allow you to travel with me.'

'Lock, there'd be a problem with your plan, see, the stagecoach is travelling in the name of –'

'Are you taking me seriously or not?'

Flynn scoffed, and reached for his costrel. 'Not.'

Lock exhaled and closed his eyes.

Enough was enough.

He booted the door open again, and as Flynn watched him with his mouth slightly agape, Lock wrenched the costrel out of his hands. With a careful step, Lock then exited the confines of the stagecoach.

The entire ordeal had left Flynn stunned, and he took a few precious seconds to exit the coach.

This time, a tone of panic had entered the Irishman's voice.

'Lock, stop, you must *stop*!'

Lock had stepped out into a scene reminiscent of the English countryside. He moved four paces on the dried mud road and into the edge of the riverbank. The fast-flowing currents would seize the costrel, and bring it all the way to the North Sea, for all Lock cared.

He drew back his right arm, and mimed throwing the heirloom into its rushing depths, before a final, desperate plea came behind him.

'*Stop*!' the Irishman roared, loud enough to compel a troop of birds to flee from their shelter.

The shout also caused the stagecoach to shudder to a halt, and the driver's eyes widened as he took in the scene.

The Irishman's shaking frame was barely a yard from Lock's. He was plainly terrified of what was to come next.

'Lock, please, that's the only memento I have of my family. Please don't *do* this.'

Lock narrowed his eyes at him, relishing every moment of the Irishman's turmoil.

But the satisfaction was short-lived.

Flynn's turmoil was real.

Too real.

The Irishman was near collapse.

Lock hesitated.

'Please... Please Lock, I'm sorry. I'm so sorry, I'm just... I'm...'

Before Lock could back down, the Irishman plonked himself on the edge of the riverbank. He stared into his empty, outstretched hands, and looked back up to Lock in appeal.

Lock still dangled the costrel over the river. Once again, he had to raise his voice above the sound of churning water.

'You need to tell me what you did, Flynn. You need to tell me what you did to my brother in 1613.'

'I *can't*!'

'Why the bloody hell not?'

'Because I am *ashamed*! Is that what you want me to say, Lock? I'm ashamed of my past. I'm ashamed of what I've done. I'm ashamed of what I've become.'

The confession was surprising, but it was not enough.

Flynn's shame would not fill the empty holes in Lock's mind.

It would not answer his burning questions.

The costrel still rested in his hand. Its edges were rough, but when examined more closely, they revealed an intricate web of Celtic design. A craft whose fruits were reserved for only the most privileged in Gaelic society.

Lock fixed his eyes on Flynn. 'This costrel, it's valuable to you, yes?'

Flynn nodded. 'It was my Father's, I told you.'

'I don't *have* a costrel, Flynn. My parents left me no heirlooms, and the only thing I got to inherit were some empty rooms in an even emptier house. Any memories I have are tainted by this mess with the black masks. Could you imagine what that would be like? Could you imagine what it would be like if your parents or siblings were killed, and you had no inkling as to why?'

The Irishman glared at his shoes.

Water leaked steadily into Lock's worn boots.

Birds sung obliviously in a clump of nearby trees.

The sun beamed down on Lock's head from a cloudless sky.

It was a beautiful picture, notwithstanding the hostage situation.

'You *know* something, Flynn. I know it's painful for you to say, but I *need* to hear it. I need to know what happened to my family. I need to know that my only memories of them won't be how I... how I failed.'

It was his greatest fear. To fail his family in their death, just as he had failed them in life. The very prospect made him nauseous, but also strangely rootless, like there was nowhere he belonged.

Father once explained what a homeless person was, and as a child, Lock couldn't fathom the concept. *'Their home must be somewhere,'* the young Matthew had insisted.

Lock was scarcely sure if Locksville would feel like home ever again. It certainly wouldn't, if he returned to Arthur's expectant gaze, and could bring him nothing.

The Irishman sighed. 'Get in the coach, Lock. I promise, I swear on Irish earth, I'll tell you everything.'

After an apology to the coach driver, and a brisk return of Flynn's costrel, hooves began to strike at the road once more.

The journey would continue, but on Matthew Lock's terms.

- CHAPTER FORTY-FOUR -

The heavy coach was no match for the four beasts.

These were larger horses than the usual palfreys used for a single cart or wagon. They were built and bred for speed, and for the speediest mode of transport then available.

With scarce pauses for food and rest, the Strasser brothers' stagecoach could comfortably travel fifty miles in a day. This was just as well, because the journey from Frankenthal to The Hague was close to two hundred and fifty miles.

Since the coach was now in Cologne, Lock estimated that the fever had wiped him out for another two days, perhaps more.

Lock kept his eyes fixed on the Irishman.

If he'd expected a reprieve, he was not about to get one.

Lock was determined to squeeze him for every last bit of information, whether he liked the answers or not.

Finally, the Irishman took a purposeful sip of his costrel, packed it away, and then sat forward on his bench with a sigh.

'Alright Lock, what do you want to know?'

'I want to know a great deal of things, Flynn, but I'll start from the beginning. Since you're such a great servant of his, perhaps you can enlighten me. Why is the Black Prince after me?'

'How do you know the Black Prince is after you?'

'Well, he's sent me three warning signs. First, a mask with a note. Second, a load of masked men in my parents' Dutch home. Third, a group of masked ragamuffins to intimidate me...'

Lock stopped speaking in response to the hand Flynn had just raised. The Irishman appeared puzzled.

'What was the second one? There were men in your parents' *home*? In The Hague?'

Lock nodded. 'I went there, when the embassy landed, to see if I could learn something about what had happened. There was no information available anywhere, just that they had died. The front door was ajar, so I walked into the place, and –'

'They were waiting for you?'

'There was blood everywhere. No one had been to clean the place, but this was another level of mess. It was like they'd ransacked the entire house from top to bottom.'

'That doesn't make sense...'

'Makes perfect sense to me. The Black Prince sends his dogs to kill my Father, with you among them... I'll get to that later. But he fails in 1613, so he tries again in 1622, and then...' Lock allowed the sentence to end. Flynn still shook his head.

'That doesn't sound like the Black Prince's behaviour, Lock, not at all.'

'They were all wearing his masks, I saw them with my own bloody eyes Flynn, those were the Black Prince's men.'

Flynn sighed. 'I'm afraid, it's not as straightforward as that Lock.'

'Of course it's not,' Lock said, half throwing his arms up in despair. His left arm throbbed with the act.

'Those men you saw in The Hague, they weren't working for the Black Prince, notwithstanding their attire.'

'Say I believe you, what reason could these men have for dressing up as men on the Black Prince's pay? What could they possibly have to gain from the trickery?'

Flynn paused, as if debating his next words.

'Are you familiar with wasps, Lock?'

Lock blinked quickly at the Irishman.

'I ask, because of course you are. Wasps are horrible, nasty things. But the one positive about wasps, they at least warn you of their fearsome capabilities.'

'Right...'

'The problem with this strategy is, you get imitators. Many insects mimic the wasp's attire, because they know when others see it, they'll steer clear.'

'I see.'

'Those men you saw, in The Hague, they were mimics. They weren't the wasps; they weren't the Black Prince's men.'

'God sakes Flynn, I could have done without the metaphor.'

But Flynn persisted, more enthusiastically this time.

'They wear black masks to scare their enemies, Lock. They get by on the reputation of the black masks, and they do essentially what they want while they wear them.'

'I understand. Are there many of these frauds around?'

'Their number isn't the issue Lock. You'll often find with those mimic insects, that even though they're not true wasps, they are still capable of delivering a painful strike.'

'So what you're saying is, the frauds are as dangerous as those that work for the Black Prince, and both are my enemy.'

Flynn nodded slowly.

'This journey keeps getting better.'

Flynn rubbed the corners of his eyes with his right hand.

'The Raven, Lock, do you remember Captain Ricardo mention him?'

Lock nodded.

The scene returned to his mind with a vivid intensity.

The captain's searing arrogance.

His cutting words.

His relish for inflicting misery.

Lock was back parrying the captain's strikes, and crippling his resolve in a pool of blood. It felt good to relive the captain's defeat. It felt good to force an enemy to choke on their own words.

'The Raven, Lock, *he's* the one those Rogues flock to.'

'Captain Ricardo, he had a stiletto. Those are reserved for only the Black Prince's best men, is that right?'

'Where did you learn that?'

'The Rogues that follow the Raven, they aren't mere imposters, they once served the Black Prince. Correct?'

'Correct. Hence, their ability to inflict a painful strike.'

'They know the Black Prince's methods, but are unbound by his code?'

'That... that is about the sum of it, yes.'

'The Raven and the Black Prince... are they at odds?'

Flynn shrugged lightly. 'Not openly. No war has been declared. They prefer to snipe at each other now and then, from the shadows. You won't find any information about who the Black Prince is, but the Raven is equally secretive.'

'Someone must know something?'

'Perhaps the Raven is within the Black Prince's organisation, perhaps he is not. Perhaps the Black Prince knows who the Raven is, but thinks it too risky to challenge him. The truth remains unknown.'

'Captain Ricardo, and that other fellow, Fabio?'

'Rogues, Lock. Unrepentant Rogues, who stopped listening to the Black Prince's orders long ago, and went into business for themselves.'

'The Black Prince cannot be pleased with all these Rogues running around, misrepresenting him.'

'He is most certainly *not*. That's why his masks are instructed to kill any Rogues on sight.'

'Yet the Black Prince and the Raven are not at war with each other?'

Flynn shook his head. 'No. The conflict between them remains curiously low level. Masks hunting down Rogues, Rogues ambushing masks, that sort of thing.'

'That's what you do, then Flynn, you hunt these Rogues down? By order of the Black Prince, I'm sure.'

'I am doing important work Lock. Good work. These Rogues are some of the vilest men you've ever met. Men drunk on power. Men enslaved by their ambitions, or passions, or sins. The Black Prince's organisation works because the masks follow orders. So long as they follow orders, matters will transpire to everyone's satisfaction.'

'You sound like you're reading from the Black Prince's own pamphlet.'

'He has a moral compass, Lock. The Black Prince is no brute. He does not deal in mindless violence.'

'He just has an agenda that you happen to support.'

Flynn leaned back into his bench, and lifted his chin at Lock.

'Let me tell you something. When I first joined his organisation, I was young, broke and alone. Do you think there were many prospects for the second son of an exiled Irish earl?'

'I would suspect not.'

'I was *hopeless*, Lock. I had no future where I was going. After one too many, I faced a particularly knavish Brussels jailor, when suddenly, the iron door swung open, and a masked man was waiting for me.'

'When was that?'

'1609. Since that date, I have worked my way up in his organisation. I have money now, Lock. I have status, and respect. I receive honour and bows from any snivelling merchants or well-to-do parvenu that crosses my path.'

'Fearing you is not the same as respecting you.'

'But they *do* respect me, Lock, because they know that I am good.'

'They know you're good at killing.'

'Killing the Black Prince's *enemies*,' Flynn said, as though the correction was essential.

'Was James Lock the Black Prince's enemy?' the question shot forth from Lock like a cannon ball.

Flynn absorbed the force of it, and then returned his gaze to the floor. 'That... that was an accident. James was never meant to die.'

'He didn't *die,* Flynn, he was murdered in cold blood by men that you worked with. If the Black Prince is so all-seeing, so all-knowing, and if he is as *honourable* as you say, then why did he not stop his men from killing James?'

'Something happened, Lock. One of the men in our group, he... he went crazy. I'd never seen anything like it.'

'If this crazy individual went against the Black Prince's orders that night, then shouldn't that mean you are all Rogues now?'

Flynn's eyebrows narrowed at the challenge, but he shook his head briskly.

'It was just one man. The Black Prince was informed, and we all swore that it was one man among us that did it. We were believed, thank God, after some... interviews.' The Irishman shuddered involuntarily at the thought, before composing himself. 'The only problem...'

'You lost him. You lost James' killer.'

'We didn't *lose him*, Lock. He vanished off the face of the earth. Any information on any of the men that took part that night, was also destroyed. Burned to ashes in an all-too convenient blaze on the night of.'

'Someone must know something about him?'

Flynn shook his head gravely. 'As was customary, we hadn't taken names that night, and nobody had shown their faces. It was the perfect way to cover up the whole thing. Someone knew what they were doing, and went to great lengths to muddy the waters as much as possible.'

'Captain Ricardo, he said that a man, Rudolf Macht, was supposed to be there. How did he know his name if anonymity was so important?'

Flynn shrugged. 'Sometimes, friends signed into his organisation and didn't disclose their past. Sometimes, you were joined by men who worked in pairs. Perhaps Captain Ricardo and this Macht fellow had a past. I don't know.'

'Considering his reputation for running such a tight ship, the Black Prince's organisation seems riven with holes.'

'Only when men go against his orders. Then, problems inevitably arise. To clean them up, he relies on men like me.'

'A *cleaner*, that's how you see yourself?'

'That's my official title. I am the most successful cleaner the Black Prince has.'

'Listen to yourself, you sound ridiculous.'

'You would not think me ridiculous if you saw the list of men I put down.'

'Explain something to me then, oh wise cleaner. Knowing what you know of the Black Prince, is it odd that he hasn't worked to discover who was responsible for James' death?'

Flynn sighed. 'The Black Prince had a better idea, to send me to investigate instead.'

'*You*?'

Flynn took another sip, before clearing his throat.

'A year ago, the Black Prince contacted me with a job. I was to reopen the 1613 event. I was to track each of the participants down, one-by-one. Through a process of elimination then, I would be able to determine who had done it.'

'Did he only contact you with the job? Why would he not round up the participants of 1613 once again?'

'Because they couldn't be found, Lock. Thanks to my high profile, the Black Prince knew I could be depended on.'

'Alright, well why the sudden interest in something that happened nine years ago?'

'I'm not told the *why*, Lock, I'm just told the *what*.'

The information was both encouraging and unsettling all at once. This terrible event, this moment which had always been a private tragedy, was at the centre of an investigation authorised by the most dangerous, mysterious figure in Europe.

'I don't know whether to feel special, or deeply concerned, to be honest Flynn.'

Flynn winced, before clearing his throat. 'I'm afraid that's not the end of the story, Lock.'

'What do you mean?'

'I told you I was sent to reopen the 1613 case. Well, the first lead in that case brought me to two names. Two men that had taken part alongside me.'

'Let me guess, Captain Ricardo, and Fabio.'

The Irishman nodded. 'Fabio was easy enough to find. The man was a clay-brained dolt. He outed himself after a few fingers of wine. He had only been the driver that night in 1613. Terrible driver he was too.'

'And then you killed him?'

'The Black Prince didn't want a load of bodies, he wanted answers, something to fill in the blanks, to get closer to the man who was actually responsible for swinging the sword.'

'But Fabio was... disappeared, in the forest?'

The flash in Flynn's eyebrows told Lock he had again surprised the Irishman with his knowledge. Von Salm's contributions had been invaluable.

'Following an informative chat regarding 1613, Fabio proceeded to tell me that he'd gone into business for himself, but was keeping the black mask.'

'Was he quite well? Did he not know your rank?'

'As I said Lock, clay-brained dolt. He thought he could entice me into a new life, free of responsibility, and filled with power.'

'Has a cleaner ever become a Rogue?'

'Absolutely not. Fabio had not a hope, and he sealed his fate with his loose tongue.'

'And then you sold his stiletto to Herman Strasser.'

Flynn smiled. 'I wondered if I'd ever see that blade again. Sharp little bugger. You should keep it, but you should probably wash it first, considering where it's been.'

Lock glanced to the left corner of the coach, where his belongings lay collected in a heap. Presumably, the stiletto was there among them.

'Fabio's deathbed confession was a bit of a damp squib. Couldn't understand a word he said. I heard the Black Prince's name enough times though.'

'He switched into a different language?'

'He did, perhaps he thought it would make a difference to my decision to strike him down.'

'But all Rogues must die, that's your policy.'

'That's the *Black Prince*'s policy Lock, and I can't afford to ignore it, or what use am I to him?'

'You killed him in the forest, and what then?'

Flynn nodded gravely. 'Poor old von Salm enlightened you? I swore I thought that man would live forever.'

Lock resisted the opportunity to reminisce. 'First Fabio, and then Captain Ricardo made your list? Did he out himself as well?'

'Fabio's loose lips handled that matter. He placed Captain Ricardo in 1613. Once Fabio was gone, the captain seemed particularly interested in Fabio's fate, more than anyone else.'

'Nobody else liked Fabio?'

'Nobody gave two shits about Fabio.'

'You knew Captain Ricardo was there in 1613, and almost certainly a Rogue on top of that, so why didn't you eliminate him as you did Fabio?'

Flynn shook his head at the interruption. 'I was getting to it, Lock, when something odd happened. My orders suddenly dried up. My handler went dark.'

'That can't be a new experience. It takes weeks for letters to arrive, and who knows where the Black Prince is posting them from.'

'But it was strange, Lock. I was in the midst of a job. And then, I get told of a new mission, with no mention of the old. The 1613 investigation was forgotten. Instead, I was tasked with chaperoning someone to a particular church in Mannheim.'

'When did you receive those orders.'

'Approximately two days before you arrived in de la Barca's camp.'

Lock went silent for a moment.

The wheels of the coach provided a consistent, rhythmic sound which he drew comfort from.

'This whole time we were travelling together, you were doing a job?'

'Yes. It doesn't mean I didn't enjoy your company, but –'

'Did you even *want* a pardon?'

'Of course I did.' Flynn reached into his front pocket and pulled out the document, bearing the necessary seal. It had been folded and refolded multiple times, which suggested it had also been read multiple times. Perhaps by an individual who couldn't believe they had finally managed to possess such a document.

'You weren't simply following me around?'

Flynn scoffed. 'Returning to my homeland is the thing I want most. It so happened that I could balance my job with my heart's desire.'

'But your job changed, under unusual circumstances.'

'Yes. I decided to stick with the new orders, but to keep my eyes open. There was plenty of room to improvise along the way.'

'Do you think it's possible that these Rogues may have intercepted your orders, and swapped them out for their own?'

Flynn's expression confirmed he feared the exact same thing.

'If the Raven has managed to direct his Rogues to this extent, then the Black Prince faces a graver threat than I had thought.'

'Were you not prepared for something like this? Surely the Black Prince cannot live forever, someone must seek to succeed him.'

'I was prepared, to an extent.'

'Really?'

'Yes, Lock. It may appear as though I was caught with my breeches around my ankles, but in truth, I suspected some complication once the correspondence with Captain Ricardo began.'

'*Correspondence*? You were writing to the bastard?'

'If I wished to arrange the surrender, I had to.'

'What did you discuss?'

'I made it plain that he should surrender peacefully, and that he should not mention anything of his involvement in 1613.'

'You thought you had leverage against him.'

'Fabio had let slip that his good friend Ricardo was there in 1613. When I confronted the captain, he did not deny it.'

'What then?'

'We kept writing, Lock. And we worked out a deal. In exchange for his safe passage out of Mannheim, Captain Ricardo swore not to reveal any details of 1613 to you.'

'You didn't know he was a Rogue?'

'I did suspect it, but you must understand, Lock, Rogues do not make a habit of showing themselves.'

'So, that incident in Mannheim church?'

'An anomaly, Lock. I've scarcely heard the Raven's name mentioned in public, and I have *never* been set upon by Rogues.'

'Yet you've killed scores of them?'

'I am *always* one step ahead.'

'Not this time. You should have been better prepared. You should have anticipated some form of foul play.'

'I was safe, by any reasonable standard. I had scoped out that church before I brought you there. God sakes, I even hired four backup plans. Those suits of armour you saw.'

'The men who *betrayed* you?' Lock snorted.

Flynn sighed. 'A Basque mercenary outfit. I paid them good money. That used to matter. Ricardo must have got to them first. Thank Heavens I packed the wheellocks, I nearly did not.'

'And you assumed Captain Ricardo to be honourable, and to surrender himself to your care?'

'I assumed him to be sensible. But then, he knew a great deal that I did not. I reckon the Raven planned this with him for some time.'

'He was miles ahead of you.'

'Fortunately, my safeguard worked. He royally underestimated you, Lock. As did I.'

'You weren't so charming when you grilled me for information in that meat cart.'

'Yes, well, I wanted to ensure you weren't some Rogue in disguise. The sudden change in orders had made me somewhat... jumpy. I was ready to kill you if necessary.'

'But then I mentioned black masks.'

'Your initial mention of them threw me, but when we were with Burroughs and Gage, and you referenced the death of your brother in 1613 to black masks, that was when I was truly flummoxed.'

'Did you suspect you had been set up?'

'Can you fathom it? That I, a mask in 1613, now investigating the incident nine years later, should be tricked into chaperoning the younger brother of the victim from that night? Like some sick joke.'

'It sounds too coincidental, like encountering a wild Irishman among the ranks of Spain's armies.'

Flynn laughed. 'I realised then that I was either being messed with by Rogues, or that God was providing me with an opportunity for repentance.'

Lock's coldness surprised him. 'It's the first one, Flynn.'

Flynn's face fell, and he turned his gaze to the carriage floor. It seemed he had expected Lock to forgive more easily. An awkward silence followed.

The grinding, repetitive sound of the wheels no longer soothed.

They had become irritating.

There was nothing to do but continue the conversation.

Lock cleared his throat. 'Captain Ricardo must have thought he'd get away with killing the Black Prince's favourite cleaner.'

'Which should make everyone, including the Black Prince, very anxious indeed.'

'Because?'

'Because, Lock, the more active the Raven is, the more likely his cover is to be blown. Although we foiled his agents, he has shown that he can do something of this size.'

'The question is, why?'

'No Lock, the real question is, what's so special about *you*?

'Me?'

'Yes, Lock. Don't you see? The Raven mobilised all of his resources to get *you* into his hands.'

'He wanted your head as well.'

'I was just a bonus, Lock, to be beheaded on the spot. He had plans for you. You were to be captured alive, and handed over to him. God knows what he would have done to you.'

'A frightful thought, I admit.'

Flynn smiled grimly. 'You didn't happen to wrong any individuals in your youth? Perhaps one of them grew up to be the Raven?'

Lock scoffed and gestured to the bench. 'Look at me Flynn, my arse is so delicate I can barely sit still on this hard wooden bench. I caught a fever after a few days of intense activity. I'm not the kind of person the Raven is looking for.'

'Are you *sure*?'

'Very. The Raven must be mistaken.'

But Lock was not sure.

He scanned his memories, even the most fleeting of fragments, to find some trace of an individual he might have mortally wronged. Billy, the rough Sherbourner, might have qualified, but he lacked the brains or the means to coordinate so many men.

This left no obvious candidates.

Two possibilities thus existed.

Either the Raven was capable of making such cardinal errors, or the truth behind his pursuit was a mystery to Lock alone.

The dilemma caused pain behind Lock's eyes.

Though, perhaps, it was just the afterbite of the fever.

Flynn chuckled. 'You know, it's not abnormal for pampered men to become ill after a few days on the road. Their bodies are not used to it. You need a few more days on hard wooden benches, Lock, then you'll have the arse for adventure.'

Lock allowed a laugh of his own, but he then grew more serious.

'How do I know I won't be followed by these Rogues for the rest of my life?'

'You don't, Lock. But until we find out what they want with you, we'll just have to do our best to dodge them. I am more interested in another question.'

'What's that?'

'Why was the Black Prince after you in the first place?'

'Should I trust you enough to tell you?'

'Do you have anything to *lose* by telling me?'

'You have already cost me a great deal.'

Flynn winced at the reply, and Lock's expression did not soften. But Flynn persisted.

'Did you wrong the Black Prince in some way? Think carefully on it.'

Lock could have erupted, but objectively, the Irishman had a point. First there was the visit to his family home in 1613, and then the son had been haunted by black masks since his arrival in Europe.

If the Black Prince didn't hound his enemies for no reason, then what could the reason be? Could it be the same motive that compelled the Raven to attack?

'What did his message say, Lock? The initial note delivered with the black mask?'

Lock hesitated, slightly perturbed by Flynn's knowledge.

But then, the Irishman had been in the organisation for more than a decade, so it made sense he would understand its processes.

'It was... a strange message. It said that I was ordered to remain in England, and not to make landfall on the continent.' Lock exhaled. It brought a measure of relief to share the encounter with another.

'That *is* strange. The Black Prince normally sends messages demanding repayment of debts, or informing the target of their wrongs... but to demand that you stay away from the continent...'

Flynn sucked his teeth as he turned the issue over for a few moments. He then raised an index finger.

'Do you think the two cases could be connected, Lock? Perhaps your Father imparted some sage wisdom within you before he died, which both the Raven and the Black Prince wish to get their hands on?'

Lock smiled at the suggestion. 'Unless they're after his leatherbound collection of wisdom and wit, inspired by Francesco Guicciardini, I doubt that's the case.'

Lock turned towards the window on his right.

His eyes had been drawn by a new feature – smoke.

Plumes of it rose high into the air. A consequence of the Spanish and Dutch skirmishing just across the Rhine, no doubt. As he watched the smoke rise, something still didn't sit right. Something that troubled him the more he turned it over in his mind.

'When those black masks ambushed me in the carriage...'

'Yes?'

'They were so determined to take me from the continent, they were willing to escort me for over a week.'

Flynn leaned back in the bench. His face was drawn in confusion.

'That... that is *unheard* of.'

'There's something else. When the Germans attacked, the leader... he... he tried to protect me. In fact, I believe he gave his life trying to protect me.'

'The Germans...' Flynn said quietly. 'Are you certain your carriage was attacked by *Germans*?'

Lock was about to nod, but realised he was not sure.

'My God, Flynn... could they have been Rogues?'

Flynn clapped his hands together. 'The same Rogues that arranged for me to deliver you to them, I would guarantee it.

'You were their insurance policy. God save us.'

'They failed to kill you in the forest, so they took more extreme measures.'

'They acted so quickly, quicker than a courier can travel. How can that be?'

'My guess is these Rogues have been planning for some time. They picked this moment, it would seem, to flex their muscles.'

'Do you think the Black Prince knew I was in danger?'

'I suspect that's why he wanted you off the continent, Lock.'

Lock shook his head. 'I don't think we need assign purely selfless motives to your master just yet.'

'How many masks did he send to escort you?'

'Three, at least. One had a stiletto, if I recall.'

'A stiletto? God's guts Lock. The Black Prince was not messing around. He made your safety a priority.'

'Perhaps it was my swift exit that he made a priority.'

'Perhaps.'

'If the Black Prince wants to keep me alive, but far away, and the Raven wants me dead, or worse, what does that *mean*?'

Flynn gathered his chin in his right hand. 'It is hard to say, Lock. It could mean a whole range of things. At least we know now, the Raven and his Rogues are your true enemy, not the Black Prince.'

Flynn had said so with satisfaction, but Lock was unconvinced.

'Not so, Flynn. I still don't know his motives, and more importantly, I don't know why the Black Prince sent you to my home in the first place.'

Flynn sighed, as if expecting the challenge. 'I don't know either, Lock. I wish I did, but the Black Prince kept it this way. We were only told to arrive at a given place, at a given time, for a given target.'

'Target? *My family was the target?*'

'Not your family Lock, God no, just... just your Father.'

The answer hung in the air.

'*Father*? What would the Black Prince want with him?'

'God's guts Lock, I don't know. We were never told *why*, we were just told *what*. A big house, perhaps a holiday home. No security. Three sons and a husband and wife. Rough the man up, send a message. That's it. Not too different from the scores of jobs I'd done before.'

Lock balked to hear the most traumatic event of his life summarised into such a mechanical job description. He cleared his throat. 'Except this time, my brother was murdered. That wasn't part of the script.'

Flynn shook his head gravely. 'It wasn't. It absolutely wasn't.'

Lock's eyes moistened, as he recalled the blur of events that followed James' death . Long sup pressed memories would now be forcibly , painfully excavated from the brain, like a grisly autopsy.

Lock found that he did not have to dig too deeply to recall the horror. Years of reliving the terrible night had brought it to the forefront of his mind, like a constant, niggling companion.

There was the physical pain as well.

The antagonist had leapt upon Lock after despatching James.

After begging for his brother's life for so long, Lock had lacked the strength or will to defend his own.

Perhaps the horrors he saw had sapped the will from him. Either way, he had been ready to die, to accept the end, only for the reigning of blows to suddenly stop.

Lock wracked his brain.

The attack stopped, but why?

He envisioned it now, lying prone, staring at the modelled ceiling, willing the nightmare to end.

He focused on the commotion that followed his sudden peace.

Arthur's tearful pleas, and Mother's screams, had made little impact on the antagonist.

That wasn't what Lock searched for.

It was the attacker's reaction to being interrupted.

It seemed so close to his grasp, and so familiar to him, but also so intangible.

Like a light through the dark, the answer surged with force into Lock's mind.

'*You saved me*,' Lock whispered. 'You pulled the killer off me.'

Flynn had turned his gaze to the window in Lock's silence, but he now snapped back to the moment.

'Aye, Lock. I pulled him off you. He was trying to kill you, after already cutting open... sorry.' Flynn cleared his throat.

'You never said? Why?'

'For the same reason you didn't tell Burroughs' men about your exploits with Benjy. It didn't seem... proper, to relish in it.'

But Lock wasn't finished. 'He *knew* you, Flynn. He knew who you were.'

'What do you mean?'

'He called you an Irish bastard.'

'Mother Mary. Lock, are you sure? Why don't I remember?'

'Perhaps because... you don't speak Dutch?'

Flynn leaned forward on the hard bench. 'How do you –'

'*Remember*? I don't know Flynn. I think that night is ingrained into my memory. I can recall details of that event I wish I could forget.'

'So, we're looking for a Dutch Rogue...'

'Or a Rogue who speaks Dutch.'

'True, Lock. But if a man swears in the heat of the moment, one expects that swear to be in his native language, unless he's showing off.'

'Also true.'

'*Shite*, that changes things.'

'This attacker knew who you were, but no one knew who *he* was? Surely that means... he knew the identity of the other masks... How does that happen?'

Flynn nodded, and signalled he was grappling with the same dilemma. 'It *doesn't* happen Lock, not on any of the other missions I've been on. We arrive, we meet with masks on, we all have the same information. We then plan who will do what. Nobody asks for names or more details about one another. We all go our separate ways when the job is done.'

Lock shifted his weight on the hard bench. He would need to stretch his legs soon.

'What did you do, after the job was done?'

Flynn sighed. 'I ran, Lock. I'd seen enough missions to know something had gone wrong. I ran as far from Frisia as I possibly could. I was caught eventually, of course, and then the... the interviews started.'

Lock stared at the coach's wooden ceiling, and relived the worst night of his life.

His brother's corpse was fresh.

It hurt to breathe through his broken nose.

His face was a bruised mess.

The damage confined him to bed for a week.

In that week, the whole world changed.

When he emerged from his room, he was the family failure. The boy who couldn't defend himself or his brother. The boy who wouldn't fire the musket when he'd had the chance. The boy who wouldn't save a life when it mattered most.

Lock cleared his throat. 'Is it possible that if my Father had listened to the Black Prince the first time, those men would never have shown up in the first place?'

The possibility that 1613 might not be his fault was irresistible.

'Lock, I don't know what your Father did, or didn't do. All I know is that I was told to be at your home, and so were six other men. Two of whom recently tried to kill us.'

'Two of whom are now dead,' Lock whispered.

'I don't like it, Lock, I don't like it at all.'

'It doesn't strike you as odd that all of a sudden, a wide range of things go wrong, and the usual rules are broken?'

Flynn became suddenly sombre. 'That is why I am afraid, Lock. And you should be too. If things are changing, and if the Black Prince's organisation truly is so compromised, then that means much of the known world could also be in danger.'

'In danger?'

'If the Black Prince's restraint was removed from the equation, or his organisation fell into the wrong hands, the power that could be wielded in the name of insidious ends...'

'We stopped the Raven's Rogues once, Flynn, and we will do it again if necessary.'

Flynn smiled gravely.

Perhaps he thought the very act of resistance to be hopeless. Perhaps he was contemplating a new plan to fight back against the Rogues. It was impossible to tell by his expression, so Lock did not try. The Irishman sighed into the silence.

'We've got many more miles to go Lock. I'll be recommending a stop in a few hours, but you should get some rest.'

Lock prepared to argue, but a quick glance at the pillow told him that his body would not object to a rejuvenating nap.

The interrogation had been surprisingly exhausting.

To aid in his rest, Flynn pulled covers down over the windows, and the coach's interior was suddenly cast into darkness.

The Irishman then gingerly opened the coach door, and swung himself into the seat beside the driver.

Lock latched onto their conversation for a moment, before the birdsong entered into his mind.

With additional clarity, would come deeper sleep.

Perhaps a conversation with Sir Horace Vere might bring a truly tranquil rest.

Perhaps the clawing nightmares might be banished once and for all.

- CHAPTER FORTY-FIVE -

M atthew Lock stared at the solid oak door.

There could be no doubt, this was the place.

After weeks of searching and misdirection, Sir Horace Vere residence in The Hague had finally been reached.

So why couldn't he rap his knuckles on it, and enter the building?

It was hardly a mystery.

Vere was not merely a source of information, he was also family – a precious commodity. Godfather was a title Lock had heard a great deal of, but the question remained, how far would Vere go to fulfil it?

Would he be generous, reserved, or furious?

The possibilities had moved Lock to ask Flynn to remain behind. The Irishman had returned to his old bolthole in the less savoury part of the city.

It was, Flynn insisted, free from masks, Rogues or any other of the Black Prince's men. Once the meeting with Vere was concluded, the Irishman agreed to go over a few more things before taking his leave.

It was early in the morning, very early, and The Hague was only beginning to stir. Behind him, carts of vegetables, seafood and butcher's meats were dragged or pushed. The smell reminded Lock that he had skipped breakfast. He'd barely had time to sit down once they'd arrived.

Following a shave – on Flynn's recommendation – Lock had changed his clothes and dunked his head in a barrel of cold water.

Seawater, the Irishman had insisted, was the best rejuvenator, particularly after a harsh fever.

Lock was confident that he'd finally beaten the illness. He felt as strong as he had when he'd first landed here a fortnight ago.

So, why did he now hesitate?

He heard Flynn's voice in his head.

'*You knock on that bastard door. Don't take no for an answer*', and the pep talk had fired him up at the time.

Yet, the closer he had gotten to the diplomatic centre of the city, and the closer he had gotten to Vere's residence, the more that confidence had ebbed away.

A small voice in the back of Lock's head told him to turn back.

Perhaps the only factor preventing this retreat was the look of scorn on the Irishman's face if he dared to do so.

Lock was wary of creating a scene, but the street was largely deserted, save for the merchants minding their own business, and preparing for another day.

He forced his hand onto the door. He forced his knuckles to rap against it. He forced himself to steady his breathing.

Now he just had to wait.

He rehearsed the speech which he had been planning since the coach's wheel had been replaced outside Cologne.

The Irishman had played the role of Vere, but really, he had played devil's advocate.

Lock smiled as he recalled Flynn's impossibly posh accent.

Then there was a creak behind the door, and Lock's smile vanished. He cleared his throat, puffed out his chest, and kept the vision of his parents front and centre.

Remember who you're doing this for.

Not just for you, but for your family name.

The heavy door heaved forward, and a servant's face greeted Lock on the other side.

Lock bowed slightly, before continuing in perfect Dutch. 'Good morning friend, I apologise for the trouble so early in the morning...'

The servant's confused face suggested that Lock's assumptions had not been correct. Lock switched to English, and the servant's face was suddenly transformed.

A welcoming smile formed on his fleshy face.

'Sir Vere is currently engaged in his duties, mister...'

'Lock. Matthew Lock. I believe –'

The servant's whole demeanour changed again. He practically jumped on the spot, before grasping Lock's sleeve, and pulling him into the doorway.

The door shut behind them.

Amidst a flurry of profuse apologies, which Lock worked to deflect, the servant led Lock into a reception room.

'Please, Mister Lock, make yourself comfortable. I will inform my master you have arrived. May we fetch you any refreshment? Tea? Perhaps an early morning tipple? My colleagues are at your disposal.'

Lock was bowled over by the attention.

Not even Locksville's servants had ever been this attentive, or warm. Mother used to joke that they had all been hired in a sale, and Father had lost the receipt.

'Thank you, I am perfectly fine.'

The servant bowed before making a slick exit. His light shoes slapped on the stone floor as he walked away.

Lock was now alone in an oak panelled room, no larger than Father's study. It was ornately decorated with wood carvings on the walls and skirtings, and the furniture was predictably plush.

Here it was, diplomacy in its essence.

Scarcely five minutes had passed, before the slapping feet returned. The servant pushed the light door aside, and bowed again before speaking.

'Mister Lock, Sir Vere is waiting for you in his study.'

Lock's heart jumped into his throat.

The servant left his presence so briskly that a slight breeze followed him.

Lock followed the servant quickly down a corridor with impossibly polished floors. The walls were adorned with paintings, which rushed past before Lock had a chance to take them in. Following an abrupt left turn, the servant paused outside another oak door.

'Mister Lock, you will find my master inside. I will leave you two alone. Please, if my colleagues can do anything for you, you need only ask.'

Lock now regretted turning down the liquid courage, unusual though the request may have been at this hour. Even after all he had done and seen, the prospect of meeting this man, this legend of Father's tales, was more terrifying than any masked Rogue.

Lock's expression may have betrayed some of his angst, as the servant paused.

'If I may, Sir, my master is eagerly looking forward to making your acquaintance. Indeed, Sir Vere has spoken of little else for the past week.'

It was a tactful way of easing one's nerves, and Lock smiled warmly at the servant for the gesture.

With a bow, the servant retreated, his feet slapped away, and Lock faced yet another door.

He exhaled quietly, before rapping his knuckles on its centre.

After a brief pause, a voice filtered through from the other side.

'Come in,' it said.

Another exhalation, louder this time.

Lock grasped the door handle and pushed.

The room he entered into was small and rectangular in shape. The space had been immaculately furnished, including a rosewood desk at the far end. Large maps hung on the walls, and Lock had to restrain himself from becoming sucked into them.

Sir Horace Vere stood, his hands behind his back, his head slightly bowed. A smile played on the man's face. He was perhaps a foot shorter than Lock, and appeared impressed by the height difference.

Lock restrained his shaky knees, and forced himself deeper into the room. As he came closer, Vere's smile spread, and he threw open his arms.

'*Godson*, what a pleasure to meet you at long last.'

He was sincere, warm, welcoming, and everything Lock had desperately hoped for.

His light brown hair hinted at a soft complexion, but there was a residual hardness in his brown eyes, a natural result of more than two decades of soldiering. His hair was beginning to turn, but was not quite grey. Vere's pointed chin was mostly obscured by a beard, which had itself escaped the taming of the razor.

Lock moved within inches of him. 'Godfather,' he managed to say.

Vere grasped his right hand and elbow for a warm handshake.

'Well, let me look at you! The last time I saw you, Matthew Lock, you were up to my knee!'

Lock couldn't find the words.

In truth he wished to embrace the man, as a Father did a son. Perhaps it was merely a symptom of the long journey, or perhaps it was a natural result of such a friendly reception.

'*Impressive*. Tall. Broad shoulders, very important for soldiering. And what's this?' Vere examined Lock's right hand. 'Callouses, from writing? You're a man of letters as well?' Vere shook his head, a touch of emotion lacing his voice. 'Your Father would be so proud to see you like this. Just as he'd always intended.'

Lock's eyes moistened, but he desperately blinked the tears away.

Vere just increased the intensity of his smile. 'You've been on quite the journey Matthew. I hear you've acquired something of a name for yourself. *Matchlock*, I believe they call you now?'

A surge moved through Lock's stomach. How had the embarrassing nickname followed him all the way to The Hague?

'Vere, Sir Vere... I...'

Vere held up a hand and placed it on Lock's right shoulder.

'Cease the formalities lad. Please, call me Horace. Or, call me Harry, if you prefer. My wife Mary prefers Harry. Never did like Horace as a name myself.'

Lock sighed, and his shoulders relaxed. 'Sorry... Harry. I have waited a *long* time to make your acquaintance.'

Vere nodded. 'That's partially my fault lad. I thought you were landing here with that embassy your Father had planned, so off I went from Frankenthal. I never imagined you would journey to Frankenthal to meet with *me*.'

'Father always used to mention you,' Lock said, as Vere retrieved a second chair from beside his desk. 'I thought that after... after what happened, you would be able to shed some light on the situation.'

Vere's face fell. 'I am... so very sorry for your loss, Matthew. Your Father was a good man. But even an evil man did not deserve that fate. And your Mother...' Vere shook his head.

'Harry, I had hoped you would know something about what happened. Have you –'

Lock stopped the question in response to Vere's shaking head.

'Believe me lad, I've spent the last fortnight trying to piece it together. I'm afraid all I have are several clues, but no solid answers. I've got my people working overtime on it. Rest assured, once something comes up, you'll be the first to know.'

Lock seated himself on the soft red armchair that Vere had produced, and Vere descended into his desk chair. The two men sat, perhaps inches apart. The room seemed to buzz with a nervous energy.

The legion of questions Lock had prepared.

The speech he had rehearsed.

All of it now forgotten in the face of Vere's reception.

Lock nodded and smiled. 'I have learned a great deal about the Black Prince in recent times, do you know if –'

Vere appeared to flinch at the very mention of the figure, and the expression caught Lock off guard.

'You must be careful, Matthew,' Vere cautioned. He gestured to the study's door. 'You met Redding, I suspect?'

'Your servant?'

Vere nodded. 'Redding has been with my household for as long as... well for as long I've had a household really. Do you know where I first met him?'

Lock shook his head.

'He was on the run, from the Black Prince's men, and he nearly collided with me at a market in Bristol.'

'The Black Prince has men in *Bristol*?'

Vere's body stiffened. 'The Black Prince has men everywhere, Matthew. Do not forget it. I scarcely think there are places, even in the New World, where a man can go to be free of his gaze.'

Lock's expression moved Vere to offer a calming hand.

'But, lad, the Black Prince did not kill your parents. His methods are underhanded, unethical, perhaps, but never so brutal or so brazen, and for a very simple reason.'

'It draws attention to him.'

Vere pointed with satisfaction. 'That's exactly right. He doesn't want lords or dukes or kings poking around in his business. He'd prefer to buy them out. He'd prefer to stay under everyone's noses, in the back of everyone's minds. Murder is his last resort, and certainly not murder like this.'

'I was told it could be Rogues.'

Vere's eyes widened. 'You've learned much then. Perhaps you know more than I do?'

Vere gestured to one of the maps on the wall.

'It is a beautiful map, Harry,' Lock said.

'Indeed it is lad, but I do not keep it in this room for its beauty alone.' Vere then stood up and walked a couple of paces, so that he was standing before it. 'This is a map of the continent, and goes as far as the borders of the Polish-Lithuanian Commonwealth.'

Lock allowed his eyes to fully absorb its contents.

Land was indicated in green, the rivers and seas in light blue. Borders were delineated in black, and around the map were black dots, to indicate cities of importance.

In among this detail was another factor.

Red pins had been placed at apparently random intervals, ranging from Italy, to Spain, to Scotland and to Denmark.

Vere cleared his throat.

'Those red pins, they denote occasions where the Black Prince's men have been active.'

Lock's eyes widened. The sheer scale of activity was immense. The confident talk of taking on both the Black Prince and the Rogues at once seemed to dissipate in the face of the mountainous challenge that lay ahead.

His eyes then latched onto another detail. Among the red pins was the occasional yellow pin. The yellow pins were less numerous, perhaps fewer than a third of the number of red pins.

Lock cleared his throat to ask the question.

'Yes, Lock. Before you ask. Those yellow pins refer to occasions where, I believe, Rogues were involved.'

Lock shook his head. 'That's a lot of Rogue activity.'

Vere placed his hand on his right shoulder. 'Indeed it is lad, and in the last year, I have had to place a great deal more yellow pins down than was customary.'

'The Rogues are becoming more active?'

Vere nodded. 'More active, and more daring, though I can't figure out why.'

Lock's eyes returned to the Netherlands. It appeared impossible that such a small corner of Europe could provide such an enormous headache for Spain, the greatest empire in the world. A yellow pin, placed in The

Hague, caused Lock's stomach to lurch.

'Harry... is that?'

Vere nodded gravely. 'I fear so, Matthew. That pin marks your parents' murder. I am *almost* convinced that Rogues were involved. As I was not certain, I didn't want to alarm you.'

'Not certain? Did you not see the destruction they caused to our house?'

Vere's blank expression sent a shiver down Lock spine.

'Vere... did you not see the house, in The Hague?'

'I finally plucked up the courage, perhaps a week ago.'

'And?'

'The place was pristine, Matthew. Absolutely pristine. Judging by your expression, that is... a bad thing?'

'The Rogues were there! They had ripped our home to pieces,'

Lock immediately regretted sharing. Vere abruptly removed his hand from Lock's shoulder.

'How do you know lad? Did you *see* them?'

How could he tell his godfather the truth? That he had entered his family's residence in The Hague, only to flee like a coward when faced with a room full of Rogues and blood.

Lock decided he had had enough of secrets. He sighed, and rubbed the corners of his eyes with his right hand.

'I saw them, Harry. When I first got here. I went to investigate my parents' home. Let myself in, and there they were.'

Vere gasped. 'Gracious me Matthew, thank heavens you escaped!'

'I know, but I...'

Vere clasped his right shoulder again. 'You were wise to escape, lad. If they'd known who you were, they would have killed you.'

'I felt like a coward,' Lock whispered, his voice partially breaking.

'*No*,' Vere said. 'A coward would not have travelled the length of the Rhine and back again just to learn the truth. A coward would have stayed in England, and buried his head in the sand.'

'I ran from danger when my family's honour was at stake, just as a coward would.'

'Listen to me now Matthew, a coward would never have gone into the depths of the underground to save a man he'd never met. A coward would not have led so many Germans to glory on the battlefield. A coward would not have rid the world of such a vile man.'

'You are aware? Sir, I can explain.'

'I read Burroughs' letter, Lock. Apparently, you have trouble following orders. Burroughs and I often disagree. The man is... how shall I put this? He is regularly full of hot air. But we both agree on this, that you, Matthew Lock, are not a coward.'

Lock nodded his head.

The simple act belied the immense weight which had been lifted from his shoulders.

He was not a coward.

If even such accomplished commanders of men thought so, it surely must be true.

Vere smiled warmly at him, and grasped more firmly at his shoulder. Lock ran his eyes over the map again, taking in the breadth and scope of the Black Prince's operations.

'He's even been to *Ireland*,' Lock said.

Vere furrowed his eyebrows. 'Indeed, lad. I hear the Irish make some of his best agents. Not much else for them to do.'

What would Vere think of Flynn O'Toole?

Lock did not wish to find out. Yet.

'Right, lad. Judging by your stature I'd say you're permanently hungry. By my watch, it's nearly breakfast. What say you to some belly cheer?'

Lock's stomach growled, as though on cue. The mere thought of a proper meal was irresistible.

'Thank you, Harry. It would be a dream not to eat from the saddle.'

Vere laughed. 'Hunger is the price we pay for serving King and Country, eh lad? That's why it's important to stock up when you get a chance. Mary is likely there already. She's dying to meet you. Shall we?'

Vere gestured with his right arm to the door, and Lock began to walk towards it. As it opened, Lock's nose filled with smells that returned him to breakfast at Locksville, his favourite time of the day by a country mile.

If he followed his nose and squinted, Lock could almost pretend he was back in Dorset, in the tranquillity of the countryside, in a time before the Black Prince.

There could be no going back to a time before the Black Prince.

Everything was different, and would be forever.

His old life was over.

He was the head of the Lock family now, but he was very far from alone. Lock silently thanked his parents for choosing Vere as his godfather.

For the first time in a long time, Lock was at home.

- CHAPTER FORTY-SIX -

The meal had filled a hole in his belly, and the conversation had filled a hole in his heart.

Horace and Mary Vere had treated Lock as though he were a long-lost son. Lock had blushed when Mary asked of love interests, before Horace had tut-tutted at her. They seemed to derive great enjoyment from the very act of feeding him, which was perfect for Lock, as he was eating to make up for lost time.

With a wave at the servers, trays arrived with a wide range of meats and an even wider variety of breads.

One particular item, a lemon sweetbread, wrapped itself around Lock's senses, and he had to push the tray away to stop himself from eating the entire stock.

Halfway through the meal, Lock learned a sad truth, that the couple had been unable to have children of their own.

Mary's declaration that Lock would be welcome here, or at the family's home in London, was sincerely meant. She had grasped his hand warmly when they had first met, insisting she was his godmother as much as Horace was his godfather, and she smiled with her whole face.

But there was a sadness behind her eyes.

A sadness that came from repeated disappointments, and long stretches of time without her husband by her side.

After Mary excused herself for morning prayers, Lock was brought to an annex off the dining room. Here, Vere explained, his guests would smoke tobacco pipes and drink coffee while they discussed matters of business.

Lock was told to sit in the seat where the Prince of Orange had once sat. Vere even promised to arrange a meeting with Maurice of Orange at one point, a prospect Lock could only have dreamed of.

Sir Horace Vere was like a walking encyclopaedia of information and memories. Once he settled into his company, Lock let loose with a barrage of questions.

Vere's experience of the 1600 Battle of Nieuwpoort, where massed musket volleys were used to devastating effect against the Spanish for the first time, was a favourite topic.

Another favourite was the Siege of Ostend, where Vere had been in command for a time. The siege had been a three-year ordeal, with eye-watering losses for the Spanish and Dutch.

And then, the conversation turned to the ongoing war in Germany. Vere's countenance quickly changed. The jovial, generous commander had evidently suffered through some bitter disappointments.

'The Duke of Buckingham was a fool,' Vere insisted. 'The Palatine ambassador chose *me* to command, and Buckingham withdrew his support from the venture as a consequence. He sulked, like a child, when the lives of good men were at stake.'

Lock hesitated to comment on the status of men so far above his own station, but Vere's demeanour relaxed him.

'Buckingham, the Prince's friend?'

'He poisoned the Prince of Wales against me, and he ruined the prospects for our expedition. We had perhaps a third of the effectives we required to get the job done, thanks to his abandonment. Even with English honour at stake, the fool couldn't see past his own ego.'

'The Duke sent a shipment of new linens to Frankenthal.'

'He did, Matthew. Smug bastard wanted to claim he had made a contribution, even though he knew how perfectly useless the contribution was.'

'I managed to put his contribution to good use,' Lock said with a smirk.

Vere chuckled, and wagged his finger at Lock. 'So I heard. Most commendable! It is so rare that we soldiers get to do something good for the poor children. But they are our future, Matthew, they will be here after we are gone. We *must* take care of them. That was a damn good thing you did.'

The burst of attention moved Lock's cheeks to redden.

Lock sipped the black contents from the delft cup and winced. Coffee, it seemed, was more favourable as an aroma than as a drink.

Vere chuckled. He had insisted the taste would grow on him.

Lock pressed for more details. At long last, he was in a position to get some answers.

'Is His Majesty truly so preoccupied in arranging a marriage between his heir and the Spanish Infanta?'

Vere held up his hands, as though captured by the same frustration.

'His Majesty scarcely keeps his eyes on the wider picture, however blessed is his name. He must know the Spanish will never restore his daughter and son-in-law to the Palatinate, regardless of whom Prince Charles marries.'

Even with his knowledge of European affairs, Lock occasionally struggled to keep pace with the varied names, connections and issues at stake in the German War. Vere navigated them all, as if no volume of detail was beyond his comprehension.

'Should Frederick have sought the Bohemian Crown?' Lock dared to ask. 'Should he not have been content with his Electoral title, and possession of the Palatinate?'

Vere gave a neutral shrug. 'I don't believe it matters much Matthew. The Holy Roman Emperor leapt at the chance to welcome the Spanish into the Rhine, to surround the French on all sides, and to bottle up the Dutch. It is all very convenient, if you ask me.'

'What will happen if the English fail to hold Frankenthal?'

Vere flashed him a sympathetic look. 'Frankenthal is lost, I'm afraid. As are Mannheim, Heidelberg, and any of the Elector's other possessions. Mark my words, the Spanish will stand in control of the Rhine by the end of next year.'

'And then?'

'And then,' Vere half chuckled. 'Then we will see where His Majesty's loyalties truly lie. Do they reside with his Protestant dependents, or with the fantasy of a Spanish Match?'

Lock did not share how sick he felt that so many lives had been lost for no material gain. General Burroughs' honour may have been retrieved by the defiance, but the Spanish would overwhelm English defences all the same. And what of von Salm's Germans? Where would they go now that their underground warrens had been exposed?

Vere then presented a question of his own to Lock. 'The King fancies himself a peacemaker, a great mediator. Can you fathom it?'

Lock scoffed and shook his head.

Vere nodded in satisfaction, and refilled his cup with more coffee as he spoke. 'His Majesty places too much stock in his own influence, and not enough in his agents. Would the Twelve Years Truce have been formalised without your Father's involvement? I do doubt it.'

It was a convenient opportunity for focusing the conversation back onto Lock's parents. Vere surprised him with a wealth of information, delivered as though Lock was already familiar with it.

'Your Father was a stellar soldier. He just needed a little refinement. I trained him for a time, did you know that?'

'You did?'

'Indeed, for much of the 1590s. Plenty to be doing in that decade. Gracious, can scarcely believe it was so long ago.'

'What did you teach him?'

'Oh, Matthew, you don't want to know about that...'

'Harry, I do, I really do!' Lock nearly flung his coffee cup across the room in excitement. The cup's small handle stuck on his large index finger, and Vere suppressed a laugh at the sight.

Vere then made a face, as though reasoning that the information would do no harm either way.

'He said his first taste of action was in 1588. A dark time for sure, particularly if you had no taste for the navy, or any desire to fight the Irish...'

Lock certainly did not wish to hear of the Anglo-Irish conflict that had ended with Flynn's family, among many others, being exiled from Ulster. He prodded Vere forward.

'He signed up for service in the Netherlands. That was Her Majesty's other great theatre, but it had a steep learning curve. Would you believe, he brought his family's longbow with him? *A longbow*, at a siege? Can you imagine it? But he was far from alone in that. We had to teach him how to fight, and I'd wager we did a pretty good job.'

'He served under you a long time?'

Vere refilled his cup with more of the steaming, black liquid, and Lock politely refused a top up.

'Indeed. By Nieuwpoort, so... July 1600, Charles Lock was one of my best men. The only man better was, I reckon, his best friend.'

Lock sat back in his chair. 'His *best friend*?'

'Indeed lad, every soldier has one. Charles' favoured comrade was a pious, grisly fellow by the name of John Louis.'

'John Louis...' Lock turned the name over, but it didn't ring any bells.

'Indeed, a real sinewy man. I hear he's mellowed in his old age though.'

'He's still alive?'

'*Alive*? Lad, John Louis is the stadtholder of Frisia. He's probably the third or fourth most important figure in the House of Orange.'

'Can I meet him?' the directness of the question surprised Lock, as it did Vere.

'Perhaps. I can try and arrange a meeting if you wish. He may do it for me as a favour.' Vere then seemed to dwell on something, his face became drawn, and he stared into his steaming cup for a few moments.

'What's wrong Harry?'

'Sorry, to harp on about it Matthew, but your parents' murder. The sheer randomness of it. Perhaps it wasn't random after all.'

Lock's heart raced. 'What do you mean?'

Again, Vere hesitated. 'Lad... there's... there's something you should know about your Father.'

Lock stopped breathing for a moment.

'He was something of a rebel, back in his youth. He and John Louis, the two of them were inseparable. Before I ground them down into better soldiers, they had their share of adventures. Not all those adventures were entirely... honourable.'

'What are you saying?'

'The Rebel and the Prince, that's what they called themselves. It was clever too. Charles was always clever like that. He being the rebel, and John Louis being a Prince of Orange. They got a third man, a captain, I believe. Augustus Frank.'

Lock could barely contain his excitement. 'Frank was there at my birth, he's a dear family friend. He's in Locksville now, guarding the family interests.'

'He's an impressive man, *a rare good man*, your Father used to always say.'

Lock found that he suddenly missed Captain Frank terribly.

'They used to call themselves the Embassy, if you can believe it. The

Rebel, the Prince and the Captain, each man a specialist in his own craft. They recruited others as well. A Frenchman, I believe, who was a master of swords.'

The information was like music to Lock's ears. 'What did they do?'

'Like all soldiers of fortune, they made their way in the world. I used to hear stories about what the Embassy had done, but I reckon many were fables.'

'*Fables?*' Lock couldn't hide his disappointment.

'Ah, don't be discouraged lad. A man's reputation is everything. Where would we be if we couldn't embellish that reputation from time to time?'

'What happened to the Embassy, in the end?'

'At some point, I think it all got too much for them, living up to that reputation. Poor John Louis got a terrible wound in the face at Ostend, damn near lost his nose. He settled into the life of a stadtholder after that.'

'And my Father?'

'Well, as you know, he settled down and married your Mother, and here you are.'

'You think... you think the Embassy may have done something, something that led to his death?'

'Do I think your Father wronged many men? I suspect he did, as we all did in our time. Do I think he wronged a man extensively enough to die as he did? Certainly not.'

'*Revenge?* You think someone killed my parents for revenge?'

Vere shook his head, apparently regretting his loose tongue. 'I don't know lad, but I know someone who might know.'

'Who?' Lock nearly fell off the edge of his chair.

'I would like you to meet with a man named Rudolf Macht. He was –'

'*Macht?*'

It then occurred to Lock that he couldn't tell Vere how he knew the name, without admitting the unsavoury way in which he had extracted the information. Nor had Vere yet been told about the other mission, to bring the perpetrators of 1613 to justice.

Vere seemed puzzled by the interruption and then the sudden silence, but he resumed.

'Yes... Macht was a member of the Embassy at one point, but I fear things ended badly in that relationship.'

'Why?'

'Your Father always said he regretted how things ended with him, but Macht was special. He was the master of letters for the Embassy's operations. If there's a whiff of information about what happened to your parents, it will have reached him by now.'

The coincidence was incredible.

Too incredible.

It could not be coincidental that Father's master of letters had been replaced in 1613. Had he known of the operation in advance, and refused to join in? Had he been involved with the Black Prince? How deeply if so?

Of all the fantastic tales and pearls of wisdom that had filled Lock's young ears, never had the Embassy or Rudolf Macht been among them. This in itself was concerning.

'If those Rogues killed my Father – perhaps for something the Embassy did – then Captain Frank and John Louis could both be in danger as well...'

'The thought has recently occurred to me,' Vere said, his face drawn into a frown.

'Then I must meet immediately with this Prince.'

Vere held up a cautionary hand. '*Easy*, lad. He doesn't have time for small fry like us. He also doesn't go by that name any longer. I suspect a that only a select few know of his adventurous past. He'd surely like to keep it that way, having built a reputation as one of the most pious, upright scions of the House of Orange.'

'But is it possible that he may know something, about what happened to my Father?'

'It is possible. It is also possible you'll be wasting your time.'

Vere walked to the corner of the small reception room. He put his hands on the long table where a number of papers rested, and uncurled scripts awaited his examination.

'So I will meet with Macht?'

Vere nodded, turning slightly back to Lock. 'I think that would be wise. I'll warn John Louis of what has happened to your parents. I am sure he'll be devastated, but he can at least make preparations to protect himself.'

'And how do I find Macht?'

'That... that is a difficult matter.'

'How do you mean?'

'Macht is infamously difficult to find Matthew. I suspect he may have fallen foul of the wrong people. He has no fixed abode, so tracking him down will be difficult, but not impossible.'

'Where should I start?'

Vere raised his hand. 'Not to worry, I'll get my men on it.'

'Harry, you are going above and beyond for me, is there anything I can do for you in return?'

Vere nodded at the question, but did not answer it. With his back to Lock, he placed his hands on his hips.

'There is something I'd like to discuss with you. Something unrelated to all this.'

'There is?'

'You have done remarkably well for a recent graduate.'

'Thank you.'

'Indeed, I dare say Charles would be immensely proud. All those years of practice paid off, eh? I heard you took down ten men with a single musket.'

Lock's face became flushed. 'You do me a great kindness, Harry.'

'But there is nothing quite like an apprenticeship.'

'An apprenticeship?'

'Yes, lad. Someone to show you how to harness and leverage those skills. Someone to prepare you for difficult situations. Someone to instil within you the confidence necessary for the career you want.'

'Is that someone... you?'

Vere turned slowly around. 'I trained your Father. Let me train you. For the next two years I will –'

'*Two years?*' Lock couldn't hide his dismay.

'You won't be confined to The Hague the entire time, lad. Rest assured, you'll be travelling, where necessary, but you'll also be learning from me. As you do, I'll provide for you. You can stay in my lodgings, eat my food, even wear my clothes if you wish.'

'That sounds like quite the opportunity.'

'And it gets better, Lock. Would you be interested in meeting Frederick V, the Elector Palatine?'

Lock's mouth fell open. 'Harry, you couldn't possibly –'

'Oh, but I could Matthew. Like I said, you will learn from me, and part of learning means meeting the brightest sparks in this war.'

'I could meet him now?'

Vere waved away the suggestion. 'You haven't heard the rest of my pitch, Matthew.'

'Oh.'

'You will go where I go, if I need you to, so that you can see what this life requires. It would be a similar experience to the last fortnight. Except this time, you'd have me to watch over you. I'll introduce you to my contacts, not as extensive a network as the Black Prince, but we get by. My people will protect you from the Black Prince. I'll make sure your loved ones are protected too.'

Lock tilted back his head and pursed his lips. 'I'm still waiting for the downside, Harry. Father always told me to be wary of offers that sounded too good to be true.'

Vere nodded. 'And that was sage advice. I will not mince words lad. I will work you hard. You will earn your keep. There is also one other thing.'

Lock grimaced. 'Yes?'

'Stay out of Germany. At least until next year.'

'But, Harry... My parents...'

'I loved your parents, Matthew. They were very dear to me. I know you are under no obligation to heed my advice, but Charles gave me this responsibility as your godfather. He would haunt my soul for all eternity if I allowed you to romp across Europe while the war was in full swing.'

'It will hardly be safer next year.'

'On the contrary, it will, because the Spanish will be in control of the region then. An occupation is always safer than a war, Matthew.'

'But how will I find Rudolf Macht, if I'm stuck in The Hague?'

Vere smiled. 'I mentioned the Elector Palatine? I have reason to believe that Rudolf Macht serves his interests. One thing about Macht which hasn't changed – he's still a determined enemy of the Habsburgs.'

'Where is he now?'

'As I said, Macht has no fixed abode, so he could be anywhere. Certainly at the moment, he'll be in hiding.'

Lock's expression moved Vere to jolly him along.

'Cheer up now Matthew. It's only to be expected. The Elector Palatine's allies are scattered after all. I'm sure you have heard of the recent losses? Such is the rhythm of war. Next year they intend to launch a new campaign.'

'And Macht will be easier to find, as he'll be among their ranks?'

'Precisely. You should know that you aren't alone in this investigation any longer, Matthew. There's a long list of people who want justice for your parents.'

'Thank you, Harry, though I must confess that all this waiting will be very difficult.'

'Trust me Matthew, this is the better course. Otherwise, you'll be sliding all over the Rhineland with nary a scrap of information to guide you. Wait for the dust to settle on this year, then next year, when the Elector Palatine raises his head above the parapet, you will introduce yourself.'

Lock considered the advice. 'What is he like?'

Vere's expression then changed. It was full of emotion. 'He's... a good man, Lock. A few years your senior, but like you, has a good head on his shoulders. I would say he's also a good ruler, a good husband to Princess Elizabeth, and a good Christian.'

'He sounds quite unlike the caricatures I have seen.'

'In another lifetime, perhaps, Frederick V would be among the Rhineland's greats. But alas, he chose the path of war, and now his people suffer.'

'The Rhinelanders, they did not all seem overly fond of him.'

'I am not surprised. Their prince chose another crown over them. He rushed to Bohemia without sufficient care for the consequences.'

'I thought you said he was a good man?'

'Good men make mistakes, Matthew. I do worry that Frederick's mistake may cost us all dearly, but perhaps there was no escaping it. Perhaps it was only a matter of time before the Habsburgs pushed matters into a great war.'

'You sound torn.'

Vere smiled wearily. 'I am torn, Matthew. For decades I've watched wars unfold. Once your Father helped the Dutch and Spanish make their truce, I truly believed that I might enjoy a career in peacetime, at least for a while.

But the wars have never ceased. And now, the greatest war of our lifetimes has arrived.'

'It is surely just another German war. Was there not one like it a decade ago?' A faint memory returned to Lock of a succession war in the heart of Germany, fought over duchies and microstates whose names always escaped him.

'This is different Matthew. There are too many issues at stake for either side to roll over this time. And even if Frederick is overwhelmed, his allies cannot accept the total defeat of his forces. They certainly cannot accept the total triumph of the Habsburgs.'

'It just doesn't seem right, to abandon the Rhinelanders like that.'

'We can't help them now. The Rhinelanders will not be the last victims of this war, Matthew.

'Can we stop it? Can we reduce the suffering of the people?' Lock couldn't help blurting out the question. Walter's adopted family, squeezed into the pitiful hut, returned to him vividly.

'If you wish to stop the suffering, you must stop the war. If you wish to stop the war, one side must be beaten. So you must decide, Matthew, which side do you fight for?'

'Surely I must fight for Frederick's side? I am meeting him next year and serving in his army, am I not?'

Vere shook his head. His smile was more mischievous this time.

'Not so, Matthew. As you will learn, there are many mercenaries in the field from all nations. Many men take decades to choose a side, and they chop and change in the meantime. But money can only push men so far. At some point, an issue more important than coin will have to enter the equation.' Vere leaned his head back and breathed deeply.

Lock cleared his throat. 'I think, at the moment at least, I want to help Frederick's cause, and I want to help the Dutch.'

Vere chuckled at the enthusiasm. 'The underdog casts a noble profile. But, if we want to fight the Spanish, and if we want to beat them, we'll have to do so in the most sensible theatre.'

Lock looked around him in rapid bursts. '*Here*? You want to fight the Spanish here? In The Hague?'

Vere shook his head. 'The Dutch are a remarkable people, Matthew. The Spanish will never get within striking distance of The Hague, Amsterdam, or any of the other major towns. But this land, *Dutch land*, is the place to fight them.'

'Are you sure?'

'Matthew, the Spanish have been fighting the Dutch since 1568. The greatest, most powerful empire in the world, and they couldn't stamp out a rebellion from a band of merchants and cattle farmers in the soggiest corner of Europe. The Dutch must be doing something right, and the key is in their defences.'

'But the Dutch have lost ground. Spinola is on the march, and he has them virtually surrounded.'

Vere nodded gravely. 'The war is not going well for them now. The Twelve Years Truce was more a curse than a blessing for the Dutch people, and they started fighting amongst themselves. When the war resumed, they were slow to react. But that will change.'

'What if it doesn't?'

Vere placed his hands on his hips again. 'Trust me, Matthew. If the Spanish flag ever flies over The Hague again, I swear on my ancestors I will climb up the flagpole myself, tear it down, and devour it in front of the new Spanish magistrate.'

Lock was drawn to Vere's eyes. They sparkled with determination. Vere believed every word he said. After more than twenty years in Dutch service, fighting the Spanish enemy, his word was good enough for Lock.

'Alright,' Lock said. 'You've convinced me. I will serve your apprenticeship.'

Vere slapped his right thigh. 'This *is* well met! We will begin our training next week. I'll ready the ruby room for the duration of your stay.'

'Harry...' Lock hesitated, but the question was always worth asking. 'While I stay here, can I be permitted visitors? I would dearly love to see Arthur, and perhaps Captain Frank.'

Vere paused his walk to the door. He turned back to Lock, and grinned widely. 'How convenient then Matthew, that I recently penned a letter requesting he and Captain Frank join us here for a spell.'

Lock shot to his feet and surrounded Vere in his embrace.

'Thank you,' Lock whispered.

He didn't care if it was considered ungentlemanly or somewhat uncouth to embrace one's friend, and evidently, neither did Vere.

He patted Lock on the back, and pressed his hands into his shoulders with a chuckle.

'Let's make you at home, shall we?'

- CHAPTER FORTY-SEVEN -

The street was seedy, and the appeal non-existent.

Men scarcely walked here after dark, or even during the day, if they could help it. For a woman to be spotted here would mean the death of her reputation. Its taverns were the haunt of criminals, many of whom had fled to join the navy in recent years.

It was that or the noose.

It certainly looked like an inconspicuous enough bolthole.

A small door to the right of a rundown vegetable shop served as the entrance. The smell of rotten turnips haunted Lock's nose, but it was better than sewage, which the Irishman claimed his old residence stank of.

The street was deserted, save for an optimistic murder of crows that had gathered near the front of the unopened vegetable market. Lock waved them away as he approached the small door.

He wrapped his knuckles on it, in the rhythm Flynn had instructed, and within a few minutes, he heard rumbling down the stairs, and the door was cracked open.

Flynn nodded at him, and opened the crack wider for Lock to squeeze through. Then the door was closed, locked and double bolted.

Flynn bounced up the stairs, and Lock followed behind him.

The lodgings were simple. A single large room which had been fitted as a bedroom. A bucket in the corner, and two cots side by side, laden with a clump of linen sheets.

A small desk with a rustic wooden chair had been moved up to the window, so that the man of letters could write while taking in his first storey view. Though the view was hardly much to write home about.

'It's a shithole, I know,' Flynn said with a smile. 'But nobody's found me here yet, and I've been here a year.'

Lock shuddered involuntarily, but sat down on the cot. Flynn took the chair attached to the desk.

'Was he much use, old Vere?'

'He offered me a position, Flynn,' Lock said. He'd intended to deliver the news more carefully, but it had just tumbled out.

'A position? A *paid* position?'

'I mean, I get meals and lodgings. In return, he's agreed to train me. To show me how he operates. To introduce me to his friends. To show me how to be the best soldier-statesman I can be.'

Lock held his breath, and prepared for a sarcastic comment or critique. He scanned the Irishman's face for a reaction. There may have been a brief flash of disappointment, but if it was present, it was quickly extinguished.

'It sounds like a phenomenal opportunity, Lock, really. You should take it.'

'The position is for two years.'

'That's... that's great. You'd benefit from a mentor like Vere.'

'He was a mine of information. He mentioned a lot of names. Have you heard of John Louis?'

'That dry bastard? Fearsome scar, don't stare at it too long.'

'Apparently he and my Father used to be friends. They called themselves the Embassy.'

Flynn's eyes narrowed. '*Your* Father, was part of the Embassy?'

'It seems he was a founding member.' Lock did his best to hide his pride.

'*Mother Mary.*'

'What is it?'

'The Black Prince used to send us against the Embassy's men.'

'You *fought* them?'

Flynn waved his hand, as though wiping the suggestion away.

'We didn't *fight*, on a battlefield, but we often found ourselves on opposite sides to Embassy men. They always seemed to... get in the way.'

'Well, this does change things.'

'How so?'

'Vere thinks the Black Prince, or perhaps the Raven and his Rogues, may be after the Embassy's founding members. My Father, John Louis and

Captain Frank.'

'So, will you be carted off to Leeuwarden shortly, to tell His Grace the news?'

'John Louis will be informed by letter that he's in danger. Scions of the House of Orange have sufficient resources to protect themselves when needs be.'

'Makes sense. So, where will you go?'

'To find Rudolf Macht.'

'Vere mentioned Macht?'

'Yes. He wasn't just replaced in 1613. He was also the Embassy's man of letters.'

'You're joking.'

'I wish I was Flynn. But it is starting to make sense. These connections cannot be coincidental.'

'When does your investigation begin?'

Lock cleared his throat. 'In the spring of 1623.'

'*Next year?*' Flynn was aghast.

'I reacted the same way.'

'What will you do in the meantime?'

'In the meantime, it seems I'll be busy with my apprenticeship.'

Flynn sucked his teeth and leaned on the hard wooden desk with his right elbow. He turned his body in the chair, and gazed out the dirty window.

'Probably for the best if you lay low for a while Lock. Maybe by next year, the Rogues will have calmed down a bit.'

'Vere also said that the war would be less complex by next year. The Spanish seizing the Palatinate should simplify matters.'

'He's probably right. Don't count the Elector Palatine out yet though. I hear Frederick is planning a campaign for next year.'

'Perhaps he'll want some company.'

Flynn scoffed. 'You, and the Elector Palatine, off on a merry adventure?'

'As far as Vere knows, Rudolf Macht serves the Elector Palatine. They're unlikely to be far from each other if that's the case. Anyway, after Vere's training, perhaps I'll have more to offer.'

'You have plenty to offer as is, Lock,' Flynn stared out the window as he said it, and Lock did his best to hide his reaction. He cleared his throat.

'What will *you* do?'

'*Me*? Don't worry about me Lock. I have a country to return to. I also need to report back to the Black Prince. He should be informed that Fabio and Captain Ricardo were Rogues.'

'What about the 1613 investigation?'

'I'll be sure to let the Black Prince know that his orders were intercepted. Perhaps he'll set me back to that task again, though it's difficult to say.'

'And what if he doesn't?'

Flynn shrugged. 'I don't know what to tell you Lock. I work for the Black Prince. I go where he commands.'

'What if the Black Prince commanded you to kill me, would you work for him then?'

'*Lock...*'

'Come on Flynn, you can't work for that bastard anymore.'

'Why do you care who I work for? I'm unlikely ever to see you again after today.'

Lock fell silent, as the Irishman stared back out the window.

If Flynn left, he'd never find James' killer.

Flynn was one of the few people in the known world who knew more about 1613 than he did. The only person that knew more than the Irishman was James' killer.

If he focused on his parents, he'd be failing his brother's memory. He could not get justice for his whole family, certainly not without Flynn's help.

The conflict was unbearable.

Despite every effort, bitter, angry tears had begun to emerge. Anger at the injustice. Anger at having to choose. Anger at the prospect of losing a potential friend.

'Oh dear... *Lock*,' the Irishman said in a half gasp, when he noted the tears gliding down his cheeks. The awkwardness seemed almost too much for him.

Lock wiped a tear away with a brisk swipe of his hand. He stood up from Flynn's cot, his fists clenched, unsure what to say, but certain he had to say something.

'That night ruined my life, Flynn. And that bastard who did it, whoever he is, has gotten away with it. That... that does not sit right with me. It can't sit right with you either. I don't want to have to choose between justice for my brother or justice for my parents. I can't do it.'

The Irishman turned away, redirecting his gaze out the window into the busy street below. There were few pleasant sights to take in from this fetid corner of the city. A girl screamed, and another laughed. A dog barked. Horse hooves clip-clopped on stone.

Still staring out the window, Flynn exhaled deeply.

'I saw him, you know, preparing his boat on the jetty, just a few hours after he'd killed your brother. The rat bastard was vulnerable. I could have shot him, or challenged him. Even pushed him into the river. Perhaps he couldn't swim? Either way, I know the Black Prince would have rewarded me for killing a Rogue. But I did nothing... I ran Lock, I ran from him and I've been running ever since.'

Lock fixed his eyes at the side of Flynn's head.

The Irishman briefly glanced back at him, before turning his face away. Flynn's head was bowed, in the same manner as when Lock had first learned of his betrayal in Mannheim's church.

'Flynn, if you hadn't acted that night, if you'd stood aside like the rest of them, then my parents... my parents would have buried two sons. Perhaps even more. I am thankful that there was at least one man of honour among you.'

Flynn shook his head. 'It is not good enough. My Father held me to a higher standard. I have failed him. I failed you. I...' the Irishman's voice broke, and he placed his head in his hands.

Heavy breaths were forced through the gaps in his filthy fingers. He couldn't bear for the world to look at him.

'Do you want my forgiveness?' Lock asked in a low voice.

Flynn slowly raised his head up from his hands, his eyes shining. 'I don't deserve it. You have no idea what else I've done.'

'I know what you can do, *now*, Flynn,' Lock said, a hint of smile growing in the corner of his mouth.

Flynn picked up on the expression. His dark eyebrows were scrunched into the middle of his forehead. 'What can I do, other than return to Ireland?'

'Return to Ireland Flynn, but once you've had your fill of the place, I want you to come back next year.'

'*Why?*'

'Excluding yourself, Captain Ricardo and Fabio, how many other men took part in 1613?'

Flynn considered the question carefully. 'We were a party of seven, so that leaves four. Four men remaining. I don't know their names, but I remember them being there.'

'The Frisian Four. I like the sound of that.'

'Lock what are you –'

'*Come with me*, Flynn. Come with me and we'll track these men down together. *That's* how you redeem yourself. That's how you earn my forgiveness.'

'*What?*'

'We'll bring them to justice. We'll also make the Black Prince happy, will we not, if we take down some of his Rogues? I don't have to like him or trust him to benefit from his power. Perhaps if we make him happy enough, he'll give us more information, and I'll be able to find out what happened to my parents.'

Flynn just stared at him. 'Lock, you're barely out of... You're not even... I...' the excuses were verbalised, but none of them finished. 'God's guts, I should have left you in von Salm's forest.'

'I'm going on this journey with or without you. I would... I would rather have you with me.'

Flynn cupped his chin into his right hand, and partially stroked the black stubble that had emerged in the last few days. He turned slightly a few times, as if at war with different sides of his brain; one logical, the other emotional. Finally, he glanced back at Lock's expectant stare, and let out a frustrated groan.

'*Alright*, Lock, alright then. Let's track the bastards down. But you can't tell Vere about what we're doing. If he suspects you're helping the Black Prince, in any way, he'll kick you out onto the street.'

'I know.'

'I don't know how, but you have to keep the 1613 investigation separate from that of your parents. Can you do that?'

Lock nodded. 'I can. I swear it.'

'Risking your neck for a bloody Englishman. *O'Toole what are you doing?*' Flynn lamented, but the lament was hollow. A smile began spreading on the Irishman's face. It was a mischievous smile, there could be no doubt about it.

Lock couldn't help but reciprocate. The two men locked eyes for a few moments, before each turned abruptly away.

Flynn coughed to clear his throat and the air. 'So, what do I call you then? *Matchlock*... is that really what you're going by now?'

Lock grinned.

'Call me Matthew. My friends call me Matthew.'

MATTHEW LOCK WILL RETURN...

Now that you've finished your first Matchlock book...

If you enjoy this book , please consider giving it an honest review wherever you get your books from. If you enjoy this book , please consider giving it an honest review wherever you get your books from.

Reviews are the ***lifeblood*** of books like these, and really do make the difference between people ignoring this book, or reading it and enjoying it (hopefully) just like you!

If you wish to keep up to date with all things Matchlock, including behind the scenes details, fascinating facts about the Thirty Years' War, and special offers, make sure you become a Matchlock Messenger by clicking here:
https://www.subscribepage.com/matchlockmessengers

For everything else *Matchlock* related, see our website
www.matchlockbooks.com

HISTORICAL NOTE

The Thirty Years War was in its infancy by the time Matthew Lock landed on the continent in spring 1622. Then, it was merely a German War, between the forces of the Habsburgs, and the forces allied to Frederick, the Elector Palatine.

Sir Horace Vere's observations would prove correct. There was much more at stake in *this* German War.

The Elector Palatine, Frederick V, had already suffered several devastating military defeats, yet he felt unable to submit to his Emperor, Ferdinand II. He was also wholly unwilling to admit that his play for the Bohemian Crown had been ill-judged.

Instead, Frederick presented his struggle as one of for the heart and soul of the Holy Roman Empire. It was an attractive presentation, if disputed. The key point was that this stance kept Frederick's resistance alive long enough for external actors to become involved. These external actors included his father-in-law, King James, and Frederick's uncle, King Christian IV of Denmark. Once this intervention occurred, the German War would cease being merely a German War.

But this is all to come in Matthew Lock's world.

I thought it would be useful for the reader if I made a few notes here on the accuracy or inaccuracy of certain characters and events.

I should begin with the obvious target. There was no Georg von Salm, and no underground village in the forest south of Manheim. I was inspired to write about these things when I visited Malta, and noted the sheer extent of the caves which had been cut into the countryside, to help the population escape Axis bombing during WW2. No tongueless guides wandered these caves. At least, I didn't see any...

Other fictional characters include Diego de la Barca, his secretary Luis Romera, his illegitimate son Gaston Phillipe, Captain Augustus Frank, Joseph Gage, Prince John Louis of Nassau and some others sprinkled in to spice up the narrative. A full list of characters can be found in the character index, which can be useful with such an extensive cast.

Nor did I rely on entirely fictional constructs. Sir Henry Vane, General Burroughs, Sir Horace Vere and Captain Monroe did exist, but their timelines have been slightly adjusted to fit the narrative here. Vere, for instance, did not leave the Rhine until 1623, whereupon he did return to The Hague. Sir John Burroughs was in command of Manheim's garrison, which didn't fall into Spain's hands until that same year.

Captain Monroe is fascinating character, and his model of soldier-statesman was one of many inspirations for Lock's character journey. Monroe is most famous for his memoirs, which still exist today as *Monro, His expedition with the worthy Scots regiment (called Mac-Keyes-regiment) levied in August 1626.*

This and many other contemporary texts can be accessed for free or very cheaply on sites such as Google Play Books. This includes Jacob de Gheyn's drill manual, which really does contain forty-three individual steps for the drill. Lock's thirteen steps, alas, are not supported by a drill book of its own. They are instead a work of my own mind, drawing from innumerable texts and tactics from the period.

Experts in musketry certainly existed. The challenge is imagining how these experts would cope with the demands of the drill. How would an expert improvise? What corners would he cut? How quickly could their new and improved drill truly be? Lock's speed and efficiency may be disputed, but he has proved the critics wrong before...

The mention of the Florentine statesman Francesco Guicciardini and his *Counsels and Reflections* was no accident. Any enthusiast curious about the values and beliefs of contemporaries of that period could do far worse than consult this tome of wisdom and advice. It was good enough for Charles Lock!

As the timeline has been deliberately, but slightly, skewed, it should go without saying that there was no struggle in the forest, and no battle for Manheim. However, these contests likely did happen, just on a different scale, and with different results, in other towns.

The Twelve Years Truce was a real event, and preserved peace between Spain and its Dutch rebels from 1609-1621. Contemporaries feared that the resumption of that war would set off several chain reactions, but then the Bohemian Revolt occurred in 1618, and it became clear that contemporaries were very bad at predicting things. This Bohemian Revolt drew in the Elector Palatine, who made a play for the Bohemian Crown, and the rest, as they say, is history.

Other historical truths were also inserted into the narrative. The Battle of Wimpfen, for example, did occur on 6 May 1622, and it was a disaster for the anti-Habsburg cause. By that point, Frederick's cause appeared doomed, yet he refused to approve of anything more than a temporary truce.

Indeed, he set his sights on the campaigning season of 1623, in the hopes that this would provide him with more leverage. But that is a story for another time...

The Black Prince, the Raven, and the masks and rogues under their command were not present in the Thirty Years War. The vizard does exist, though it was used for more innocent purposes than the cloak and dagger conspiracy it appears in here.

Was the Black Prince a *total* fiction?

Perhaps.

It is almost certain that he was.

But then again, if the Black Prince wished to remain anonymous, surely maintaining this illusion would be in his interest?

Perhaps, like so many legends, we will never know for sure...

FURTHER READING AND INFORMATION

The interested reader can locate a wide range of non-fiction materials, which will deepen their knowledge of the Thirty Years War and the era. These materials include books, but also content in audio format. Audio programs, known as podcasts, are freely available, and if listening is preferable to reading, they can be a brilliant way to pass the time, or avoid going insane while ironing, walking the dog or (sigh) going to the gym.

With this in mind, I would like to humbly present my history podcast to the reader, as it is within this podcast *When Diplomacy Fails* that I have taken up the task of covering the Thirty Years War from beginning to end. The podcast can be found in the usual places; Apple Podcasts, Spotify and Podcast Addict. The podcast also has a website, www.wdfpodcast.com where the latest episodes are uploaded. You can find my author page, with links to all my written projects, in the same place.

If you'd prefer to read, you should know that my book examining the Thirty Years War, *For God or the Devil* is undergoing a re-release for its second edition, and should be available by mid-2022. Readers should also keep an eye out for *Warfare in the Age of Matchlock*, an examination of warfare in the period, which will really help add some meat onto the bones of warfare in Matthew Lock's world. If you would like to keep up to date with these projects, and more Matchlock books, please consider subscribing to my email list.

It should go without saying that the Thirty Years War boasts many other excellent studies as well. Anything by Geoffrey Parker or Peter H. Wilson will be worthwhile; an older, but arguably more accessible study by C. V.

Wedgewood is also welcome. It should be added that the latter is available in audiobook format. In time, depending largely on the success of these books, I intend to invest in audiobook versions for the Matchlock series, and for my other works. So watch (or should that be, listen to?) this space!

When Diplomacy Fails was where I first started exploring history to my heart's content. It's where my passion for history was first nourished, only to then explode. You can find many other episodes and series in that podcast's back catalogue, including examinations of conflicts such as the Korean War, the Great War, Ireland's 1916 Rising and more.

As the name suggests, we also examine why war happened, so check out our July Crisis Anniversary Project, and the sequel, the Versailles Anniversary Project, for massively detailed studies in audio format. It deserves repeating, this is all available absolutely free of charge.

I am so excited to see where Matchlock can take me, and my podcast, and I would love for you to join me for the journey. If you'd like to chat with like-minded history friends, make sure you join the Facebook group [When Diplomacy Fails Group] and follow me on Twitter [@wdfpodcast].

Together we can fulfil the vision I first developed all the way back in May 2012, when I first started doing this. To present history in a way that is fun, accessible, and fascinating, and to make history itself *thrive*.

Thanks for being part of it!

- CHARACTER INDEX -

[Historical characters are underlined].

<u>**Ambrogio Spinola**</u>: Renowned Spanish commander of Genoese origin; commanded mostly in the Spanish Netherlands.

Arthur Lock: Younger brother of Matthew Lock, b. 1604.

Benjamin 'Benjy' Blare, 3rd Earl Blarefield: Veteran soldier and second son of prolific Yorkshire family.

Billy: Unrepentant troublemaker from Sherbourne.

Black Prince: Mysterious commander of the black masks, with interests stretching across the known world; identity unknown.

Captain Augustus Frank: Charles Lock's right-hand man, Locksville's physician, and a second father to Matthew and Arthur.

Captain Monroe: Scottish soldier hailing from warlike Monroe clan, renowned for skill and ingenuity.

Captain Ricardo: Present in 1613. A brutish beast of a man, former mask, turned rogue. Attempts to hand Lock over to the Raven, but it costs him his life.

<u>**Cardinal Richelieu**</u>: Foreign Minister of France, and rising star in King Louis XIII's administration.

Catherine Lock: Wife of Charles Lock.

Charles Lock: Husband to Catherine Lock.

Diego de la Barca: Alcoholic Spanish commander who took the town of Woodrest, south of Manheim, as his base.

<u>**Emperor Ferdinand II**</u>: The Holy Roman Emperor, and the main rival to Frederick, the Elector Palatine. Leader of the Austrian Habsburg

dynasty.

Enrique Zuniga: Dour-faced pikeman normally seen by de la Barca's side.

Fabio: Present in 1613, is disappeared by Flynn.

Frederick V, Elector Palatine: Leader of the House of Wittelsbach, temporarily King of Bohemia, earns him sobriquet Winter King. Declared an outlaw in the Empire, lives in exile in The Hague.

Francesco Guicciardini: Famed Florentine who wrote extensively on matters of diplomacy, philosophy and statecraft, notably in his Counsels and Reflections. Major inspiration for Charles Lock, who adapted his teachings for his son.

Flynn O'Toole: Second son of an exiled Gaelic Earl, one of the Black Prince's most able agents – a cleaner, and an enemy of rogues.

Gaston Phillipe: Illegitimate son of de la Barca, and an all-round terrible knave.

Gonzalo Fernández de Cordoba: Commander of Spanish forces on the Rhine.

Georg von Salm: Vengeful former militia commander at Woodrest, shorn of much of his tongue and four of his toes.

James Lock: Elder brother of Matthew and Arthur, killed during an encounter with black masks in March 1613.

Jean le Renne: Renowned master of swords, and Lock's French tutor during much of his youth.

Johann Tserclaes, Count of Tilly: Overall commander of Habsburg forces.

John Louis, Stadtholder of Frisia: Son of William Louis, and distant cousin to Maurice of Orange.

Joseph Gage: Burroughs' less successful counterpart.

King James I and VI of Britain: r. 1601-1625.

King Louis XIII of France: r. 1610-1643.

King Philip II of Spain: Arguably Spain's greatest King, of the 'Armada' fame; r. 1560-1598.

King Philip IV of Spain: King Philip II's grandson; r. 1621-1666. Leader of the Spanish House of Habsburg, largely recognised as the more important of the two lines, for now.

Lady Jane Digby: Concerned mother of Sir John Digby, and purveyor of useful information.

Lady Mary Vere: Wife of Sir Horace Vere.

Luis Romera: Assistant to de la Barca at just the wrong time.

Matthew Lock: Our hero, b. 1602.

Maurice of Orange: The Prince of Orange, military innovator extraordinaire, and de facto military-political leader of the Dutch Republic; d. 1625.

Patrick Murphy: Pepper and spice merchant of Irish origins.

Pieter Kleppe: Owner of a ramshackle inn along the Rhine, helps replenish Lock's stores.

Prince Charles: The Prince of Wales and heir to the thrones of England, Scotland and Ireland. Infamous today for his sticky end.

Raven: Commander of rogues, and potential threat to Black Prince's position; identity unknown.

Sir Henry Vane: An MP and rising star in the British political establishment.

Sir Horace Vere: The quintessential soldier-statesman, and a veteran of Anglo-Dutch operations; d. 1635.

Sir John Burroughs: A commander of English forces on the Rhine.

Sir John Digby, 1st Earl of Bristol: Britain's Ambassador to Madrid, and owner of Sherbourne Castle in Dorset. Charged with making the Spanish Match idea work.

Strasser brothers: Theo and Herman Strasser, owner of Strasser Brothers Fine Meats in Manheim, Palatine loyalists, determined opponents of the Spanish.

Terri: Stable boy on Locksville estate.

Tommy: nephew of Gage, bars the door for Flynn and Lock.

Walter: Occasional soldier in von Salm's ragtag army; full-time father for many children, mostly not his own.

William Louis: Known as the father of the drill; worked with Maurice of Orange to develop the new tactics, which were put to good use in the 1600 Battle of Nieuwpoort.

Printed in Great Britain
by Amazon